T0272655

THE LOST DIARY OF MARY MAGDALENE

Johnny Teague

THE LOST DIARY OF MARY MAGDALENE

HISTRIA CHRISTIAN

Histria Christian

Las Vegas ♦ Chicago ♦ Palm Beach

Published in the United States of America by
Histria Books
7181 N. Hualapai Way, Ste. 130-86
Las Vegas, NV 89166 U.S.A.
HistriaBooks.com

Histria Christian is an imprint of Histria Books dedicated to books that embody and promote Christian values and an understanding of the Christian faith. Titles published under the imprints of Histria Books are distributed worldwide.

Library of Congress Control Number: 2024931095

ISBN 978-1-59211-450-4 (hardcover)
ISBN 978-1-59211-486-3 (eBook)

Dedication and Thanks

The Lost Diary of Mary Magdalene is dedicated solely to the Lord Jesus Christ, God's only Son, the Savior of the world. It is my yearning that in reading this, all will grow to know the living, eternal Jesus personally.

I thank God for my publisher, Histria Books and their partnership in this endeavor. They are such a blessing to me. I especially thank Dr. Kurt Brackob for his walk with the Lord.

I thank the Father for my wife, Lori, for her love and living example of what a woman in Christ looks like.

I also thank the Father for the Church He has given me to pastor – Church at the Cross. They are my Church family. They bear with me as their pastor, ever reaching to be transformed in the image of our Lord Jesus Christ through His Holy Spirit.

Contents

The Discovery

On March 10, 1976, Father Virgilio Canio Corbo and his partner of archaeological excavations, Father Stanislao Loffreda, had finished their work for the day at the site of ancient Magdala. Their foreman, who had collaborated with them in Capernaum and at the Herodium, Giuseppe Campise, was left to barricade the site and cover it from observers or intruders. As was his custom, it also gave him time to chase his curiosities, which the two friars permitted upon completion of the daily tasks. They found valuable insights from Giuseppe. Often, he would dig outside the grid on his own on a hunch, carefully adhering to the stratigraphic excavation techniques to keep the time periods intact. This was the only requirement of the friars, just on the notion that he did find something.

Near a hill overlooking the Sea of Galilee, Giuseppe liked to sit and think of what an amazing view this was. He thought of how, if he had lived back in the first century, he would have wanted a home on that very spot. The more he enjoyed the place where he sat, the more he felt this would be a great site to dig. Previous archaeologists had ruled it out a decade earlier, but in his mind, he just felt they missed something. With the blessings of Friars Corbo and Loffreda, he was given latitude to do a personal excavation upon the spot. It was an exceedingly small matrix because he had little time. Days before, he had not dug thirty centimeters when he found the top of a wall. He expanded the matrix to discover that at the location was what appeared to be a first-century cistern.

Giuseppe had kept his bosses apprised of his progress. They were interested, but it was outside the scope of their current endeavor. Once Giuseppe was certain of the perimeter of this ancient cistern — five meters by six meters —, he began to dig within the confines. Brushing the inside of the walls carefully, he found plaster with carvings. The etchings and words indicated that at some point, prisoners were isolated within this cistern. He was intrigued. Friars Corbo and Loffreda were too, but again, Giuseppe's quest was outside their purview.

The curious foreman kept digging. On this particular day, March 10, 1976, a rush of excitement overwhelmed him. At the depth of six meters, he touched the lid of something. He fell back, trembling. He laid aside his small plastic spade and used a dirty toothbrush and a rag to very gently move buried dirt away from this fixture. Finally, it became clear. What he had uncovered was a sealed clay pot. Giuseppe instinctively knew this was what he was destined to find. He brushed around it. Then, he looked to make sure no one saw. Laying his instruments aside, he carefully laid his right gloved hand on the center of the artifact, his left gloved hand digging underneath its bottom. He said a silent prayer and then lifted. The ground resisted as if it did not wish its encasing disturbed. With hesitation, he continued cautiously. The pot released. Giuseppe now beheld his discovery from the cistern, broken free from the first-century hold of ages past.

Never before had Giuseppe Campise found anything like this. He thought of the Bedouin shepherd in Qumran who discovered the Dead Sea Scrolls. Could this be something in that sphere of significance and value? Giuseppe was employed by the two friars and had been for several years. Quite inherently, the thought of personal fame and fortune crossed his mind. He wanted the credit and the benefits if this small clay jar had any importance. Yes, he worked for famous archaeologists, but could he not aspire to be one himself, freestanding? Beyond that, Giuseppe was superstitious. Would this find harm he and his family for generations to come? It was hard on him, but he had to think. Here was something he could not share. Many had said he was wasting his time, there was nothing there. Why not let them think that a little while longer?

With that, now that night had fallen, Giuseppe wrapped his find in dirty worn gray cloths. He placed it tenderly in his wheelbarrow, insulating it with cloth upon cloth, then placing his tools around it, with his hat upon it, to appear as he always appeared each evening, just a laborer taking his tools to his hotel room for the night.

He arrived at his hotel. Everyone had locked themselves in for sleep. Guiseppe did the same. He placed a "Do Not Disturb" sign on his door, though the hotel services were unlikely to appear. Many days had passed since they had cleaned his room or made his bed. The very first night in this room, his sheets had the aroma of some previous guest. Cleanliness and sterility were not a priority here, which was probably the reason for their long stay at this establishment. He knew of his supervisors' sparse daily allotment. Even so, he could not risk a cleaning now.

The foreman placed the clay pot on his dresser and quickly washed his face and hands. His heart was pounding again. What is inside? The lid was held to the pot by a wax seal. Giuseppe gently ran a warm moist rag over the seal, while pecking at it with a toothpick, peeling away the layers bit by bit. He then twisted on the lid to see if it had loosened. It had not. So, he wiped the rag over the seal and picked at the layers again. He tried to twist again, but to no avail. He repeated the process for almost an hour and then a slight turn came to the lid. By the nightstand's lamp light, the only light in the room, he wiped with the warm moist rag and picked where the lid seemed to stick. With the towel, he twisted the lid again. It popped open. Dust seemed to escape like a breath from the inside. He leaned the lamp toward the opening in the clay pot.

Down below, Giuseppe could see a bound book of some sort. It was dingy and frail. Its rigid form was lost as if the top had been pushed one way and the bottom pulled another way, loosening the binding that held pages of something written. It sat at the bottom of the pot almost as mush. What to do? If he lifted it, would it fall apart? If he left it, there would be no answers. Were he to break the pot around it, he might find that the value of this treasure was the pot itself and not the perceived book below. The thing he hated the most was the contemplation of archaeologists. They seemed content to make a discovery, leave the discovery in place, and chase theories of what the thing was, rather than picking it up and answering the question. He knew the ultimate wisdom was their procedure, but this was not his bent. He would reach in, with care and precaution and the protection of gloves — not for his hands, but for the object his hands would clasp.

Giuseppe reached, trying not to touch the sides of the pot with his arm, nor to rub the bound object against the sides of the pot to the detriment of either object. His hand would have to grab hold of the object, then set it upright, then grab it again at the top, and finally lift it out of the jar. Nervously, he wiped the sweat away to ensure no foreign element was added. He loosely grasped, turned it upright, and gently lifted the contents through the opening. Raising the object above the clay pot, he could see it more clearly. He was relieved it did not fall apart. It was a binding of parchment pages. He could not make out the cover's title. He laid it on the lamp table, let go, and leaned back. He felt like a man attempting to disarm a World War II unexploded bomb found in the basement of a fully occupied building. One wire cut, now the next one. Clay pot opened. Content extracted. Now to the content itself. Giuseppe waited. He poured a glass of water from the pitcher on his dresser. He thought. He dreamed. He dreaded. He feared discovery. He fretted reprisal. He gasped with excitement. Time for the next step.

This man had come a long way from a personal dig — to a discovery — to a transport — to another discovery — and now to the heart of the unearthing. With gloves still on, Giuseppe placed the lid to his ice bucket beside the book so that when he opened the cover, it could rest on the ice bucket lid to protect the fragile binding. As he rolled it from right to left, he could see faded writing. He looked closer and realized it was Koine Greek, which he immediately recognized. Of all the languages, this was consistent with the first-century people who had lived in this area. It also happened to be the only language he had learned to read from all his studies. He looked for a name or a place or a date. He could make out a date. Even more astounding, he made out a name on the first page, on the top line — Mary.

With great caution, he turned to the next page. It would take better lighting and a thick pair of glasses to actually discern what was written, but the one word was frequent — Mary. Giuseppe thought of the place they had been digging — Magdala. He knew that in the first century, Jesus Christ had been to this site, which was the main interest of the friars. He also knew Magdala was a major fishing factory for the Sea of Galilee, at one point perhaps a residence for forty thousand people, but more so, he knew Magdala was known for its famous daughter, Mary Magdalene. Racing through his mind was the question and the secret, have I possibly found a writing by Mary Magdalene?

Days would pass. Giuseppe would translate the text using all the skills his employers had taught him. He would oversee the excavations within the grid for Father Corbo and Father Loffreda. On occasion, they would ask why he had quit digging on his own. His answer was simply, "I am so tired each day. My mind seems to be focused elsewhere at night." They assumed some loneliness felt by the separation from his family was the cause. They would kindly encourage him, reminding him of his value to them. They never caught on to the fact their foreman had made a discovery on a whim of his own. Maybe he would tell them, he thought. Maybe he would not.

Was this a joke? Was this a fake? Was this another Gnostic finding? Giuseppe was uncertain. What he was sure of, was this book he found read like a diary. It told the story of Mary Magdalene, seemingly from her own hand. This book detailed personal encounters and conversations with Jesus of Galilee, the One who lived not far from here in the city of Capernaum. The foreman read it from start to finish, slowly and patiently. The translation required that anyway. He examined it carefully. Ultimately, he needed to make a decision concerning these objects before coming forward. Here is what he found:

The Lost Diary of Mary Magdalene

The Eighteenth Year of Tiberius Caesar

In the eighteenth year of the reign of Tiberius Caesar, on the first month, on the second day — I am Mary, the daughter of an exceedingly kind Jewish tax collector named Jared and his wife, my sweet Roman mom, Adriana. How did I get in this mess? I am chained to the walls in the depths of Magdala's old, dried cistern.

For the life of me, I have no idea why I do what I do. One minute, I am fully competent, helping my father in his tax booth. I visit with the fishermen as they bring their catch. I confirm their port of origin. I document what they have. I question them to assist. I go over the inventory of the salt merchants. I review the records of the shipments of pickled fish going out. I write down the number of customers using the fish tower. I ascertain the territories crossed to reach our port. I make copious notes of what they all have and then pass it on to Poppa for his assessment of various taxes and amounts owed. Things are normal.

We go home for our family meal, often in our courtyard overlooking the beautiful Sea of Galilee. We are a tight-knit family. How can we not be? When your Poppa is the tax collector for the village, especially the busiest village along the Sea of Galilee, there are no friends, just names. We are called "dogs", "traitors", "heathens", "Achans", "Korahs", and even "Jezebels". These are our neighbors, relatives, and former friends who do this. They once were close to us when Poppa worked at the fish factory. He was regarded, promoted, and given greater responsibilities. He had gone from a single fisherman operation to a consortium of men like him for negotiating purposes. With his experience, the factory hired Poppa as foreman of processing. Finally, he was assigned the task of operation expansion. In that position, he made good profits for this community, working on commission, to help them find better markets for their fish. This job required lots of travel and many evening meetings.

The bad thing about his job was he was never home. Momma threatened to leave him. It was then that Poppa accepted an offer from the Romans to be their tax collector for the village. They knew he had full knowledge of the local industry. He would know where the money was made and how it was hidden from taxation.

Poppa knew the job would be frowned upon, but it would have steady hours, great pay, and constant protection. He was home at night after he accepted the job, but little did he know, our social circle would decrease to us three.

Men of our community refuse to court me, but the Roman soldiers and the Gentile fishermen fill that need. Being with these men seems freeing. Nothing is off-limits. It has been an adjustment from our Jewish life of purity. They do not worry about what food is clean or unclean. They have introduced me to delicacies unimagined. They have no restraints. If they think it, they say it. If they consider it, they try it. With these "Gentiles", they have no shame. Nothing embarrasses them. They can talk about sex just as easily as talk about fish. They speak of going to the synagogue for good luck and praying to Neptune for a good catch.

They revere Jupiter as the head of all their gods. They eat pork. Their indulgence of wine is ravenous. These men laugh. They flirt. They touch me in public and show no restraint in private. When I fear judgment for partaking in these things, they take me to fortune-tellers who tell me my future. They even know secrets about me I have never shared with anyone.

Thinking back, this may have been when I started having these overwhelming fears. I write all of this because Poppa was able to arrange for a revered Roman physician, who was passing through, to see me. His name is Gaius Xenophan. He is the personal physician to Emperor Tiberius. Because of my father's reputation among the Romans, the soldiers were able to arrange an examination for me here. Poppa and Momma were present. They wept as I shared things that were all too embarrassing for them in the presence of one so esteemed.

Xenophan arranged some concoction for me to drink two times each day. It tastes horrible. He also asked that I begin to note what I feel and think during the day. He gave me a bound parchment to write on. Since Poppa taught me how to write and record things for the tax collector files, it was a natural thing for me. The good doctor promised that in a few weeks, he would pass back through Magdala to monitor my progress and take further action. This last statement shocked me

— "in a few weeks." How long do they plan on keeping me in this dank and dreary hole in the ground?

I must try to understand why I am here. Surely if I write it out, I can make some sense of it all. I must get out of here NOW! Back to my recent terrors. I am sometimes paralyzed by suspicion. It seems someone is following me, that people are watching me in the market, along the shore, and through my bedroom window. At times like these, I cannot be alone. I must have Poppa or Momma with me constantly. I see the same people every day, at all hours of the day, on Harbor Street where our home sits. These shadowy beings stand in the dark corners watching me. I point them out to my parents, but they conveniently do not see what I see, or maybe the trackers hide when my parents look out from our front door. Poppa has passed it off by saying I need help. Momma says no one is there, that I need to overcome such paranoia. They both say these feelings are not real, but they do not see what I see. I know I am being watched.

At times, I break out in a violent rage. I tore Poppa's shirt and slapped Momma's face three days ago. I curse. I swear. I accuse. I run out of the house screaming. All the neighbors are sheepish around me. No one hardly looks me in the eye. My suitors bring me comfort from a bottle and some magic arts they practice. All of this they say they learned from their worship of the underworld god, Pluto. My fits of anger cause the men to hold me down, undress me, and take their turn upon me. This soothes my temper. My yearnings find satisfaction for a few days.

Sadly, Poppa came upon one of these events recently near the Roman tavern. His guard, Linus, had instigated the activity and then feared when I swore I would tell my father. The next thing I know, he leaves just to return with Poppa acting as if he had nothing to do with the bestial feast. I have never seen such hurt in my father's eyes. He cursed the men, threatened them profusely, grabbed my stola, and ashamedly led me home.

Momma was waiting. She saw the stark look in Poppa's face. She inquired, but he delayed the answer. He and Momma had me clean up. They then put me to bed. I am thirty-two years old. How offended I am to have them try to control me. I write this, but even as a thirty-two-year-old, I have kept this part of my life away from their knowledge. Even my courters and male friends play innocently distant from me at the tax booth. I cannot explain it. I am proud to indulge, but ashamed to reveal such to my parents. I suppose it is true: What is done in secret will come to the light. This revelation has overturned our home life.

Years ago, Poppa entered the tax booth for fear of losing Momma. Now he and Momma speak of him leaving the tax booth for fear of losing me. From my feathered mat resting upon my bed on the second floor, I heard my father and mother do something I had not witnessed in years. They spoke of Adonai, of God. I heard them kneel in their room next to mine. I heard the trembling voice of Poppa pleading with God for me, their daughter. I began to weep. It dawned on me that I am breaking their hearts. I am ruining our lives. I do not think they slept that night. I know I did not, but I will not join them in prayer. My Gentile companions have made such things look silly. All gods seem to me of late to be nothing but lucky charms and things to call upon when desperate. I clearly am stronger than that. I suppose that makes me stronger than Poppa and Momma.

I was surprised on the seventh day of the week to see our leisurely morning change. Poppa woke me. A morning meal was prepared. He and Momma were dressed. They told me to get dressed as well. I had wondered what the occasion was. They told me we would be going to the local synagogue. I quickly objected, "But Poppa, they hate us there." He nodded and said, "Perhaps for good reason Mary. I am going to try to make amends. I am going to announce my plans to leave the tax booth. I am going to be seeking different employment. I am going to repent before them, ask for their forgiveness, and request their help." That came out of the blue like the violent storms that come from nowhere suddenly to pound us on the shore of this sea. Being a tightly bound family of three who has faced so much together, how could I not join them in this new direction? I cannot help but think Poppa must be going through some crisis. They can infer or act as though it is because of me, but I know it cannot be because of anything I have done. I am no different than any other Galilean young lady. This city of Magdala is well-known for women involved in much more salacious activities than the little light moments in which I partake.

It had been a long time since I had entered this synagogue. Our community is unique. We are a strong Jewish community, though we are also at the intersection of the world. We do not have just one synagogue. We have two — one near the shore for the visiting Jewish fishermen and their families who devoutly honor the Sabbath regardless of where they travel, while the other is not far from our home.

It is for the locals. I pass by the first one often as we make our way to the tax booth, but the second one is up from our house, deeper into the community. It is these neighborhoods we have ceased to frequent since Poppa took the tax job. Yet, there we were walking up Harbor Street, making a right on Way Street to the front of the synagogue for the locals.

I had forgotten how impressive the pillars and columns were to this facility. The mosaic floors always delight me. The walls are plastered, decorated with beautiful colored frescoes, and also many beautiful rosette designs. Ornate ritual baths are present with water flowing from a tunneled water system. The remainder of the building has black basalt floors to match the outside walls. No expense was spared in the construction of this synagogue.

The pride of our Magdala community is the bimah, the stone table on which the Torah is placed. I watched the visiting synagogue ruler, Jairus, go into the closet to retrieve the scrolls. He then laid them upon this most unique bimah in the whole area of Galilee. Many visitors doing business at the fish factory make a trek to this place to see this table. As Jairus searched for the text, I could see the familiar six-petal rosette relief carved into the top of this huge stone. The front of the table before us had carvings depicting the seven-branched menorah with water jars on each side. I was unable to get up at that time, but I did remember years ago, Poppa, a once devout Jewish worshiper, showing me all four sides. Each of the two sides of the stone had etchings of four arches with sheaves of grain and an oil lamp included. The back side of this bimah had carvings of two wheels and a depiction of fire representing the Holy of Holies. My Roman Momma whispered in my ear, "I love the bimah. It is an accurate miniature replica of the Temple in Jerusalem. This synagogue allows those seekers of God to visit the Temple without ever leaving Magdala. You know I was brought up to worship many gods until I met your father. He is the one who led me to certain knowledge that there is just one God, the God of Israel. He is the One we are to worship and to share with the whole world." I felt as though she was attempting to recapture me in the ancient faith of our fathers. Her sincerity touched me, but her words turned me off.

As Jairus began to read from the prophet Amos, I felt a burning anger in my breast. He called a local rabbi to come speak on the text. I did not hear him. What I heard was a racket, a clamor of voices inside my head. Hate was spewing within me. The room was spinning. The sweet little faces of these attenders sickened me.

These haters of my Poppa, not one sat near us. All acted as if we were lepers who forgot to shout, “Unclean”. I had grown up with some of these. I heard them whisper when we walked through the doors. I saw the eyerolls of disdain. Worst, I saw two men who had been at the shore with my Roman friends a few days before. They had undressed me. I had undressed them. Now, here they were pretending with their wives to be men of honor!

I lost it. I remember now as I write. An uncontainable disgust hit me. Suddenly, I was reenacting their actions a few nights back. I tore my clothes off to reveal my breasts, pushing the guest speaker away. I climbed upon the bimah where the Torah was laid and writhed in unmentionable actions. I began to scream out profanities at all those in attendance. I screamed with voices I did not recognize. I exposed two of the well-regarded men by name for their sexual activities on the pallet of the seashore. I wanted them to see my body, the one they tantalized.

I challenged them, “If it was okay then to do what we did, it should not be forbidden here. Why don’t you touch me now? You undress too. You said there was nothing for which to be ashamed. You said you couldn’t keep your eyes off me, your hands from my hidden places. You said it was natural. Come on then! Let’s do it!” They showed no restraint outside this house of worship, then what prevented them inside now? Wives looked at their husbands, but then wrote me off as a lunatic.

Poppa and some men grabbed hold of me. I heard one woman say, “I told you when they walked in, they would be trouble. I told you that this is the kind of people tax collectors are!” They forced me outside. Poppa trembled. I could hear the speaker and the worshipers sing while they drug me out. Quickly, Momma put part of my clothes over me, holding them with her hand so that the covering would not come apart. The local Roman guard who protected Poppa, who had instigated the activities on the shore just hours before, piously had his men throw me in this prison of a cistern. They roughly chained me. When no one was looking, one of the guards slid his hand underneath my robe and rubbed his hands over my body with a mocked grin, saying, “Mary, I will be back to pleasure you. Just hold tight. I know what you want.” Outside, I could hear the familiar brokenness of Momma weeping.

As I record this on the second day of this first month, I find no healing in these words. What does a physician like Xenophan know after all? I will enter the next day's date now. We will see what tomorrow will hold.

In the eighteenth year of the reign of Tiberius Caesar, on the first month, on the third day —

NO!!!! NO!!!! NO!!!! xxxx oooo bb cze (Mary's writing indiscernible)

45 fish, 12 pounds of salt, 2 talents of gold, 1 talent of silver, 5 shekels of perfume

I cannot go today. I have things to do for my Momma.

Oh guard, come here. I have something to trade you for my freedom.

Lying guard. I gave what I promised and more. He still has me chained. He laughs. Curses upon him and his family.

The voices are calling. Why do the guards not fear the voices?

I have no idea what day it is. Why is everyone watching me? Someone is sneaking in at night. They have their way. And I have mine.

Blood. There is blood all over me. I sit in a pool of it.

Two men chained beside me laugh. These beasts mock. Ones I see and ones no one but me sees.

In the eighteenth year of the reign of Tiberius Caesar, on the first month, on the twenty- second day — Poppa and Momma just visited. I am better today. Momma washed me up.

In the eighteenth year of the reign of Tiberius Caesar, on the first month, on the twenty- third day — Poppa and Momma came today. They were able to walk me out of the cistern unchained. Xenophan has a new treatment plan. He says it is best I heal with family. How grateful I am to be home. I feel a peace, but for some reason, deep down inside, I feel an unexplainable anger.

In the eighteenth year of the reign of Tiberius Caesar, on the second month, on the third day — Things have been better now. I have not been able to go out with my friends at night. I have this longing to go with them, but it is interesting how much happier I am when I do not venture beyond Poppa and Momma's presence.

I have helped around the house. Poppa says he needs help at the tax booth. He said that he hopes I will feel up to going with him to work tomorrow. I am willing to try, but I am extremely nervous. I so do not want to disappoint him. I am also afraid of how I will act when I am around other people. It is as if something comes over me. I become powerless to some type of evil force inside. Or, at least, that is how I can describe it. Maybe Xenophan can read this and make some sense of what might be wrong with me.

On the second month, on the fourth day — I was unable to go with Poppa today. I got dressed, but when we stepped outside, I saw all kinds of people looking at me. As we made our way down Harbor Street, two men and a woman were following us. The farther we walked, the closer they got behind us. They had horrific expressions on their faces. I panicked and ran back home. Poppa followed me through our front door. I was frantic. I hid under our dining table. Momma knelt down to soothe me. She asked Poppa what happened. He said that I thought people were following us, but no one was behind us. This just angered me. He has two eyes just like I do. If he cannot see the people following us, then maybe he needs to see Xenophan. I told him as much. He left in anger. I cried out for him not to go. It just may be that they were following him and not me. He is the tax collector after all. Maybe it is his enemies that are torturing me to get to him?

On the second month, the fifth day — I stayed in today. Poppa and Momma wanted to go to the synagogue by the harbor but were afraid to leave me alone. They spent the morning reciting scripture and praying. They asked me to join them. I have no desire. I am doing fine.

On the second month, on the tenth day — Momma felt I needed to get out. She enticed me with a trip to the market to get me a new colorful ornamental robe.

Loving new clothes, that was the bait I needed. We had a wonderful time. We ate fresh vegetables from the vendors there. We bought me the most beautiful robe. Momma bought herself a new shawl. We even bought Poppa a new outer robe for formal business meetings. We sat on the shore afterward and watched the fishermen unload their catch. Thankfully, I did not see any of my Gentile male companions. I waded into the sea a bit. The wind blew softly. The smell of the air was crisp and fragrant. I saw beautiful birds. The hills around us were so appealing. Mount Arbel stood over the whole village with such grandeur. We heard some speaking of unrest with Rome. Some Jewish families are moving into caves on Arbel. I am unsure what their fears are.

Speaking of fear, I did not see anyone following us today. It may be that Poppa is the one in danger. I used the money they gave me to purchase an amulet for Poppa to wear around his neck for safety. He is against such good-luck charms, but I will just tell him that I liked the design. Deep down, I hope it brings him good luck. When Momma went to buy some food for the evening meal, I bought a tintinnabulum to hang inside the covering of my window. This wind chime is supposed to ward off evil spirits. I hope it will help keep me calm. I hid it in my new robe until I could get it into my room.

Poppa came home. We had a great meal of lamb and artichokes. We then modeled our new purchases for him. He loved his new outer robe. When I gave him his amulet, I could tell it disturbed him. With a slight grimace, he saw my face. He quickly pretended to love it and put it on. I know Poppa and Momma are walking very gingerly around me. They fear they can set me off. I feel I am well. I have quit drinking my medicine. Even if Poppa does not wear the amulet, at least he put it on. This may ward off any danger. I will clutch my tintinnabulum before going to sleep and think positive things for him.

On the second month, on the thirteenth day — Poppa asked me to try to go to the tax booth with him today. His work is piling up. I never realized that what I did for him helped so much. He promised we could work just a half day if I began to feel bad. We went. People with whom we had to deal were waiting in a long line. I am so glad I was there with Poppa. I questioned each merchant and citizen. I recorded what they had. I even caught a man lying about the number of fish he had caught. I saw his boat when we walked to the booth. He had two baskets on his ship, yet he only brought one to count. When confronted, he acted as if he had forgotten the second and went to retrieve it. I heard him call me a name under his breath when he was about ten paces from me. Such is the life of a tax collector. They hate us, but in front of us they are greatly respectful. They drown us with compliments, even bringing little gifts of appreciation. They all acknowledge our work is hard. They each say our job is one they would not want. Then they reveal a fraction of their displeasure when Poppa gives them their bill. They would really let us have it were it not for the Roman guard and our ability to tax them even more. Their greatest fear is that we will take their possessions or home.

Probably in the tax booth is where I grasp the reality that, in this line of work, all we have is our immediate family, just the three of us. I understand Poppa wanting to leave this animosity. However, the money is great, and the hours are steady. Of all the tax collectors we encounter, Poppa marks up the taxes for our bonus less than any others I know. Since I have not had another episode like at the synagogue, the talk of his career change has subsided.

On the second month, on the fourteenth day — Things are feeling normal again. Even more so when we have our typical blow-up at the tax booth. Simon from Canaan, also called Simon the Zealot, showed up with a band of his ragtag men protesting Rome. They threw over a few of our tables near our booth where first-time shippers register. Thankfully, Linus and the rest of Poppa's guards made quick work of Simon.

With bitter name-calling directed toward Poppa and the Romans, Simon was led away to the cistern to serve a ten-day sentence. I hate the thought of that cistern, even for Simon. I have no fond memories of being there.

On the second month, on the seventeenth day — An occurrence today reminds me more of why Poppa needs me at the booth. I know these fishermen. I have dealt with them ever since Poppa let me work the tax booth with him. Zebedee's fishing company was waiting in line today to pay their duties. When it was their turn for me to inventory their fish, I noticed their card listed their port of origin as Capernaum. I looked at the kind old man. His sons, John and James, fidgeted around, acting all hot, bothered, and not slightly inconvenienced. I said, "Sir, it says here that your port of origin is Capernaum. Now, I know you live in Bethsaida. You came from there two weeks ago. You have signed 'Bethsaida' for the last two years. Have you moved?" Peter, one of Zebedee's partners, spoke up, "He didn't move. My brother and our families moved.

We now base our business out of Capernaum where we do all our fishing."

People do this all the time. Bethsaida is in the jurisdiction of Herod Philip. Among other villages, Capernaum and Magdala are in the jurisdiction of Herod Antipas. As long as merchandise does not cross another jurisdiction, just one tax is levied. However, if the goods cross over from another jurisdiction, two taxes are levied — one for this tax district and one for the other. If more districts are crossed, additional taxes are levied for those. I had no choice but to tax them for both jurisdictions until one of our soldiers could verify that the Zebedee fishing operation not only changed ports, but remained solely in the jurisdiction of Antipas.

John had a few choice words for me. His brother James hollered. Peter got into a shoving match with Linus. Finally, the old man and Andrew, Peter's brother, pulled the men away. The tax law is the tax law. Poppa and I visited later today about the incident. He says Zebedee's men are as good as Galilean fishermen can be, but he does believe Peter and Andrew moved with the express purpose to reduce taxes. This is where my father is very compassionate. He said he would probably have done the same.

On the second month, on the eighteenth day — We have had a full week. I was able to work with Poppa all six days. I feel stronger now. I did see some of my partying companions at the booth, but I was so busy getting information from our clients, I hardly had time to think on anything but work. Poppa seemed so grateful to have me. He loves me dearly even if I do nothing to help, but with me helping, his load is much lighter. He is able to finish a week with no work to carry over to the next week. When I am not there, he has others who help, but none do so with the care or efficiency that I do.

On the second month, on the twenty-second day — Poppa had a meeting to go to, so the tax booth was closed. Momma and I are going to the market today to shop and eat.

On the second month, on the twenty-fourth day — I am awake now. Yesterday was lost to me. Momma had to tell me what day it was. So I am writing. Something happened at the market. Momma is not talking about it. I have bandages all over my arms, my legs, and my breasts. I am hurting. What happened? Momma will not say.

She changed my bandages. I was able to look at the wounds. It was like I was punctured all over my body with gaping skin folds sutured back closed. I do not get it.

Poppa had to work. He returned home. They both sat with me talking about nothing. They seem so concerned and scared. Scared of what?

On the second month, on the twenty-seventh day — I was able to help Momma today. We had some honest conversations about the world, the tax booth, and the neighbors. The one area not discussed was the market. I let it pass most of the day. Momma began to share about her childhood, about her father, and her sisters. She seemed very nostalgic. Since she was sharing, I asked her to please tell me what happened to me at the market.

Momma began to tear up. She said that she does not want to upset me, that what happened at the market was gruesome and unexplainable. I told her to go ahead. I am okay. I am home. I feel safe. I asked her to please tell me. Momma then told me that we had been having a great day. She went into the fishing shop to get Poppa some hooks. Though he no longer fishes for a living, he loves to take time off in the water, cast nets, and hook fish. While we were in the store, Momma said I began to tremble. She said I picked up a fishhook, used a voice so deep, she thought a man was behind me, but my lips were moving. The guttural voice was coming from me. She said I started talking nonsense. Then, I began to take the fishhook, stab it into my arms repeatedly, ripping it out, tearing skin. She said everyone looked in horror. Momma tried to grab me. She said I pushed her away. She asked some men to help. She said I displayed such strength that I threw three men out of the shop singlehandedly. I ripped my skirt off, stabbing my legs with the hook laughing. I then opened my robe, puncturing my breasts with it repeatedly, ripping flesh out. She said I began to lick the blood from my arms.

At this point, the owner of the store cast a net over me. I was entangled. Then the men were able to subdue me. They carried me out, Momma said, while the customers of the store shrieked, cried, and prayed aloud. It was only after I was home that she said I settled down. They kept the net on me until Poppa could get home. He closed his booth and rushed to my bedside. A local doctor sutured my wounds. Only then did they remove the net and dress me.

Now all my wounds make sense. Bruises surround the puncture sites. I am very sore. How could I do this to myself? And why do I think it is funny? I turn toward the window to hide my pleasure. Yet, I am mortified that I did this to my body. What is wrong with me? What will the Magdala townspeople think of me? How does this help Poppa when he has to face an angry public every day? I fear our neighbors will say, "It serves him right. He made a deal with the devil of Rome. Now he is paying for it. I hope the money helps him sleep." Maybe it is time for Poppa to change jobs. Maybe it is time we move to another town. My only fear is that the trouble we are having is not outside these walls as much as inside my room.

In the eighteenth year of the reign of Tiberius Caesar, on the third month, on the seventh day — Momma did not wake up this morning.

In the eighteenth year of the reign of Tiberius Caesar, on the third month, on the eighth day — Momma was laid in her tomb this morning at the base of Mount Arbel. I wore my ornamental robe she bought for me. They said I should wear black or sackcloth. I refused. I would see her off wearing the outfit she had chosen. She was buried with her colorful shawl we had bought at the market. The doctor said her heart just stopped. Momma was no more than forty-eight years old. Our home now is draped in black. Poppa wears sackcloth. His face is ashen.

Why so young? What caused this? Murmurings of Magdala are saying this is what a tax collector deserves — a daughter out of her mind and a dead wife. The tax business is taking its toll — more than money can cover. Poppa will not speak to me. No one else in the town comes to console us. The only visitor we had was the synagogue ruler, who acted as if he did not want to be with us.

On the third month, on the ninth day — Poppa and I returned to Momma's tomb. He had a stone box for her bones, to be used a year from now. It was surreal to read her name on the ossuary: "Adriana, a Magdalene, wife of Jared, mother of Mary." I had never imagined my name on the side of an ossuary. There, etched in stone, the three of us — Momma, Poppa, and me.

The day was beautiful, so after the committal of the box for Momma, Poppa decided we would climb to the top of Arbel. We walked around to the backside, crossed a little stream, and made our way up the rough jagged side. The climb was steep, zig-zagging back and forth on an old path. At one point, Poppa had to give me a boost. With great arm strength, he then pulled himself up. We got to the outcrop on the very top. We both sat on an outgrowth of rock crowning the peak. The wind was strong. The view was breathtaking. Every worry melted away. Grief disappeared. We saw the beautiful Sea of Galilee. We looked down. Poppa and I took turns spotting different buildings and sites around our city. We could see our two-story house and the courtyard on Harbor Street. We could see the tax booth near the shore. Fishermen were sailing in and out.

Others were casting nets near the sea's middle. We saw ships moving from Decapolis toward Magdala. We saw activity in the direction of Tiberias in one direction, Capernaum in the other. We saw the neighborhood synagogue where I had my meltdown. We could see the market where we bought our clothes. Sadly, I glanced, then looked away from the fishing shop where I had pierced myself with fishhooks. Below us was a reminder of joy and sadness, but from this height, all pain seemed so distant.

Mount Arbel had a feeling of home, because inside of this mount lay my Momma. This mountain is a fixture of our community, now it is our sentimental base. I told Poppa I will come here often to check on Momma. One day, we will all three be together in the earth of this mountain. Poppa quoted scripture: "Precious to God is the death of one of His saints." He then recited a favorite passage from Job: "I know that my Redeemer lives, and that in the end he will stand upon the earth. And after my skin has been destroyed, yet in my flesh I will see God; I myself will see him with my own eyes — I, and not another. How my heart yearns within me!"

Poppa asked me if I knew what that meant. I told him it is the belief that there is life after this one. Beyond that, it was hard to be honest. I do not believe there is life after this one. That is an old folktale. I believe we live out this life however we want. We should make ourselves happy. If this life is all, I want no regrets. If there is life after this, I will trust in my efforts to be good. No need to cover this on the day we sit above the grave of my dear mother.

Before we arose to leave, Poppa looked me square in the eye. He said, "Mary, we have had a very difficult last few months. I love you. I love Adriana. It has been the three of us for a long time. Now there is just two of us. Let us make a new start. Let us remember your Momma. Please do not break my heart. I cannot bear the thought of losing you, too. Please do not go near those men. Please, if you feel a spell come over you, just let me know. We can close the booth and go home. Will you try?" I gave him a hug. I promised I would try my best.

On the third month, on the tenth day — I am doing the cooking for Poppa. I am not particularly good at it, but I am all we have. We walked together to the tax booth alone. I did not feel like going today. Poppa will not leave me by myself. He hardly speaks still. Does he blame me? Does he blame himself? Is he afraid — of me or the people who follow us everywhere we go? Yes, they still are.

We work together. Poppa only speaks with regard to the necessities of business. We come home. He eats. He bolts the door. He sleeps on a mat beside it. It is as if he is afraid someone will break in. Or maybe he is afraid I will break out. Does he not know I have a window? The only thing keeping me here is me. He seldom looks me in the eye. I know he loves me. Grief hits people in different ways. I love him. I love Momma. I grieve too. I am tired of grieving though. We must snap out of this. Life must go on. Tomorrow is my birthday. I refuse to welcome thirty-three in drab.

On the third month, the eleventh day — Poppa brought me my gift this morning. Inside were the most beautiful skirt and a purple linen veil. I was so excited. Not only were they striking, but they were also extravagantly expensive. Poppa did not say it, but I think he was trying to express my value to him. I put them on before we went to the tax booth. I hate to write this, but I cannot wait to show my male friends down near the shore. I am going to celebrate with Poppa this evening, and then when he goes to bed, I will celebrate with my companions. They know how to have a good time.

Our work was hectic. Poppa had a special lunch delivered to us. He told Linus and his guards that today was a special day. They asked what made it special. He told them it was because this is the day that I was given to him and Momma. He shared how he can still see a lot of Momma in me. They congratulated both of us. We had a delicious dessert made with honey and grapes. It was incredibly good.

Poppa and I had a great meal at home. Again, he paid someone to cook for us. We laughed. We fellowshipped. At bedtime, he saw me to my room. Gently kissing me on the forehead, he wished me a good night. I almost feel bad leaving him. He has set his mat by the front door. Because he is such a diligent worker, sleep is sweet to him. It was also readily available. He was out within minutes. I have packed my birthday skirt and purple veil in a sack. I am climbing through the window onto the balcony. I will grab hold of the fig tree branch as I have done so many times before. I will then lower myself to the ground. I will put on my skirt and veil below. I am so excited. I deserve a night on the town. I know the men will be glad to see me.

On the third month, the thirteenth day — They tore my skirt. They stole my veil. All I am wearing is my undergarment. The men were happy to see me — all of me. I told them that I just wanted to celebrate, nothing more. But after a few drinks of strong wine, I was dancing with every one of them. Then they had me dance for them. They began to shout for me to undress. I told them that I was not going to do that. This was my birthday, not theirs. That was when they started pulling at my clothes. I wanted to leave. I wanted to stay.

I wanted to do right. I wanted to do what they wished. Atticus is a young man who has recently begun to run with my Gentile friends. He is handsome. Of all the men, he was the one for whom I wanted to do whatever he asked. Egged on by his buddies, he made the move. I accepted in a semi-private part of the shore. No sooner had we made love, another came. I resisted. Inside a voice pleaded to let him in. I did. Then came the next. Another voice in my head, came out my mouth, saying "Let's love on them all." That is the last thing I remember.

My friends say I then began to speak to them with seven different voices, taking seven different names. One minute they said I identified as Sarah. The next minute, another voice called Horatio came out. At first, they were amused. Then they were scared. They said I was begging for fishhooks. The men knew better. Poppa's guard, Linus, appeared. I was surprised when he told them to leave me alone. I ran from him barefoot with just my undergarment. I swore. I howled. I ran to Mount Arbel among the graves of my Momma and others.

On the third month, the fourteenth day — Poppa gathered me up from Arbel. He looked so alarmed. He kept saying, "Mary, you don't look the same. Mary, why are you talking in those voices?" I could hear them, too. I could feel them. But I could not control them. It was as if I was no longer an individual, but many. I am writing this down. I am not sure if any will read it, but I am now afraid myself.

On the third month, the twenty-first day — Poppa left his assistant to run the tax booth. Rome is giving him leniency. He is not simply good at his job, he is also a good manager and delegator. He packed for the both of us. He told me we are going to find someone to help with my sickness. Our first stop will be to see Judas the Galilean. He claims to be the Messiah.

On the third month, the twenty-third day — It is told Judas has divine powers. I have heard of stories of people he healed. Poppa and I met with him today. I carry my bound parchments to take note of any guidance he can give. He asked Poppa to let me stay in his home for the night. He says he will take the evening to pray to the gods for a method of treatment. A reference to plural gods made Poppa hesitant, but he concurred. He is desperate.

I wish Poppa had not left me. Judas came into my room. He touched my forehead, had me remove my robe. He acted as if he was examining me, but his touch said something different. The next thing I know, he was being intimate. He said it was all part of the treatment. I have received this treatment many times. It was neither Messianic nor medicinal. He left. He warned me not to share this with anyone. Otherwise, the cure will not work. His men are guarding my door. They are not friendly looking men. They are men of swords and armor. They carry bows with quivers of arrows. They threaten me. They pledge harm to my father. I cannot sleep.

On the third month, the twenty-fourth day — Judas the Galilean is no Messiah. He is a liar. He acted as if he had run me through several treatments and I should be fine now. He told Poppa I was a little out of my mind, hallucinating sexual acts, but after the medicine set in, I calmed. Judas is a fake. After raping me, I heard him share his intentions with his men. He plans to gather the Jewish people to take down Rome. Then, he says Israel will be his.

Poppa was very caring. He wanted me to speak. I could not. He asked if everything went well. I stoically answered, "Yes Poppa." He said he hopes this will work. I told him I think it will not. He then asked, "Should we try someone else?" A voice came out of my mouth, "Quit trying. She is ours now."

On the fourth month, the sixth day — We entered Jerusalem today. I have been too tired to write. There has been nothing that I want to write. I spent this trip listening to voices in my head. I heard voices come out of my mouth. Poppa is more afraid each day. He will not sleep for fear I will run away. Poor man. Linus has accompanied us, as well as his Jewish servant, Thaddeus. They are here to help Poppa. Even so, my father cannot sleep. His eyes fill with tears every time he speaks to me. He has hope now, though.

We entered Jerusalem from the Mount of Olives. As we topped the mount, Jerusalem and the Temple spread out before us. It was simply breathtaking. It had been a while since I had accompanied Poppa here. I remember the last time, it was the three of us. Momma always loved the view from the Mount of Olives. She was so enamored with the sight. She would always say that as much as she loved the bimah stone in the Magdala Synagogue as a replica of the Temple in Jerusalem, nothing could compare to the actual Temple. The last time we made the journey, Momma stopped at the top of the Mount under the shade of a massive old olive tree. She refused to budge. Poppa and I sat beside her for almost an hour. She would not speak. She just smiled in awe. I wish Momma were here now. I paused as we topped the Mount. Poppa saw I was not following. He walked back. I think he knew my thoughts. He simply put his arm around me. We looked below the glistening Temple, at the walls of Jerusalem, enjoying the aroma of the sacrifices. "Pleasing to God is this city. This is His Temple," Poppa said. "Come, let us go down to worship." With that, we made our way down.

We crossed through the Kidron Valley. We entered the city through the Sheep's Gate. We passed by the Pool of Bethesda. It is here that we are told healing can occur. It very well may be here that we return. It all depends on what the priest tells us to do.

We walked to the Temple. We entered the court of the Gentiles. Buyers and sellers were everywhere. Poppa bought a lamb for a sin offering. I know he is a good man. He is honest. He is fair. Perhaps, he believes his sin caused the loss of Momma. Maybe it is because of his sin I am facing what I am facing. I do not think Poppa's life has anything to do with any of this except perhaps why people follow me everywhere. He still does not see them. I have been followed all the way from Magdala to here. It is very scary.

Just west of the Temple, Poppa entered the mikveh. He asked if I wanted to do the same. I declined. Poppa then led the lamb past the Court of the Gentiles, through the Beautiful Gate into the Court of the Women. He had me wait there. He then entered the Inner Court with the lamb. There was a long line, so I just waited against the wall, next to the gate. Why all this fuss? I pity these. The thought that a person can do wrong, kill an animal, and everything is then okay makes no sense to me. I know it is my heritage, but I have never understood it. We should do whatever makes us happy. This is how I have lived.

I write that here inside this gate. A woman is walking toward me.

This Jewish woman introduced herself to me in the middle of my writing. She said, "Hello, my name is Maria. Are you lost? Is there anything I can do to help?" I could tell she was very caring. Her face beamed sincerity. She had a peace about her. What is it about me that makes her think I need help? But Maria reminded me of my mother. I let her know that I was just waiting on my Poppa. I caught her eye glancing down at my parchments. I quickly closed them. I stared at her for a minute. I nodded as if to say, "Goodbye". With that, she walked away.

Back to my writing; where was I? Oh, that's right, we should live to make ourselves happy above all. That is what I have done. For some reason, these words ring convincingly. I have done what makes me happy. Then, where is my happiness? I am sure not happy people are following me. I am not happy that I have these voices inside my head. The voices coming from my mouth that do not match my normal voice do not please me at all. I am not pleased with the scars from the fishhooks. It bothers me that men use me for their pleasure. I am grieved knowing that I still let them. I am not happy that I have upset Poppa. I am not pleased at all that the stress I brought may have contributed to Momma's death. I am thirty-three years old and not married, have no home of my own, and cannot be left on my own away from Poppa. Has what I have been doing made me happy?

Here in this Temple court, I have mocked all things religious. It has all seemed like a crutch. Yet, I saw Poppa walk into the Inner Court, wet-headed from the mikveh. He looked at peace, leading that lamb to slaughter. It was as if he had found the answer to life's woes. I see the woman, Maria, caring, concerned, as if she has it all together. Am I happy? I feel empty inside except when the voices speak. Then I am in horror. Is religion what I need? If so, which one? Spiritual matters seem to have a great variety of choices. Most people seem to try one, then another, then return to the one they preferred, albeit half-heartedly. Even the most religious do not seem serious about their religion. It is like a shawl people choose for certain occasions, just to be returned to the drawer when the need passes. I do not think that is for me. Yet, I am empty. I am hurting.

Something about gazing at this Temple, I feel I can almost see Adonai hovering above. The clouds float over us, the smoke rising seems to display a heavenly, open arms gesture receiving what the smoke is delivering upward.

That was a long pause. Is God there? Does He see? Have I ruined it with Him? I feel a tenderness, almost a sustenance offered from above that my soul needs.

Here comes Poppa. He has blood on his hands, a deep red spatter on his robe. He laid his hands on the lamb. He cut the throat of it. The priest took the blood and placed it on the altar. Parts of the animal were burnt.

Once the lamb was walking in, with no idea why. Now Poppa walks out alone. He seems at peace.

In the eighteenth year of the reign of Tiberius Caesar, on the fourth month, the seventh day — We are waiting our turn to see the high priest, Annas, which is an exceedingly rare privilege. Few get to see him. Poppa has become well-known to the governor here, Pontius Pilate. It is Governor Pilate who has asked Annas to see us. He agreed. It seems the Jewish priests and the Roman government are at odds, yet work together at times. I know Simon the Zealot hates this! They do favors for each other as efforts of goodwill. I am a little nervous. So we wait.

They escorted us into Annas' house, a beautiful, elaborate home just southwest of the Temple. As we passed the courtyard, beautiful flowers were everywhere. What was surprising is the high priest has his own private mikveh. He also has a cistern within the walls of his complex. Everything is so extravagant. Who says religion is a vocation of poverty? Not here. Annas even has his own army. Poppa has Linus and a few guards. Annas has an army of soldiers at his disposal. They are calling us in. I pray he will not use his army on us.

That was strange. Annas was like the physician Xenophan. He asked many questions. He wanted to know if I had ever made any sacrifices to foreign gods. Poppa looked at me. I said, "No." Annas asked if I had ever worshiped the moon or the stars. Again, Poppa looked at me, and I said, "No." Annas asked if I had any idols in our home. I felt this one hit. I had given Poppa an amulet for good luck, but I have not seen it since the day I gave it to him. I still have the tintinnabulum bells in my window to ward off any evil. They have not worked so far, so I owned up to them with Poppa and the high priest. He felt they may be the problem. He ordered that we get rid of them immediately. He handed us a jar with water and the ashes from the red heifer. Annas ordered that we go back to our home and sprinkle them throughout our house. Sadly, what he did not know was that I was having issues before I bought the tintinnabulum. In fact, it was because of those struggles that I bought the charm of bells.

The high priest ordered I be immersed in the mikvah. Afterward, I am to make an offering of fine flour for my sins. Poppa asked, "Is that all?" Annas said, "Yes." Poppa then asked, "Will this make my daughter Mary well?" Annas answered, "We pray so. Let us pray now." There I was, as if I were just a sick lamb with no input or need for my consent. Annas did pray beautifully. Poppa wept; he could not quit weeping. After the prayer, Annas asked if he was okay. Poppa told him about the need to change jobs, about Momma's death, and gave details about my indiscretions. We went to see Annas for me. I fear this was more for Poppa. My father then gave Annas a sizeable offering. I was a little bothered by that. This high priest does not need anything. Why are we paying him? But then again, we paid Xenophan.

We left the high priest. Poppa dropped by the praetorium to thank Governor Pilate. I was not allowed inside. We then went back to the mikveh on the west side of the Temple. It was then I was struck by all the limestone. This whole city is like one big limestone block except for the gold Temple, which is so bright in the sunlight, that I can barely look at it. Poppa told me that is intentional. Just as we cannot look at the Temple in the sunlight, so we cannot look at God in His glory. Of all that I faced these last two days, that made the most sense to me.

Poppa bought some fine flour in the Court of the Women. He then went with me to give my offering to the priest, who burned it. With that, Poppa said, "Let's go home. We must purify our house. I will dispose of the tintinnabulum in your window."

In the eighteenth year of the reign of Tiberius Caesar, on the fourth month, the twenty- ninth day — We made it back home. Poppa went immediately to my room and tore my charm of bells from my window. He pulled them apart and burned them. He half-way apologized to me. I told him there was no need. They had no power that I could see. He said that more than anything, he wants me well.

Poppa then led us outside. He took the jar of water and ashes from the red heifer the high priest gave us. He clenched the jar between his hands and prayed. He then began to sprinkle the house outside, all around the black basalt stone walls. He entered our front door. I followed. He prayed in every room as he sprinkled. He went upstairs. He repeated the prayer, sprinkling in my room, by my window, and then in his room.

With what was left in the jar, he climbed an outside ladder to the branches and clay of our roof. He emptied the purifying water left in the container there and placed the container in our storeroom.

After the cleansing duties, we sat in our courtyard facing the Sea of Galilee, eating our noon meal. We talked about Poppa's plans. He keeps speaking of leaving the tax booth. He then speaks of the work ahead at the tax booth. I do not think he wants to quit. It keeps him busy. It keeps him engaged, and it gives me work by his side. That is fine. We are a great team.

The question for the evening in my room was, did all this ritual stuff work? For the moment, it seems to. I feel normal. I have heard no voices since we made our sacrifice. I even prayed before the altar: "God, if You are there, let this work. Give me peace, please. Forgive all the things I have done that you see as sin. Amen." That is my prayer again this evening.

On the fifth month, the first day — We attended the synagogue at the harbor. Those there on the shore seem less pious. None of them know us very well, either. There were no whispers. Some of the fishermen even greeted Poppa, though their motivation may be for less taxes assessed their next visit to the booth.

This synagogue has a normal bimah, nothing ornate like the neighborhood one. It does have a main hall with two side rooms, though. Six pillars are here, too, to hold the roof up. The plaster-covered walls are decorated in more extravagant colors than the other in our town. This one has the Torah closet, but the way it is placed, it seems to have been an afterthought. Many more candleholders are there, along with more ornate glass bowls.

The synagogue ruler read from the Torah about the cleansing rituals. It is ironic that the day after we perform these rituals, we are taught in this synagogue about them. I wonder if Poppa told this rabbi something? I am sure he needs someone to confide in locally, especially over spiritual matters. Oh well, for some reason, I felt comfortable. The words spoken from the text resonated with what we did in Jerusalem. It was a timely affirmation. Maybe we are on the right track.

On the fifth month, the second day — Today was a great day. We are back in the tax booth — father and daughter. Everyone has been truly kind to us. Linus and the men have been very tender toward me. They have been quietly submissive to Poppa. Even the people coming to pay their taxes were more respectful.

Zebedee's sons came with a large catch of fish. They were delighted that we only charged them one tax, as we confirmed that they are now operating solely in Herod Agrippa's jurisdiction in Capernaum.

I have been neglectful to record the money we make from the tax booth. If a person paid approximately ten percent on their goods, produce, spices, or land, Poppa's mark-up amounted to about one third of that.

Needless to say, this Magdala port makes us approximately twenty times a citizen's daily wage per day. That sounds exorbitant until you realize that Poppa is well-educated, greatly experienced, and extremely hated. When you consider those factors, it makes the pay about right. We have also gained a portion of lands confiscated for refusal to pay taxes. Our holdings have been substantial. I qualify this in that our tax booth is the most fair in the area. Poppa's peer, Levi in Capernaum, lacks the volume and variety at his booth, so he increases his percentages to extortionary levels.

Over the years, Poppa has accumulated productive vineyards, a fleet of boats he rents, shops he leases, lands he cultivates, and gold he stores away in a safe place. He even owns the land upon which our booth sits. He rents it back to the Romans. He has been incredibly wise in his management of assets. We live in a nice home with the two stories and a courtyard on an outcrop with nothing to block our view of the sea. Poppa could have built a bigger home, but he tries to keep our wealth indiscernible. I am not sure I will ever marry. I am content with that. I have shared a bed with many men, as well as the shoreline. I do not find a need for a man. With that said, if I do join myself in marriage to a man, I dare say he will be quite pleased with his dowry.

On the fifth month, the third day — Poppa and I took a break for lunch today to visit the marketplace. I was a little nervous, but Poppa held my hand. We passed by the fishermen's supply store. A few people saw me nearby. They crossed over to the other side of the street. Do they not know that it is me I hurt, not others? That is, unless someone is trying to stop me from doing harm to myself. I pray all that is past.

Funny I wrote that: I pray. I am praying some of late. The sacrifices we made at the Temple, the cleansing ritual we performed at home, the message at the synagogue two days ago — all of these have given me calm. No voices.

On the fifth month, the fourth day — Poppa received a certificate of honor today from the town clerk. He brought it by personally to our booth. It reads, "To Jared, the local administrative revenue official. Let it be known this day that the city of Magdala sends this certificate of appreciation for the generous donation made to complete the city's new harbor pier." It had the seal of Herod Antipas. I am glad the city sees that my father is a wise businessman who also believes in giving to the community. We immediately posted it upon our tax booth for every person to see as they meet with Poppa to satisfy their assessment. A few dignitaries then accompanied us to the dedication of the pier. How great to see Poppa smile. I do not think it will make us loved in this village, but it does take the edge off.

Our supper was one of celebration — just Poppa and me. We enjoyed our courtyard. We reminisced about Momma. We discussed a few of the psalms of David. Then we parted for sleep. I am writing this now before I turn in. I do not miss the tintinnabulum in my window. I feel God is wanting me to have peace with Him. We have many trees in the Lower Galilee. The one we need is the butma tree. My understanding is this is the tree where people meet to make up for a fight. I do not feel Adonai has been fighting with me. I am the one fighting with Him by how I have lived most of my years. If only I could find a butma tree. How I would love to have Him meet with me there, face to face, so that I could know that I am right with Him. It would also help me find assurance that He exists. If only I could meet Him in His person.

On the fifth month, the sixth day — Atticus showed up at our booth today. I have not thought of a man in a good while. He was so kind. He had a small tax to pay. He then gave me a sweet bottle of perfume. He is a few years younger than me. He seems so innocent compared to the men with whom he works.

On the fifth month, the ninth day — Poppa and I made it to synagogue again yesterday. The reading came from a proverb of Solomon about the management of money. I kept looking at my father. Every principle shared was what Poppa has practiced his whole life. No wonder we have been blessed. Some say Poppa is a thief stealing bread from the mouths of families. As I wrote before, I believe a workman is worth his wage. Poppa is just carrying out what the ruling authority of Rome requires.

On the fifth month, the eleventh day — We took the day off to go to Mount Arbel to visit Momma's tomb. Everything was in order. It was a sweet time to talk of Momma. I almost felt she could hear us. It was like it was the three of us again. Poppa and I sat beside the stone cover facing the sea. We had a few pickled fish and some bread. It was a delightful picnic.

Later, we climbed Arbel. It is wonderful to get exercise at such a meaningful place.

On the fifth month, the fourteenth day — Atticus came back to the booth this afternoon just before we were closing. He asked if we could walk along the sea for a bit. I asked Poppa. He was hesitant. I know why. Things have gone so well with me in his sight. I knew his feelings. I let him know all would be okay. He relented.

We had a nice walk. I did not let Atticus walk me home. We returned to the booth and I left him there. He is considerate, not pushy. I know we have had intimacy. I think he realizes now that is behind us. We need to go about this the right way. Inside, I want him, though. I pray he cannot tell. It would not take much to push me over. I hate that I feel that. When I do right, everything is simple. When I do what makes me happy, the wrong things I want, everything falls apart.

On the fifth month, the twenty-third day — It has been an incredibly busy few weeks. Everyone is pressing to meet Rome's demand for fish. As their empire expands, the need for food grows. With the catch and the pickling, the taxes on the two grow. This is the required process before things are shipped out. Poppa and I are working long hours. We have added a couple of helpers. I oversee them. Poppa still is the final stop for all merchants.

We have not been able to go to synagogue, nor have we reflected on any scripture. Poppa is tired and a little short on patience. He snapped at me today, bringing an ire that I have not felt in a good while.

On the fifth month, the twenty-fourth day — Poppa has left the booth so my male friend Atticus could help me pick up the booth to prepare for the next day. He asked me to a party for his uncle this evening. It is late, so I am going straight from here with him.

On the sixth month, the third day — Everything has come undone. I am at the bottom of the cistern, chained. I have blood on my hands. My robe is torn. They say I stabbed a man in a rage. The doctor says he will live. The judge is coming by today. Two witnesses say the man was raping me. His men deny it. Atticus is nowhere to be found. The voices are calling. Three others from that night are chained on the other side of this hole in the ground. They are separated from my sight by a poorly constructed wooden wall. I am angry. I have been wasting my time doing good. No more of that. Others can act out on their pleasures. They do not face the complications I face. Why?

Eee xxx tu woookken isesesseaxxtt

Llleeee seven seven seven seven seven seven seven

7 7 7 7 8 no 7 7 7 (Mary's writing indiscernible)

Momma, you are here! I miss you Momma. Get me out. Poppa is no help.

6 shekels 12 talents our new pier

On the sixth month, the fifth day — I went before the judge today. The man I stabbed will be okay. He will serve no time. The judge was going to let me off, but then I began to scream at him in a guttural voice, calling him things I dare not write. With that, I have been given thirty days in this dank, dark, humid, and hot cistern. As they dragged me out, I overpowered eight of their guards. Just as I was about to run out, Poppa stepped in front of me. I tore his shirt. Horatio inside my head growled, "Move, Jared, or I will kill her." I waited for Poppa's response. He did nothing. Something in me drew back to slap him, but I was able to restrain it. I broke down, crying, "Help me, Poppa. Forgive me, God." Ten Roman soldiers, Linus among them, escorted me here. Poppa followed close behind.

How do you like that Mary?!

Xooxxvebe **?? (Mary's writing indiscernible)

You belong to us now. Let us rule you. Do not resist. This will be easier, Mary. Write that down. Remember what we are telling you.

On sixth month, the eighth day — I am laying on a mat in the cistern, but my right arm is chained. The pallet is soaked in blood. This time, not from a man, but from my own neck and arms. What happened?

Now I remember. The guard slid me a knife. He told me if I did not like my treatment, this was the way out. He motioned the knife across his throat. He handed it to me, saying, "Now you copy that, Mary, but closer. Make contact. It will all be over." I remember weeping, begging. He left me with it. At some point, I must have tried.

On the sixth month, the ninth day — Poppa came to see me. He said I tried to kill myself. I asked him how I got the knife. He told me I stole it from the scabbard of the guard while he was bringing me food and water. Yes, of course. That is what the guard told my father. What else would he say?

Poppa just held me. I sat limp. I would not return the embrace. Why would he love me? I do not think I love him or anybody else. I just want to be happy.

On the sixth month, the twelfth day — Poppa came to see me again today. He has not missed one day. He works the booth. He looks so tired, but he comes to see me every day. Today he was upbeat. He said he met with his counterpart from Capernaum, Levi. Poppa believes there is a cure for me. There is a doctor for me. He is a rabbi from that area. Poppa shared with me that he believes the town clerk, the judge, and the Roman authority will let him take me to see this man.

I was consoled that my father had a sign of hope in his eyes, but I remember the last rabbi he took me to — Judas of Galilee. All he did was rape me and pretend he did his magic. Have I not been through enough?

Even the high priest and the Temple were temporary pacifications. I protested. Poppa said it is that, or isolation for another thirty days. Funny he said that. I looked around. I had not noticed. I am in this cistern alone.

I am writing by the moonlight that shines through the gap between the wall and the roof. I hear the sea stirring. I feel the cool lake breeze. Laughter is emanating from a local tavern. The cut on my neck is sore and itching. I dare not scratch it. I fear infection leading to sickness will make this place even more miserable.

I felt I had made some steps to healing when I was in Jerusalem. I want that again. Can this rabbi in Capernaum help? I doubt it. I wonder what his name is. I had heard of another supposed Messiah named Theudas. From what I am told, he is no different than the Galilean, Judas.

"God, will you help me? I am in the bottom of this pit. The dogs are all around me. The enemy seeks to destroy me. The voices haunt me at night. Are You there? Are You real? Please show Yourself to me. Please. If not for me, for Poppa. Please?"

On the sixth month, the thirteenth day — Poppa bought me a new skirt to wear. He is finishing his paperwork. He assigned his new assistant to run the booth. We are going to Capernaum. I hear this rabbi moved there permanently. I asked Poppa his name. He says it is Jesus. I love that name. It is our Greek form of the Hebrew Joshua — "God is salvation." I prayed last night for God to come to my rescue. Maybe He will save me. How I pray God will use this rabbi for my good.

We are about to leave. It will not be just me and Poppa. The judge required ten Roman guards to accompany us. They do not trust me. Poppa argued, but to no avail. He says it is worth everything to get me well.

We have walked for three hours. We are now in Capernaum. For the devout Jewish worshiper, that distance is way too far for a Sabbath-day walk. Poppa understood that, but there was no time to lose.

We checked in with Levi. He was very cordial to us. He told us we had come on a good day. He told us to go to the synagogue and ask Jairus, the synagogue ruler, where the rabbi was. We knew Jairus from his visits to Magdala. Levi chose not to come with us. He does not go to the synagogue. He keeps his distance. He cares for his family. He tends to the tax business. Besides, people in these parts hate him, even more so than we are hated in Magdala.

Levi's house is on the Magdala side of Capernaum. We did not get a mile away when we were overwhelmed by crowds and crowds of people. It was not a Jewish festival here. There were no games here, no arena like the one in Magdala. We had no clue. We only had a vague idea where the synagogue was. Linus asked one of the Capernaum soldiers if an uprising was occurring. The man said, "No. A miracle."

A miracle? Linus inquired as to what kind of miracle. It turned out, the Rabbi Jesus was speaking in the synagogue that Jairus oversees, and a demon-possessed man began to scream out, "What do you want with us, Jesus of Nazareth?" I was overwhelmed with nausea. Poppa had me sit. One of the men brought me a cool rag. The Capernaum soldier looked at me leerily. He asked, "Are you here for the same reason the other thousands are?"

Poppa did not know what he meant. "That is a good question. What is this crowd here for?" The soldier replied, "They are gathering outside Simon Peter and his brother Andrew's home. They are hoping to catch a glimpse of Jesus. They are pleading for Him to heal their loved ones. Young lady, are you sick?" Poppa looked at me. I looked at the guard and honestly answered, "I am very sick." He told us we had come to the right place. He directed us to the home of Simon Peter and Andrew. I was struck by the oddity. Those two fishermen had actually moved from Bethsaida to Capernaum, and the tax collectors from Magdala are going to their home? Someone in the crowd yelled out, "James and John! Please have Jesus heal my wife!" James and John, partners of their father Zebedee, those two hotheads are present with the Rabbi also?

The hours have been many now. The crowd is crushing us forward. People from up ahead are running out, shouting with glee, "I am healed!" Another, "Hallelujah, I can see!" A lady is carrying her mat, the one she swore she laid upon for twenty-nine years, unable to move.

Time is passing rapidly now. The closer we get, the more excited we become. Poppa has me sitting with the soldiers guarding me. I am able to write. It is as if I am Herod's daughter, someone of importance, not a criminal. With such a guard, no one cuts in front of us. The time is late. Poppa says we will stay in this line all night if that is what it takes. I agree.

Someone else has had demons cast out of them. I heard them shouting. I asked Linus what the soldier told him about the man in the synagogue screaming about demons. He said that while the Rabbi Jesus was preaching, the demon-possessed man cried out, "What do you want with us, Jesus of Nazareth? Have you come to destroy us? I know who you are — the Holy One of God!"

I began to writhe in pain. Voices began to come from my mouth — not one at a time, but all at once. The Roman soldiers flinched. One drew his sword. Another thrust his shield forward. Poppa did not move, but said, "Hold her. This is why you are here. You are soldiers trained for battle." They did.

I am calm again. I am taking notes. My thoughts are racing. The Holy One of God. A demon calls Jesus that? This term is for the Messiah. Judas the Galilean said he was the Messiah. Theudas claimed he was. Both are fakes. No demon called them that. These two men called themselves that. It makes sense that only One with real power can evoke such a response from demons.

I said the name, "Jesus."

I am on the floor again. Linus brings the damp rag. Why is this happening? The voices inside, the beings inside me, the "we" who claim I am theirs; I sense their fear. I will say his name again. "Jesus."

I fell into seizures. They placed the cloth in my mouth.

I am calm now. I say this man's name and they tremble. A voice screams from my mouth, "DON'T SAY THAT NAME!" Everyone is looking at me. I just lower my head to write.

The men had not heard me say His name. Poppa asks, "My daughter, what name did we say that offended you?" He must have been reflecting back on some of the men who abused me by the shore. I said, "Poppa, that was not me." Poppa turned pale. "If it was not you, who was it?" I told him it seemed clear to me now. It must be demons inside. Poppa said, "Put down your pen."

We are near the door. I can see the Rabbi. Urgently, Poppa had the soldiers push forward. We passed others in line ahead of us. Poppa yelled, "There's no time to waste! Please let us through. This is an emergency!" With the guards opening the way before us, for some reason, no one voiced objection.

I see Him. I dare not say His name again. I cannot lose my place. We are so close. He smiled at the little girl before Him. He looked at her parents with the most concerned attention. He nodded as they spoke. He opened his eyes wider as they shared some symptom. He looked at the girl. I could see the girl, too. She stood in an uneven manner. Her parents spoke of her fever and recalled her muscle pain. The Rabbi knelt down to touch her left foot, which dangled above the ground, while her right foot was squarely stationed on the soil. He then looked up to the sky. I heard Him pray. I watched His eyes glisten with joyful tears. He looked down. I looked down. Now this little girl's left foot was planted parallel to her right foot. The little girl, with a "Weeeeee!", jumped up in the air. She began to move her legs up and down as if running in place. Her mother covered her face weeping. "Thank you, Rabbi! Thank you, Lord!"

Next man up. Poppa made the guards stand between me and the older gentleman. He has no ears. He has sores. Everyone gave him room. A leper here in this crowd? I had never seen one. I had heard of leprosy. My father and mother had prayed that disease would never hit our family. They had described such a condition to me, but I had never seen one with this malady. What is this Rabbi going to do? I would say His name, but I am too close to getting help.

This Rabbi touched the man, left hand on the man's right ear. Right hand on the man's left ear. I was so disgusted. I looked away. But I could not for long. This Rabbi looked to Heaven. He just sighed. When He removed His hands . . . When He removed His hands . . . When He removed His hands, the man's ears were there. His sores were gone. The man hugged the Rabbi. He screamed with joy, "Rabbi, I AM CLEAN!!! I AM CLEAN!!! Did you all hear? I AM CLEAN!!!

Now it has been four hours. We are staying in Levi's guesthouse. Poppa prayed with me. He is staying by my side. An excitement has come over me. I yelled for all of Capernaum to hear, "I am delivered!!! Did you hear me say that? I am delivered! The voices have gone! The demons have been cast away! I can think. There is no anger. There is no conflict. There are no voices."

I did everything to stir them. I said His name, "Jesus," and nothing but peace flooded over me. Love fills my soul. I am made well! I can hardly write. I just want to run. But I must write. How could I record the assets of a merchant and not put to paper the best discovery ever? I will try.

Before I could grasp what I saw with the leper, the Roman soldiers parted in front of me. I stood directly in front of this man. He looked at me with such kindness. I felt forgiven immediately. The flour sacrifice in Jerusalem was nothing to this. He said to my father, "Jared, how can I help your daughter Mary?" Poppa looked at me. I glanced back at him for a moment. We said nothing, but felt the same thing: How did He know our names? Could it have been because of the soldiers? Had my father's reputation preceded him? Did Jairus share some things, or maybe Levi? I looked behind him, there was Simon. Maybe it was Simon. He knew us all too well, and not fondly. However, Simon seemed different. He looked as shocked as we did when Jesus (I said His name again, and no shrieks) said our names.

Poppa answered Jesus. He told Him about all that I had been enduring. Jesus did not rush Poppa. He did not demand the bare facts. He did not interrupt all the details. He listened as if no patience was required. Jesus looked at me as Poppa talked. His eyes of compassion told me that He understood — that I was in good hands. Poppa told Him about the fishhooks, about my stabbing a man, about my sexual activity, about the knife I took to my own throat. Poppa also told Him about the voices.

It was then the Rabbi Jesus interrupted. "I could see them when you first arrived in Capernaum. I felt their fear while you waited in line. Even when Lucias, the Roman soldier, was telling Linus about what the demon of the man screamed in the synagogue, I felt the trauma they were putting you through, Mary." He said my name as He seemed to be not just telling Poppa this, but me, too. He knew the name of the soldier Lucias. He also knew Linus's name.

Then He asked, "How bad are the scars from the fishhooks and knife cut? How hurtful are the scars of the rapes and sexual abuse?" Poppa said they were terrible. Then the Rabbi Jesus — I love His name . . . still no response of anger, still no voices — then the Rabbi Jesus said, "Mary, God loves you. I am here to prove that. I saw the guard run his hand beneath your cloak. I saw the trade you offered him for freedom. I saw you when you lost your mother. I know the guilt you have faced. I saw at the shore when Atticus and the men assaulted you. I watched the guard hand you the knife. You fought it and then gave in. I kept you from bleeding out. I saw when the demons entered you back on that shore when the magic arts were presented to you, and you joined in willingly. I saw the tintinnabulum on your window, the demonic thing you welcomed even unknowingly."

At this point, the demons inside began to scream. Jesus commanded, "Silence!" Then not a sound was heard. The Rabbi said, "Mary, there are seven in you. I am going to cast them out." He raised His head to Heaven, and with a voice like the sound at Creation, He said, "Come out!" I fell to the ground. He took my hand. With a clarity in my eyes, I fixed upon His. "Mary," He said, "you are free. Worship God. Receive Me as your Lord and Savior. You asked to see God face-to face. You wanted to see His person. Now you have."

The Roman guards with us did not bat an eye. Linus fell to his knees before Him. The Rabbi touched him. He said, "Linus, I offer you the same. Jared, you too. I know your hurt. I know your grief. Old things are passed away. All things are made new."

Is this how it happened? I am writing it, but to be honest, with my record, I do not know. When a moment comes upon you like that, when demons are one minute fogging your brain, then a total cleansing — all the words and actions do not seem to come to my mind. They do not seem to matter. I met Jesus today. I have seen God face to face in His Son. I am not sure how to understand that. But I am free. I am saved. I am not writing the Holy Scriptures. I do not know many of them, anyway. I cannot add to what God has done. All I know is, once I was possessed, now I am free.

I wanted to linger before Him, but there were many behind me. I left His presence. As I walked away, I glanced back. Six men ushered before Him a young boy on a stretcher, barely breathing. He gave them the same attention He gave me. He never looked away from them. At that moment, this young man was the most important thing in His life. Just like a few minutes before, I was the most important thing in His life. Just like an hour before, the girl with the uneven leg was the most important thing in His life.

In the eighteenth year of the reign of Tiberius Caesar, on the sixth month, the fourteenth day — Poppa let me sleep in. I could hear him and Levi talking. Outside my window, I heard the Roman soldiers of our guard recounting what had happened the night before. I have never slept this well in my life. I would wake up. Try to rouse. Feel the softness of this mat, the smoothness of the fine linen covers. I had no need to get up. I have not rested in years. I would hear the sound of their stories. I could not help but smile. I did an internal inventory. Nothing inside me but me — and a whole lot of love that only God can give. I drifted off to sleep a few more times.

Poppa peeked into my room. I heard him. I looked up. He came, kissed me on the head. He quietly walked out after saying, "Sleep, dear child." Peace.

I finally roused around midday. I could smell a fine meal wafting through the house. Poppa heard me stir. He brought me the finest breakfast choices I have ever seen. I sat up. I asked him to join me. He said, "I thought you'd never ask." He sat beside my bed this morning. We spoke about only one main topic — Jesus. We had seen a miracle. It happened to us. Jesus performed it for us. Just knowing Jesus was in this town made me not want to leave. I told Poppa I wanted to stay. I wanted to see Him again. Just as I never wanted to be out of Momma and Poppa's presence, now I do not want to be out of His. Poppa asked me, "Do you still feel like people are following you?" I could honestly answer, "No Poppa. I have absolutely no more fears." He smiled. So glad we made this trip. No comparison exists between Xenophan, Judas the Galilean, or Annas the high priest. Okay, maybe a little difference between the two former and Annas.

I begged Poppa to stay in Capernaum. I wanted to be with Jesus, to hear Him, to watch Him. Maybe, just maybe, I could get to know Him personally, talk to Him as a friend. Poppa relented. He said he would talk to Jairus to see where Jesus would be speaking today. With that, he left. I got dressed. Everything was new.

Poppa just returned. I cannot say bad news, but it definitely was not what I wanted to hear. Jesus had left Capernaum. Some saw Him walk out early this morning as they were coming in from a night of fishing. His friends, Simon, Andrew, James, and John, went after Him. No one knows where they are off to. Jairus says that's how rabbis are. They travel from synagogue to synagogue. He supposes Jesus is no different in that aspect, but so different in every other.

An interesting thing Jairus told us. He said Jesus always follows our Jewish faith to the letter. He observes every Sabbath. He forgives. He is kind even when people are ugly toward Him. He listens. He honors every holy day. He tithes. He pays His taxes. He never is alone with a woman, and if a female approaches Him, He always moves out in public so all can see. The prophet John, who was the son of a very well-respected Jewish priest among our people, baptized Him. Suddenly, I have a passion to live out our faith as Jewish people adhering to the Laws of Moses. If One with such power submits to God in this way, how can I not? Poppa and I agreed that from now on, we will follow the faith of Abraham, Isaac, Jacob, and Moses without exception.

We are leaving now for Magdala. Two synagogues are there. Perhaps Jesus is headed to our hometown. I sure pray so, and I do pray now — constantly. There is one God, the God of Israel. There is no Neptune, no Jupiter, no amulet, no praying to a star or the moon or the sun. God created all of these. How proud Momma must be if she can see us now!

In the eighteenth year of the reign of Tiberius Caesar, on the sixth month, the sixteenth day — This morning, Poppa and I began our day with prayer. We then headed to the tax booth. Many walked on the other side of the road as we made our way to work. This was not uncommon, as many choose to show their hatred for Poppa's position very subtly. They also held a fear, I think, of me. After all, I was arrested for stabbing a man. Of course, this town knows he is a scoundrel of the most wicked sort. If I could hear their thoughts, I am sure some were thinking, "That dog had it coming. It's a shame she didn't finish him off and then herself."

The hatred is strong still for us. It is understandable. It is also unimportant. What God thinks of us is what is important. Now that we are seeking Him, nothing else matters. And I am free. No more demons. A newfound delight and a freedom are present that I have never known. I feel as though I am walking on air.

The sea breeze is sweeter. The aroma of the shore blesses me. The flowers and the trees delight. The birds' singing makes me walk in silence to pick up every tune. No drink can give such joy. No fellowship can match the one Jesus brought us with God, Adonai.

The line at the tax booth was heavy. Poppa levied the taxes, but today he made no extra charge for our services. He would exact just what the Roman authorities requested and nothing more. This meant the taxes people paid were about one-third less than normal.

News spread quickly. People who were not due to see us this week showed up early. Poppa did the same for everyone who came. No one likes to pay taxes, but everyone likes to pay less taxes. Our new assistant chastised Poppa, but he is the authority, not our assistant. When evening came, we had gathered more money in a single day than ever before. To top it off, as we made our way home, men gave us cordial acknowledgements. Some even dared to say, "Have a good evening, Jared and Mary." What a blessing!

On the sixth month, seventeenth day — Today was another great day. We opened the day in prayer just as we closed the night before. This much pleasure has not existed since the early days when Momma was with us in my youth.

The line of taxpayers was even longer today. Our work was heavy. Our burden was light. Real light has penetrated our corner of the world. Our Roman superiors are ecstatic. Our neighbors are pleased. I do believe, though, that Poppa's peers will be incredibly angry. Taxing without our mark-up will bring pressure upon other collectors. This could endanger us from people who have the ability to hurt us without consequence.

Tonight, I shared with Poppa my concern. Poppa smiled. "Mary, you have no fear. This is our last week collecting taxes. We have enough to provide for me in my lifetime, you in yours, with plenty to spare for others." I am delighted this evening. I am also a little concerned. What will we do with our time? The tax booth has been our existence for years now. It is where I developed my expertise. I asked Poppa. He told me he had no idea. All he knew was we are at peace. In our prayers tonight, we thanked God for Jesus. That one meeting in Capernaum has made all the difference for us both.

On the sixth month, the eighteenth day — Atticus came by the booth today with his partners. They paid their taxes. They then returned with a kind gift of wool for me. Atticus spoke on their behalf, telling me how sorry they all were for the way they had abused me. I could tell Atticus was very worried about my response. I thanked them all. I told them that what they did was wrong. I shared with them that what I had done was also wrong. I should never have been there to begin with.

It was then I had the privilege to share what Jesus had done for me. I told them about the Rabbi from Capernaum. I told them about the change in a few of their acquaintances, Simon Peter, his brother Andrew, James, and John. I no sooner finished saying their names when Zebedee walked up with his catch. He greeted me by name. "Mary! I am so glad to see you. John told me about your visit to Simon's home in Capernaum. I have hardly been able to enter the town for all the people visiting. John and Simon (he simply goes by Peter now) said they did not know all of the people who lined up at Simon's front door the other day, but they surely recognized you. John was ecstatic to tell me of how Jesus cast the demons out of you, how the tortured look on your face disappeared in an instant. Mary, I am so happy for you and your father. Will you please make a note in your records. You will not see my boys or Simon and Andrew here anymore. I do not want you to think they are not paying their taxes. They have left the fishing business entirely. I am downsizing to just me and a few hands. You will see me, but they are going to follow Jesus as His disciples. I am not sure what lies ahead for them, but I trust Jesus. We know God has sent Him to us for some reason. He clearly has power like none we have ever seen before." With that, Zebedee paid his taxes. He then left with a kind word.

I am sitting in my room now. It is late. Poppa and I have said our prayers. God really has responded. We have never really seen prayers answered until now. I am sure God was answering them, but we never really noted them. As I kept copious notes at the tax booth, I am going to start taking notes of all God is doing for us.

Anyway, I am jealous for Simon, or Peter, if that will be his sole name. They have had the privilege to leave everything and follow Jesus. I want to do that. With my past, I do believe I could harm any ministry that Jesus has. I am from Magdala after all — the land of loose women. I am the one who many men have violated many times. Most of the time, I did so willingly. I am the tax collector's daughter, a puppet of Rome to our people. I am the one who was demon-possessed, who stabbed fishhooks into myself, cut my own throat, and stabbed a man. I fear what the presence of a woman like me would do to His ministry. Before long, all would say He is no different than Judas the Galilean or Theudas.

In the eighteenth year of the reign of Tiberius Caesar, on the sixth month, the twentieth day — This week closed with the greatest of joys. We began our morning with prayer. We then attended the synagogue in our neighborhood. Poppa let the local synagogue ruler, Simeon, know ahead of time we were coming. Poppa also arranged for a moment to speak to the people gathered. I was nervous. I remember the scene I made the last time we were present with Momma. I know the people remember. They have reminded me every day with whispers and glares, but now everything for me is different. I attended with Poppa, remembering the words of the psalmist: "I lift up my eyes to the hills. Where does my help come from? My help comes from the Lord, the Maker of Heaven and earth." God honored our faith!

The scripture was read from Isaiah. I was thrilled at what was read. Tears flowed down my face. Everyone watched me. I am sure they thought I was about to break out among them again. If only they could see I am not the woman they saw a few weeks ago, but what made me weep was the joy as if God provided this particular text for our very visit:

> The Spirit of the Sovereign Lord is on me, because the Lord has anointed me to preach good news to the poor. He has sent me to bind up the brokenhearted, to proclaim freedom for the captives and release from darkness for the prisoners, to proclaim the year of the Lord's favor and the day of vengeance of our God, to comfort all who mourn, and provide for those who grieve in Zion — to bestow on them a crown of beauty instead of ashes, the oil of gladness instead of mourning, and a garment of praise instead of a spirit of despair.
>
> They will be called oaks of righteousness, a planting of the Lord for the display of his splendor.

Everything Isaiah wrote was what I experienced in Capernaum at the door of Simon the fisherman. My broken heart has been bound. I, the captive, have been set free. I, who was once in darkness in a cistern in chains, have been released!

I waited for the guest speaker to share on this text. I was shocked when Simeon introduced a special guest to speak — my father! Poppa got up. Great rumblings radiated throughout the synagogue. A couple of families walked out. Simeon quieted the crowd. He said, "Let Jared speak. You will understand if you just listen." Poppa walked behind the bimah, the replica of the Temple in Jerusalem that Momma loved so much. He was about to speak, but broke down for a moment. Simeon stood. He walked to Poppa's side, put his left arm around Poppa's shoulders, squeezing with a reassuring grip. "Take your time Jared. We will wait."

No one sat near me. No one reassured me. I sat on the bench alone. I did not feel alone, though. My Help was there right beside me. My Help was there by Poppa, too. His words were so meaningful, I dare not think I will ever forget them, even word for word. Poppa said, "I want to start with an announcement. I have resigned from the tax booth effective yesterday." Someone yelled out, "I guess you have fleeced us enough!" Simeon raised his hand to silence the disruptions.

Poppa continued. "You are right to be angry, but my books are open. I did charge you fairly for your taxes, and I did charge you the additional one-third for my fees. Please compare that to any other collector. You will find my charge was always a fraction of theirs. If you find one who charged less, I will repay you the difference." No one spoke. I think all knew Poppa was telling the truth. No one challenged him, though they were welcome to try. I have kept the most accurate of records, including signatures upon payment.

My father then shared about my mother's untimely death. He explained the stress our family was under was most likely the cause. He shared that the last time we came, he was going to resign from the booth and seek their help. He told them, "Now I come to announce my resignation without any help. My daughter has been very ill, as you all know. You can call it a curse I deserve, or a punishment she deserves. Either way, it was a curse and a punishment to us. I had tried everything to help her. Nothing worked. My wife and I thought we had a daughter out of control. We even ventured she might be insane. Recently, after dear Adriana's passing, I realized it was much darker than insanity. Demons possessed my daughter, Mary. During this time, I began to call upon God, knowing that if the devil is this real, then how much more real is the Living God? We traveled everywhere to find healing. We went to Judas, whom some said was the Messiah. He is not. We traveled to Jerusalem. We made sacrifices for our sins. We were immersed in the mikveh there. We had a personal visit with the high priest, Annas. He prayed for us. He gave us purifying water with the ashes of the red heifer. We cleansed our home. We prayed. All went well for a short while. Then Mary grew worse, more violent, even stabbing a man. I am sharing all of this, but you know most of it, or at least have heard. Last, we went to Capernaum when we heard of the Rabbi Jesus there. I do not know what you may think of Him".

"Clearly, most of you here who have had a need have gone to see Him in Capernaum. You have left His presence, like we did, healed, whole. Jesus healed my daughter. He turned us back to God. Mary and I have made the decision that we will follow the faith of Abraham, Isaac, and Jacob. We will live by the Law God gave Moses. We will worship God in some synagogue, somewhere. We ask that you let us worship God here with you. You are our neighbors. You were our friends. I have done business with you. I have represented you. And, yes, I have taxed you. I have also given you taxes with no mark-up the last week. I have donated a pier to this community. I do not seek any leadership position, I just wish to be a laborer by your side for God and for you. Mary and I will leave now. Whatever you decide, please know we love you. We will be your friends, no matter what. If you have a need, we will meet it, even if you decide you do not want us to be in fellowship with you."

With that, Poppa and I left. You could see the change in the whole synagogue. All skepticism seemed to leave as Poppa left the bimah. I cannot describe how proud I am of him. I cannot write the elation my heart feels because of what God has done for us through His Rabbi — Jesus.

Jesus. This is such a common name in our nation. I grew up with a boy named Jesus. I have taxed three or four men named Jesus. When I say the name and think of them, there is no power. But when I say the name Jesus and think of this special Rabbi from Capernaum, goosebumps come up on my arms and neck. A divine authority is present when I say the name as His. I cannot explain it.

Back to Poppa — I am so proud of him. I am so glad to be his daughter. We prayed tonight that the synagogue would accept us. I know Simeon has his work cut out for him. Either way, as for Jared and his house, we will serve the Lord.

On the sixth month, on the twenty-first day — Poppa and I handed over our books to the Roman authorities. Poppa's replacement will be named later. His assistant will fill in for the time being. Poppa let them know that he will only go to the tax booth for personal taxes assessed. If they have questions on the operation, he requested they come by our home. Poppa does not want any of the townspeople to ever think that he might reverse his decision.

Simeon dropped by today. He had great news. The synagogue dismissed after worship. He called them back that evening after each had time to pray. They decided to receive us into their fellowship, provided I have no more outbursts. They also stipulated that if Poppa returns to the tax booth, they will exclude him from the synagogue. To be honest, there is no chance of either ever happening again, by God's grace.

We ended the night in praise. Our God has supplied all our needs. He has lifted our burdens. We have never felt Him closer. I wonder, how can anyone live apart from Him? I suppose the same way we did — in misery, in emptiness.

On the sixth month, the twenty-fifth day — Poppa and I have mapped out our future. He has many revenue sources, all of which he managed loosely, for we had a steady income. If one did not pay rent, or was short on their harvest of the vineyards, Poppa usually let it pass. I have no idea how much revenue we have lost over the years. We have decided to deal compassionately with everyone. We only ask our renters to fulfill their contracts. If they fall on hard times, we will make concessions. We want good relationships with everyone. We also seek that everyone follows God's direction — do what you say, let your "yes" be yes, your "no" be no.

We divided up Poppa's business enterprises between us. I will oversee the shops he leases. He will oversee the fleet of boats. Together, we will check on the cultivated lands. I know what Father is doing. He is keeping me from the shore. I am glad. It is near the shore where I had committed all my indiscretions. I was exposed to other gods and witchcraft when I was with those men. Father fears the foremen and workers of the vineyards around me. Everything he is doing is to protect me, to guard our peace, our joy.

The renters are a little sensitive. With the eyes of a tax collector, we can clearly see that many have not been paying what they promised. Their resentment to oversight only reinforces our doubts about them as honest stewards. That is fine. They will do right, or they will lose their privileges. My father is a kind man. He is also a savvy businessman who knows how to enforce the law.

On the sixth month, the twenty-sixth day — Atticus came to call on my father. I had a hunch of what he was up to. They visited for a good while. Poppa then came to tell me, with Atticus by his side, "Mary, this young man has asked permission to court you. I have given my permission on the condition of yours. My one requirement is that his visits are restricted to this house and always with me present, to our courtyard, or amongst our vineyards, as long as I am nearby. I do not want him with you near the shore or the fishermen. I have also told him that he must break off friendships with a few of his friends. I have let him know I will alert Linus as well. Atticus has agreed to my terms."

I was embarrassed. I am thirty-three, yet I felt like I was fifteen again. Rather than taking offense, though, I am gratified. I have never felt safer. After all I have done, after all that men have done to me, it is a shock that such a handsome boy as Atticus would want to share my company. I nodded with approval. I pray my smile did not make me appear over-anxious. A girl must make the young man know he must earn her love.

Atticus ate with us tonight, with Poppa's eyes and ears open to every conversation. We sat in the courtyard. Poppa sat inside (I am sure near the window) pretending to read by candlelight. We listened to the sea. We talked about his family. He shared his dreams with me on this first night. He asked if I had any dreams. I told him just one — to be able to hear the Rabbi Jesus as often as I could. I shared with Atticus all that Jesus did — again. He asked many questions. Now, in Magdala, the news of Jesus has spread. My encounter is just one of many. It seems everyone would like to visit with a person who Jesus has healed. The beauty of my healing is that it is apparent to all here in this town. Our whole lives have changed!

Atticus asked if he could go to synagogue with us. I told him how much I would like that, but not tomorrow. Our first attendance after their decision to allow us in should be with just Poppa and me. They admitted just the two of us, so it must be the two of us they see.

In the eighteenth year of the reign of Tiberius Caesar, on the sixth month, the twenty- seventh day — Poppa and I prayed this morning after we got dressed for the synagogue. We had a light breakfast. I asked Poppa if he was nervous. He smiled and assured me he was — just like me. Never before have we attended synagogue after being formally accepted. We will take no privileges. We will be faithful. We will learn. We will serve.

The synagogue ruler, Simeon, welcomed us at the door. Many inside finally broke their separation. The greeting was not family-warm, but it was kind. For the first time, ladies in the synagogue actually spoke to me as another lady in their midst. It was very awkward for me. It is difficult, even with this new life, to blend in after all the years of being cut off. They were making the effort. I could tell it was a bit of a task — perhaps even humbling for some of them. The men greeted Poppa the same. He seemed to have easier success blending with them. A fear still looms when I think of me among the women. God reassured me that, in time, I would feel comfortable. The one constant was the bimah table. I looked at it and thought of Momma. She would fit right in here. She would also have been the connection between these and me. Without her, I would have to do what I could to connect with God's Help.

The text Simeon read from David was a great comfort:

> The Lord is my shepherd, I shall not be in want. He makes me lie down in green pastures, He leads me beside quiet waters, He restores my soul. He guides me in paths of righteousness for his name's sake. Even though I walk through the valley of the shadow of death, I will fear no evil, for You are with me; Your rod and Your staff, they comfort me. You prepare a table before me in the presence of my enemies. You anoint my head with oil; my cup overflows. Surely goodness and love will follow me all the days of my life, and I will dwell in the House of the Lord forever.

I truly felt this scripture in that synagogue at that moment. In all my restlessness, the Lord has been my Shepherd. He has guided me through the valley of death. He has led me to green pastures with Poppa. He is leading me along the paths of righteousness. These who were once my enemies now see God prepare His table before me. Surely, goodness, and love will follow me all the days of my life. The love of Poppa is with me. The love of Atticus may be. The love of God will always be with me.

I thought about the connection I needed from Momma to be with these ladies. I now think as I write, Jesus has become my connection to God. It is because of Him I have this relationship with the God of Abraham, Isaac, and Jacob. My praise abounds beyond the walls of this room. They exude beyond the walls of that synagogue. I pray all can see on my face the glow of His glory.

Poppa and I dined at home after synagogue. We rested all day. On many past Sabbaths, we did catch-up work at the tax booth to prepare for the next day. We have much to do even now to get our businesses back in order. We discussed a little of what this coming week required. We then laid that aside. We talked of all the Lord has done for us as our Shepherd. We have seen the quiet waters of the Sea of Galilee this afternoon. He has prepared His table for us. We feasted on the psalm this morning. We feast on some bread today which I made yesterday. All is good.

On the sixth month, the twenty-eighth day — We are about to leave for Capernaum. I woke this morning to the sweet aroma of breakfast. Poppa made it to surprise me. However, he had a better surprise in store. Poppa said he had heard Jesus was back in Capernaum. He told me that our business for the week could wait. "Why don't we go to Capernaum to see Jesus? I want to thank Him for giving me back my daughter." I cannot describe how thrilled I am.

We are back in Levi's home. I must say, he was a little cold toward us when we arrived. He has caught a lot of complaints when news spread that Poppa had not charged his commission the last week at the tax booth.

Poppa explained. He related it back to our visit here a few days earlier. Poppa told Levi then that he planned to leave the booth. Levi just did not like the way he did it. Thankfully, they are good friends.

When we were on the outskirts of Capernaum, we were alarmed at the massive crowd along the shore. At first, we thought there must be some unrest in the village with the Romans. However, the closer we got, the more smiles we saw on faces. We were hearing cheers from time to time, not yelling. As Poppa pressed his way through the crowd, we saw the Rabbi Jesus. We heard a call for a boat. The next thing you know, everyone passes the word from the lake back to us: "Sit down. Be quiet." Compliantly, Poppa and I sat down. We learned long ago, in dealing with the Romans, to respect authority. Once everyone was seated, we saw men boarding the boat. I heard one of the men say, "Don't worry. He is not leaving. We are just getting a boat closer for His safety. You all have pressed Him into the water. Just wait while we move the boat nearer." Jesus stood there with His disciples around Him. He was visiting. They were smiling. Laughter ensued. I was overwhelmed at how approachable He is. He is famous, but not separate. People seek after Him, but He acts as if He is just our neighbor in Magdala.

We waited. As we looked around, we saw people from all over the region. We recognized some from Judea. We saw a few we recognized from Jerusalem, including a few priests. We saw many of our old clients from regions across Galilee. We listened to a man in front of us explaining to some visitors who Jesus is. In the lull of their conversation, Poppa asked the man, "What did we miss?" The man said he had been at the synagogue in Capernaum earlier at the invitation of Jairus. That synagogue was extremely packed. They now leave the doors open so people outside can hear when Jesus speaks.

He stated that today a real commotion occurred. A man had traveled a long way to see Jesus. He had a shriveled hand and was unable to work to provide for himself. As Jesus got up and took the scroll, the man approached the bimah. He sat on the floor below some Pharisees who had arrived from Jerusalem. The man said he had supposed the Pharisees were coming to join Jesus. Sadly, he said that he had overheard them attempting to argue with Jesus, but He would not join in the argument. They threatened Him for using His power. They dared Him to tell where He received such abilities. The man said he felt extremely uncomfortable because of the Pharisees' attitude. These were considered to be the most holy of the holy. Even as the synagogue service began, they were quietly baiting Him.

We looked toward the shore. The fishermen were drawing up anchor in their boat. They were pushing it closer to Jesus.

The man said Jesus then broke from the text. He commanded the man with the shriveled hand to stand before them all. The man rose to his feet in front of the Pharisees. Jesus asked a basic question, directing it to the Pharisees on the front row. "Is it lawful on the Sabbath to do good or evil, to save a life or to kill?" The man reported you could have heard a rope tied around one's waist. He said the pause of Jesus was awkward. With a mocked impersonation, the man said he saw one of the Pharisees fold his arms as if to say, "I am not here to answer You. I am here for You to answer me." He said Jesus then looked compassionately at the man with the shriveled hand.

I turned to Poppa, "I know those eyes. He looked just like that at me." The man stopped his story. He asked me, "What is your name?" I told him. He asked, "What was your illness, young lady?" Poppa looked at me as if to warn, "Don't say. We don't know this man." I pressed ahead. "I was demon-possessed. He looked right at me." Others sitting around us were listening. They looked at me.

We all looked at Jesus. We then looked at each other. I told them, "He knew my name. He knew all I had ever done. He spoke. The demons trembled. They left. I was set free. I am still free today. He changed my life." A small cheer erupted from those around us. The man hugged my father.

The man then continued as the fishermen dropped anchor a few yards from the shore. The man said the Rabbi went from compassion for the man to anger for the Pharisees. Jesus would not speak to the Pharisees, but defied them by saying to the man with the shriveled hand, "Stretch out your hand." This amazing narrator of events said that in just a split second, the man stretched out his hand, completely restored. You could hear excitement from all the people around us who were listening to this stranger speaking to us.

Just as he finished, Jesus began to speak to all of us. Oh, that voice! All I could make out was a blessing upon us. I hoped that He would speak more. The next thing I heard was James, John's brother, invite the sick and the hurting to come forward. Row by row, His disciples brought people to Jesus in an orderly manner. We felt welcomed to watch as He poured out the power of God on friends, neighbors, and strangers. One by one, He healed everyone who came forward of their diseases. Surely people heard our roar of praise and celebration throughout Capernaum and across the Galilee.

I hugged Poppa. "This is a great gift." He looked as joyful as me. Tears were constantly welling in his eyes. Poppa whispered in my ear as someone was escorting another person to the Rabbi, "I love Him. I don't know Him, but I love Him. I love Him in a way of loving God. I cannot understand it." I have never heard Poppa speak of such emotion. I pulled myself to his side. I told him, "I know Poppa. I feel the same. I would beg you, let's never leave Him." Poppa nodded with a wishful agreement.

No sooner did Poppa nod, I heard the voices again. The demonic voices were calling out. Every so often, we would hear them again. Someone would walk up to Him. They would fall down before Him. Then we would hear the voices of the demonic. It was not me alone hearing them. It was not Poppa only. The entire crowd heard. Many moved back. Some people jumped up and ran. I do not know whether they were afraid, or if the demons inside some forced them to retreat, but I knew the voices. Poppa knew the voices. The most impressive thing was every time they yelled, they spoke one phrase and stopped. What we could make out was something I had never heard them say: "You are the Son of God."

They exclaimed that. Jesus silenced them. They uttered not another word. Jesus cast them out. He made each person whole — just like me. There I was, once possessed by demons, seeing others with demons set free, too. I cannot write how thankful I am that I am whole, that I am not afraid. I know God. He knows me. In that moment on the shore just outside Capernaum's town limits, I asked God to come inside, to stay inside. I will be His. I want Him to be mine. All of a sudden, a fresh fullness came over me. I felt fully safe, fully guarded.

With that, Jesus dismissed our crowd. As much as we wanted to follow Him, it seemed we all wanted to obey. How can we offend One so kind? How could we not honor the smallest courtesy to One who has done so much? His face was brilliant, radiant in love, but it was easy to see He was very tired. I did not want to leave Him. Out of love, we did.

We are staying the night with Levi. We will return home in the morning. Levi wants to speak to Poppa about taxes. He keeps getting irritated. Poppa wants to talk to Levi about Jesus. I hear them in the other room. They have compromised. Tax discussion first. Poppa and Levi stepped outside. I am here, back in the room where I rested after Jesus delivered me. I want to finish my writing for the night. I am tired, too. My one last entry will be a question. I pray to know the answer one day soon. What did the demons mean when they declared to Him that He was the Son of God? He is a man. He has power that only God can give. I know God endows people from time to time. He allowed Moses to part the Red Sea. He allowed Elijah to pray for rain. By Elisha, He healed the sick, but nowhere have I ever heard any of these called the Son of God, much less a son of God. But the demons declare this Rabbi staying here in Capernaum, the man named Jesus who gets tired, is the Son of God. How can this be?

On the sixth month, the twenty-ninth day — We returned home midday. Poppa and I are both hoarse. We had few moments of silence. We talked about Jesus without end. Then we would get quiet for a moment to consider what we saw. Mere seconds passed. We talked more about Jesus. We got tickled at our enthusiasm. No one has ever touched us like this One from Capernaum, this mystery of mysteries. Who is this One? Is He the Son of God?

Atticus dropped by. I filled him in on what we had seen until it was almost inappropriately late to have a single man in a woman's home. I would say a young lady's home, but I am no longer that. Atticus had so many questions. I could tell he was not making small talk or trying to invent interest in my stories. He had a hunger. His questions were very personal — about himself. Atticus is looking for something. He is empty. I shared with him how I asked God to come into my heart, to be my God, to let me be His daughter. I told Atticus he should think about doing the same. He wanted to, there in our courtyard. I have had little exposure to our faith. He has had almost none. I told him he needs to see Simeon. If he can talk to Simeon, perhaps go through some of the lessons they teach our own boys, perhaps he will have enough knowledge to know what it means to follow the Living God. He was grateful. I told him he had to leave. Poppa came in to say the same. Atticus left with a promise to reach out to Simeon. He asked if he could go to synagogue with us this Sabbath. Poppa said yes. I exuberantly concurred.

When can I see Jesus again? As much as I love Poppa as my father, I want to see Jesus. As much as I may love Atticus (too early to tell), I want to hear Jesus. As I watched Him heal, I just could not get past the longing to know Him personally. I want Him to know me more personally. Obviously, He knows my name. He knows all I have done. I am not sure if someone told him. Perhaps Simon whispered what he knew in His ear? I do not know. I just want to know Him, to be His friend as long as that will not sully His name.

On the seventh month, the second day — We received good news. Rome approved the purchase of the land where the tax booth sits. Poppa is so smart when it comes to business. He is giving a generous donation to the neighborhood synagogue. The rest we will set back. We thank God for His constant provision.

On the seventh month, the third day — We had a surprising visit today. Levi came to see us. His face was brilliant. His words were animated. This was not the Levi I grew to know through Poppa. I always sensed he felt a competition with Poppa. Our family had made much more at the tax booth than him. We had more possessions, yet lived very frugally. We charged less than Levi, but made more. That was based more on our location in Magdala than anything else. Levi had no other interests but doing business and making money. This explains why, the last time we saw him in Capernaum, Poppa wanted to tell him about Jesus. Levi wanted to talk about business. Regardless of what he made, he never seemed content. So why this change in countenance today?

He told Poppa and me he was gathering taxes yesterday in Capernaum. Everything was going as usual. He would assess the tax. The payor would complain. Threats ensued. There was name-calling. Then the soldiers would come forward. The debtor would pay, then leave in a huff. Next customer.

Levi expressed something to us he had never intimated before. He had been considering leaving the tax booth. "Why?" Poppa asked. Levi said it began when Poppa came to Capernaum a few days before with the shocking news he had left his tax booth. Levi said it was a silent arrow with no warning. He felt that he and Poppa would spend their lives competing with each other. He assumed they would die in their booths. Then out of the blue, Poppa comes with the news, not that he was thinking about it, but that he had already left. Levi said it was like a slap out of a dream. Now, instead of thinking of new ways to make money off the masses, he contemplated life without it. He was going through his head if he had enough money to live on. He had been wondering if it was time for him to quit, too.

The turnover rate for tax collectors of the Jewish persuasion is huge. One can only take hatred and insults so long. When a man first enters the business, all he sees is gold, possessions, and security. Once he gets in, the money is intoxicating. No amount of pushback can change the excitement of the wealth. After a while, the tax collector reaches a dilemma. How much money is enough? How much hatred can a person bear? The soft- hearted do eventually leave, but much later than Poppa. The greedy just grow harder-hearted. One would think that after years of vandalism, refusal of service, people walking on the other side of the street, ugly names, rejection from synagogues, even the greediest among us would fold, close shop, change their names, and move to a Roman port. Poppa had said Levi was the hard-hearted type who would be in his booth long after the vast majority had retired. He thrived on discontent.

What Levi was telling us did not mesh with the man we knew. Levi continued. With all these thoughts of leaving, the last incident drove home the need to decide — does he harden to push forward or soften to quit? He said a lull occurred right after lunch. Unexpectedly, he heard a voice of authority. Assuming it was a Roman official, he looked up. It was no Roman at all. It was the Rabbi Jesus. Levi said he expected a criticism such as, "Why are you fleecing your own countrymen?" But it was not that at all. Levi said, "You would never believe what He said to me." He paused. We waited. His eyes flashed. I asked, "What did He say, sir?"

Levi's eyes moistened. He smiled. He simply said two words: "Follow me." Poppa looked at me. I looked at Poppa. We looked at Levi. He wiped his eyes with the sleeve of his tailored shirt. Poppa asked, "What are you going to do, friend?" Levi answered, "It's not what am I going to do. It is what did I do." With a flame of satisfaction, he said, "I nodded my head goodbye to my Roman guards. I closed the booth there on the Damascus Road cutting through Capernaum, leaving every penny in it. I followed Jesus!"

I cannot tell you how jealous I am of Levi. Oh, by the way, he said, "Don't call me Levi. Call me Matthew. My name 'Levi' means joined. I have joined in everything the world has to offer. I have been empty and miserable. Most have never seen me smile. My name is Matthew now. The name means 'gift of God.' I have been given a gift by God to leave this old life. I will be following Jesus as a student. He will be my Rabbi." As he spoke, I thought, how interesting. Simon no longer wants to be called Simon. Levi no longer wants to be called Levi. We have had four business taxpayers follow Jesus. Now we have a tax collector friend follow Jesus.

Levi, or should I say, Matthew, then gave Poppa and me a gracious invitation. He is having a banquet at his home tomorrow evening for Jesus. He came personally to invite us. He invited us first. He told Poppa that it was Poppa's visit that first warmed his heart toward this One. Then Jesus came to his booth. It was Poppa's words that made him willing to consider his life and the life that comes with following God's direction. It was Poppa who gave Levi the softening to listen to Jesus as He approached. So now, he has invited us and will soon invite all his other tax collector friends, along with Roman dignitaries he knows. He wants us all to meet Jesus in person.

What a thrill! I want to know Jesus personally. I want to be like Levi — I mean, Matthew. I want to be like Peter, Andrew, James, and John. How can a woman from Magdala become part of His circle? I am willing to change my name, too. I would love to disassociate myself from my past and from this town. I want to freely listen to Him. I want to learn as He teaches. I want to see lives change and the hurting healed. Oh God, please let me follow You and this Rabbi who seems to point completely to You.

On the seventh month, the fourth day — We arrived at Matthew's house a little after noon. (Poppa and I are both struggling with the name change.) I have stayed in Matthew's home many times. It is a gigantic house. It is the largest home on this side of Galilee. Where we have lived very humbly to avoid the ire of the neighbors, Matthew — or should I say, Levi — never worried about the anger. He had the money. He wanted extravagant things, so he purchased them. Poppa invested in things that made money. Levi (I use his old name for his old way of life) spent all that he received on whatever whim he had at the moment. He has things. Poppa has investments. But judging from our visits, he has set enough money back to support his lavish needs.

Regarding his mansion, we have always entered from the back. We have stayed in two of his many bedrooms. The front of the house is grandiose. We were told he had a great room in the front for entertaining. We had never been in that room until today. It was spectacularly huge. It was like a vacuous cavern, so large that no amount of furniture could reduce its immensity. Do not get me wrong, there were fine furnishings in it, enough to seat all of Herod Antipas's officers and his Galilean army comfortably.

A long table was set up with a variety of foods Matthew had paid to be prepared. Rich purple silk covered the table. He had cooks, servers, and greeters in elaborate uniforms. He opened his cellar to allow everyone the enjoyment of his collection of exquisite wines. Matthew himself was dressed in the finest clothes shipped in from Rome. My first thought was — this must be what it was like to dine at our forefather Solomon's table. This was the event of all events. This was the most special occasion this area has ever seen.

We thought we would be there to help, but we found he needed no help. He treated us as special guests, almost as his own family. We retreated to our rooms as guests began to arrive, to put on our own dressy clothes. When we reappeared, every guest had dressed the part for this monumental event. A doorman checked in each person who came. He searched the invitation list to ensure that none but the invited entered. I am sure others were trying to get in, as I heard a little commotion at the door. I assumed he was turning someone away to their chagrin. I was surprised no fishermen or discontented citizens were outside protesting such opulence, which was clearly at their expense.

At exactly the twelfth hour, a silence filled Matthew's banquet hall. Jesus walked in with His disciples. He had no fine clothes. In fact, He was wearing the same clothes I had always seen Him wear. Other than Matthew, His disciples were dressed no better. If one were to drop in from Decapolis and see this banquet, they would assume some poor had slipped in past the doorkeeper. That was not the case at all. In fact, all who were there in their exceptional clothing, gold, and jewelry were there to see the man dressed as a pauper. No one felt worthy to be with Him. I say that. I surely did not feel worthy. I wanted to meet Him. Now that He had arrived, I was overwhelmed with nervousness. I could hardly breathe. I could not speak. I simply stared. I could not take my eyes off Him. No one felt comfortable speaking. Everyone seemed to just want to hear Him speak.

Matthew walked to the door with obvious anxieties. He shook the hand of Jesus. He turned, and with a trembling voice, he said, "My friends, I have invited you here today for one reason. I want you to meet the man that you have all been hearing about. Jesus, I am honored You would come to my dwelling. I want You to feel at home here. This place is Yours. All I have is Yours. These are my friends. I want to thank You for coming to my tax booth. I want all here to know that Jesus so graciously, humbly, just as He is today, came to my tax booth and made an offer to me of all people. He has asked me to follow Him. I am announcing today officially, I have quit my job as a tax collector. I am going to follow Jesus."

It was then the talk amongst the guests ensued. They expressed sounds of shock. Questions were asked concerning this decision, but an overwhelming feeling was also present that there was a power in this cavernous hall that filled it completely. His name is Jesus. The chatter of the people stopped again as Matthew spoke. "I have invited Jesus here to thank Him for sure. But more, my main purpose of this banquet is for you to come and personally meet Him. Jesus is open to visit with each of you. You can ask Him any question you desire. Over the coming days, I cannot wait to get to know Him more and more. Please meet Him. Please hear Him. I genuinely believe He has the words of God."

This was that for which I was waiting. Everyone was hesitant to step forward toward Him to visit. After a few awkward moments, He walked through this reception hall. People spread out to make way. He walked up to the banquet table, took a plate, but instead of helping Himself to the fine cuisine, He handed it to one of the guests. Motioning His hand for this man to eat, he followed the Rabbi's direction. Others soon followed in line out of compulsion. I do not think anyone felt like eating. I believe we all could have just had Him stand up on the table while we watched without a blink. Perhaps He would speak. That would be even better. We quickly learned this was not why He came. He came to meet us individually.

As people got their food, no one seemed to notice what they were putting on their plates. With one hand, they held their plates. With another hand, they placed whatever food was before them. Their heads turned away from the table to fix their eyes upon Jesus. Again, it was so awkward. Poppa nudged me toward Him. I obliged. As I made my way, I was the daughter well-known to this crowd. I was the insane adult-child criminal of the tax collector from Magdala. That was my label. I felt their eyes move from Jesus to me, back to Jesus, then to rest on me again. They wondered, I could tell, what Jesus would do with such a one as me.

As I got within five feet of Him, His face broke out in a huge smile and He said, "Mary!" He remembered me! He knew my name. And He said it for all to hear. He asked how I was doing. I visited with Him about the change He had brought. I could not wait to tell Him of my newfound devotion to God, to the worship of God in the synagogue. I shared how Poppa and I pray every evening. He nodded as if He already knew. I told Him about traveling to Capernaum to see Him. I shared how I was on the shore that day when He was healing.

Then came my confession. I told Him that I hope to know Him more. I confessed that I want Him to know me more, but I felt He already did. Jesus was so gracious. How awesome to visit with Him after the demons were gone. How wonderful to see Him after the change He had brought. I felt I could stay there all evening, just He and me. He did not seem rushed at all. A room full of guests to meet Him surely would have brought pressure on Him to limit His time with each, but He did not show it.

Everyone in that great room seemed to need to see one person interact with Jesus before they would dare try. I stepped away. Poppa then greeted Him. He called out my father's name: "Jared!" He congratulated my father on his retirement. He wished him the best. John and James did not grimace in the least. People began to come forward to Him. Each shy. Every man seemed embarrassed by how they had dressed. Never before had they been embarrassed to wear their expensive clothes. I believe they realized they had misplaced their priorities. I heard some begin with an apology. Others brought a worry. Some shared deep feelings, but in hushed tones, fearful of who might hear.

Men left their conversations with Him uplifted, smiling. It was as if they met the person of their dreams. I saw women approach Him. They came away with a glow. I thought of Moses when he saw the back of God. His glow was frightening to the Israelites when he descended the mountain. This was the glow I envisioned, being seen right here in Matthew's house. A prophet from God was in our midst. We knew at least that. He is more than a rabbi. He comes dressed in tattered worn clothing but all we see, in awe, is the person.

A line formed. Single file they came. I watched Him converse with each person. Once they walked past, they gathered on the other side just to watch. Andrew, Peter's brother (Simon's brother) tapped me on the shoulder. His first words were, "Isn't He awesome!" I felt a kinsmanship with him that I cannot explain. Here was a former enemy, a taxpayer talking to me, a tax collector. We had many differences in Magdala — Andrew's brother Peter even more so. Poppa and I were ridiculed, criticized, and called horrible names in the past. This night, Andrew and I stood side by side in full agreement. It was almost as if we were now brother and sister. I cannot explain this.

Peter came up. He tapped me on the shoulder and slid to the other side. When I turned, no one was there. I looked the other way. Peter met me with a smile, saying, "Mary, I am so glad you are here. What a difference Jesus has made in our lives. I am no longer the contrarian that I was. I am no longer your adversary. Neither are John and James. I do not think anyone, other than your father, could be happier to see Jesus heal you than us. What a blessing to see you here, wanting to be near Jesus. We have seen many healed by our Rabbi over the last few weeks. Most get what they want and leave. Here you are. You have been healed, but you have not forgotten Him. We saw you at the shore a few days ago. The crowd was just too great to greet you personally. How are you?"

Peter was right. We had been adversaries. He did not like us for what we did. I did not like him for how he responded — especially toward Poppa. Then in my weakest moment of life, we were at Peter's door, pleading with Jesus to help me. Peter and Andrew were there at that door behind Jesus. They closed their eyes to pray while He spoke to me. They watched as He cast the demons out. They smiled as they saw my countenance change. I remember now how Peter shook Poppa's hand with his right hand, wrapping his left arm around Poppa's shoulders. Not only has Jesus healed my soul and body, He has healed our relationships. He has made us one.

I shared that with Peter. I motioned Peter's eyes toward Jesus. I then repeated what Andrew had said: "Isn't He awesome!" Peter responded, "Yes, He is! We will follow Him no matter where He goes, if He will let us. Every day with Him is a gift of grace from God. Mary, Jesus has turned our hearts toward God. Everything He shares by the campfire or on my fishing boat as we travel is in adoration of God. He calls God, 'Father.' He tells us we can do the same. Jesus says God sent Him to us. We do not know what all this means. He said to follow Him. He will explain more in the days ahead. I cannot wait!"

Shyly, I told Peter my heart's desire. "Peter, I want to be with Him like that, too. I know I am a woman. I know that I am one with a terrible reputation. I realize what the reputation of the village of Magdala is compared to that of your Bethsaida and now Capernaum. But, somehow, some way, I pray to be able to be with you disciples from time to time." Peter responded, "Pray that Mary. Who knows? Maybe God will make a way."

That is my prayer at this moment. Our evening lasted late into the night. Jesus visited with each and every person there who chose to visit with Him. Hardly anyone ate. We all just watched in wonder. God's presence was stronger in that house than in any Sabbath in our synagogue. But I feel that that experience is what God desires every Sabbath. Perhaps this is a lesson He is teaching us through the Rabbi. Finally, after all had visited with Jesus, Matthew dismissed the crowd. Jesus' disciples left first, followed by Jesus. No one else would go until then.

One last thing to write. A slight commotion occurred as Jesus was exiting. Some Pharisees, who Matthew did not allow in, were waiting for the gathering to break up. They accosted the disciples, demanding very loudly an explanation as to why they would eat and drink with tax collectors and sinners. James and John, typically happy to mix it up, seemed stymied. The Pharisees yelled even more, wanting all to hear their accusations.

Matthew heard the arguing tones, and grabbed Poppa. Both ran to the outside. I followed close behind. Before Matthew could stand between them, Jesus spoke. At His first utterance, every voice fell silent. With a voice as crisp as thunder, Jesus said, "It is not the healthy who need a doctor, but the sick. I have not come to call the righteous, but sinners to repentance."

What was the Rabbi saying? That the people who were at this banquet were sick, that we were sinners? Not one of us objected to His words. He was right. We were glad He came to be with us. Clad in our finest garments this night, not one of us felt we had covered over our sins, blotted out who we really were. No perfume can offset the scent of rebellion. I, for one, stood before Him days ago, broken. No fig leaf on earth could cover over my transgressions.

The Pharisees seemed emboldened. Instead of falling in with our crowd of sinners, they raised themselves above as righteous. It was always their opinion. They were our zealous leaders in the faith. Their history was one of strength and holiness. Their presence was nothing more than a charade. This self-righteous bunch then accused Jesus, saying, "John's disciples often fast and pray, and so do the disciples of the Pharisees, but yours go on eating and drinking." I heard grumbling from our party. I knew why. These Pharisees dare to boast of John. They hate him. Yet, for their benefit, they tout him as a role model. Besides, I was at this lavish meal held in Jesus' honor. With the finest wines money could buy, no one hardly touched a drop. Jesus was our only focus. No one wanted to be caught inebriated with such a great One in our midst.

Jesus' answer was curious. "Can you make the guests of the bridegroom fast while he is with them? But the time will come when the bridegroom will be taken from them; in those days they will fast." I agreed with the premise, but how does that answer their question? Is there a bridegroom among us? We had not gathered for a wedding, but to see Him. Yet, His answer was about His disciples and feasting. I do not know if He is the groom, but in this context, He was the guest of honor. We did seem to be His guests in Matthew's home.

Jesus had not finished with these. He told them, "No one pours new wine into old wineskins. If he does, the new wine will burst the skins, the wine will run out, and the wineskins will be ruined. No, new wine must be poured into new wineskins. And no one after drinking old wine wants the new, for he says, 'The old is better.'"

The Pharisees were talking about drinking, so Jesus addressed wine. He spoke the truth that new wine in old wineskins will burst the containers. People put new wine in new wineskins, but everyone just wants the aged wine. With that, strangely, the Pharisees separated. Jesus walked between them with His disciples following. Matthew literally walked out from his own home, left it to his attendants, I suppose, and went with Jesus. I wanted to leave Poppa. I wanted to follow Jesus, but unlike Matthew, He had not asked me.

On the seventh month, the fifth day — We spent the night in Matthew's palatial home. Matthew never came back. This morning, you would have thought we were the owners of the house. No one else was in a bedroom, but Poppa in one, me in another. It felt so odd this morning. We got dressed. We made our beds.

We met in the hallway of this home. Poppa walked through, looking for Matthew. He was nowhere to be found. Poppa shrugged. He opened the door for me. I walked through. He closed it behind us, and off we headed for Magdala. We walked the shoreline, hoping to see Jesus or the disciples, or at least Matthew. We just saw fishermen going about their trade.

All we could talk about was the night before. How wonderful is this Jesus! How powerful He is! How great that He never shrinks back in the presence of Romans, dignitaries, or Pharisees. He dresses the same as He always does. He speaks the same. He loves the same, but His authority is unmatched when He speaks. The demons know it. So do our so-called religious leaders.

Poppa and I had our evening meal. We sat in our courtyard. The sunset was spectacular with splashes of color in every direction. We watched the myriad of colors change almost every moment. It was sad to see the sun drop below the mountains just on the other side of the Galilee. A quiet breeze blew from the lake (as we often call Galilee).

It has been hard to go to sleep. I have sat up a couple times writing my thoughts. I pray this is my last entry. I am overrun with thoughts of where Jesus is tonight. What is He doing? What is He saying? Who is getting to see Him tonight? Do they realize how fortunate they are? Do they not know I want to be there, too? I am praying more than ever. I seldom write my prayers, but God hears. Or, as Peter referenced Jesus' words, our Father hears. He has blessed me. I know it sounds selfish, but I want more of His blessings. For what would I ask? A simple request: let me be with Jesus, following behind Him. Give me more of Him. My longing is not that of a woman for a man, but of a living being wanting more of God. Somehow, I find that in Jesus.

On the seventh month, the sixth day — Poppa and I took flowers to Momma's grave. We sat outside her tomb, laughing at what she would say to all the changes that have happened in the last few weeks. I believe she sees us. I miss that she did not get to live this with us here. I honestly believe what God has done for us was our life's prayer. It is good to toil. It is better to toil and see the fruit of our labor. Mother labored for me in particular. She saw the horrors. What a relief today must be, even from her vantage point.

On the seventh month, the seventh day — Poppa and I had breakfast this morning. I prepared it last night as today is the Sabbath. I am getting much better at cooking. We are fitting in nicely in the synagogue. There are still faint references to my past. People cannot help it. I notice they almost slip off in embarrassment for broaching my history. That is okay. To appreciate where I am today, it is important for people to know what I once was before Jesus brought God into my life.

The speaker spoke about our Shema from Deuteronomy. I was so refreshed to hear God call to my soul, "Hear, O Israel: The Lord our God, the Lord is one. Love the Lord your God with all your heart and with all your soul and with all your strength. These commandments that I give you today are to be upon your hearts. Impress them on your children. Talk about them when you sit at home and when you walk along the road, when you lie down, and when you get up."

For so many years, this has been a prayer of ours. Nothing more. Now it has become our life. God is our God. He is One. I no longer find true religion in any other. I do love the Lord my God more than ever. He has forgiven me, protected me, touched me. This is even more true now because of the Rabbi Jesus. I am praying to love God with all my heart, all my soul, and all my strength. I also want to love Him with all my time. Poppa and I talk of God when we are at home, when we are in our courtyard, when we see the sunset, when we walk to Mount Arbel, when we walk to Capernaum, when we walk to synagogue, and when we pray together to Him when we rise every morning.

I join Momma in the appreciation for the bimah in our synagogue. It reminds me of Heaven's Temple - the original temple that the Tabernacle and Solomon's Temple were to represent. I wish I could have seen Solomon's Temple. I know it was destroyed. I know it was rebuilt. At that time, the men wept, for it was no match to what Solomon had built. Herod has tried to expand it to match the original. We are told it still falls far short. That is okay. It is like our forefather Solomon intimated : it is God who makes the Temple the Temple. It is God who can Tabernacle with us here in this neighborhood synagogue.

It seems since Jesus hit these shores, all eyes are more on God than ever. Some are skeptical of Jesus, but even so, they are more sensitive to God. Prayerfully, in time, they will see Jesus for the prophet Poppa and I believe He is. He seems to be more than a prophet, more than a rabbi. We just cannot explain it. I surely cannot. I want to follow Him. If He would call me like He called Levi, I mean, Matthew, I would follow. Poppa said the same. In a conversation with Poppa about my disappointment that I cannot follow Him daily, Poppa said, "If He calls us, we will follow Him wherever He goes. And if He doesn't call us, we will follow Him here in Magdala." I have to say, that brought an inner peace to my soul. I love Poppa.

On the seventh month, the tenth day — Poppa and I fasted all day. Today is the Day of Atonement. I spent the day confessing my sins to God, asking for His forgiveness. I trust He will do as He promised. He always does.

On the seventh month, the fourteenth day — I have not written in a few days. Poppa and I have been working through our businesses. We truly are getting them in profitable shape. We have made some hires. We have also cut a few workers. Poppa's chief concern is honesty. It once was simply frugality and profit. He is still frugal, but he will no longer tolerate even a hint of dishonesty. I am not saying Father was ever dishonest. One can be dishonest not by lying only, but also by not disclosing all the facts. Father wants full disclosure in all business transactions. He is willing to take the hit. He says we are doing business before God's eyes.

On the seventh month, the fifteenth day through the twenty-third day — We have not done this in a long time. It is the Feast of Tabernacles. Poppa constructed a booth for us to live in for the next eight days. While Poppa was the tax collector here, we never participated in this festival to God. We were excluded from synagogue. We were hated. There was danger to do much outside our home. Now, we have left that business. We are faithfully participating in synagogue. Back to the Deuteronomy Shema. We must love God. To do so, we must obey all that He has spoken. To be honest, it was genuinely nice, Poppa and I in the same booth at night. I forgot how much he snores. I admire Momma even more!

Each night after prayers, we visit until falling asleep. We never fall asleep at the same time. One would still be talking. When no response came from the other mat, the talker would decide it was time to sleep, too. We had fun seeing who would go to sleep first. We threatened mischief, but neither would dare carry it out. I cannot help but smile.

I never have heard Poppa share his heart as I have this week. I am good at sharing mine. He is somewhat reserved. Seemingly, even with his adult daughter, he is compelled to maintain the fatherly position. I am glad. In another way, I am disappointed. He has allowed me to get to know him better. He has shared things with me that I have never heard from him in my thirty-three years. He has hopes. I knew that. He also has fears. He wakes up from dreams where his qualifications as a tax collector are questioned. He has not been a tax collector for a while. I would think such dreams would cease. In his dreams, he still works the booth. He feels inadequate for business. I know of none more qualified.

Other times, he says that he has the worst of all dreams. His nightmare is that Jesus is speaking to a large crowd. At some point, Jesus tells the people, "I will not continue speaking until that unworthy Jared leaves us." "That haunts me," Poppa says. I assure him Jesus would never say that. He invites the unworthy.

Otherwise, I would still be possessed.

Those are the dreams that recur in my mind — the demons pulling me to the pit of Hell. I have nightmares of the nights on the shore where I engaged in unspeakable sexual immorality. I dream of wanting to do such. I dream of men forcing me to do such. I dream of the voices calling my name. I feel them throw me into fits of rage. I still have nightmares of how I tried to harm myself. The fishhooks and the knife cutting at my neck. I awake weeping. I then call on Jesus' name. His face appears. I say His name again. The demonic dream ends — at least for the night.

Other dreams are sweeter. I had many this week in the booth — not the tax booth, but the Feast of Tabernacles booth that Poppa made. I see Jesus in a field. The twelve disciples are present. I am present with them, too, but sitting a little separated, which I suppose is proper. He speaks. Matthew asks a question. Jesus explains. Peter makes a statement of humor. We all laugh. Jesus laughs too. He has the most wholesome laugh. I ask a question that seems so foolish. He smiles. The disciples nod as if they have had the same question. Jesus answers my question while looking at the disciples, too. We are all learning together. In my dreams, I see families restored in His presence. I see lepers healed. I see blind people given sight. I even envision Jesus being at the bed of my Momma. He speaks. She gets up, well. I heard He did something similar for Peter's mother-in-law.

On the seventh month, the twenty-fourth day — Matthew just left our home with Poppa to visit some Roman friends who have come to Magdala. Once, Matthew was a man to himself. He has been transformed. He no longer looks to see how much money he can make. He wants to see how many people he can tell about Jesus. From what Matthew has seen and heard, he has shared with us that he earnestly believes Jesus is the Messiah. The Messiah? That makes sense! How else could any explain the miracles He works, the words He shares, the lives He has changed? The Messiah. The Promised One of God. Our Deliverer!

The Messiah? With His power, He can be the king of Israel. Matthew says He is from the lineage of David. Poppa stated that was a requirement. Matthew tells us also that He was born in Bethlehem. For some reason, that fact seems to hold significance. He could be our king. Look at all the people He has helped. In my limited time near Him, it is amazing how He is able to put His enemies, even the religious ones, in their place. He gives them the correct perspective without attempting to disrespect their positions.

That did not help my unhappiness of not being able to be joined with Him. Matthew told us that the other day, Jesus took twelve from the crowd following Him. He chose twelve to pour His teaching into. In a way, I am glad I was not present. It would have crushed me not to be selected. The men He chose are an odd bunch. Let me think — Matthew named them. There were Peter, Andrew, James, and John. Those four did not surprise me. There is Matthew, of course.

Jesus gave him the personal invitation at his tax booth. I do not think Jesus would have done that if He had not decided beforehand to have Matthew with Him.

There was that other friend of Zebedee's boys, Philip from Bethsaida. That makes sense, though I do not know him. Some men I had never heard of: Nathanael (also called Bartholomew), Thaddeus, another man named James, and a Thomas. One who is a part of the twelve is named Judas. I have to be cautious with my attitude toward him since my experience with Judas the Galilean. It is sad that the names of people who have hurt us carry emotions along with bias. I hear he is from Tiberias.

The one name that shocked me was when Matthew named Simon the Zealot. Simon the Zealot! This is the man who protested at our tax booth. He is the one who threatened us. He is the one we thought had vandalized our booth. Now, he is a follower of Jesus. More, he is now one of the few, the twelve disciples. I am anxious to see Simon the Zealot. I want to see for myself if he has been changed. How he treats me will be a sign one way or the other.

I have been sparse in my writing of late. On this day, I feel I could write all day from the things Matthew shared with us. He told us he got to meet Jesus' mother and brothers a few days ago. Another dissatisfaction for me. I would love to have been there. I wanted to know what they were like. Matthew said His mother was surprisingly young. I asked if he got to meet Jesus' father. Matthew said that His father was a carpenter but that he was not with them anymore. Matthew said he was hesitant to ask why.

I asked Matthew, "What about Jesus' brothers? How many are there? What are they like?" He said, as he understands, Jesus has four brothers and some sisters. He could not remember the names of the brothers, but he thought the main spokesperson for the family was named James. Jesus and the brothers had a strong resemblance to their mother. They all were very respectful to her. Then Matthew dropped a shocking bit of news. He said that Jesus' mother and brothers fear Jesus is out of His mind. Matthew said that what was worse, at that same gathering, the Pharisees were accusing Jesus to His face, saying he was possessed by Satan. I was aghast.

How this hurts Jesus! It is something I suppose we should all question. I feel terrible writing that. The Pharisees are our religious leaders. They have been coming after Him with an unexplainable vengeance. They never went after Judas the

Galilean that way. Based on my experience, he clearly could be of the devil. They never went after Theudas. I hear he is more of a fake than Judas. Why is it that the Pharisees are not concerned about these men who have no power? All they had was a spirit of revolt. Here is Jesus, no revolt. He speaks truth. He confirms His words with power. The Pharisees have worn on all of us. Their hypocrisy has driven many from the temple. They are profiteers in the same vein as the worst tax collector.

Had I been there, I would have told the Pharisees, "Trust me, when He spoke to the seven demons inside of me, there was no collegial interaction. His name alone made the demons inside me quiver. The closer I got to Jesus at Peter's door in Capernaum, there was no kinsman feel. I sensed what was in me was in complete enmity with the Rabbi at the door. When Jesus commanded that they leave, they left. When Jesus told the demons at the water's edge to be silent, they did not close their mouths willingly. His force closed their mouths."

But His family? Family should be quick to defend their loved ones. His family says He is out of His mind. If I had been there (I wish I would have been), I would have asked, "What is it about your son and your brother that makes you think He is out of His mind?" I heard Him speak on a few occasions. I have never heard anything but the purest wisdom. He is like none I have ever heard. Nothing wild-eyed was said. No word was spoken that did not make sense. Everything He does resonates within my spirit. No warning shoots through my mind. "Be careful." If something was wrong with Him mentally, Matthew certainly would have caught it. If he would not have, I know Poppa would have. These tax collectors are taught to read a person's face. They learn how to ferret out a lie in any statement. Instead of finding fault in Jesus when He spoke, they each found fault in themselves. His words are like a seining net, bringing what is wrong in our lives to the forefront.

Out of His mind? He would be if He could not do what He said. He would be insane if He claimed to heal a leper before our eyes, and then the leper left as spotted as when he arrived. He would be insane, if He said He would cast the demons out of me, only to find the demons act out and laugh at His words. Even more if He commanded the demons out, just to find them attacking Him. I have watched Jesus. No demon wants any part of Him. No wise person has been able to outsmart Him.

It makes me wonder what His mother saw when He lived in her home. Did she think He was insane then? Did she ever have Him committed before? Did the brothers have to seize Him from a public place? If so, why did they not seize Him before the crowd? Could it be the crowd believes, but they do not? If they are so sane, why can they not persuade Him? Or could it be that they are the mistaken ones?

What is wrong with these people? What do they see that I do not? Better yet, what am I seeing that they refuse to see? I believe that is the better question. Regardless, I will watch Him. I will listen. At the first sign of contradiction, I will stand up to Him. How can I even write that? I am whole now because of Him. His smile. His goodness. His words. I feel as though I am sinning even to question Him.

Poppa returned this evening. We talked into the night about all that we heard from Matthew. I asked Poppa, "Do you think Jesus is out of His mind?" Poppa said, "Honey, if He is, then how much crazier are we?" Poppa reassured me that he would listen closely for any warning signs. I remarked to him we had not seen any yet. I have a strong feeling that we never will.

On the seventh month, the twenty-fifth day — Matthew sent a message to Poppa from Capernaum. He wrote that the town of Capernaum looks like Jerusalem at Passover. Masses have come to town. We are just coming off the Celebration of Booths. He said it looks as though everyone has moved their booth to his fair town. He said Jesus is speaking nearly every day, and that we should come up so as to not miss anything.

Poppa smiled. The next thing you know we are packed and walking out the door. How grateful we are to have a man inside the twelve!

On the seventh month, the twenty-sixth day — Matthew was right. The crowds were the largest I have ever seen. It was as if you could see them for a mile. I could not see Jesus. Judging from the way the crowd faced, He was somewhere on the edge of the water. The crowd kept pushing forward. How can He not be soaked by now? Poppa stood upon an olive press there in Capernaum. He said he could make out fishermen rowing toward the front of the crowd. I waited.

Poppa then told me he saw Jesus helped up into the boat. When he said that, I feared we had traveled all this way for nothing. If He left the minute we arrived,

I would be heartbroken. At that moment, Poppa said, "He's not leaving. He is asking everyone to sit." As people were getting seated, Jesus waited. Finally, all were on the sandy shoreline — us included. He spoke. With all that crowd, I cannot believe that we could hear Him so clearly. I could hear a few birds. I could actually hear the water's small crashing sound into the shore. I saw a fish jump. I heard its splash as it reentered the water. These did not distract. They seemed to enhance the mood of this gathering. It was as if all of nature were taking part.

Jesus then told a parable, a story with a lesson. I cannot begin to write the exhilaration I felt to actually hear Him teach. Up until today, I had seen Him deal with individuals. I had seen Him greet people. I had seen Him defend Himself against the Pharisees about tax collectors and sinners. I had heard Him up close and personal as He healed me. But today, I was so blessed to get a taste of His teaching willingly offered. It was like He had something to say. This was the moment to say it. There was a purpose for this lesson today. I know He has spoken in synagogues around our area. I have never been there on time to hear Him. Before that, I was not in any shape to be in attendance. I was not wanted. I did not want to be there. All that has changed.

This is what He said: "Listen! A farmer went out to sow his seed. As he was scattering the seed, some fell along the path, and the birds came and ate it up. Some fell on rocky places, with not much soil. It sprang up quickly because the soil was shallow. But when the sun came up, the plants were scorched, and they withered because they had no root. Other seed fell among thorns that grew and choked the plants, so that they did not bear grain. Still other seed fell on good soil. It came up, grew, and produced a crop, multiplying thirty, sixty, or even a hundred times. He who has ears to hear, let him hear."

I am amazed at my memory. I feel like I just wrote word for word what He said. I suppose I truly listened as He commanded. After He spoke, He and His twelve sailed in the boat to the other side. I wanted to go in that boat with them. I was not asked to join. Neither was Poppa. I guess it is as he said — we will follow Him from Magdala.

As we walked back home, I tried to reason what His words meant. First and foremost, these were not the words of a mad man. I recounted them with Poppa. A farmer sows seed. We are familiar with that in our vineyards. Jesus said that some fell on the path. We never plant on the path. It is too hard. Birds, as He said, do truly eat the seed. He is not a farmer, but He clearly observes the country around Him. The farmer's seed also fell on rocky places. We have seen that. It will spring up, but it does not grow very much beyond the ground. It yellows from the heat with no access to water. It quickly dies. We always hate that because it is a waste of seed. Father is frugal, you know!

Jesus then said some seed fell amongst the thorns. It grows, but the thorns choke the plant so it cannot bear fruit. We have seen that when we grow our vegetables. Often in the spring, after our tax collecting day was over, we would tend to a garden behind our home. We drew the lines for the plants. We meticulously planted the seed. We watered them daily. Sadly, sometimes the tax business hours were long. We neglected our garden. Weeds grew up around our plants. In fact, often, we could not tell the difference between our plants and the weeds. If we left it as it were, the plants never produced. The weeds soaked up all the moisture, the vegetable plants made nothing. Sometimes we tried to pull the weeds around the plant, just to find the plant was so intertwined that to pull a weed meant to pull the plant, too. Either way, no vegetables for Mary, Jared, or Adriana.

Jesus said that some seed fell on good soil. That plant produced. That vine also did where the seed was planted. I told Poppa, "I understand the facts of the parable. But why did He tell us about farming? I know His words are good for daily life. However, there had to be more to it than simple gardening best practices." Poppa said, "Absolutely. Did you notice His charge, 'Let him who has ears to hear, let him hear'? Jesus was attempting to drive home a point. I am not sure what it was." For Poppa to say this made me feel better. If Poppa cannot understand it, how will I be able to understand? With that, he said, "There is something about hearing. David always wrote that we are to meditate on the words of God. I believe Jesus only speaks the words of God. We must meditate on them."

No sooner did he say that, I had a thought. "Poppa, you said David wrote that we should meditate on the words of God. You said Jesus speaks the words of God. What if the seeds going into the ground are the words of God, finding a home within our lives? Think about it. Jesus speaks. The Pharisees argue with everything He says. We all know how mean they are toward the common Jewish person — more so with Jesus. His words go into their ears, but they will not let them penetrate like they have with us, Poppa. He said some seed hits rocky soil and they sprout, just to die. Do you remember what Peter said to us at Matthew's home?

He said Jesus heals many. They get what they want and leave, never to be seen again. Peter said that is why it was so good to see we had not forgotten Jesus. I suppose that is what it is like to hear the words, to get what you want from them, and leave with no real desire for God."

Poppa acknowledged with pleasure. "Okay, daughter, then I guess the seed that lands among thorns that gets choked out is like those who come to synagogue, who make a decision to follow God, but then they get tied down at the fish factory with promotions and are never seen again at the synagogue. They got too busy for God." "Yes Poppa," I said. He then confessed, "Mary, that was me. I got my promotion. I got my breakthrough job. I started making money. I started gaining assets. I grew too busy for God. Before I knew it, I almost lost you. In a way, I did lose you."

I answered him, "Ah, but Poppa, we are good soil now! Here we are. We are hearing the words of God through Jesus. He is redirecting our lives to follow Him in every way. We are becoming fruitful. Matthew is the living example. He went from wanting more money to wanting to follow Jesus more. Peter went from fishing for fish, to helping the Rabbi lead masses." I wonder if we got it right?

Once we got home, we thanked God in our evening prayers for opening our eyes. These are questions I want to ask Jesus personally. Perhaps He has achieved what He desires. He caused us to listen, to reason. He prompted us to ask God. In doing so, we have analyzed our lives. I feel we grew one step closer to Him.

In the eighteenth year of the reign of Tiberius Caesar, on the eighth month, the sixth day — Poppa collapsed nine days ago. We were walking in the market by the shore. I heard a sound of something hitting the pavement. I heard some people gasp. I turned to ask Poppa if he knew what that noise was. He was on the ground. It was Poppa. He was frantically attempting to get back upright. He seemed confused. He could not answer me. As he tried, only his left side was functioning the way you would expect. His right side was limp. Some men came to help as they saw his struggle. They convinced him to lay still. They yelled out for a physician. Cassius, a physician from Tiberias, responded.

The doctor examined Poppa. He said that he feared it was dropsy, or some form of palsy. I was, and am, devastated. I do not know of anyone who has ever recovered from this. There is no known treatment. Some workers from the fish factory helped me get Poppa home. They had great difficulty getting him on a mat. It was as if one limb of Poppa's would go one way, the other another. It was surreal.

We moved his mat from his room to the main room within the entrance of our home. Ladies from our synagogue came to help me. It has been five days now. Poppa will not eat. He barely drinks. He tries to speak, but I cannot understand him. I have tried to get him to write, but what he puts to paper is not intelligible. All I see in his eyes is fear. How could this have happened?

I am so distraught. Going through my own pain was difficult. At least it was happening to me. Losing Momma that morning was traumatic. Thankfully, it was sudden, in our home, and with great peace. I have grieved for Momma. I have also rejoiced to know where she is. But, laying on our floor in the home he built is Poppa. After all the good he has done, this is his outcome? I have moved my mat beside him. I have prayed with him every morning and every evening. Oh God, will you heal my beloved father? He loves You. He follows You. He has believed in You. He honors Your prophet, Jesus.

Jesus! That's the answer. I will send for Jesus. Atticus has been with me every day to help when he gets off work. Linus has received Roman permission to give us a few hours every day. I am so thankful for these two. Linus has changed radically since our meeting with Jesus in Capernaum. Atticus is still considering what all this means. He has never been deeply religious. His past is one of superstition and mediums, but since he has been going to synagogue with us on occasion, he seems to be turning to God. I fear it is for me. It must be for Him. God has given both of these men to help. I could not make it without them. I am asking Linus to see if he can find where Jesus is. I know Jesus is our only hope. Linus promised he would.

On the eighth month, the eighth day — I left Atticus with Poppa so I could pray in the synagogue. God healed Hezekiah. God extended his life. How I long for our God, our Father to do the same with my father. Where is Jesus? I need Him now. I know He would be here if He knew. There is no way He would abandon me and Poppa. If we could reach Matthew, I know he would let our Rabbi know.

I returned home from synagogue. I asked Atticus if he would go to Capernaum for Matthew. Matthew loves Poppa. Matthew is a disciple of Jesus. I know Matthew would help if only we can get word to him. Atticus swore he would not quit looking until he found Matthew. As he was leaving, Atticus gave me a comforting hug. His last words were ones I had not heard him utter before. Atticus told me he loves me. I did not return the gesture. I longed to hear those words from a man like Atticus. But not now.

On the eighth month, the eleventh day — Cassius the physician left. He says Poppa does not have long to live. His breathing is shallow. He does not open his eyes. I am here alone with him. Thankfully, the ladies from the synagogue have brought food for me. A few have stayed some nights by our side. Linus returned this morning. He said he heard Jesus was somewhere on the other side of the Galilee near the Decapolis. If Jesus is there, then I can expect Atticus will not find Matthew, either.

What am I going to do? I have not felt this powerless since the demons left. Jesus cast out the demons. He could also cast away this palsy from Poppa. If only.

Poppa awoke with a fright. He was trembling. I wonder if he had that dream that Jesus sent him away? Or did he see Momma? God, please heal my father. I know You love us. I know You have Momma with You. Do you seek to reunite Momma with Poppa? If that is Your Will, I will accept it. But Father God? I am not ready for that. Please take that into account. I am not ready for that. Please consider me in Your plan.

Job came to my mind. I have never suffered like Job. He lost all his children, all of his possessions, then his health. His words were, "Though He slay me, yet I will trust in Him." This is where I must be. I will trust God knows best. I will trust He does all things for our good. I will trust that we are eternal beings, to live here or to live there with Him. Oh God, please help my unbelief.

In the eighteenth year of the reign of Tiberius Caesar, on the eighth month, the twelfth day — Poppa is resting now. He breathed his last a few hours ago. Linus was here. Atticus was, too. Several ladies wept with me. I clutched his sweet head in my lap. I watered his face with my tears. "Poppa, I love you. You have been with me from my birth. You have never stopped loving me. You always cared for me. You would not give up on me. When the whole of Magdala walked in disgust of me, you held my hand in public. Poppa, we worked the tax booth together. We bore the insults together. We treated people kindly, just as you taught me. Even when they spewed hatred, you taught me to be kind in return. Poppa, you led me to synagogue. You took me to find help when I was unmanageable. You rushed me to see Jesus. You waited in line with the masses by my side. You were there when He made me whole. You surprised me with a special trip to see Jesus speak at the shore. You faced Jesus with me at Matthew's banquet. I spent the nights with you in our booth for Tabernacles. We shared our hearts. You taught me how to write. You taught me how to do math. You taught me how to pray. I climbed Mount Arbel with you after visiting Momma's grave. Oh Poppa. I love you. You have been our rock. You have been our provider. You have trained me to carry on without you."

In the eighteenth year of the reign of Tiberius Caesar, on the eighth month, the thirteenth day — We buried Poppa beside Momma today. Linus and Atticus were by my side. I stayed at the tomb for hours. Sometimes I would face the tomb and weep. Other times, I would face Galilee. I let the breeze dry my tears. I would then turn back to the tomb and refresh them again. Linus and Atticus sat down near the shore. They faced the lake to give me privacy.

After a few hours, I ran to the other side of Arbel and began to climb that familiar trek to the top. The men called. I yelled back, "I am okay. Please wait."

I climbed the mountain. Sitting on the outcrop that Poppa and I always used, I looked over the whole of Galilee. I could see Magdala. I could see our home. From this vantage point, it looked like it did a few years back. I could imagine Momma and Poppa in the house preparing the meal. I could almost see us in the courtyard, sharing our evening meal together. From this vantage point, it seems nothing had changed down below. Sadly, that home is now empty. It is mine and mine alone.

I glanced down to the shore below the mountain. I saw Linus and Atticus. They visited. I could tell because their heads faced each other. They would then cast their eyes to the Sea of Galilee, I assume to ponder life and me. I know they both feel the grief of losing Poppa, especially Linus. To think, Linus had the unenviable job of being a Roman soldier, battle-hardened, protecting a Jewish tax collector. It was not enough that we Jewish people hate Rome. He had to guard a Jewish man hated by the Jewish people. That was almost a double dip of distaste. Yet, he grew to love Poppa. My father rewarded him handsomely for his efforts. Monetarily, yes. But more. He made Linus feel a sense of family.

Why this climb? It is from here that I find a peaceful perspective. Job's words come back to me: "I know that my Redeemer lives, and that in the end he will stand upon the earth. And after my skin has been destroyed, yet in my flesh I will see God; I myself will see him with my own eyes — I, and not another. How my heart yearns within me!" I will one day see God. He lives. He raises the dead. I will see Momma and Poppa again too, with my own eyes. I will see them — me, and not just others. Though He slay me or Poppa or Momma, yet I will trust Him. There is no other way to live.

If this life is all there is, how tragic. The very existence of the unseen demons have convinced me more things are unseen than seen. The very power Jesus displayed over them emboldens me that God can do all things — not just for life, but beyond death. I find peace up on Mount Arbel. I have one thought: I am so thankful Jesus did not call me apart from Poppa to follow as Matthew did. Had I been with Jesus, I would not have been with Poppa when he needed me most. How gracious is our God.

On the eighth month, the fourteenth day — I attended synagogue today by myself. It was exceedingly difficult to be there without Poppa or Momma. I am so grateful; the people were so kind. I have never felt so much love in my life in this one place. It seems my past is behind me. I feel as though they now accept me as a true member. Old things are passed away.

On the eighth month, the seventeenth day — It has been a busy few days. I am getting Poppa's businesses all in order. I am grateful he divided the duties with me. I have mine in order. Now I am attempting to learn his. I know he did not want me to deal with things near the shore. I have hired Linus to assist me in that area. He was more than willing to do it without pay. I reminded him that a workman is worth his wage.

I am still honoring our prayer times each morning and evening. It is sad in one way. Poppa is gone. It is also comforting, because God is our Everlasting Father. He will never leave me. In my darkest moments, He has been here. In the lonely times, He is ever present. I do not know how I survived without Him.

On the eighth month, the eighteenth day — What an amazing visit I had today with Matthew! Matthew loved Poppa so much. He called Poppa both his competitor and his role model. He was so saddened to hear of his passing. We spent several hours just recounting the years with my father. It was a tearful, yet joyful, walk down memory lane.

I did not want our whole visit to be about Poppa. I wanted to know what it was like being a disciple of Jesus. Matthew just returned from being with Him at the Decapolis. Let me start this note by saying we have seen great miracles of Jesus already. We have seen Him heal the leper. We have seen Him cast out the demons. We have seen Him heal the sick. His words penetrate the hearts of His listeners in ways no other rabbi has ever been able to do, but what Matthew shared with me was simply overwhelming.

His eyes were bright. He was exhilarated at the mere repeat of what he saw. I am writing what he said from memory. Even as I try to put it into words, they cannot express what he shared the way he did. Matthew said his own words cannot come close to describing what he saw.

As I recorded before, Poppa took me to Capernaum to hear Jesus speak. He shared that parable about the farmer. Jesus then left in a boat with his disciples. We found out later that they had gone to the Decapolis. This was why we could not find Him to see if He could help Poppa. Matthew told me that when they set out in the boat, Jesus had experienced a long day. I cannot imagine how difficult it is to deal with so many people, to speak, to heal, to cast out demons, and to deal with Pharisees. I had exhausting days at the tax booth. That pales in comparison to what He does each day. Matthew said Jesus laid down in the front of the boat to sleep. He said he was glad Jesus slept, giving him and the disciples time to visit about all they had seen.

The wind began to blow against the boat, slowing their progress. Some fought the sails. Others rowed against the wind. A few hours later, they, too, were suffering exhaustion. That is when it really got bad. A squall broke out upon the Galilee. Matthew, not a seasoned sailor, had heard of these things. He had been enamored by the stories. That is all fine and good if you are not in one. Matthew said he knew of the ferocious winds that blow out of the Galilean hills. He had felt them at shore. But on the sea, at that moment, the water began to collapse onto the boat. It seemed the boat was breaking apart under them.

Matthew said he looked at James, John, Peter, and Andrew for comfort, but they were as afraid as him. They began to scream at each other for help. No one could hear the other over the storm. They looked in the front of the boat. Jesus was still sound asleep. The way the boat was built, He was shielded somewhat from the wind and waves. Even so, no one could sleep through such trauma. The boat lifted way up into the air, then crashed down into a vacuum as the water escaped beneath. Water was accumulating in the boat, moving front to back, side to side. There was no way Jesus was not being splashed. And yet, He slept.

Matthew said it was then that one of them (he could not even make out who it was in the deluge), hanging onto the rigging, made it to Jesus. He heard one statement, almost indicting, "Master, Master, we're going to drown!"

Matthew said Jesus roused from His sleep. He sat up for a minute, wiping His eyes, He looked at the twelve staring at Him in terror. In that moment, He did not make fun of them. He also did not panic. He simply stood up. Grabbing the mast, He commanded at the top of His lungs, "Quiet, be still!" Now, I was hearing this from Matthew's own lips. I am picturing it in my head. Jesus commanded who? That was my first thought. I was thinking He was telling the disciples to be quiet, to be still. We know that we are often told to be still and know that God, He is God, but that was not who Jesus was commanding.

Matthew continued. He said at that very moment, the wind died down. The sea was completely calm. He said in an instant, the noise in their ears was gone. All they heard was the gentle ripple of waves brushing against their boat. I cannot imagine it! Jesus can command the weather? This, to me, is much bigger than healing a person. Doctors can bring cures. Jesus just does it instantly. Doctors also can't heal some. Jesus has no limits to illness. Demons can scream, but He silences them. That is His Power over those spirits, but to order the wind to stop, the water to be still? Can He kill a tree with a word? Can He make one appear from nowhere? Can He shut lions' mouths? Can He make the sky bronze, halting all rain?

Matthew said Jesus then looked at the twelve. He asked, "Why are you so afraid? Do you still have no faith?" Still have no faith? They had just been with Him a short time. How quickly does faith come? I would like to see that myself. I am growing in faith at a slow pace. Then again, I am not with Him all day long, seeing all He can do. I suppose their faith should have grown unquestionably with all they have seen. It sounds to me as if Jesus then laid back down to get a little more rest. Matthew did not say. I was still in awe of the miraculous act. The disciples, Matthew said, then began to visit. "Who is this? Even the wind and the waves obey Him!" I am glad they had that question. I do, too. How I love Jesus! We have never seen anyone like Him, ever.

Per our conversation, I learned Jesus was back at Peter's home in Capernaum. Once I confirm our businesses are in order, tomorrow, with my good friend Linus, I am going to Capernaum to see Jesus. I cannot wait!

On the eighth month, the nineteenth day — What a spectacular day today has been. I am resting now in Matthew's beautiful home in my usual room. I miss that Poppa is not in the room beside mine. I am comforted to know he is in a much better place with Momma.

I arrived in Capernaum a little after noon. Linus was happy to cover for me back home. He knows my longing for the Rabbi. Rome keeps him from having the freedom God has given me. As I entered Capernaum, the crowds were as large as ever. Every time Jesus is in town, the city is abuzz with visitors. None of the locals complain. Businesses thrive during these almost divine appointments where God does a mighty work through Jesus. This is the first time I have written such a phrase. The more we talk amongst ourselves, the more we realize it has to be God working through this Rabbi or Prophet.

We had heard Jairus' daughter has been sick. The synagogue in Magdala has been praying for her and Jairus' family. The Rabbi did not come one moment too soon. As I walked with Matthew to where he was to meet Jesus, Jairus cut frantically through the crowd. He fell at Jesus' feet, begging Him to come to his house immediately. His daughter was dying, gasping for breath. I knew Jairus had a family, but we never had the opportunity to meet them. Jesus obliged without hesitation. He has become the featured guest at the synagogue in Capernaum. I assume Jesus and Jairus have a strong relationship. I am a little surprised Jairus has not become a disciple. It may be that he feels his calling is to guide this synagogue. Or he may not want to leave his salary. He may also have too many questions about Jesus to leave everything. I can understand that.

I followed at a distance. On the way, a disruption occurred by a woman in the crowd. Jesus was asking, "Who touched Me?" To be honest, everyone wanted to touch Him. Any who could touch Him, did. I did not hear beyond that. Then, He kept moving. The crowds separated as He reached the street of Jairus' home. That allowed me to move in closer. No sooner did I get within a few yards of Him, I heard a group come toward Jairus, weeping uncontrollably. I knew at that moment, having just lost Poppa, his little daughter was gone.

One of the men from the town, a friend of Jairus' family, put his arm around the synagogue ruler and said, "Your daughter is dead. Don't bother the Teacher anymore."

I remembered Poppa's passing. Now this family is facing a fate worse. We expect our parents to die before us, but never our children. I was saddened. Tears would not stop rolling down my cheeks. I turned to look away. I saw the Sea of Galilee. In an instant, I remembered Matthew telling me that Jesus made that horrible storm just stop in its tracks — like making a charging lion sit at His feet to be petted.

In the middle of this thought, I turned back to hear Jesus say to Jairus, "Don't be afraid; just believe, and she will be healed." Healed? They said the girl was dead. I believe someone dead cannot be healed. Though, at Poppa's side, I wanted him healed. I would have welcomed the healing before or after death. Jesus kept walking down the street toward the house. He was undeterred. It was if He was determined to do something about this problem.

Jairus ran into his home ahead of us. Jesus was about to go in. He turned to the wailers and said, "Stop wailing. She is not dead, but asleep." Asleep? I trust Jesus, but I know the difference between sleep and dead. The crowd around gave the most devilish laugh. They mocked Jesus.

Here in the time of Jairus' greatest tragedy with no hope, they have the audacity to laugh? Even as Jesus said that, I was shocked too, but I did not think it was funny. How can any of us doubt what He can do? He cast the demons out of me. He healed the leper. He gave sight to the blind. He calmed the sea and the storm!

Jesus made everyone leave the home but Jairus and his wife. He then called for Peter, John, and James to come in with Him. What a threesome — Peter, John, and James; fishermen I well knew. Fishermen changed to disciples. Such a transformation. Had I not dealt with them in the tax booth, I would never have grasped the dramatic turn for these three.

Matthew, the other disciples, a few people I did not know, and I, were left outside. I waited. It seemed like a long time. I walked away from the crowd and around the house. I hoped to see something within the home. I was so blessed. I could see the window to the girl's room. I saw Jesus present with the parents and the three disciples. He hugged the mom. He walked up to the mat of the young girl. He said something I could not hear.

Immediately, this prone, still girl sat up! Her mom gasped, covering her mouth. She looked at Jesus. She then fixed her eyes on her daughter. The daughter stood from her bed. Jairus, weeping without restraint, clutched his daughter. His wife closed in with arms around the two. I could see Peter shake his head in disbelief toward his friends James and John. I saw them look at Jesus. He just gave a very faint smile. I saw Him say something to the parents. With that, He motioned toward His disciples in the room. They were leaving this sweet family to themselves. Again, the tears just rolled down my cheeks, checkering my robe.

I made my way back toward Matthew. I whispered to him only, "He did it." Matthew looked at me in confusion just as Jesus walked out with Peter, James, and John in tow. Matthew looked at Peter. Peter nodded with approval. Nothing was said aloud.

I cannot get a grasp of Jesus. Every time we think we have seen Him do all that is imaginable, He does something more. Either that twelve-year-old girl was dead, or she was at the point of death. Judging by the experts who were with her, including Cassius, our area physician, she was dead. Jesus said she was asleep. I cannot help but think she was dead or on the slender line that separates life and death. Jesus raised her up miraculously. It goes back to what I have written: the God of Moses is working through Jesus.

On the eighth month, the twentieth day — Matthew left early for Peter's house. He left me a note. They were headed several miles southwest to a place where Jesus loves to teach. Jesus had already left by boat ahead of them. Matthew gave me directions. I really did not need them. When I left his house, there was a long drawn-out crowd walking in that direction, following the disciples with hopes to see Jesus. I simply fell in behind them.

I could hear all kinds of people talking about Jesus. Some were talking about what they had seen. Some visited about what they hoped He would do for them. Most were just following with the yearning to do no more than to sit and listen to Him speak. The vast majority were missing work to be there. Some took off. Some chose not to go to work. Some were private businessmen who sacrificed a day's income. Most were traveling as families, their children pulled from whatever activities in which they generally engaged.

I recognized an older lady, but I could not place her. She recognized me, too. I began to walk with her. We struggled for a little while to remember where we had seen each other. Then it dawned on me. This was Maria, the lady I met at the Temple inside the women's court. She said that I appeared a lot different than when she last saw me. I was able to tell her what Jesus had done for me at Peter's home several weeks ago. "Remarkable!" she exclaimed.

I wanted to know how she had heard of Jesus. She explained she had heard Him speaking on the Temple steps inside the Gentile courtyard. The crowds were massive. She had been around the Temple her entire life. She loved God, studied under numerous priests and rabbis, but had never heard God's Word explained so thoroughly and so simply. Maria said that too often, the scholars of Jerusalem, her hometown, try to impress people with their big words. She said it is impressive. The sad thing is, no one understands. Even worse, no one wants to let on like they do not understand. The result: "We learn nothing."

She continued. "But when Jesus came to Jerusalem, He overwhelmed us. God's Word just opened up. He brought truth to our reach. Our hearts pounded. Our love for God grew in ways never imagined. Since then, I have made trips when I have had time. My friend Juanita makes the trips with me. We believe He could be the Messiah." (This is the second time I have heard someone refer to Jesus as the possible Messiah. Matthew was the first.) She said, "We believe." My question was, who is "we"? I asked her. She said talk is all over Jerusalem about Jesus. "Our religious leaders denounce any reference to Jesus as Messiah. Most follow their lead like Roman soldiers under Pilate's glare. In the closed doors of homes all over Judea, whispers from many conclude there is a good chance He is the One."

Juanita spoke up. She said He fits all the prophecies. "He was born in Bethlehem." I have heard many now referencing that place of His birth. She went on, "The prophets foretold Bethlehem as being the place from which will come the Son of David. King Hezekiah referenced it as well." Again, this would explain so much about the Rabbi, a prophet with power from on high. Messiah. It makes sense. I am hesitant to use that word after my experience with Judas the Galilean and Theudas' reputation. It has almost taken a derogatory mockery of late. It is shocking how evil can take things of God and distort them in such a way as to make them untenable.

Before we could talk more, we had climbed a grassy hill overlooking the Sea of Galilee. The disciples went through the crowd, getting everyone to sit. "Jesus is going to teach us!" Quickly, everyone fell on the grass where they stood. The Rabbi began. Not one-side conversation was going on. No children were running. No one was getting up. We all sat in rapt attention.

He stood at the lowest point of the hill where the grasses meet the sandy shore. His back was to the sea. Our faces toward it — more so toward Him. When He spoke, His voice boomed. It echoed up and down the hill, clear as crystal. Every syllable was understandable. What blessed me the most? Every word seemed to resonate with my spirit. I never really felt I had a spirit until Jesus drove the evil ones from me. I now feel as though He is tuning me to match God's yearning for me. His words were shaping me just as a stoneworker hammers on a piece of stone to make it fit into the wall he is building. Maria and Juanita sat with their mouths wide open, as if they were drinking in every word. They did not even break eye contact with Jesus to see if I was doing the same. I was.

I did not miss a word He said, but I was interested to see if all those seated on that hill were getting the same spiritual nourishment. It seemed as though all confusion was leaving the crowd. Every problem melted into the ground. Countenances once grimaced turned to peace. I wish I could write all that He shared. When we first sat, I pulled out my parchments to write, but found that when I wrote, I was missing the wonder of listening. I decided God would bring to mind what I needed to write. More than anything, I did not want to miss one word or meaning behind each lesson. I still am not at a place where I can logically write what He said. It is as if I am digesting it all.

What I can write is that we were there a long time. Some who had to relieve themselves quietly got up. Men exited to the right of the hill. Women and children to the left. It was that orderly. Jesus spoke for hours. At times, He offered to end His teaching, but we all begged Him to continue. No one wanted this moment to end. Everyone refused to leave His presence.

Facing the Sea of Galilee, the sun began to set behind us. It was at that moment I saw a few of the disciples walk up to Jesus at a pause. I moved closer to Him every chance I had. He looked right at me at times when He spoke. Nothing was better than that. Maria and Juanita were now a long way back, sitting where they had initially knelt. I heard one of the disciples say, "This is a remote place, and it is already getting late. Send the crowds away, so they can go to the villages and buy themselves some food." Matthew was with them, but I do not think it was him who suggested that. I was not hungry. I did not want to be sent away. I came to Capernaum for this. I walked to this solitary hill for this. At this moment, Jesus is all I want.

Jesus, what a friend! His answer was almost a defense of my sentiments. He said, "They do not need to go away. You give them something to eat." I could see the disciples flummoxed. They left His side for a little while. Jesus continued to speak. We were relieved He picked up where He left off. To not have this day end was my wish.

A little while later, the disciples returned. One had a small basket. The disciple said, "We have here only five loaves of bread and two fish." I heard him. I looked around. Thousands were on that hill. Five small pieces of bread. He called them loaves. I do not think they were large enough to be called loaves. Two small fish. I was content for Jesus to eat them. He was the One doing all the work.

I watched Jesus. He said to the disciples, "Bring them here to me." They did. Following close behind, I saw a little boy. It was clear that this was his lunch basket they were holding. He was cute. Where was his mother? Was he alone here? It looked to be so. Who would let their little boy go off with a crowd like this? Perhaps it was because never was a hint of danger present when Jesus was around. All those who wanted to hear Him appeared to pose no danger. What was it about this young man that would make him want to leave his friends and games and follow Jesus? Is he that mature? It just shows the impact Jesus is having on the young and the old. We are all being changed. Our natures, youthful and set in our ways, are being changed.

A few people had reluctantly gotten up. Jesus asked His disciples to have the people sit again on the grass. We all obeyed expectantly. There Jesus was with the backdrop of the Sea of Galilee. He held this lunch basket up to the sky. He gave God thanks for the food He held. He then pulled apart a loaf of bread. He gave that to the disciple next to Him. As the disciple was about to leave, Jesus had him wait. He took that part of the loaf and pulled it apart, again handing it to the disciple. He would not let that one leave still. He handed so much bread to that one disciple, he had to extend his robe out to hold all the bread. When his robe extended was full, he was then sent to distribute it.

Matthew came next. Clearly, more than five loaves had already been given out, more like ten times five loaves to one disciple. Yet, He reached into the basket for another loaf. He pulled that one apart, too. Matthew learned from the first disciple to stand pat. The Rabbi did the same multiple times. With Matthew's extended robe full, he left to distribute. One by one, Jesus did the same with each disciple with the bread. When they returned, He sent them out again with more bread. From that little basket, bread just poured out like rain from the sky that falls on us in endless supply.

When all had received the bread, Jesus repeated the same miracle with the fish. Because I was close to Him, my group was served last. I never fretted about not getting fed. Food was not what I wanted. I heard His words. Then I saw His magnificent miracle. Every time I am near Him, or hear of Him, the far reach of His power widens. By the way, it was the best bread I have ever eaten. I thought Momma's bread was the best. I had never had bread as good as hers. That is, until today.

The fish? I am accustomed to good fish. We live in Magdala, the home of the largest fish factory in our nation. I have been exposed to the best cooks on the shore. Honestly, never has fish tasted so — dare I write it — so divine. If this is what the manna from Heaven tasted like in the wilderness years of our people, I can understand how they could eat it daily for years. Granted, they longed for meat. God sent them doves until they could vomit them out. God has given us bread and the meat of fish all in one setting. They were almost as delicious as His words.

Jesus spoke while we ate. They gathered up what was left. I had a little left over myself. I gladly handed to Peter what I had not eaten. Right in front of me were twelve baskets full of leftover food. It all started with one small lunch basket. Now we saw twelve overflowing baskets and a hillside of thousands with full stomachs. It was incredible!

Jesus then told the disciples to leave. Matthew bid me goodbye. They boarded the boat Jesus had taken to this solitary hill. He then sent us home with His blessing. He walked away from us. I wanted to follow. I am sure others did, too. What prevented us? A realization fell over us. He needs His time alone, and alone with God. The only word I can think of is "sacred." One does not walk into the Holy of Holies of the Temple, nor pull the Torah from the Torah chamber on a whim. One prepares himself. It seems Jesus needs this too. I watched Him walk until He faded over the brink of the hill.

I am now back in Matthew's home. He is hardly here anymore. It has become my second home. I have almost finished with my daily record. The one thought I had was, who is feeding Jesus? He fed thousands today. Who feeds Him? Who provides for His needs? Poppa left me with many businesses. I have all the money I need. I have plenty to spare. I am able to pay Linus a handsome salary to help. All of our vineyard workers do well. Poppa always believed if we pay the best what they deserve, we can keep the best in our employment. Nearly all our business associates have been long-term. If I cannot be a disciple, I can certainly be a contributor. The one impedance is I am a single woman from Magdala.

It does Jesus' reputation no good to have such a woman as me following Him. Even if I am just with the disciples, too many sordid stories would spread. Jesus has already shown He will do nothing that could be construed as sin. When he is accused, like of drunkenness at Matthew's reception, there was hardly any alcohol on anyone's breath. The witnesses of that event could clearly testify in Jesus' defense. My task now is to gather some other women to join me. If many women are staying together, helping where we can, with no fraternizing, we can care for Jesus without rumor. I am sure Maria and Juanita are two such women, if available. They live in Jerusalem. Perhaps they can help Him when He is there. Maybe women from our Magdala synagogue will join me. I am sure Jairus will have many who can help from Capernaum, especially after his daughter's healing. This will be my project. This may be my calling.

On the eighth month, the twenty-first day — Since I was in Capernaum, I attended the synagogue of Jairus today. I could see great elation all over the room. Jairus' twelve-year-old daughter was there, helping her father. Everyone there knew she had been sick. Most everyone knew she had been labeled as dead. Yet, two days later, she is as healthy as any twelve-year-old we have ever seen. I expected Jairus to speak about the miracle in his home. He did not. People asked questions. He just said, "God blessed us with our daughter. Let's just treasure our children while we have them."

Some pried, almost demanding he tell them what Jesus did. He would say nothing other than talk of how Jesus is a blessing to his family and this town. "But what did Jesus do when He sent people out of your house?" they kept asking. I saw through her window, but I did not know for sure what Jesus did, other than say a few words. His words have power. That is all I know. He does heal. We all know that.

Jairus walked to the bimah. He opened the scrolls to David's familiar psalm. He read:

> The Lord is my shepherd, I shall not be in want. He makes me lie down in green pastures, He leads me beside quiet waters, He restores my soul. He guides me in paths of righteousness for His name's sake. Even though I walk through the valley of the shadow of death, I will fear no evil, for You are with me; Your rod and Your staff, they comfort me. You prepare a table before me in the presence of my enemies. You anoint my head with oil; my cup overflows. Surely goodness and love will follow me all the days of my life, and I will dwell in the house of the Lord forever.

Jairus then expounded on the text himself. We all hoped Jesus would walk in the door. He never did. The psalm is so beautiful. I pray no one asks me what I thought of his message. I have no idea what he taught. I could not help but think of that text and yesterday.

Now in my home away from home, I must note why this psalm moved me so. Jesus had led us up a grassy hill. He had us sit in the green pasture. He had us listen beside the still water. My soul was refreshed. "Though I walk through the valley of the shadow of death" — we had just seen Jairus' daughter brought out from that shadow. Fear no evil? That little boy carrying the basket lunch feared no evil in a crowd, though all by himself. He prepared a table before us — from five loaves and two fish, He fed a multitude, including me. Our baskets overflowed. If I am with Him, every time I am with Him, surely goodness and love follow me.

I want that for the rest of my life. I want to dwell in the house of the Lord, the house of God, forever, with Poppa and Momma. I am struck by the timing of God to have this scripture read the day after Jesus taught and fed so many, two days after He made Jairus' daughter well. I am in awe. My praises for God cannot end. I want to run as fast as I can with my arms raised celebrating, worshipping God! I want to scream "Hallelujah!" at the top of my lungs! What would this town of people think? I dare not. The excitement within me wells. My cup overflows. Thank you, God! I cannot imagine leaving for Magdala. I want to serve God. I want to care for Jesus. Is He the Messiah? That is the question. If He is not, I cannot imagine who would be.

In the eighteenth year of the reign of Tiberius Caesar, on the twelfth month, the first day — I have been neglectful to record the events over the past few months. I have been busy attempting to get all things in order with Poppa's businesses so that I may have the freedom to travel, if allowed, to support Jesus and His disciples. I have had success in meeting several women who are willing to assist me in this endeavor. I was certain the wives or mothers of the disciples of Jesus would be the easiest to recruit.

Salome, the wife of Zebedee and the mother of James and John, was the first. She loves her sons and has the best sense of humor. She shared with me how incredible it was to see her temper-ridden sons change. I love to hear her tell about the scrapes they had with other men. She said that often at their dinner table, there would be her and her husband seated across from one or both sons with blackened eyes, bloodied noses, scrapes and bruises, still fuming from their latest brawl.

Now, she sees them with Jesus. They are calm. They are thoughtful. They think before they speak. They are patient. They no longer take offense at slight insults. Most importantly, they pray. James and John seem to know the Torah and the Writings better than our scribes. Salome attributes it to one person — what God has done in them through Jesus. She was worried about Zebedee running their business alone. Thankfully, the Lord provided others to fill the gap. Now her husband has what he needs. Her sons are in a good place. She has the freedom to travel some, not to mention she is the best cook I have ever met this side of Momma.

Another disciple's mother has joined to help. She is Mary, the mother of James (not the brother of John, but another disciple with the same name). Her husband is Alphaeus. She calls him by his pet name, Clopas.

Alphaeus is a leader in Bethsaida. He is an astute businessman with little time for anything else, including family (to hear her say it). He struggles with an overinflated ego. I think this is why she calls him by a pet name. It is her way of humbling him to a degree.

Mary calls her disciple son "James the Less" with good humor. Her son is smaller than John's brother. He is also quieter. Beyond that, he is opposite of his father Alphaeus. Where Alphaeus thirsts to lead, her son James seeks to follow. Clopas, as she calls her husband, seeks the stage. James, her son, seeks to serve in the shadows. He is James the Less by his choice. I see this as a great attribute. Since her name is Mary, I am content to be called Mary the Less. I suppose being Mary from Magdala is no different. Any woman from my hometown is considered less than other women. My history reinforces that perception.

Mary and Alphaeus have a second son, Joses. He is not a disciple. I seldom see him nearby. He does work as an independent businessman apart from his father. Mary has taken great interest in both of her sons. It seems to me she tries to fill the gap left by her husband. Or it could be she fills the gap of an absent husband with her sons. Either way, she loves them. She seeks to see her son James cared for. However, this is not her primary reason for helping. She has fallen in awe of the Rabbi Jesus. We have had meals together over the last few weeks of planning our ministry. She has never seen such meaning to life before. She has actually begun a relationship with God. This was never something that concerned her before. Though Jewish, her family lived outside the synagogue relationship. They followed more of a Hellenistic mindset to things. Business was key. Making money was the quest of life. Family was seen as a means of internal belonging. Mary expressed how empty this all was.

One day, James the Less was on a business venture for his father. He saw the crowd in Capernaum and wandered up to see what the commotion was about. He heard Jesus speak. He felt this warmth overflow his soul. For the first time, he heard a rabbi speak of God as Father. With the distant cold experience of an earthly father, Alphaeus, James assumed God to be the same — all business.

All of scripture seemed to reference "the God of your father". However, James' father had no god. He was his own god. Jesus spoke as if God was a loving, listening Father who cared more for His children than any other thing. James liked that idea. He had seen other fathers caring for their kids. He saw other fathers walking with their arms around their children. Such a relationship, he had never had. It was something he longed for, though. At Jesus' words, James the Less began to consider God in a different light.

James attended synagogue later that week. To his surprise, Jesus was speaking there, too. The synagogue ruler, Jairus, read a passage from Exodus. God said, "Therefore, say to the Israelites: 'I am the Lord, and I will bring you out from under the yoke of the Egyptians. I will free you from being slaves to them, and I will redeem you with an outstretched arm and with mighty acts of judgment. I will take you as my own people, and I will be your God.'" He tied that passage to one from the prophet Isaiah,: "Can a mother forget the baby at her breast and have no compassion on the child she has borne? Though she may forget, I will not forget you!"

James had never known a father with the love of a mother. He had never conceived of God as wanting him to be His. Just then, Jesus got up to speak. He brought all of this together. James the Less told his mother how tears filled his eyes. What he had been missing his whole life was right above him in the person of God.

Mary said her son changed in that moment. He lost interest in the business. He was respectful to his father, but he also was clear he had no more interest in following in his footsteps. At some point, Jesus called James the Less to follow Him, just like Matthew.

Later, James invited his mother, Mary, to hear Jesus. She traveled to Capernaum. Her son sat her with the crowd on that hillside a few days back. She heard the lessons I heard. She saw the multiplying of that little boy's lunch like I did. We visited about the thrilled look on that little boy's face to not just see his lunch given out, but to receive his lunch basket back, fuller after the meal than before. Mary said she was glad I reached out. She had been trying to figure out how to help

Jesus, since He had no food for the masses, much less for He and His disciples. Now we can fill that void.

I met Susanna in Capernaum. She has been very active in the synagogue. Her interest in Jesus began when He would speak in their local synagogue. She said it peaked when she saw how Jairus' daughter was made well. From that point on, she fell in love with Jesus. She truly believes He is a prophet from God. She is industrious.

Since Jesus began to stay in their city, Susanna discovered a talent within her. People needed places to stay. She saw some land and an old building a family was trying to sell. The price was affordable. She bought it and was able to get it restored. Now she leases rooms out by the week. It seldom sits vacant. Families rent rooms to be near Jesus when He is in town. When He is out, they willingly rent so they can have a place to stay until He returns.

That was her first business foray. Susanna bought a corner lot in Capernaum. She allows traders to rent spaces. She also sells some of the clothing she makes from wool and flax. Just in the past year, she has accumulated much wealth. Yet, Susanna lives humbly. She cares for her children. Her husband died several years ago. This void forced her to assume the role of provider for her family. Since being introduced to Jesus, at least from a distance, she has been consumed with the idea to help Him in some fashion. She heard of my project from some ladies in the area. Naturally, she reached out to me to help.

With these three ladies (and I pray for more), we can serve as a sort of Levite tribe for the Rabbi. We can be His assistants, though we are not qualified to be one of His disciples. I say "qualified". I knew Peter, Andrew, James, John, and Matthew before. They clearly were not qualified, either. I have come to the realization that it is Jesus who qualifies, not the disciples themselves. Regardless, I feel like David. I would rather be a doorkeeper in the Temple than to be a king (or queen) someplace else. I am content to be a sparrow living inside the porch cover of the Temple than to live in a palace on a throne. I feel when I am near Jesus, I am in the Temple. It is hard to explain. That is the experience I have, just being near Him. I yearn to follow Him. Poppa said we could follow Him from Magdala. I will do so if that is His will, but I am trying to be nearer to Him. If I can be of service to Him, perhaps I can follow, too. I rejoice that this is the shared yearning of Salome, Mary, and Susanna.

On the twelfth month, the fifth day — I attended synagogue today in Capernaum. I had hoped Jesus would be back. He was not. We had a great time of worship.

After synagogue, we met at Susanna's home. Mary and Salome joined us. Salome informed us that Jesus went alone to preach in other synagogues. Her sons James and John, Mary's son James the Less, along with the other disciples, were sent out from Him months ago to continue His work. Salome indicated she is anxious to hear what this means. We speculated — would their sons be speaking to crowds as Jesus does? Would crowds come to hear them instead of Jesus? Even if they are speaking under His authority, is there any guarantee people will come? Susanna interjected that crowds like Jesus' would only come if these disciples were able to work miracles.

Salome scoffed lightly. "My sons, James and John, work miracles? I cannot see that. I believe it is a miracle they have changed. People in Bethsaida would come to hear them. These neighbors of ours have seen the change. But people who do not know them? I just cannot see the interest. And the only miracle I have ever seen my boys do was to make the food on their plates disappear." We all laughed. Mary agreed. She said James the Less is a shy boy. He prefers to help. He is always the last to speak. When he does speak, it is almost in a whisper after looking around to make sure no one but his intended listener can hear. James the Less working miracles? She cannot see him do such a thing. Alphaeus, his father, is the one who thinks he can work miracles in business, not their son.

It is almost surreal to imagine ordinary men working miracles. Peter? Can Peter work a miracle? I know he can speak. I know he is assertive. He is the oldest of all of Jesus' disciples. He seems extremely comfortable in the role of leadership. But Peter working miracles? He was barely a good fisherman.

Then there is Matthew. I almost picture Matthew accounting for the expenditures, going over the money they have on hand. I see him as an administrator to the Rabbi. Nothing more. Matthew speaking to crowds? He never was one for loving the common sort. Matthew working miracles? I cannot fathom it. I wish Poppa were here to consider this with me. He would relish such a discussion.

We had a great meal. I returned to Matthew's home. I am glad I have this place to stay. He is hardly here, anyway. The questions linger in my mind. Jesus sending the disciples out. He has them, supposedly, in areas all over the Galilee and Judea. I can see them as lambs going out, unprepared. I am anxious for their return. I cannot wait to hear what all of this means. Moreso, I want to see Jesus again. I pray He will let us care for Him.

On the twelfth month, the ninth day — I returned to our home yesterday. I can hardly write what a spectacle I saw this afternoon! After checking with Linus on our vineyards, I walked up to our home. Right here on Harbor Street, in front of our house, were royal chariots pulled by four horses each. They bore the seal of King Herod Antipas. Servants were walking alongside. The wagons contained piles and piles of baggage. Soldiers on great horses readied for defense, startling the neighbors. Enamored children peeked out their windows at the display. Mothers were herding others on the streets into their homes. Men stood outside their homes wary, yet submissive. The question was, have we done something wrong? Has Rome become angry with our village?

We had seen Roman wagons weekly gathering our salted and pickled fish. We have always had soldiers in our community to guard tax collectors like Poppa and me. We had frequent visits of soldiers sent to carry the taxes we accumulated to Rome. We had soldiers stationed in every area to keep peace. Moreso, soldiers were ever present to remind the locals who is still in charge of this nation. Some days we would see them at every corner. Herod Antipas held his position upon the promise he would do Rome's bidding.

So why were they here today? I slowly and leerily walked around them. The eyes watching this parade seemed to all focus on me. But why? As I made my way to our courtyard, I saw her. She was dressed in a decorated tunic. A stole wrapped around her shoulders, cascading down. She had an ornamental medallion around her neck, accompanied by many gold necklaces. Her hair was exquisitely arranged. My heart began to race. My first thought since we left the tax booth was, were they coming to take our home? Had we made some mistake in our count. I did not think so. I did the math myself. Poppa always double-checked it. An accounting was always made to the centurion picking up the money. Never in all of our years did they note one error. But could Tiberius be needing money? Perhaps the emperor had been killed. It was not uncommon for the military to overthrow a ruler. I was nervous. I thought of walking by as if this was not my home. I felt that maybe I should get an idea of why they were there before I presented myself.

That idea faded when I saw Linus standing beside her. As I got closer, Linus pointed at me with a smile. I felt betrayed, even more afraid. Then the woman in royal apparel smiled at me too. She gently said, "Mary, I am Joanna, the wife of Chuza, Herod Antipas' steward and business manager. May I come in to visit?" Only one answer is appropriate when the wife of one in great authority makes a request. That reply is restricted to "yes".

I nervously opened the door. Joanna motioned for the soldiers to remain outside. That included Linus. Then I thought, was Rome angry I had distracted Linus from his duties in the service to Emperor Tiberius? Or was Herod Antipas sending her to recruit me to some tax booth that would benefit him? That would not be beyond Antipas.

She asked for a drink of water. I poured her some. She asked if she could sit. I nodded my head in approval. Standing, she motioned for me to sit at the table next to her. This was strange. It was as if I was being prepared for some type of horrible news. Daniel, enter the lion's den, have a seat. Do not mind the roar.

Joanna then asked me to tell her about Jesus. He was my favorite subject, but why would a woman of such power appear at my door in Magdala? I casually asked her what made her come to Magdala to ask me? She said that she had met Susanna in Capernaum, who had told her I was gathering women to help meet the needs of the Rabbi. This was meant to soothe me. It should have, but I felt even more on edge. I knew the Pharisees did not approve of Jesus. I knew our priests were not fond of Him, either. The priests work hand in hand with Rome and Herod. It made sense that perhaps she was here to find a way to put an end to His teaching.

With great anxiety, my voice wavered as I explained to her of how I had been in a very dark place. I feared going into too much detail. With general descriptions, I told how Poppa and I had gone to hear Him. Before I could go further, Joanna interrupted, saying, "I know you are nervous. All of the horses, wagons, chariots, servants, and soldiers have you shaken. I know you were a tax collector. Linus informed me of that. Let me call in my guard for a moment." With that, she stepped outside. She called. At once, at the door were ten Roman soldiers. She led them inside. This was not making me less nervous. What she said next reduced my fears.

She said to me, "In the presence of these Roman soldiers, I am admitting to you that I want to follow Jesus. I had the privilege to hear Him when He was in Jerusalem, teaching in the Temple courts. There was so much talk about Him. Other rabbis were there speaking. It seemed only their immediate families stayed to listen. Priests, Pharisees, and scribes all spoke at our last Passover. They had no audience. I heard of this Jesus from Nazareth. They said He was the One gathering all the crowds. I made my way to hear Him for myself. Along with the Temple guards, my guards accompanied me. The crowd split for our entrance. Jesus saw us. He made no special note. He neither gave us special acknowledgement nor asked people to get up so that I might sit. That was the first thing that impressed me. I did not want any special attention. I wanted to hear Him speak with no regard for status. Many of our spiritual leaders have two concerns — money and privilege. To get both, they bow to the right people. They also moderate what they say to appease. We have only had one other rabbi who seemed to speak with sincerity, who was no respecter of persons. His name was John. They called him 'the Baptizer.'"

With this, she dismissed her guards. No sooner did they shut the door, she said, "I am making myself vulnerable to you so that you will trust me, I pray. Herod Antipas, whom my husband works for, had John killed because John had the audacity to confront him in Antipas' affair with his brother's wife. All the palace staff were incensed that he and Herodias would flaunt such a sordid thing. Herod is part-Jewish. He knows the law. He seeks to appease Rome, yet he has no desire to appease God. He is Jewish by convenience, not by values. I had been lost without John's teaching. When I heard Jesus those days on the steps of the Temple, my heart warmed within me. Every day He spoke, I was there. He does not know me, to my knowledge. When He speaks, everything He says answers the questions deep down in my soul. When Passover was over, He left. I decided that when my husband traveled with Herod, I would look for Jesus. I have found Him a few times around the Galilee. My longing, when able, is to be near Him. I cannot get enough of His teaching. God has given me position for a reason. I choose to use my resources for His ministry. I say all that to ask, "'May I join you in your work for Him?'"

Here is a woman of wealth, power, and position. She is risking everything, I believe, to follow Jesus. It was not that long ago in our history that Antipas' father, Herod the Great, killed thousands of babies for fear one of them was the long-awaited Messiah. Can his son be any different? Is Jesus the Messiah? That is the question I dare not mention in this first visit with Antipas' steward's wife. I pray I can trust her.

I decided to take a step in faith. I asked Joanna to join us in Capernaum in two days. We expect Jesus to return any time. Salome says that her sons intimated that it would be around the middle of the month they would return. Joanna agreed with a smile.

I saw her to the door. All my neighbors were still watching through their windows. The men stood as statues in the front, outside their homes. Joanna was helped into her chariot. Off her military detail rode in the direction of Capernaum. I suppose Susanna has a place for them to stay. I motioned to our neighbors that everything was alright. An ease settled over the village as the sun set. I sat in my courtyard, feeling the Galilean breeze. I watched as her train vanished out of sight. Could it really be that a woman of Joanna's influence is joining us? I will pray to Adonai regarding this. I looked up into Poppa's room. He is not there of course, but I could not help myself "Poppa, can you believe what just happened?" I asked.

On the twelfth month, the tenth day — Linus and I had a great laugh about yesterday's events. I told him how mad I was when I first saw him point at me. He teased me a tad about my lack of faith. He said that I pray to God daily. Where was the faith? If God cast demons from my life, could He not keep a few soldiers away? Linus was right.

I prepared things for my trip to Capernaum. I am set to go. Atticus dropped by. He has been away with his work. He said he drops by nearly every evening, leaving disappointed that I am not home. I apologized. I caught him up on what has been happening. He agreed to accompany me in the morning. He has business in Capernaum for his foreman. We had a good meal in our courtyard. I dare not let him inside my home.

People will get the wrong idea. Besides, I cannot trust myself to another man until marriage. It is for the good of both of us. I do not wish to sully myself further.

I want to serve Jesus. He does not need anyone to bring question to the kind of man He is.

This evening after Atticus left, I am thinking on Herod the Great. Matthew and Maria both said Jesus was born in Bethlehem. That little village sits beneath the Herodium, the palace of Herod the Great. I remembered the story Poppa told me about Herod killing the babies in Bethlehem and Ramah. He shared with me how Jeremiah foretold this. I do not know how old Jesus is, but I do believe He is of the approximate age to have been born in that area at the time of Herod's massacre.

This draws me into the question again: If Herod were trying to kill the Messiah in the Bethlehem area, and Jesus was born in that area at the same time, could it be Jesus is the Messiah, the coming King, from the line of David? Is He the Promised One? He works miracles. He speaks like no one else. He is no respecter of persons. When He speaks, demons comply. I know that firsthand. He knew my name before I ever introduced myself. It is difficult to imagine that in my lifetime I would see such scripture fulfilled. Even more, a woman of my ilk. God is indeed merciful!

On the twelfth month, the eleventh day — What an exciting meeting we had today. Susanna, Mary, and Salome met me at Matthew's house. Then Joanna rode up. Her parade did not follow. It was just her immediate guard following behind her chariot with a driver, pulled by four fine horses. At first, everyone deferred to Joanna. She quickly corrected us. She told us she was just a housewife seeking to do something for Jesus. She declined any leadership role. She even asked us to give her orders. The stress left the room.

In our responsibilities, we each need to provide money for any lodging He may need. We also want to cover His and the disciples' food needs. We can buy supplies to cook. Or, we can have others prepare meals when that is more convenient. We also want to send money with Him so that, when we cannot, or we are not allowed to, be with Him, He will have what He needs. I suggested that Matthew be the one we trust with the money. Salome did not like that idea. Her sons were still a little distrusting of the tax collector in their ranks. They asked me not to take offense. I assured them I did not. We decided to let Jesus decide who will carry the money for Him. He might even choose to do so Himself. However, this seems out of His character to carry money, much less care about money. How different He is from Judas the Galilean.

When possible, we will travel with Jesus. We decided we would camp away from Him to avoid any gossip. Joanna asked if we thought He would be willing to use her chariot, horses, soldiers, and wagons for baggage. Susanna believed that would make Him look like He is coming to be a king. Nothing would jeopardize Him more. Mary said that from her visit with her son, James the Less, she has the perception that Jesus is put off by such shows of importance. Salome says James and John report He walks in old sandals. He walks. He does not ride. He stays most times outside. He sleeps in meadows. He prays on mountains. He catches any boat heading in the direction He wants to go. He is humble. He relates to everyone. He sees people just as people. He stays in homes only as an invited, not assumed, guest. He stays with Peter only because Peter requested it.

We five women made progress. We are not content with five. We need to grow our numbers so that no matter where Jesus goes, someone is present to look out for Him. Joanna took this as her personal duty. She knows righteous women all over our nation. She is familiar with friends of Jesus in Bethany near Jerusalem. She knows of people in Gamla. She has acquaintances even in the Decapolis. Some wives of some of Governor Pilate's officers in Caesarea may be willing to help there. The two places we probably do not need to worry about are Capernaum, because of Peter, and Nazareth, because of His own family there.

Now all we have to do is wait. We agreed to gather an amount of money each to be ready for when He returns. With that, we prayed together. Each of us returned to our daily lives.

In the eighteenth year of the reign of Tiberius Caesar, on the twelfth month, the twentieth day — Matthew is back, as are all of Jesus' disciples! He cannot be far behind, we pray. Matthew sent a messenger to call me to join them in Capernaum. Salome let them all know what we had planned to do. It sounds as if they are excited. Matthew also wrote that he has some exciting news that I will find hard to believe. Needless to say, I rushed off to Capernaum the moment I got his message.

Matthew was waiting outside his house with James, John, Peter, and Andrew. They had a glow on their faces I could not describe. Matthew gave me a brotherly hug. He welcomed me with excitement. He asked Peter to tell what they had been doing. Peter told me Jesus had sent them out by twos throughout the land. He related, "He commanded us that we should take no money, no bread. We were to wear only the sandals on our feet, carry a staff, and one coat. He said everything we need will be given to us." James piped in. "Mary, He gave us the power to cast out demons. We had no idea what that meant. We saw how He worked with you and so many others. We were always afraid when they would speak out. He never was. He never is. To think, when we left, that He gave us that power was beyond comprehension. It was as if we were excited to try out this power. We were also afraid to even try. What if we failed?"

John spoke. "Mary, we had been men without Jesus. We had lives long before Him. But I'll tell you, when He sent us out without Him, it was more than any of us could bear. Then to split us up into twos? It seemed the world would be against us. He said it would be. He told us not to fear. He said to preach about God and about Him. He said that He has come to be the Good News for which our people have waited."

That could only mean one thing, He is the Messiah. I was about to ask, but they continued. One by one, they told me their stories. One could hardly get the words out before another jumped in. Sometimes they spoke over each other. One would start. Another would interrupt. I was tickled at them. These did not seem like men. They seemed like boys telling of their first all-night fishing expedition with their fathers. A whole new world had opened to them, a whole new realm.

They said they never went hungry. When it grew cold, people gave them coats. Most people let them stay in their homes. If no one from a town did, they dusted their feet off and went to the next one. They preached God's Word. They explained the scriptures in synagogues, on shores, on street corners, and in family rooms. I told them we had visited about their speaking. We feared no one would come to hear them like people did for Jesus. Andrew, the quiet brother, spoke. He said, "Mary, when I spoke, there was a power in my words that I have never felt before. I try to duplicate it away from people. It will not come. Strangely, when a crowd is near, or I have this unction to speak, at that moment everything is mapped out before me. When one truth is spoken, another follows. People listen to me, to us, like we are the Rabbi. I have listened to Peter speak. It is his voice, but the power is that of Jesus. The experience is the exact same. I cannot explain it."

They met Jesus outside of Capernaum. They stated they each had the opportunity to tell their stories. They said Jesus smiled from ear to ear. I wish I could have been there. They said He was so delighted, not the least bit surprised. He drew more joy from their joy. Each pair had the same experience. Crowds were following them wherever they went. The numbers grew with each village.

Somberly, John spoke. He reported what was more amazing was that there was no need for miracles. He said, "The words that the Rabbi had shared, we were repeating." He went on. "Lives were being changed. But, just like the Rabbi, each of us at some point encountered screaming demons at the mention of Jesus' name. It was then we saw His power over them exercised. In His name, we commanded them to leave. At His name, they left. In His name, lepers were made whole, the deaf could hear, the blind could see, and the lame could walk. Mary, everything you have seen Him do, He enabled us to do. We all celebrated. He then reminded us what was most important — that our names were written in Heaven."

Written in Heaven. I want my name written in Heaven. I asked them how they were able to get their names there? Was it because they were His disciples? I want to get my name there. After the others left for their homes, I asked Matthew. Matthew said that as best he could tell, anyone who follows Jesus, who listens to Him, who does as He says, their names are automatically written in Heaven. If that is the case, that will be me. I will make sure it is. I cannot have it any other way. I pray the names of Momma and Poppa are there, too. I am sure they are. How could they not be? They followed God. They would be here with me had they lived to see this.

In the eighteenth year of the reign of Tiberius Caesar, on the twelfth month, the twenty- second day — Jesus arrived today to join His disciples here in Capernaum. The reunion was grand. News traveled fast. Soon, people from all over the area were coming in crowds of thousands. Susanna's properties were full.

Matthew again gave me an introduction to the Rabbi. I say he introduced me, but Jesus needed no introduction. Before Matthew could get out my name, Jesus welcomed me by name. He expressed His sympathy regarding my father. It is funny. Every time Poppa is mentioned, I get sad. When Jesus referenced his passing, I had no sadness at all. I felt a comfort all over, as if Poppa was doing great, as was Momma, just from the look of assurance in Jesus' eyes.

I let the Rabbi know what the women and I had planned to do to help Him and the disciples. His expression was overwhelming. It was not a look of gratitude from desperation. It was as if He was signaling an appreciation we had accepted an invitation to join Him in His work. Nothing was said. It was just His look and a feeling in my heart. I told Him that, when possible, we would like to follow Him. We want to meet His needs. We desire to cook for Him and His men. We would be happy to clean their clothes. We can help secure places for them to stay. We would also like to give money for any expenses or taxes that He must pay. It is only suitable that a former tax collector considers taxes owed. How amusing that must be to those who know my past vocation. I shared with Him that we would like to begin with a donation up front. I suggested Matthew could keep it for them. Jesus instead directed me to give any money to Judas Iscariot. He had been helping with that part of His work. Matthew agreed. He had managed the money. For some reason, it seemed Judas showed an aptitude for those kinds of things. He had the respect and trust of all the disciples.

With that, Matthew took me to meet their treasurer. Judas greeted me in a rather formal manner. He acted as a man imposed upon. I can understand that to a degree. These men are pulled in many directions. Surely, they have a sense that anyone who comes to them simply wants to use them to get to Jesus. As Matthew introduced me, Judas seemed to be looking past me. When my friend told him I had money to give for the Rabbi, only then did he look me in the eye. His whole attitude changed. He was cheerful. He asked questions about me, my family, my upbringing. I returned the questions.

I was delighted he showed such an interest in me. He let me know he was not from the Galilee, but from Southern Judea. He even boasted at being the only disciple not from Galilee. We Galileans are accustomed to that response. Most consider us Galileans a lower class of people. We are primarily a mixed race. I am a perfect example — a Jewish father, a Roman mother. His accent was different from ours as well. Judas sounded more like Joanna in speech. He is proud of his heritage. That can grate on a person, but in a way, it is good to be thankful for your origins.

We passed by all the get-acquainted formalities. He then looked me in the eye and said, "Now you have money to give for our work?" I felt that was a little assumptive. When did it become "their work" as opposed to Jesus' work? After all, Jesus started all of this. They were His disciples, not partner rabbis. Perhaps I am being a little too judgmental. I pulled out my purse. Judas' eyes opened with a glimmer. He smiled as if he were licking his chops for a fine delicacy of food like Matthew served at his house. Judas then returned to his normal expression — all business. I emptied my purse to him. I informed him that, as they have need, to please let me know. The ladies and I will be happy to provide for any of their needs as God provides for us.

He did not write down what I gave. He did not even put it into some sort of money box for safety. He placed the money in his own purse. I looked at him. I am sure my expression was clear. He said, "Don't worry. I will place it with the other monies. I don't want to be seen carrying it around in the open." That made sense, I suppose. Not everyone has the experience of a tax collector. I am not sure what Judas did before becoming a disciple. Nor am I certain what qualifies him to be the Rabbi's treasurer. Then again, he may be like Joanna, a man of wealth accustomed to his own way of managing money. Regardless, I was giving it to Jesus. I will watch with the tax collector's eye to ensure, at least when I am around, that the Rabbi has provision. That is what matters. Besides, if He trusts this man from southern Judea, how can I question him?

On the twelfth month, the twenty-third day — Jesus withdrew from us to pray last night. I stayed at Matthew's. The disciples stayed in Capernaum, some with Peter, others in rooms of Matthew's home. Judas rented a room elsewhere.

This morning, Jesus had the disciples meet Him at Peter's house. I was invited, as was Susanna, Salome, Mary (the mother of James), and Joanna. Joanna had already left for Jerusalem with her personal guard. Passover is near. She went to prepare for Jesus' arrival. Joanna is excited. Jerusalem is where she met Jesus. If the normal crowds come, along with all these going where Jesus is, it will be one of the biggest feasts they have had there in years. She is hoping to get the priests to give Jesus more time to speak. Her great ambition is to see her husband, Chuza, and the officials of Herod Antipas hear Him. She is unsure of Herod. He had John killed.

He has the paranoia of his father. That is the other reason Joanna left. She is hoping to provide some sort of protection for Jesus. I have a feeling Jesus is safe no matter where He goes. He has authority that makes every power buckle.

We received good news. Jesus is allowing us to travel with Him! We will be going to Jerusalem together. He plans to stop in Nazareth, His hometown, to see His family. We will stay there for the Sabbath. We will then go up from there to Jerusalem. I am excited like Joanna. One, I get to go with Jesus. I can hear Him speak. I can see His miracles. I can have an attachment for which I have longed. Two, I can meet His mother. I have many questions to ask her. I pray I will be able to ask them. I pray also that she will see her son for how we see Him.

On the twelfth month, the twenty-fourth day — Last night, we stayed a short distance from Nazareth. The women and I stayed on one side of the hill. Jesus and His disciples camped on the other side. Before we parted for the night, we made a meal for them at the fireside. The men seemed to enjoy having real cooking for their journey. We had packed all the ingredients that we would need. I brought along our famous salted fish from Magdala. The Galilean men make it their staple. The Judean, Judas, seemed incredibly pleased with it. He says he is getting to like our cuisine more and more. The homemade bread was delightful. We also brought some honey, making a sweet treat for them all. It was a blessing.

I enjoyed watching Salome care for her two sons, James and John. I do not think any mother dotes on their children more than she. What's more, these are not boys. They are rugged, grown men. They are fishermen, comfortable with the discomforts of being in the elements. Yet, they soften at her care. They are bold. When Salome is around, they are submissive. She reminds me of the rudder on a boat. She is small, yet directs her two sons with just a look. When the food was served, she was quick to get her boys their food first. Salome seems to pay no mind to the other disciples. She lets them care for themselves. Thankfully, no one appears offended. They see it, as I — just a mother caring for her children.

How different is Mary to Salome. Not only does Mary serve the other ten disciples, but she also has her son James the Less serve them with her. James eats last of the men. His mother eats last of all of us. Susanna has taken the lead among us. As industrious as she is, she designs the menu, and orders each of us to bring a portion of what is needed. She always has in her bag any ancillary items needed. If you need a needle, she has it. If you need an extra jar, she finds one in her pack. I stay near her. The two of us have no children among the disciples. I have no children at all.

I watch Jesus like Salome watches her sons. I had the pleasure to bring Jesus His food. He was very appreciative. He is the head of this group of men. He is the reason we are all here. Yet, He is humble. He is modest. He lets others walk in front of Him. He asks those in our group questions about our lives. He has a sincere interest in us. The ladies and I have not walked with Him twenty-four hours yet. Still, we have seen Him spend time with each of us. My favorite is when He walks alongside me. He talks about Poppa. He visits about my life. He never brings up the demons. He never intimates any knowledge of my past sins. He also never pretends we are perfect.

The hill in which we were staying is part of the Lebanon Mountain Range. It is in this area Zebulun's people settled. Down below, we could see the Plain of Esdraelon where the caravans of travelers were camping. With that said, I tried to imagine myself with the children of Israel following Moses. I am a child of Israel — at least, half a child. Jesus is easily comparable to Moses, to me, and these people here, anyway. Tonight, Jesus just so happened to speak about Moses. He talked with the disciples about the bread we had just eaten. He was very complimentary. I assume it reminded Him of His hometown, which is not extremely far from here.

Jesus took a piece of the bread we served. He reminded us of the manna that fell from Heaven during those forty years. He said, "I tell you the truth, it is not Moses who has given you the bread from Heaven, but it is my Father who gives you the true bread from Heaven. For the bread of God is He who comes down from Heaven and gives life to the world." Jesus paused. A disciple or two asked Him some questions. I was helping the ladies clean up after our meal. I did not hear their questions. I stopped to listen when He spoke. I resumed cleaning when the disciples visited.

Then I heard His voice again. He declared, "I am the Bread of Life. He who comes to Me will never go hungry, and he who believes in Me will never be thirsty.

But as I told you, you have seen Me and still you do not believe. All that the Father gives Me will come to Me, and whoever comes to Me I will never drive away. For I have come down from Heaven not to do My will, but to do the will of Him who sent Me. And this is the will of Him who sent Me, that I shall lose none of all that He has given Me, but raise them up at the last day. For my Father's will is that everyone who looks to the Son and believes in Him shall have eternal life, and I will raise him up at the last day."

The fire crackled before Him. Its light shone upon His face. In the shadows were the disciples. I looked over at Susanna. She did not break her fix on Jesus. With that, Jesus smiled. It was as if He was encouraging us to go to our places of rest. He was giving us time to consider what He had just said. So here I am on my mat, next to the fire Nathanael built for us. If this first night is any indication, Nathanael is to be our caretaker on this journey. He sets up our camp. He builds our fire. He is upright. Not a hint of insincerity is in his being. Though I have never heard him speak much, he appears to be the strongest of the twelve. He also appears to be the most unbending from what is right. He calls out before he crowns the hill to our camp. He makes sure all are decent. He does not hang around. He retrieves things we need. He then leaves.

I am writing notes. I wish Judas would keep notes on offerings. I do not know why that encounter is still bothering me. I must let that go. Jesus said that He is the Bread of Life. I have never heard anyone describe themselves in that fashion. He even said He will make sure those who are with Him never go hungry or thirsty. When I was with Him south of Capernaum on the hill above the Galilee, He spoke for hours. None of us wanted food or drink. We were content to be with Him alone. No physical needs were important. Is this what He means? If that is the case, I find it true. Or does He mean that if we are with Him, we will not go hungry? He fed over five thousand men and many more women and children out of a small basket of food from a little boy. Maybe He means when we are with Him, He will be sure we eat. If that is His meaning, I can say, "Amen." I have seen that also to be true.

Jesus said any who come to Him, He will never drive away. I have found that a fact as well. I came to Him possessed by seven demons. I also came sullied. He did not drive me away, but healed me. Even now, I hear people call me Mary Magdalene in Capernaum. I know people use such descriptions to delineate people with the same name. There is James, and then there is James the Less. There is Mary, the mother of James the Less. There is Mary, the mother of Jesus. And there is Mary Magdalene, a woman from Magdala.

I regret to write that many may use this latter description to sully who I am, to remind people of who I used to be. It can also be regarded as a slur, because women from Magdala are considered immoral. I would rather be called Mary, the daughter of Jared. I say that, but then some would say, "Yes, the daughter of a treacherous tax collector. Let's not forget that!" I have a fear my past could bring question to Jesus' character. But then again, He allowed me to come. He is wise beyond all men. He knows hearts, or so it appears. He also can know assumptions people will make, yet He asked me to come anyway. So, yes, He does not drive away those who come to Him.

The three most shocking things Jesus said are: He has come down from Heaven. He will give eternal life. He will raise up the last day. I am flummoxed by what I have heard. I am forced to think. Even confused, how awesome to be here! Is this what the disciples have had the joy to hear all these weeks? I was right to want to be here. I was right to pray to follow Jesus. God has heard my prayer. Of all the people in the world, I am one of the few in this camp. Me, Mary from Magdala, share a meal with Jesus. He speaks with me. I can now say I know Him — at least in a small way.

Back to the three shocking things. Jesus came down from Heaven? How can that be? Is this figurative? He was born in Bethlehem, from what I have been told. Manna came down from Heaven. Jesus? It would explain the miracles. It would explain calming a storm. It would make Jairus' daughter's healing make sense. It would give reasoning to the demons fleeing at His name. Many believe He is the Messiah, but Messiah was to be from Bethlehem, from the line of David, not from Heaven, not in the line of Adam, whom God came down to make. I will have to watch for that one. Maybe a disciple will ask a question regarding this. Perhaps they did while I was cleaning. I am going to have to listen to Jesus and the questions. I hope they ask a question that I have. If not, I will try to pose one through my confidant, Matthew.

He will give eternal life. Job wrote that though he die, God will raise him up in his own flesh, that with his own eyes, he will see God. Eternal life, life without end. Jesus says He gives eternal life. If Jairus' daughter indeed was dead, and not asleep, this gives some credence to that statement. That would also help explain that Jesus will raise up people on the last day. I suppose the last day of their breath, He will restore it. So, will Jairus' daughter never die? Or never die again? I will have to keep an eye on that. She is much younger than I am. The chances of me seeing her in her old age are not particularly good.

I am riddled with questions. I will ask Matthew about these if I can get him to the side. I am not sleepy. I am ready for another session of lessons from Jesus. The ladies around me are asleep. Our fire has now become a glowing pile of orange embers. I decided to get up for one last look. I walked to the crest of the hill. I was hoping Jesus might be sitting with His disciples still.

As I looked down, I could see their fire still burning. All thirteen of them were laying on their individual mats. I could see Matthew laying on his expensive mat with warm covers. I could see Judas there with the most unique mat. I am sure it is awfully expensive. It definitely was not made anywhere around the Galilee. Off to the side, I could make out Jesus. He was with them, but a little offset. I can only make out some rough garment spread out on the ground. He sleeps.

I am not sure, but I never envisioned Him needing to sleep. I know Matthew said He slept in the boat during the storm. That was what Matthew said. I was not there to see it. Now, I see Jesus sleeps. He must be tired. I would be. I sat on that hill looking down. The stars were overhead in bright, brilliant display. They are always brighter away from the city. It is very breezy on this hill. The whistling sound makes me think nature is speaking in a language I have not learned. The fire flutters. At some moments, it illuminates His closed eyes and mouth. He rests peacefully. Other times, it brightens upon the disciples. They must feel very safe. They appear amazingly comfortable in His presence.

If I were sleeping near Him, like I did when Poppa was ill, I would just watch Him. Does He dream? Are there any nightmares? Does the vision of Pharisee attacks haunt Him at all? I wonder, does He grieve over His family's belief He is out of His mind? Clearly, He is not. What comes from that mouth is different from anything we have ever heard. That does not make it untrue. When I think of what He says, it is hard to understand. Then again, I encounter a lot of things I do not understand. That does not make the issue insane. It usually is a reflection of my lack of knowledge, not the loss of senses from the originator. I could sit here all night. If I do, then I will be worthless tomorrow. Who knows what wonderful things tomorrow holds. I do not want to miss a moment. I must be clear-headed.

On the twelfth month, the twenty-fifth day — We entered Nazareth this morning. Jesus' mother, Mary, met us in front of the synagogue. His brothers soon followed. His mother is sweet. He introduced the women of our group to His mother. Mary showed great appreciation that we were there to take care of her son. She also looked at us closely. I think she was trying to gauge our competence.

His brothers arrived. They greeted Jesus with a hug. They traded topics like brothers do. They ribbed each other in love. They also caught up on what was going on in each of their respective families. Jesus introduced us as His family. With that, we headed into this small little synagogue of Nazareth.

As we walked in, many of the older people greeted Jesus as a favorite son. They shared with the disciples some of the stories of His childhood. Most reflected upon His activity in the synagogue there. They said He never missed a day. They also talked about how often He was asked to share His thoughts on particular passages from behind the bimah. It was then the synagogue ruler walked up. The people parted so he could welcome Jesus personally. He talked about how thrilled he was to see Jesus had become a rabbi in His own right.

I suppose that is exactly the case. Here we are, His students, His followers, learning of God through Him. The synagogue chief also spoke about the news that has been spreading all over about the crowds that follow Jesus. He said he has heard even rumors of miracles Jesus performed. I was behind the disciples. I felt a few of them look back at me. That's right, I am one of those miracles. I became extremely nervous for fear the ruler would ask me to share my story. Thankfully, he did not. Not that I would not. It is just not my comfort to speak before crowds. Especially when Jesus is my focus. I did not travel this way to hear me. I traveled to hear Him.

The synagogue ruler told Jesus he would be delighted if Jesus would share with the crowd now entering the synagogue. He acknowledged there would be a large attendance today, because news spread the minute Jesus was seen meeting His mother outside the synagogue. People coming to worship ran back to get family and friends. The noise level of people approaching and talking was deafening.

The ruler ushered us inside quickly. He let us sit near the front. This was the normal scene in Capernaum. It is one with which we had become familiar. But to be in this old childhood worship place of Jesus, to see His family and neighbors gather, to hear the stories of His childhood, to see Jesus so comfortable, to even gaze upon His brothers, was surreal. I thanked God on the spot for letting me be here. I actually began to weep. Salome handed me a cloth to wipe my eyes. She put her arm around me. I understand why John and James respond to her the way they do.

The synagogue service began. The ruler welcomed everyone. He said that as he looked down at Jesus. He then went to the Torah closet, bringing out the scrolls. We all stood in reverence. He told the crowd how blessed they were to have a special guest. He said, "Most of you know our native son, Jesus, the son of Mary and Joseph. We are delighted to have you with us today, Jesus. We are also thrilled to see you follow God as a rabbi. Your disciples are welcome among us, too. We also want to thank the women from the Galilee for coming with you. We would all be pleased if you would come pick the passage from Isaiah of your choice. Share what is on your heart."

With that, Jesus stepped forward. Again, I began to weep. I am here in Nazareth with Jesus. I am with the disciples. How I wish Momma and Poppa were here. For some reason, I feel they do see. Jesus affirms eternal life.

Jesus unrolled the scroll of Isaiah. He searched through it. I could see His face light up at one point. He began to read, "The Spirit of the Lord is on me, because he has anointed me to preach good news to the poor. He has sent me to proclaim freedom for the prisoners and recovery of sight for the blind, to release the oppressed, to proclaim the year of the Lord's favor."

Jesus then rolled the scroll back up. He gave it to the synagogue ruler's attendant. He then sat on the chair identified as Moses' Seat. Every eye was glued. Not one baby whimpered. Not one person stirred in their seat. It was silent. All eyes were fastened on Him. I did not look around, but I could sense by the heads around me, not one turn. All looking straight ahead. I could almost feel the stares going through me from behind.

Jesus began to speak. He said to us, "Today this Scripture is fulfilled in your hearing." I heard one old man behind me ask his wife, "Isn't this Joseph's son?"

Jesus then spoke again. His words were alarming. I felt this would be a cozy affirmation of who He is. I thought of how Caesar's hometown would welcome him after his crowning. This was not what happened today.

Jesus said, "Surely you will quote this proverb to me: 'Physician, heal yourself! Do here in your hometown what we have heard that you did in Capernaum.' I tell you the truth, no prophet is accepted in his hometown. I assure you that there were many widows in Israel in Elijah's time, when the sky was shut for three and a half years and there was a severe famine throughout the land. Yet Elijah was not sent to any of them, but to a widow in Zarephath in the region of Sidon. And there were many in Israel with leprosy in the time of Elisha the prophet, yet not one of them was cleansed — only Naaman the Syrian."

This was not what I expected at all. The rumblings began. He was no longer allowed to speak. The synagogue ruler got up to approach the bimah in a move to get Him to leave it. Jesus did so very respectfully. There was yelling, even cursing. They stormed past us toward Jesus. He did not resist. They shoved Jesus out of the synagogue, yelling at Him as He walked out. We followed behind. I moved closer to Matthew. Salome moved toward James and John. Mary moved toward her son, James the Less. I looked back. Jesus' mother and brothers stood still. They stayed in the synagogue for a moment, then moved out quietly away from the crowd toward where they had walked from when we first met them.

I had wanted to follow Jesus. I feared this was the beginning and the end of our journey with Him. They pressed Him to the cliff on which the town sat. We had climbed that very cliff to get to Nazareth. It is steep. They pushed Him to the point where it was a straight drop from a great height. Any fall from there was certain death. The men were yelling, "Push Him off! He is no son of ours! He is out of His mind! He is of the devil! How dare He say such things to God-fearing people like us!" Others with sarcasm, screamed out, "Where did this man get these things? What's this wisdom that has been given him, that he even does miracles! Isn't this the carpenter? Isn't this Mary's son and the brother of James, Joseph, Judas, and Simon? Are not his sisters here with us?"

Not one disciple came to His aid. It was as if they were saying, "This is your town. These are your people." I sound harsh. I was behind the crowd with the disciples. I do not know if any could have squeezed between them to get to Jesus even if they wanted. The women screamed, "Kill Him!" As they moved forward, I thought they might have already pushed him off the cliff. Total silence fell over the crowd. Was the deed done?

They then spread out. I thought it was to allow others to see His broken body down below. Instead, as they spread, I saw Him — Jesus, with a stern look that I had never seen before. He walked toward us. He motioned for us to follow Him. We did. A hush ensued. There were glares of anger, also of a supernatural fear. Jesus did not say a word to any of us for a good distance. We did not speak to each other. Everyone was left to their own thoughts.

Mine? A prophet is not accepted in his own hometown. So, Jesus was admitting that He is a prophet. I remembered what our forefathers did to other prophets. I also remember what was recently done to John the Baptizer. Most of our people believed he was a prophet, too. Is this the outcome One so great must face? Am I following a martyr? And if He is killed, will I be part of the bloodbath? I can say that from all I have heard and seen, I love Him that much. I will take it with Him.

But they all came to welcome Jesus in Nazareth. The crowds all came to hear Him speak. I did detect some dismissive tones when the synagogue ruler referenced His miracles. When I write that, perhaps that is why the crowds came on this particular Sabbath. They wanted to see a miracle. Is it not what people go to see in Capernaum? I admit, I do go to see miracles. I went at first to receive one. How can our nature not want that? A prophet who works miracles. I think of Elijah. I think of Moses. I think of Elisha.

We were a few miles south of Nazareth. We were on our journey to Jerusalem for Passover. Many of these who attempted to kill Him will be in Jerusalem too. Will there be another confrontation there? I hope not. I will let Joanna know. She has already gone before us to make arrangements in Jerusalem. She even spoke of security. If Herod Antipas is leery of Him, if the religious leaders distrust Him, and if these from His hometown follow Him, certainly trouble lies ahead. What can I do to help? I will pray to God for His protection. I will do all I can to make His journey a blessed one.

Jesus interrupted our thoughts. He simply said, "Only in his hometown, among his relatives and in his own house, is a prophet without honor." That does make sense. I am not honored in Magdala. I will say, it is for good reason. But Jesus, the model son? He is honored in every village. Crowds by the thousands take off to follow Him. People rent rooms in Capernaum to wait for His arrival.

He has healed thousands. The blind see because of Him. The deaf do hear. The lame do walk. The imprisoned are set free. That includes me. We are seeing God's favor with Him. How can everyone see it but His hometown — and the religious leadership, of course. I believe the leaders' animosity boils down to jealousy.

Needless to say, He performed no miracles in Nazareth. Jesus informed us it was because of their lack of faith. They lacked the belief God could do such things, or that God could do such things through a person. If that is the case, they should throw the scrolls out of the synagogue. God has always done miracles. He does not change. He even uses people to do those miracles. I believe.

On the twelfth month, the twenty-sixth day — It is evening. We have walked all day toward Jerusalem. It has been a great day of listening. Before we left this morning, Jesus reiterated what He had shared with the disciples a while back. He knew we were incredibly bothered by the activities of yesterday. We did not mention them to Him last night. We feared it was too soon to cover a hurtful event. I do believe rejection by your hometown leaves a deeper wound.

Jesus said, "Blessed are those who are persecuted because of righteousness, for theirs is the Kingdom of Heaven. Blessed are you when people insult you, persecute you, and falsely say all kinds of evil against you because of Me. Rejoice and be glad, because great is your reward in Heaven, for in the same way they persecuted the prophets who were before you."

Truly, He hit the nail on the head. He is being persecuted. He has done nothing wrong. He does not tell people what they want to hear. He tells all of us what we need to hear. He is no respecter of persons. He speaks with power. His miracles support His words. He is insulted. I remember the religious leaders attacking Him outside of Matthew's house. They say false things about Him. This is why this lady from Magdala keeps her distance. He does not need another avenue for accusations.

He smiled when He said, "Rejoice and be glad, for great is your reward in Heaven." There it is again. This talk of eternal life, of Heaven. I suppose if life does not end, if reward awaits us, whatever we face here is bearable. Truly, He is being treated no differently than the prophets before Him. You would think we would learn our lesson. The very prophets our forefathers killed are the ones revered today. John the Baptizer made it clear we are still capable of the same. After all these years of observing all the religious feasts, we have not changed one iota in our hearts.

Jesus then gave us encouragement. I think what He said is the reason we are continuing this journey to Jerusalem. He said, "You are the light of the world. A city on a hill cannot be hidden. Neither do people light a lamp and put it under a bowl. Instead they put it on its stand, and it gives light to everyone in the house. In the same way, let your light shine before men that they may see your good deeds and praise your Father in Heaven." I get the feeling He is using this moment to teach the disciples. The ladies and I are here to assist. They are the followers of the Rabbi.

I will not let His words rest solely on twelve men. I can be a light, too. I can share God with others. I can share the life of this Rabbi with others, too. Whatever I do can bring praise to God. He calls God our "Father". I love that. Our Father who is in Heaven. My earthly father is there under His care. Jesus says if we do what is right, people will insult and persecute us, and people will falsely say all kinds of evil things about us. That is something to which I, Mary Magdalene, am awfully familiar. Insults have been my daily bread as a tax collector's daughter.

The Nineteenth Year of Tiberius Caesar

In the nineteenth year of the reign of Tiberius Caesar, on the first month, the first day — We had a great meal tonight. Salome led in its preparation. We had bread, oil, and a delicious stew. She said it was James and John's favorite dish. I could see why. We shared some stories of our youth. I told about how Poppa and Momma climbed Mount Arbel with me. Momma then let me play with a few friends. We sat for a picnic overlooking the Galilee. It was their favorite place of leisure — of course, after an arduous climb.

James and John shared stories about their father, Zebedee. I chimed in about how much I respected their father. I loved the way they told some funny stories about Peter. He even seemed to appreciate the stories. Naturally, he denied them. He then looked at Jesus. What followed was a good-natured confession that all they said was true. We asked Jesus to tell us about His childhood. He shared about working with His father Joseph in the carpentry shop. He never really spoke much about His father. We figured He would tell us more if He wanted. Otherwise, we would let the matter drop.

He did open up about an event that happened to Him when He was twelve years old. He and His parents were traveling to Jerusalem for Passover, like we are now. He said they went every year without fail. He spoke of His love for the Temple, for the Passover, and for learning the scriptures. He said a huge Nazareth crowd of family and friends was always making the journey to Jerusalem with them.

We expect the same crowd this week. Again, this is what concerns me. We did not leave Nazareth on good terms. Anyway, Jesus said as a boy He traveled with His parents a few days, then joined other friends of His age for part of the trip. We were taking the very same journey that He took as a boy. He pointed out different sights that always caught His attention. It was awesome to gaze upon the same landmarks He enjoyed as a boy. He said that toward the end of the Passover, He caught some priests teaching. His friends got up to leave. He did not.

Jesus' parents and their friends set out for their return to Nazareth. Mary and Joseph did not see Jesus near them, but they assumed He was walking with some of His childhood friends from the neighborhood of Nazareth. They knew He was in safe hands. The parents of Nazareth looked after all the children from their village. As long as an adult was nearby, no one worried. At the end of each day, all the children returned to their parents for a meal and then a night's sleep. All the children were with their parents at dark — all but Jesus. Mary and Joseph began to search among their relatives and friends for their son. He was nowhere to be found. They then searched with other travelers ahead and behind. No sign of Jesus.

We were on the edge of our mats as Jesus told this. He said they finally turned back to Jerusalem to look for Him. For three days, they searched for Him. I cannot imagine how frantic His parents had to have felt. We know of the dangers in the Judean Hills. We know of the violence that sometimes occurs within the city walls. I was panicked as I listened. I do not even have children, but I know what it is to worry about someone. For three days, they did not know if their son was dead or alive. I am sure their imaginations got the best of them. I can see them praying. I can see them kneeling in the Temple courts, beseeching God for their son.

After three days, they found Him in the Temple courts, sitting among the teachers, listening to them and asking questions. Mary no doubt ran in and interrupted the teaching session. I have never met Joseph, but I would imagine he was apologetic to the scribes. Jesus said the teachers seemed undisturbed. They told His parents they had never seen a young man with such insight. Not only did He ask questions, but He also answered them. His viewpoint was of a learned scholar, decades older than his current age. Joseph must have been gratified — first, that his son was safe, and second, that others saw in his son what he had seen early on in his life.

Jesus said His mom was fit to be tied. He quoted her, cheerfully mimicking her voice. "Son, why have you treated us like this? Your father and I have been anxiously searching for you." We all laughed. We all wondered what this twelve-year-old Jesus answered. Before we could ask, He said with a sincere voice, "I answered her, 'Why were you searching for me? Didn't you know I had to be in my Father's house?'"

With that, He encouraged us to turn in for the night. I helped Salome gather our utensils. Nathanael led us to our resting place. He made sure our fire was lit.

He checked to make certain all was safe around us. We slept on one side of a shallow ravine, the disciples on the other.

I laid down with the rest of the ladies. My mind was racing again. I sat up. I looked across the ravine. I could see the disciples laying on their usual mats. Nathanael was the last to lay down. I could not see Jesus. He was on the other side of the fire. He sleeps. Jesus said He had to be in His Father's house. He said He has come from Heaven. He calls God, His Father. Some say He is the Messiah. He works miracles. He speaks like no one I have ever heard. The demons tremble at His voice. We are going to the Temple, to the house of the Living God. He calls it the house of His Father. I am fortunate to be here at this place and time. I thank God for this. I am trying to call Him "Father" in my prayers. It is not natural for me.

On the first month, the fourth day — Today was the Sabbath. Jesus led us in prayer. He then began to give us some understanding of the Sabbath. The disciples asked how the priests enforce the rules ruthlessly, but then break them with clever planning. Thomas is the most inquisitive of the disciples. Philip is a close second. They want to understand what is permissible according to God. They all acknowledged it is God who is the authority, not some religious leaders.

Jesus stressed to each of us that our leaders are right to see the Sabbath day as holy, but they go beyond what God intended. He reminded us of the time David had taken consecrated bread to feed himself and some men. It was ironic that no one judged him for that. The priests apply a different law to everyone else today. I do believe these religious leaders would have judged David severely. They say they regard the prophets of old, while they attack the prophets in our day.

Jesus talked about the practical nature of the Sabbath. "If any of you has a sheep and it falls into a pit on the Sabbath, will you not take hold of it and lift it out? How much more valuable is a man than a sheep!

Therefore, it is lawful to do good on the Sabbath." He closed His discussion with the fact that the Sabbath was made for man, not man for the Sabbath. With that, He left us to go and pray by Himself. We took from His example that we should do the same.

Each of us went to an area away from everyone else. Alone, we each prayed. I could see some just looking around. I saw others with their heads bowed with their hands open toward Heaven. I noticed Judas walking around. He did not seem too interested in praying. This may be my bias. I saw James and John not seated far apart. They were both praying. John has a sweet spirit about him. Rugged Peter was on his knees. I could even hear his voice in prayer, though I could not make out what he was saying. Nathanael was sitting under a tree. He seemed completely engulfed in prayer.

The ladies and I were a little distance away in our own area. Mary held my hand until we got to a place to divide. She knelt in the most earnest of ways to pray. Susanna took her mat. She sat on it and prayed. Salome went back closer to her sons. She did not get near them, but I could tell she wanted them within her line of sight. I sat near the ravine. Jesus did not instruct us how long to pray. Our Rabbi simply told us the Sabbath is a time for prayer. So, we followed His example.

After a while, Jesus returned to the camp. I heard talking. I looked up to see that the disciples had joined Him. I got up, as did the ladies. As I approached Him, I saw that His face held a peaceful glow. I gathered that this was His most favorite thing to do. He loved to pray to His Father. He loved to be in the Temple. He loved to study and share God's Word.

Finally, the disciples made a simple request: "Jesus, teach us to pray, please." His response was eye-opening, "When you pray, do not be like the hypocrites, for they love to pray standing in the synagogues and on the street corners to be seen by men. I tell you the truth, they have received their reward in full. But when you pray, go into your room, close the door, and pray to your Father, who is unseen. Then your Father, who sees what is done in secret, will reward you. And when you pray, do not keep on babbling like pagans, for they think they will be heard because of their many words. Do not be like them, for your Father knows what you need before you ask Him. This, then, is how you should pray: 'Our Father in Heaven, hallowed be Your name, Your Kingdom come, Your will be done on earth as it is in Heaven. Give us today our daily bread.

Forgive us our debts, as we also have forgiven our debtors. And lead us not into temptation, but deliver us from the evil one. For Yours is the Kingdom and the power and the glory forever.'"

What a great lesson. Prayer is such a private matter. It is something that honors God. It is not an act we do to honor ourselves. I love the simplicity in coming before God. We can acknowledge our needs. We can ask and find forgiveness, and there is a reciprocation that we must make toward others. All things come from God.

Have I written lately how glad I am our Father (there, I am getting better) has let me be here? I am learning so much. Even more exciting, I am here with the disciples and these ladies. I cannot wait to share with Joanna all that we have seen and heard. She will regret leaving for Jerusalem early. Then again, maybe our Father has her doing different things to help Jesus.

On the first month, the seventh day — I had packed my bound parchments with the supplies. I thought I had lost them at camp a few days back. Thankfully, I found them. We are near Jerusalem. I do not see the city, but the crowds let us know we are near. The closer we get to the Temple, the more fearful I am. We have been blessed not to see any of the people from Nazareth in the crowds that are walking with us. What awaits us? I remember the attacks from the Pharisees in Capernaum. I was horrified at the attempt to kill Jesus in His own hometown. If both of these groups are together in Jerusalem, can anything good come of it? I am more relieved than ever now that Joanna has gone before us. She has the weight of Herod behind her — or at least behind her husband, Chuza. She has the guards. I know she will do whatever it takes to protect the Rabbi.

No sooner had I been fretting on such things, the Rabbi took us up away from the crowds for the night. I am surprised they did not come with us. They all flock around Jesus. His reputation has spread far and wide.

People hammer Him with questions. They make all kinds of requests. People have invited Him to every town, every synagogue, and welcomed Him to stay in many of their homes. In all this, He does not grow arrogant. He is also not dismissive. He never appears inconvenienced. He entertains every person — man, woman, or child. He is just so beautiful in His attention to others. His character brings forth the passage from Isaiah: how beautiful are the feet of those who bring Good News. He certainly does that!

Back to this evening. Before bed, Simon the Zealot gathered the wood for the fires. He got a fire going for the Rabbi. He then got one going for us. What a difference in this man! He once spat in Poppa's face. He protested us. He hassled us. Now, I see him sitting with Matthew as if they are brothers. I feel uncomfortable calling him "the Zealot". That was what he was. I do not like my past remembered in the identification of Mary Magdalene. Then again, those names are markers. Like Poppa marked my height on the inside of my door. Those markings showed where I was in stature at different times. One year, growth would be substantial, minimal the next. My name Magdalene, my origin noted, does remind me of who I once was before Jesus. I will take that as a good thing.

Jesus gathered us together. He clearly seemed regretful to have spent little time with us of late. We should be in Jerusalem late tomorrow evening. We will be staying at some friends of His in Bethany. To our apprehensions, He said, "And why do you worry about clothes? See how the lilies of the field grow. They do not labor or spin. Yet I tell you that not even Solomon in all his splendor was dressed like one of these. If that is how God clothes the grass of the field, which is here today and tomorrow is thrown into the fire, will He not much more clothe you, O you of little faith? So do not worry, saying, 'What shall we eat?' or 'What shall we drink?' or 'What shall we wear?' For the pagans run after all these things, and your Heavenly Father knows that you need them. But seek first His kingdom and His righteousness, and all these things will be given to you as well. Therefore, do not worry about tomorrow, for tomorrow will worry about itself. Each day has enough trouble of its own."

How did He know? I loved that He dealt with the insignificant things we worry about — food and clothing. He then expanded it to the big things we worry about — like tomorrow when we arrive in Jerusalem. There will be enemies. There will be multitudes. His Name has spread. The crowds could crush Him. I am reminded how He had to have a boat close by at the shore of Galilee, for the masses were pushing Him into the water.

Jealous mobs could also attack Him. Jerusalem is a place where Rome kills people for insurrection by crucifixion. It is also a place where Jewish leaders stone those caught in sin. The Temple is a place where Governor Pilate killed Jewish worshipers while they made their sacrifices. We were never sure what prompted such an atrocity toward our people.

I felt Jesus was telling me, do not worry about tomorrow when we arrive in Jerusalem. Our Father knows our needs — food, shelter, even clothing. He also knows our need for protection. We need to focus on righteousness, on doing right. Let God take care of everything else.

I felt a little silly, too, in my quest to provide for the needs of Jesus and His disciples. In one way, the ladies and I are cooking, cleaning, and providing money, when God could handle that without us. Then again, I was uplifted. Maybe God was using us to meet Jesus' needs. The Rabbi has encouraged us in our service. I suppose it is the latter — God is using us to care for them.

Jesus' reference to Solomon also blessed me. We are going to the city Solomon's father, David, built. We are worshiping at the rebuilt Temple, which stands where Solomon's once stood. God took care of David. God took care of Solomon. God does not change. He will take care of Jesus. As my Father, He will take care of me too. I cannot see myself on their level. But, if God takes care of the lilies that are here today and gone tomorrow, how much more will He take care of Mary from Magdala?

On the first month, the eighth day — We arrived at the home of Lazarus. He appears to be a special friend of Jesus. The Rabbi speaks to us as people for whom He has a great responsibility. He speaks to Lazarus much more casually. Lazarus greeted Him as an old friend. They hugged. They laughed. His sisters Martha and Mary came out. They all embraced in a circle, bouncing up and down in celebration of their reunion.

Jesus then introduced us to His friends. They greeted us with a warmth that made us feel like they had loved us from long before. Martha made a meal for us, while Jesus spoke with Lazarus. His sister, Mary, sat beside me. Another Mary! Mary, the mother of James the Less. Mary, the mother of Jesus. Mary Magdalene. Now Mary of Bethany. How many are there of us? Anyway, Mary was as fixed on Jesus as I was. Lazarus shared stories with us about how he first met Jesus.

They then asked Jesus to catch them up on what had been going on with Him in Galilee. He told how the people had come from all over to hear Him teach about our Father. He shared how God was able to do great works through Him. He talked about His Spirit. He told how, by His Spirit, He had cast out demons.

That piqued my attention. He told Lazarus how He had sent the disciples out and His Spirit spoke through them. I looked at Peter, James, and Matthew, who were seated not far from Him. God's Spirit spoke through them? I suppose it was His Spirit that enabled them to work miracles. The Spirit of Jesus was shared in their bodies to do great things? I had a lot of questions, but this was not the time.

Just then, Martha came into the room. She interrupted her brother. She looked down at Mary with a frown. She then said to Jesus, "Lord, don't You care that my sister has left me to do the work by myself? Tell her to help me!" I was a little disturbed by her complaint. I had offered to help, as had Salome, Susanna, and Mary, the mother of James the Less. She told us we were her guests. But Mary of Bethany was supposed to help her per Martha's words. I can understand the frustration. It took four of us comfortably to feed thirteen and ourselves. Now Martha alone is trying to feed twenty, including herself?

I expected the Rabbi to ask Mary to help. His response was surprising. He said, "Martha, Martha, you are worried and upset about many things, but only one thing is needed. Mary has chosen what is better, and it will not be taken away from her." That was remarkably interesting. Jesus had just taught us about worry. Martha, too, was worried and upset. Jesus said Mary has chosen what is better.

I tied that back to seeking God's kingdom and His righteousness first. Everything else will be taken care of. Perhaps it would have been better for Martha to join us at Jesus' feet. She could be fed with His words. Later, we could all get up and help prepare the meal. That made sense. Instead, Martha huffed back to prepare food. A little while later, Mary got up to help her sister. We had a fabulous meal. We are all on our mats for the night. Something occurred to me. I heard Martha call Jesus, "Lord". It is the word we generally use for God. It is also used for an earthly master. I have not ever thought of Jesus in these terms. I am barely getting used to calling God, "Father". Is Jesus "Lord"? He came down from Heaven? He said that. God is Lord, Master. I would have no problem with Jesus being my Lord if that is not an affront to God. He works miracles. He casts out demons. He walks through a crowd of attackers unscathed. He feeds thousands with a kid's lunch basket. He calms the storm with just His voice. Lord?

On the first month, the ninth day — My friend Matthew took me aside this Sabbath morning before we left for the Temple. He said he had seen me writing notes in my parchments. He wanted to know what records I was recording. I assumed he thought I was keeping up with our inventory of food and money. I was delighted he asked. I told him I began to take notes in the cistern after my first attack. The doctor, Xenophan, had recommended it for my sanity.

Since Jesus healed me, I have found them particularly useful to think through things I am facing. I joyfully told him that of late, I have been taking notes with regard to what Jesus was doing, what He has taught us, and what I have thought from His teaching. I reminded him that keeping records was a sign of a good tax collector. Matthew grinned as if this was a great idea. From our visit, I do not doubt he will be taking notes, too. He has been with Jesus a lot more than I have. There is no telling the things he has seen.

Jesus is calling. We are heading to Jerusalem. How amazing to be in Jerusalem, at the Temple, on the Sabbath. Years before in Magdala, we met in our local synagogue near the bimah that was a miniature replica of the Temple. That felt like the Sabbath. This does so much more.

We are back in Bethany this evening. It has been a long day. My recollections? First, when we climbed the Mount of Olives from Bethany, Jerusalem in all its grandeur shined before us. It is so fascinating. You walk up the hill. You are tired from the climb. All you see is limestone, olive trees, and other trees of various sorts. You are walking with all these people, some you know, most you do not know. We are all going to Jerusalem, I assume for the same reason. We have come from all over Israel and beyond to worship God. We come to remember the beginning, how God provided deliverance from Egypt for our forefathers. We go to remember God loves us. He has power. He will look after us. We go because He said to. We are to remember this day, the first month of every year.

So we walk. Trying to go fast enough to not anger the people behind. We also are cautious not to go too fast to run upon the heels of the people in front. Our eyes are down as we walk with this in mind. Then all of a sudden, the hill levels. We walk a few paces. Unfolding before our eyes is the whole of the city of Jerusalem. The diamond on the band, the Temple stands bright. The sun hits it exactly right. We have to cover our eyes.

Many walk on past. They never stop to take in the sight, but Jesus stopped. He placed His hand on the nearest disciple to stop him. The rest of us with Him stopped. We moved off to the side so as to not block people making their journey.

I looked at the city. I looked at Him. He just stared right at it. He lifted His eyes toward Heaven. He looked back down at the Temple. I could almost read His thoughts. I know that is presumptuous. If I were in His righteous sandals, I would be thinking, that is the house of God. God promised He would dwell there for our nation. He would be there to hear our prayers. If we needed a place to connect with Him, this is the place. It is here, and only here, that we can make sacrifices for our sins. It is here, only here, that we are to gather to remember all He has done. We can worship Him everywhere, but it is here He commands us to gather, to be with Him alone with all His children. God is in that Temple.

I saw all the people wandering around in the city. I saw people passing it by like they would pass by a neighbor's house, with no special attention given it. I saw people walking down, commenting on the smell, the crowds, the worry of finding where they would stay. So many are worried about what they will eat. They miss why they are here. The pause on the mount was needed. I needed it. If Jesus would have gone on down, I would have followed. I would have also missed this moment. Peter looked at me. I smiled. Old crusty Peter, the oldest of our group, smiled back. How he has changed.

We made our way down the mount facing the city. Salome was walking with her sons. Mary was walking with her son. Lazarus, Mary of Bethany, and Martha walked next to the Rabbi. I walked beside Susanna. We were all anxious to be reunited with Joanna. It dawned on me that we had no idea where she lived in this city. Besides, who wants to leave Jesus to look for her? We do not want to miss a thing. Hopefully, she will find us.

We crossed the Kidron Valley. We then entered the Sheep's Gate. I made this trip with Poppa. Sadly, at that time, I was in a totally different state of mind. We came the last time to find help. We found very little. This time, I entered the city a new woman. All of this because of the man I am following — Jesus.

We passed by the Pool of Bethesda to our right. Jesus turned back to go inside the archway of this pool area. I walked up to be near Matthew. He has been here many times for their tax collector gatherings. Matthew saw the puzzled look on my face. He whispered, "This is the place where the sick come to find healing. Many came here because they heard that on some magical moments, the water will start to bubble. The word is that whoever is first in the water will be healed of whatever malady they have." I told Matthew that if I were sick, I would stay in the water until it stirred. He told me it might stir once in a decade or more. I giggled. That would sure make my skin wrinkle horribly.

We followed our Rabbi. He walked around the Pool looking at all the sick. In one sense, they seemed to be hopelessly waiting for a miracle. In another sense, they had the expression of resignation. If you are going to die, it might as well be here. We saw nothing but outcasts — the blind, the lame, the paralyzed, the diseased. Jesus walked around the five colonnades. He then went back to a man lying near the edge of the water. The Rabbi very gently walked up to him. He knelt beside where he lay while the nineteen of us looked on the scene. He asked the man, "How long have you been in this condition?" The man replied, "Thirty-eight years."

Jesus then asked him, "Do you want to get well?" That was an odd question. Does the sick want to be made well? My assumption is that every sick person wants to be made well. I have met people, though, who seem to delight in being sick. They love the attention. Others like playing sick to avoid work. I could see those not wanting to be made well. That is an exceedingly small minority. This man was not one of those. He answered Jesus, "Sir, I have no one to help me into the pool when the water is stirred. While I am trying to get in, someone else goes down ahead of me." Jesus then said to him, "Get up! Pick up your mat and walk." Oh my goodness! Immediately, this decrepit old man, who looked like he would die at any moment, stood up, cured. He picked up his mat. He walked as easily as a robust Nathanael walks. No water was stirring. It was Jesus' words that stirred in the man. I do not know if anyone at the pool even realized what had happened. This man was a loner. No one knew him. No one cared for him. I do not think anyone knew a name for any others who waited by this pool. He was sick. He was healed. He was gone. No one, but us and the Rabbi, knew any different.

Jesus then led us to the quarters where the Sanhedrin meet. I cannot speak for Judas the Judean, but for the rest of us Galileans, this was an extremely uncomfortable place. I felt more comfortable at the Pool of Bethesda than at this place of power. No sooner did we walk up, a member of the Sanhedrin, a Pharisee, walked out. He greeted Jesus very formally. It was as if Jesus was this man's high priest. The man's name was Nicodemus. I tried not to listen in, but I did catch him reference the thought of being born again. I had never heard that term before. Obviously, this man had at some point.

He then introduced himself to us. He said, "Greetings, I am Nicodemus. I have had the privilege to know your Rabbi for a short while. I met Him one night because I was so enamored by His teaching. I have heard the greatest lecturers in the world, including our very own Gamaliel. It was not until I met Jesus that all scripture was opened up to me. I have always seen God as a God of do's and don'ts, of rules and regulations. Your Rabbi has caused me to study much. I now see God as a God who loves, who sacrifices, who forgives, who reaches down, who wants to save. Jesus has also reinforced my belief as a Pharisee, that there is life eternal. The one thing with which I have struggled is He says I must have a new start. I must be born all over again. I have wrestled with this truth. I do believe it is true. How else can I get past my sins? I cannot undo them. I need a fresh start. I need everything washed away. It goes along with what David prayed in the Psalms: I need a new heart created."

Jesus smiled. Nicodemus excused himself. Many pilgrims were coming. He had many duties to deal with before the high holy day of Passover. He bid us farewell. Jesus continued to lead us to the Temple. Crowds saw Him. They hurried to be in His audience. Jesus had them sit near the Temple steps. Before He could get started, some of the Jewish leaders interrupted. They said they had seen a man carrying his mat away from the Pool of Bethesda. They said that they chastised him for doing work on the Sabbath.

I was confused. What work was he doing? They answered my unspoken question. "Carrying anything on the Sabbath is work. People here know better than to do that. When we asked him, he told us that he did not know your name, but he described what you looked like. We realized it was you, Jesus. We have heard you in the Galilee. We have questioned you there. We question many things you are doing. They violate our law.

Now you have come here. We will expect you to follow what we say when you are in our jurisdiction."

Every eye was on Jesus. They had come to hear Him speak. We had, too. Now we all waited to hear His defense. This was a key moment for me. Could Jesus withstand the indictments of the religious establishment? If He failed before them, then He had to be considered something different than what I was being convinced He was.

He turned it on their heads. He said, "My Father is always at His work to this very day, and I, too, am working. I tell you the truth, the Son can do nothing by Himself; He can do only what He sees His Father doing, because whatever the Father does, the Son also does. For the Father loves the Son and shows Him all He does. Yes, to your amazement, He will show Him even greater things than these. For just as the Father raises the dead and gives them life, even so the Son gives life to whom He is pleased to give it. Moreover, the Father judges no one, but has entrusted all judgment to the Son, that all may honor the Son just as they honor the Father. He who does not honor the Son does not honor the Father who sent Him. I tell you the truth, whoever hears My word and believes Him who sent Me has eternal life and will not be condemned; he has crossed over from death to life."

The religious leaders reached down, grabbed dirt, and threw it into the air. I have no idea what this really means. I suppose it was to show their contempt for Jesus.

Jesus was calling God His Father. He was attributing the work He did to God. He referenced the fact that God raises the dead. We have read that about Elijah and Elisha's history. Clearly, God did the work, not them. We also know God gives life, as He did for Adam and Eve at the very beginning. Jesus promised to give eternal life. He has said this before. Eternal life is what I want for Poppa, for Momma, and for me. Jairus' daughter was raised to life, I genuinely believe that is what I saw.

My thoughts were interrupted. As the Jewish leaders shrunk back into the crowd, but while they were still in hearing distance, Jesus said, "I have testimony weightier than that of John. For the very work that the Father has given Me to finish, and which I am doing, testifies that the Father has sent Me. And the Father who sent Me has Himself testified concerning Me. You have never heard His voice nor seen His form, nor does His Word dwell in you, for you do not believe the One He sent. You diligently study the scriptures because you think that by them, you possess eternal life. These are the scriptures that testify about Me, yet you refuse to come to Me to have life."

Wow! What an affront to these pompous religious leaders. I wish Nicodemus could have been here to vouch for — should I say it? — for the Lord. It seems that is what Jesus is claiming. He said the Father has sent Him. He has said He comes from Heaven. He intimates He has seen the Father, that He has come to testify that He has seen and heard God. Even more, the crowd grasped an important fact: these religious leaders do study the scriptures, hoping to find eternal life. Jesus says the very scrolls they read testify about Him, but they will not come to Him. I know the law, the prophets, and the writings testify about the coming Messiah. I do not see Jesus' name there, but if He is the Messiah, then He is there.

With hatred in their eyes, the religious leaders left in an instant. The crowd applauded with delight. I think they applauded because these who lord over them, who act as an elevated sort in their midst, who want to be recognized and bowed to, had been put in their place. I think they relished their exit. I believe they also cheered for Jesus. They had come to be amazed. They did not leave disappointed. We had hoped He would share more, but I guess He thought that was enough for one day.

Jesus then led us into the Temple courts. He and the men went farther. We stayed in the women's court. It was here Joanna joined us. She had been in the crowd at the steps. She said she knew where Jesus was. She said you could always tell by the crowds. If there were huge crowds on a Holy Feast, Jesus was present. It had been that way for two years now. Joanna had reserved a place for us to observe Passover. She had her guards on alert, both to keep the peace, working with the High Priest's soldiers, and to defend Jesus if need be. We told her all about what we had seen on our journey. I could tell by her face that she felt she had made a poor choice in going ahead of us. Jesus had told Martha that Mary of Bethany had made the better choice in staying with Jesus. I was comforted that we had made the better choice in traveling with Jesus rather than enjoying the luxuries of Joanna. Regardless, we all have had a part to play. I am so glad a woman of power is our friend.

Matthew told me on our walk back to Bethany that while the men were in the inner court of the Temple area, Jesus saw the man He had healed at the Pool of Bethesda. From the confrontation on the steps of the Temple, we all wondered what this man had told the Jewish leaders. Jesus walked up to him in the Temple courts and said, "See, you are well again. Stop sinning, or something worse may happen to you."

Matthew said they had never seen this man before today. They did not know the man. None of them had any idea why he had been an invalid. Had it been from birth? Had it been because of some accident? Maybe he was caught in an affair and beaten by his mistress' husband. Perhaps he was injured while robbing a man's donkey. There were so many unknowns about him. But Jesus knew.

Jesus said that he was well again? Had he been made well before? Jesus told him to stop sinning or something worse might happen to him. It sounds certain his condition was because of some sin. If he was so quick to betray Jesus to the authorities, could it be that he is a profiteer or a manipulator? Maybe he is a yes-man, telling people what they want to hear to get what he wants. Clearly, Jesus knew things about this man He could not possibly have known in the natural sense.

This reminded me of what Nathanael told me of his first meeting with Jesus. He was a friend of Philip. When Philip met Jesus, he decided right away that Jesus was the Messiah. He ran to tell his friend from Cana.

Nathanael said he had his doubts. He had heard of what Jesus was doing. He had also heard He was from Nazareth. He had the same assumption many have about that town — that nothing good comes from there. I know the generalization. They say the same about Magdala.

What I remember most is Nathanael saying he was sitting under a fig tree, praying, when Philip approached. At Philip's constant urging, he got up to see Jesus for himself. Jesus called Nathanael at first sight. He said Nathanael is a true Israelite in whom nothing false abides. Nathanael questioned Jesus about how He knew him. Jesus said He had seen Nathanael when he was sitting under the fig tree. Nathanael told me that was miles away from Jesus. He also told me he approached Jesus, walking with Philip. There was no way anyone would have had the opportunity to tell that to Jesus. How could He have known unless... unless... He is the Son of God?

Jesus knows about each person before meeting them? He claims God as His Father. Today, for the first time, I have heard Him say that He is God's Son. When Nathanael told me he thought Jesus was the Son of God, I took that in a generic sense. We are all sons and daughters of God. But today, I am becoming keenly aware that Jesus, my Rabbi, is deity. What will I think when I read my parchments years from now? Will I scoff at how simple I was, how naïve I am at this moment? Perhaps how gullible I am to believe this? Or will I read this, years from now, utterly amazed at the Divine revelation that came to us little by little? This is the One sent from God, His Son Jesus.

The ladies and I are sleeping in the bedroom of the sisters (Martha and Mary). We talked a little before slumber fell upon us. I shared how worried I was at the danger that might loom for us in Jerusalem. The beginning of my fears played out today. Could they be worse tomorrow? I would think the religious leaders would be ready for Jesus tomorrow. I will hold to what Jesus said: we are not to worry. Our Father knows our needs.

On the first month, the tenth day — We awoke to a nice breakfast. Mary made it. I am sure Martha was relieved. Jesus sat with us — not at the head of the table. That was where Lazarus sat. He offered it to Jesus, but He declined. It was then He told us how we should react if we are favored with status. He said, "When someone invites you to a wedding feast, do not take the place of honor, for a person more distinguished than you may have been invited. If so, the host who invited both of you will come and say to you, 'Give this man your seat.' Then, humiliated, you will have to take the least important place. But when you are invited, take the lowest place, so that when your host comes, he will say to you, 'Friend, move up to a better place.' Then you will be honored in the presence of all your fellow guests. For everyone who exalts himself will be humbled, and he who humbles himself will be exalted."

Lazarus spoke, "Yes Lord. I invited you to sit at the chief seat after You have taken a seat around the table with everyone else." Jesus then stressed He had not come to be served, but to serve. He even said the greatest among us must be the least. He then said the one who has the greatest love will be the one who is not just willing, but who does lay down his or her life for their friends. Lazarus capitulated to the Rabbi's resolve. He then asked Jesus to thank God for our food. This was His frequent duty everywhere we went. He would take the bread and hold it to Heaven, thanking God. He would then break it to distribute around the table. The custom was always beautiful.

We left Lazarus's home. We walked up the Mount of Olives. It leveled off. We moved to the side, pausing to gaze upon the beautiful sight. Jesus then led the way down the hill. We crossed the Kidron Valley. We entered through the Sheep Gate. We passed by the Pool of Bethesda. I looked inside quickly to see if I could see the man Jesus had healed. His spot was vacant. I wondered if he had changed how he was living. I conjecture he had a face for one person, another for the next, and an altogether different face for the third. I am reading into him too much perhaps.

My impression is that if he is to stop his sin, he needs a whole new life. It is as Nicodemus described — that man needed to be born again. If I were born again, I would not have the scars from cutting my throat. I would not have the self-inflicted puncture scars from the fishhooks. If I were born again, I would be a virgin. If I were born again, there would have never been the voices, the exposures, or the welcoming in of the demonic. To be born again — the man at the pool needs this. I feel as though I have been born again in a way. I still feel the pangs of sin. As long as I am with Jesus, though, they are faint.

We arrived at the Temple. The crowds were waiting for Jesus. Everyone was milling around until they saw Him. Then, they all converged at His feet. He stood on the top of the steps. Men in their priestly robes gathered around, too. Jesus spoke about prayer. He taught again how we should pray. He spoke about the Sabbath, which had just passed. He tenderly told us what it was for and for what it was not. He went over the commands of God given in the Torah. He then began to elaborate on how men had added to those in error. He spoke of purity. He talked about the necessity to be clean — ceremonially and otherwise.

Then, some Pharisees spoke up. One cleared his throat to get the stage as Jesus was closing His sentence. Another took that as his invitation to address Jesus in front of the crowd. His statement was indicting. He said, "Why do your disciples break the tradition of the elders? They don't wash their hands before they eat!" I think it was an exact example of what Jesus had just taught us. The traditions of the elders versus what God had commanded.

They had observed the disciples, and I guess us, too, not washing our hands before eating. I am from the Galilee. Washing hands was a necessity only when they were clearly dirty. If no dirt was apparent, then why wash? That was my Gentile world on the shore where fishermen eat. This is the land of Judea. The land of Judas. The man who carries his own special high-priced mat. The one who acts as though being near the other disciples would bring about a contagious disease. I see that in him. The other disciples do not. They seem to adore him. Of course, they do not have the tax collector's eye for duplicity. Then again, I may be a cynic.

Jesus replied, "And why do you break the command of God for the sake of your tradition? For God said, 'Honor your father and mother' and 'Anyone who curses his father or mother must be put to death.' But you say that if a man says to his father or mother, 'Whatever help you might otherwise have received from me is a gift devoted to God,' he is not to 'honor his father' with it. Thus you nullify the Word of God for the sake of your tradition. You hypocrites! Isaiah was right when he prophesied about you: 'These people honor Me with their lips, but their hearts are far from Me. They worship Me in vain; their teachings are but rules taught by men.'"

I had no idea that this was what these men did. How could they not care for their parents? The very scriptures they study say we are to honor our parents. That is the first command with a promise of blessing. Yet, these would let their parents suffer. I could never do that to Poppa or Momma. I would not allow that for anyone I know. How hypocritical these must be! I wonder if any in the crowd knew this was what they were doing? That brings the question: how many other things do these religious leaders do in secret? Would they not be driven from their comfortable positions if those were to be known in this holy city?

What I loved most? These are the experts in the law, or so they claim, but it is Jesus who quotes the scriptures to chastise their traditions. I am finding the more I listen to Him, that He is grounded in God's Word. Nothing can shake Him. When He quotes God's very words, there is no rebuttal. With Jesus' recitation, the Pharisees left seething.

Jesus called the crowd back to Him. He said to all of us, "Listen and understand. What goes into a man's mouth does not make him 'unclean,' but what comes out of his mouth, that is what makes him 'unclean.'" What comes out of our mouths makes us unclean. It is from our hearts that we speak. Jesus said our hearts are deceptive in all their ways. Our mouths are just a reflection of what is inside. I am inherently corrupt. I need to be born again.

Jesus had one more thing to say before He dismissed the crowd. He said, "Watch out for the teachers of the law. They like to walk around in flowing robes and be greeted in the marketplaces, and have the most important seats in the synagogues and the places of honor at banquets. They devour widows' houses and, for a show, make lengthy prayers. Such men will be punished most severely."

A quiet applause arose from the crowd. Smiles covered their faces. It was like they had someone who would represent them against the powers that rule over them. We all had someone who spoke our language. He understood our hurts. He noticed the oppression we all were silently bearing under other men. We all sensed this was the best way to conclude our lesson for the day.

Jesus gave a wave of the hand, signifying His time to speak was over. They began to walk away. We turned to go, too. Just then, He motioned for just the disciples to follow Him beyond the entrance of the Temple. He looked back at Salome, Mary, the mother of James the Less, Susanna, Joanna, Mary of Bethany, Martha, Lazarus, and me. With a nod, we were beckoned to follow. He brought us to the money box where people were giving their offerings. I gave an offering of what was owed to our Father. I say 'owed'. I owe Him everything. I gave what He required, then some more. The ladies with me did the same. Joanna gave an insurmountable amount from what I could tell. Each disciple gave. Jesus gave. I thought we would leave, but He pulled us to the side to watch others bring their offerings.

Jesus sat down opposite the place where the offerings were put. He watched the crowd putting their money into the Temple treasury. We joined Him there. Some looked at us oddly. Some gave facing us with the offering box between us. They wanted us to see what they gave. I could see that others were uncomfortable having people see them give. They stood between us and the box, with their backs to us. They gave. They stood for a moment. They then walked away without ever looking at us. Rich people threw in large amounts like Joanna, but not with nearly the same reverence.

Just then, a poor widow came. She did not notice us. She was oblivious to anyone being in the Temple. It was as if it was just her and God. She looked up to Heaven with her eyes closed. She emptied the contents of her purse into her hand. I expected a lot of things to fall out. Nothing did except two exceedingly small copper coins. They could not have been worth perhaps a fraction of a penny. She stood a little longer. She uprighted her empty purse. She bowed. A feeling of finality settled. It was as if she dropped off her last penny that she could have used for a bit of flour to make one small roll. She left in a ragged old shawl. As she walked away, I could see the sandals she wore were held to her feet by a thread. One of them had split from the sole. It made a repetitive pop when she walked. I was moved. To what was she going home? Does she even have a home?

She came alone. She came poor. She left alone with an empty purse, a ragged shawl, and sandals that would not last many more miles.

Interrupting my sadness, Jesus called us to Him. He said, "I tell you the truth, this poor widow has put more into the treasury than all the others. They all gave out of their wealth; but she, out of her poverty, put in everything — all she had to live on." Jesus knew about the man at the Pool of Bethesda. He knew that man's story. He knew Nathanael's position miles away under a fig tree. He knew my name at the door of Peter's home. Why would He not also know this woman's extremity?

I was even more touched by this woman. She was everything I thought before Jesus spoke. But more. Jesus confirmed what she gave was all she had. She dropped into the Temple treasury all she had for food. All she had to buy new sandals with, she dropped into that treasury box. What about rent? What about the unforeseen? She gave it all to God. Why? She loves God that much? She is willing to die of hunger if that is what it means to show God what He means to her. She is willing to wrap herself at night in the cold in the only cover she has of that shawl and robe, if that is what it takes to love on God.

How much do I love God? I fear it is not that much. I am spending from the wealth Poppa left me. I am not giving every cent. I still have a nice home. I have an extended line of businesses and properties. So does Susanna. So does Joanna. Mary has her husband, Alphaeus. Salome has her husband Zebedee's business. I take comfort in giving to the ministry of Jesus, even if it means entrusting Judas with our money, and then I worry about how that money will be spent. Here this lady gives into an offering box, not worrying if the priests are buying themselves flowing robes. Here is a widow whose money is funding the priests who have nice homes, while hers is in jeopardy. Why would she give? If I could catch up to her, I think I know what she would say: "I am giving to the Lord. If they misuse my gift, that is something God will take care of. As for me, I love Him so much."

"But you are poor," I would reply. "You have nothing," I would plead. I think she would say, "Yes, but God has given me life. He has promised me eternal life. He has blessed me with all my needs. I do not have nice sandals, but I have sandals. I only have one robe and shawl, but I have been given a robe and shawl. You have not seen the ways He blesses me. He prepares a sunset for me every evening. I anxiously await each one. He feeds me almost every day. I have reached this old age because of His grace. I have food He gives me, of which you have no idea. I have enjoyed my youth. I have learned. I have been spared the punishments I deserve. He woke me up today. I have not been promised wealth or health. My life is more than that. I am here to glorify Him until He brings me home. I will do so no matter how long I am given." I could imagine her saying all of that. I am humbled.

We returned to Lazarus' home this evening. I am finishing my notes on my parchments. I thank the good doctor for giving me this binding of parchments. It overflows with blessings for my life. It will be a ready reference in the days ahead. I thank God. If I have much or little, I have a reason to give to Him all that I have, all that I am.

On the first month, the thirteenth day — The last two days have been a whirlwind. Jesus has gone off by Himself to the Temple. The disciples had some chores He assigned ahead of our Passover tomorrow.

Joanna has our location, but many preparations are to be made. It seems the disciples are in charge of this meal.

Joanna took the time to show us her home. She introduced us around to her friends who love Jesus the way we do. I had seen several of them in the crowds, but did not know any of them. That is the wonderful thing about the Rabbi's crowds. There are the rich and the poor, the powerful and the neglected, the important and the criminal. People who come to hear Him speak come from different countries, with all shades of skin. They come respectfully. They come empty, looking to be filled. They come confused, searching for someone to make sense of it all. They come, more than anything, just looking for God.

I think this is the greatest need we all have — God. We try to fill that need with position, as the religious leaders do. Others try to do it by wealth, like many of our tax collector friends. Some try to find it in family, like James and John did. Others attempt to cover the need with sex, like the fishermen. More seem to try sorcery and other religions. I imagine all who come to hear Jesus fall into one of these descriptions. I am sure these are just a tip of the mountain of vain pursuits.

We caught up with Jesus as He was leaving the Temple. He welcomed us with the warmest face. We can tell Him anything. We can ask Him whatever comes to our minds. He is patient. He is understanding. He even relates to what we feel.

He often anticipates our question before it is even asked. I am here in Jerusalem with Jesus and the disciples. My prayer is answered.

In the nineteenth year of the reign of Tiberius Caesar, on the first month, the fourteenth day — This evening we celebrated Passover. The lamb was roasted. Peter and John had prepared it. To go with the lamb, we had unleavened bread, olives, bitter herbs, and a sweet mixture of dates. We had the cups of wine. As Moses prescribed, we followed the tradition of our ancestors to the letter. As rote as it all seemed, Jesus was the master of the ceremony. He made it all come alive. We actually felt we were held up in the slave quarters of Egypt. We could almost hear the cries of the families losing their firstborn. We felt we were about to exit this slavery, that Moses was waiting at our door.

There was more meaning, though. Jesus talked about our slavery to sin. He spoke of how God sent Him to set us free. He talked about how we had all been walking in darkness, but God had sent a great light. Though, in His righteousness, we all felt unworthy. He said God did not send Him to us to condemn us, but that through Him we might be saved. I thought of Joshua who followed Moses. His name means "God saves" in Hebrew. Jesus means the same in Greek.

Moses led them out with great miracles. Through Moses, they were fed. God worked miracles through Jesus. He fed us for sure in the Galilee. Joshua led the children of Israel into the Promised Land. Jesus says He has come to lead us to eternal life, if I understand His Words. The symbolism and the parallels were too easy to identify.

Throughout the whole meal, the ladies looked at me. I looked at them. We felt as if we had sneaked into an event uninvited. The disciples fixed their eyes on Jesus. They were taking mental note. One would think they were holding all these things in their hearts so they could replicate them at some future date.

Afterward, we sang a hymn. We then headed for Bethany. Jesus took the twelve to an olive grove to pray. The ladies and I returned to Lazarus's home, with Lazarus as our escort. We prepared for bed. No one spoke. Each needed time to think. That went without saying.

On the first month, the fifteenth day — The disciples and Jesus returned this morning. They had not slept on their mats. Mary and Martha prepared our breakfast. They also sent some bread for us to enjoy as we traveled. I asked Matthew where they had been. I feared I missed something. He said Jesus loves this particular grove called Gethsemane, which is filled with olive trees. It is just across the Kidron Valley from Jerusalem, up on that side of the Mount of Olives. This is where the mount gets its name, I learned. Matthew said it is interesting. For a sight so near, no one stays there. I asked him what they did. He said they separated and prayed. I asked him if they prayed all night. He stated Jesus did. They tried, but they got tired after an hour or so. Jesus taught us what to pray. Learning the length of prayer is different.

We were all tired on the first leg of our journey back to Galilee. Even Jesus seemed very tired. Regardless, all were in good humor. There was a great sense of family now. We had made this journey. We had been drawn to Jesus. He had drawn us together. I am excited to see what He has in store for us. I pray I can be with Him some more. Our coffers have run thin after our journey. When we return home, I will gather more money and give it to Judas for the Rabbi's use.

Nathanael walked us to our side of the camp. Simon has our fire going. As in the journey, we were all too tired to speak. I did my usual practice before turning in for the night. I laid on my mat until the ladies drifted to sleep. From where I am this evening, I can see the disciples' camp at a distance. They are on the other side of some trees.

I want to write my thoughts on praying. The disciples reported that Jesus was able to pray all night. They said they could pray no more than about an hour. I do not know if I could make it a whole hour, especially late at night. Writing in my parchments allows me to think and pray. We covered a lot of miles today. Without writing, I certainly would fall asleep after a short time in prayer.

I think I know why. I fear that when I pray, I just tell God what I need. I often pray to Him as if He is not there. Sometimes I just think my prayers are joining thousands of others. We all lift our petitions into space, then go about our business, hoping they found God's ear. When I talk to Salome, I do not fall asleep. She speaks to me. I listen. I speak to her. She listens. When I talked to Momma, we could talk all night. She and I fueled each other. There was the give-and-take in our visits. I miss her greatly. I think that is what it is like for Jesus to talk to

God. We call it prayer. I believe it is more a conversation. The disciples and I talk to God. We tell Him what we want. We do not engage Him. I seldom have asked God what He wants.

My desire is to learn to converse with the Father as the Son does. That makes sense. Mary, the daughter, with Adriana, the mother, visited with no concept of time. I gained from her. She gained from me. The Father God can gain little from me. I will give Him my worship. I will also give Him an attentive ear to hear what He would like done here on this earth. His Will be done on earth as it is in Heaven. So I pray, "Father, teach me to pray to You. I have needs. You know them, but I will share them to acknowledge that I need You in all I do. I will also ask You to tell me what You want me to do. I will seek first You, Your kingdom, and Your righteousness, trusting everything else will be added unto me.

On the first month, the sixteenth day — Today, we paused in our journey back to the Galilee. It is the Sabbath. Jesus is profoundly serious about following God's Word. We gathered to pray. Our Rabbi quoted a passage of scripture. He then shared with us what it means. It is so wonderful to be able to sit and listen to Him. People flock to Capernaum to hear Him, as they do every other synagogue He enters, but we are given the special privilege to have His personal attention.

Jesus took time today to emphasize how important it is for each of us to learn the scriptures personally. He says it is the only thing that will brace us for the days ahead. He then shared an experience He had a few years back when He began His ministry. There is so much we do not know about Jesus' past. How I would love to sit with His mother and brothers to glean what I can to understand what makes Him the way He is. I need to also question the disciples. What I have learned on this trip to Jerusalem cannot compare to the times they have spent with Him. What have they seen? What have they been taught? Are there things He has told them not to share? I look at Him as He speaks. What has He seen with those eyes?

Jesus said that after fasting forty days and forty nights, he was hungry. The tempter came to him and said, "If you are the Son of God, tell these stones to become bread." Jesus answered him, "It is written: 'Man does not live on bread alone, but on every word that comes from the mouth of God.'"

Then the devil took him to the Holy City and had him stand on the highest point of the Temple. "If you are the Son of God," he said, "throw yourself down. For it is written: 'He will command his angels concerning you, and they will lift you up in their hands, so that you will not strike your foot against a stone.'" Jesus answered him, "It is also written: 'Do not put the Lord your God to the test.'"

Again, the devil took him to a very high mountain and showed him all the kingdoms of the world and their splendor. "All this I will give you," he said, "if you will bow down and worship me." Jesus said to him, "Away from me, Satan! For it is written: 'Worship the Lord your God, and serve him only.'" Then the devil left Him, and angels came and attended Him.

I was able to write what He shared. He seems not to mind me writing while He speaks. Everyone in our party is now accustomed to my notetaking. I am thankful for that. It is not as if I am writing secrets. All of this is for my good. I pray it serves the good for others, too. If for nothing else, it will remind me as I try to share how wonderful Jesus is.

Jesus allowed us all to go and pray on our own. He also encouraged us to think on what He had shared. He wanted us to think on how useful the words of God are for our daily trials. In reflecting back to His lesson, He opened up a period in His life that none here had ever been told before. He said He was led by the Spirit into the Judean wilderness. He said the Spirit led Him there specifically to be tempted by the devil. Why would God's Spirit lead Him to be tempted? Was it to test His mettle? Does God allow me to be tempted? I know I have been. I know that nothing happens without God's approval. We learned that early on as the visiting scribes taught us about Job.

I know I write a lot of questions. I look back over my writing. I may get frustrated when I reference these parchments. Then again, if I stay at it, I may be able to come back to these questions to write the answers. How I pray that will be the case!

Jesus said the devil came to Him. The devil himself. I wonder, was he in the flesh? I wish I would have asked Him. I get so enamored by His words, that I dare not interrupt. The devil that appeared to Adam as a serpent, that devil came to Jesus. Adam is called the son of God, the first son. Jesus says He is the Son of God. The devil obviously came to both. I would have run. I have seen his handiwork in my body, in my mind, and in my spirit. I trembled when Jesus mentioned his name. I also felt a peace. Jesus can handle the devil. He cast out the devil's demons. Where Satan is one we should not play with, Jesus can speak of him and address him because Jesus has full authority over evil, it appears. Nonetheless, the devil came to Jesus. I suppose, then, that it is no unique experience for the devil to come to any of us.

Jesus spent forty days and forty nights in the desert. He was hungry. The desert has no food. The desert has little or no water. People who go there often never return. The devil came to Him in the desert, a dry and weary land, seemingly the most appropriate place to find the devil. The devil said to Him, "If you are the Son of God, tell these stones to become bread." In a moment of hunger, the devil tempted Him to meet that hunger. It is when we are in need, that I suppose the devil slithers in to get us to fill the need in the most expeditious manner, discarding the considerations of right and wrong. What would I have said? If I am hungry, if I can turn a stone into bread, or a little boy's basket to a lot of bread, what would be the harm in that? If I were Jesus, I would see no difference between turning a stone to bread or taking a basket and feeding thousands.

Jesus answered, "It is written: 'Man does not live on bread alone, but on every word that comes from the mouth of God.'" I suppose if the devil makes a suggestion, we should do the opposite, no matter what. Who knows what he has planned? He tempted Adam and Eve to eat, too. They had all the fruit in the world. They were not in a desert, but in Eden. The difference was, God told them not to eat of the Tree of the Knowledge of Good and Evil. He did not tell Jesus not to turn a stone into bread. But again, who is making the suggestion? I will be sure to not live by the suggestions of the devil or those who follow him. I will live by the words that come from the mouth of God. If God says, "Do it", Jesus would do it. God told Moses to speak to the rock for water. He struck it instead. Doing so cost Moses. God had told Moses to strike it the first time, speak to it the second time. We should follow what God says, when and how God says.

I think further implications exist. The earthly needs of this body are not as important as the spiritual needs. It means more to please God than to please our own desires. If we live by the Word of God, I believe He will meet every need in time. David said that He has never seen the righteous forsaken or their children begging for bread. If we obey our Father, He will meet our needs. We should never do what the devil suggests.

Instead, we should wait on God.

The Rabbi then said the devil took him to Jerusalem, the Holy City. The devil was able to take Jesus to the highest point of the Temple. This means so much more to me after walking around the Temple with Jesus a few days earlier.

He said the devil said to Him, "If you are the Son of God, throw yourself down. For it is written: 'He will command his angels concerning you, and they will lift you up in their hands, so that you will not strike your foot against a stone.'" That the devil actually used scripture to tempt Jesus was interesting. Jesus said we live by God's Word. The devil then takes God's Word to challenge Jesus to prove it out.

The Temple is so tall. Some have said it is at least 150 feet high. The devil was able to go into the Temple, to go up to the top of the Temple. I know King Herod began the work on the Temple and that construction has been ongoing for over fifty years now. It continues well beyond his death. No end of the construction is in sight. Because of that, there was certainly a means by which Jesus and the devil could get to the top, though I did not notice a way up a few days ago. Then again, I am restricted on where I can go as a Jewish woman (there would probably be more restrictions if they knew I was a half-Jewish woman from Magdala). As sacred as the Temple is, with trained soldiers guarding every inch, how could the devil have access to this holy structure? Is the devil allowed in the Temple? Judging by some of our religious leaders, I would say they welcome him. They are hypocrites. They love money. They make laws that they do not follow. They attack Jesus every chance they get. They do not care for their own parents. Their actions match more the devil's disposition than God's.

From that high pinnacle, the devil quoted scripture, saying that if He is the Son of God, He could throw Himself down and the angels would rescue Him. I wonder. I think about the angry crowd in Nazareth. They took Jesus to the cleft of the hill. They were going to cast Him down to kill Him. Jesus walked through them, but what if He had not been able? If they had thrown Jesus off that cliff, would the angels have caught Him? What a great question! If He is the Son of God, I imagine nothing can harm Him, that no one can ever harm Him. What a sweet thought that is. I do not ever want to lose Him. I do not want harm to come to Him. I had worried heading to Jerusalem for His safety. The religious leaders were there. The people from Nazareth surely would be. I felt He was in extreme danger. Jesus addressed that, saying we should not worry. Our Father knows what we need, including protection. Thus, if Jesus were to be cast down, or jump down, God would send His angels to save Him — if He is the Son of God.

Jesus answered him, "It is also written: 'Do not put the Lord your God to the test.'" I suppose if Jesus would have jumped, that would be testing God, attempting to prove God will do what He says. To me, to test God is to doubt God. It would have made sense for Jesus to step off in accordance to God's Word to show the devil. Then again, the first thing I am learning as I write, is if the devil suggests it, do not do it, no matter how right it seems.

Last, the devil took Jesus to a very high mountain and showed Him all the kingdoms of the world. He told Jesus he would give all these kingdoms to Jesus if He would worship the devil. To me, this seems to be the weakest temptation. Why bow to the devil? Jesus is more powerful than the devil. The demons that belong to the devil flee at Jesus' name. Jesus silences them, though the devil tells them to speak. Why bow to one less than yourself?

The nations will be given to Jesus? If the crowds are any indication, the nations are already coming to Jesus. We see people from all over show up in Capernaum. More wait to see Him in Jerusalem. People take off work. They bring their children. The nations and the generations are turning to Him. How can the devil promise this? Or is he seeking to deceive Jesus? I do remember John mentioning to me one day that the Rabbi said the devil is the prince of this world. I can see evil joining the devil. Maybe he meant all who are good and all who are evil will serve Jesus if He will only bow to the devil. What good would it be to have all the nations of the world if you have to submit to one so evil as the devil? I do not think that would be worth it.

I guess some will sell their souls to have evil, or to have money, or to have power. I could see the strength of the temptation in timing. The nations are turning to Jesus, but the devil says they will come to Him instantly, I assume. I could see that. Who wants to wait when we can have what we long for now? I do not get the feeling Jesus' chief longing is to rule nations as much as to please God, His Father.

Jesus told us He then gave His command to the devil. "Away from Me, Satan! For it is written: 'Worship the Lord your God, and serve Him only.'" How awesome is that! The devil asked Jesus to bow to him. Jesus commanded him to leave.

I think the devil is confused about who is in charge. I think we make the same mistake in our lives. I know I have. I thought I was in control in Magdala. I had money. I had freedom. I could slip out my window any time to join the men at the shore. I was in command. I learned quickly that something else had taken over. I was not in charge. I was doing what I wanted at the demons' behest. I thought I was making myself happy. Instead, I was destroying my life while breaking my family's hearts. I was blatantly defiant, even physically violent with my mother and father. It breaks my heart to think of that now.

Jesus is the One I will follow. He is the One in command. Wherever He leads, I want to go. I will walk with Him. I will follow behind Him. I will do as He says, for He does what the Father says. What a great Sabbath today has been! Thank you, Father, for Jesus, Your Son. Help me understand that, please.

On the first month, the seventeenth day — We are making good time in our walk. We are going to bypass Nazareth. Matthew says an alternative route exists through Nain. I walked with the ladies. Jesus led with the disciples walking beside Him. I wanted to hear what He was saying, but I felt He made a gap for a reason. I know He called them to be His disciples. I figured He was investing some time in answering their questions. I will be content knowing He will include me as He sees fit. Though He takes time with them, I do not feel left out. I am still with Him. I shared things with Momma, but not Poppa. I would sometimes share things with Poppa, but not with Momma. It was not because I sought to hide something. I had a love relationship with both equally. It was just that at times, I felt a topic more suitable for her. I imagine Jesus feels the same about those with whom He shares. Besides, I have enough to digest from yesterday.

Jesus said the angels came to attend to Him after the devil stormed away. The devil tempted Jesus to do wrong to make the angels appear for His rescue. Jesus refused. He did right instead. Then the angels came to help. If I do right, I pray to see the same help. May I move farther and farther away from the sinful instincts that still war within my flesh. I still feel sinful inclinations. I no longer hear the demons. They are nowhere within me, but sin is still lingering. I get jealous. I can be selfish. I still feel drawn to men. I sometimes want to let my hair down to revel. When I am with Jesus, those desires fade beyond reach. When I am walking farther behind Him, I find those thoughts reappear. What will it be like when I am not with Him and the disciples? I pray I have the same resolve to serve Him. I think this is why Jesus took the time to share about how we need to know the holy scriptures. That is what will carry us in times of temptation. It is a ready resource — one I am unsure how to use.

On the first month, the nineteenth day — As we were drawing closer to the Galilee, many from our area caught up with us. For pilgrims to Jerusalem to pass each other up along the way is normal. Sometimes we will pass by a group. Later that same group will pass by us. There are always smiles. It is almost a competition of sorts. We are in no hurry on our end. Jesus is with us. How can we rush these moments? We are never sure what things will be like when we get home. Jesus has many to see. He has crowds waiting.

These many days of our trip have afforded us much time alone with Jesus.

That all ended today. Crowds recognized Jesus. They are all walking with us now. The ladies and I have fallen back. We prepare food in the evenings. We have our prayers. Nathanael ensures our safe camp. Simon has our fire lit. Even with the crowds all around, these two continue to do that for us. Jesus, though, is flocked by people. Needless to write, we have had no private time of visiting among ourselves with Him.

In the nineteenth year of the reign of Tiberius Caesar, on the first month, the twentieth day — This is one of the most monumental days I have ever lived. I had a feeling Jesus could raise the dead. I think that is what He did with Jairus' daughter, but no one will confirm it, not even Peter. But today, all doubts were removed. As we approached the village of Nain, the crowd ahead of us ceased talking. A call for silence rang out throughout our ever-growing caravan. As I drew closer, I understood why. Great weeping ensued. Judging by the clothing, I saw a widow walking behind a dead one on a mat. I assumed it was her husband. We moved to the side to let them pass. I had seen a place of burial less than a mile back.

As the body was passing by me, I realized the length of the coffin was much smaller than that of a man. I gathered it was this lady's child. I do not know how large Nain is, but, by the numbers, it must have been the entire town following. When an adult dies, people mourn. Those who know the person pay their respects.

When a child is taken from us, everyone grieves — family, friend, and stranger alike. For a child to die before the parent is unacceptable to our minds. I tried not to look, but I could not help but glance at this grieving woman in the face. She would not look up. A lady on each side were helping her walk. She was so heartbroken, I imagined it would not be hard for her to lay down and be buried next to her child. That was the grief I saw.

Jesus was following behind us. A few adoring acquaintances had slowed Him down. I looked back at Him. I could see He had the same feelings I had. Tears filled His eyes. I love that Jesus can relate to each one of us. It is a gift He has, one of many. He bowed His head. I bowed mine, too, for a minute. I looked back again. He suddenly turned, following the procession, moving toward the grieving mother. Was He joining the funeral? Did He know the woman? He had surely spoken in this town before, I am sure. Those walking with Him stopped to wait. Just then, I heard His voice, "Don't cry." Don't cry? I expected Him to give her words of encouragement. He had talked about giving eternal life. I knew if nothing else, He would speak of her child being joined with our fathers in Heaven. But that is not what He said.

He walked right up and touched the coffin! As Jewish people, we avoid touching the dead unless they are our own. It makes us unclean for seven days. We avoid this. But not Jesus. He walked up and touched the coffin. The men carrying the child stood still. I was curious what He was going to do, what He was going to say. I moved closer to catch every word. I could see in the faces of the grievers they were greatly alarmed.

Many crazy people take advantage of the grieving. Others are unbalanced and believe they have some word to say about someone they have never met. Still some feel they can explain why someone has died prematurely. The seldom seen is when some so-called prophet claims a healing. Usually, that is reserved for the living. I have never seen a deranged person attempt to raise the dead, but I have heard some have tried. I clearly understood the fear when this man walked up and stopped the funeral procession.

Jesus said to the coffin, "Young man, I say to you, get up!" My first thought was, how did He know the child was a young man? Nothing about the funeral walk gave any indication that I caught. This is Jesus. How can I question Him? He knows. He said to the coffin, "Young man, I say to you, get up!" I wonder how many times after he died did his mother demand her son to get up. How many times did she cry out, "Don't do this to me! Come back to me!", just to see nothing happen? Jesus said, "I say to you", not your mother, not your doctor, not your synagogue ruler of Nain, but I, Jesus, say to you, get up! Just then, the lid popped open. The dead man sat up. He began to talk to Jesus! He then talked to those carrying him. I think he told them to put him down. He got out of the coffin. The crowd scrambled around him and Jesus. I think I saw him clutch Jesus' hand. I could not see well. I assume Jesus smiled. James said Jesus then gave him back to his mother. Tears of joy flowed, including mine. I think Jesus was wiping His away, too, with a satisfying expression.

I write down in my parchments. Make no mistake, Jesus can raise the dead! Oh, I wish He would have been around when Poppa died. I wish He would have been by Momma's bedside when we awoke to her in the dead of sleep. He raises the dead. He gives life! What is left to say? What more does He have to prove?

Nothing to me. I have made my choice. I love Him as I love God. The love I have formed for God has been elevated above the love for anyone else. But today, I have seen God in Him. I pray I am not wrong to write this. I love Him as I love God, and, in the same way, I love God with all my heart, soul, mind, and strength. To say this, I have an assurance I am not violating the first command, "Thou shall have no other gods before Me."

What prompted this statement today? I know it is because I saw Jesus bring a boy back to life, but I am not the only one to feel this. I heard there, outside the gate of Nain, all the people were filled with awe. They began to praise God with Jesus there. Someone said aloud, "A great prophet has appeared among us. God has come to help His people." They said God has come to help His people. God? It was Jesus who came to that town gate, who stopped that procession, who raised that dead boy to life. God has come. Jesus is the Son of God. They are One? I can love Jesus the way I love God. I do not think I will live to fully grasp this. I pray I am not wrong to love Jesus this way.

On the first month, the twenty-second day — We arrived in Capernaum last night. Today, everyone was getting acclimated. We had a meal together this evening. We are going back to our homes in the morning. Jesus has things He must do. He has dismissed the ladies and me. I am not excited about leaving Him. I know He is right to send us off, though. I need to see how our businesses are doing. I need to catch up with Linus on our business affairs. I do not write this to tie the word "affair" to the next statement, but I do long to see Atticus. He has been on my mind a lot. More than anything, I want to share what I have seen and learned from Jesus these last few weeks. I want Atticus to know God. I want Atticus to follow Jesus, too. I believe if he will, we have a future together. I know he wants a future with me. I am content being single, but there is a gnawing to be married. I am sure I cannot have children now, after all my body has been through.

My age also is prohibitive. Then again, Sarah had a boy at age ninety. Nothing is impossible with God.

While we were eating our evening meal, two of John the Baptizer's disciples came to see Jesus. They did not come to see us, but no one asked us to leave. I think for a while, Andrew and Philip were considered disciples of John. I have never had the opportunity to discuss this with them. We have all had our conversations centered around Jesus. When he spoke, I do know John's biggest messages were that we should repent, and that the Messiah was coming. I have also heard John baptized Jesus. Many believe this is why He can speak the way He does. They see John's effect on Jesus to be comparable to Elijah's impact on Elisha. I see many similarities to what I have heard of them and what I have seen in Jesus. I do not believe John the Baptizer ever worked a miracle. Jesus has worked them all. I know both Elijah and Elisha worked miracles. Our synagogue ruler viewed Elijah and Elisha as peers, equals. I do not see that Jesus has any equals, regardless of how great John may have been. Besides, Herod Antipas beheaded John for confronting him about his affair with his brother Herod Philip's wife. Elijah rode off to Heaven in a chariot.

I digress. A few of John's disciples came to visit with Jesus. He said great things about John to us and the crowd around us. "What did you go out into the desert to see? A reed swayed by the wind? If not, what did you go out to see? A man dressed in fine clothes? No, those who wear expensive clothes and indulge in luxury are in palaces. But what did you go out to see? A prophet? Yes, I tell you, and more than a prophet. This is the one about whom it is written: "I will send My messenger ahead of you, who will prepare your way before you.'"

I overheard John, not the Baptizer, but James' brother, tell his mother Salome that this is exactly what Jesus had said to two others of John's disciples when the Baptizer was alive. John was in prison after testifying that Jesus was the Christ. He was imprisoned, not for that, but for calling out Herod Antipas. He must have been having doubts. He asked his two close disciples to ask Jesus if He was the Christ, or if there was another one. John then stood up. He was incredibly careful in his recitation. He stated Jesus had said to tell John the Baptizer, "Go back and report to John what you have seen and heard: The blind receive sight, the lame walk, those who have leprosy are cured, the deaf hear, the dead are raised, and the Good News is preached to the poor. Blessed is the man who does not fall away on account of Me."

I slipped over by Salome's side. I asked her son John, "Did you say that Jesus sent a message to tell John that He raises the dead?" John knew where I was going with this. He said, "Mary, Jesus did say that. Did we not see that the day before yesterday?" I shook my head to acknowledge. I will be honest — I trembled a little. I then asked John if Jesus had raised Jairus' daughter. Before he could answer, Nathanael joined us. He said he felt Jesus was the Christ at the very first meeting. Jesus' words just confirmed it through His testimony regarding John the Baptizer. Matthew joined us, too. He had not heard what Nathanael had said. Matthew gave his own personal conclusion. He believes John the Baptizer fulfilled what God had said about an Elijah coming to prepare the way for the Messiah. He stated Jesus even said as much. We were all in one accord. God was opening our eyes.

On the first month, the twenty-third day — I arrived home last night. It is the Sabbath. I walked down to our neighborhood synagogue. The text chosen by the synagogue ruler, Simeon, was shockingly pertinent. It was from the prophecy of Malachi, 'See, I will send My messenger, who will prepare the way before Me. Then suddenly the Lord you are seeking will come to His Temple; the Messenger of the covenant, whom you desire, will come,'" says the Lord Almighty. "But who can endure the day of His coming? Who can stand when He appears? For He will be like a refiner's fire or a launderer's soap. He will sit as a refiner and purifier of silver; He will purify the Levites and refine them like gold and silver. Then the

Lord will have men who will bring offerings in righteousness, and the offerings of Judah and Jerusalem will be acceptable to the Lord, as in days gone by, as in former years."

That was simply amazing. I looked around our synagogue. I am so glad I can call it "ours." All these people are listening to the Word of God, yet, none of them grasp that this scripture is being fulfilled in Galilee. I heard Jesus say that very truth in Nazareth in His home synagogue. Everyone is going about their business. They, I pray, are seeking God. They are seeking to honor our faith and our religion. They reverence our forefathers. They genuinely believe God's hand is upon us. The messenger, as found in John the Baptizer, has come. He has prepared the way. Suddenly, in Capernaum, He has come. Many in this synagogue have gone to Him as a doctor. They have gone to Him as a gifted speaker. They have questioned His sincerity. Some have used this opportunity to say His own family does not believe Him. They have not seen what I have seen. But haven't they?

They may not have seen Him raise the dead. The people in Nain have. They should visit with them. They have not seen Him calm the storm. They should think back to that day a few months back. We had that squall hit the Galilee villages. We are accustomed to those. They are dangerous to all who live on these shores, just more so for those on the water when the winds from the hills hit. Thinking back, I remember distinctly sitting in our courtyard. I remember the storm hitting. I ran inside. I heard the wind. I felt the drop in temperature. The rain was pounding. Usually, that means we are in for a long night, but this time the storm stopped suddenly. I had no idea why.

Maybe the disciples should remind these around these parts about that night. We all talked about the sudden stop of the storm the next morning. We spoke with gratitude how we had been spared any damage. The disciples could use that as a reference to say they were in the boat when that latest storm hit. The village can check with those who saw them drift ashore soon after. The storm soaked the disciples, but the wind and the rain had ceased in an instant. They could attest as to why. Jesus calmed the storm. I am not sure any here would believe that. I doubt I would have then. I had not yet seen the miracles God has blessed me to see since following Jesus.

Regardless, I am hearing scripture in the synagogue. I leave the synagogue to see it played out before my very eyes. He is refining me. People are bringing offerings like that poor lady at the Temple. I am bringing my offerings to Him, along with Salome's, Mary's (the mother of James the Less), Joanna's, and Susanna's. All that we have been taught about the Messiah is going on near our neighborhood, but few seem to associate what is seen with what was written.

I want to tell them! I want to stand up! I want to plead with them to open their eyes! But who am I? A tax collector's daughter who was out of her mind, sexually active, who punctured herself with fishhooks, cut her own throat, and stabbed a man. Surely someone better could tell them, but I am not sure John or James have any clout here. I do not think Peter does. Perhaps Andrew. Maybe Zebedee. Certainly Jairus could. So far, I have heard nothing from him. Is it up to me? No one listens to women here. Even in court, we do not have the weight as eyewitnesses. I know Nicodemus could in Jerusalem. Joanna's husband could, too, if he would only go to hear Jesus. So far he refuses. I pray Jesus makes Himself known for who He is. The religious leaders discount Him. They even hate Him. All the more reason for Nicodemus to speak up.

On the first month, the twenty-fourth day — I walked to the vineyards to find Linus going over the day's work with the foremen. He was awfully glad to see me. Many in the vineyard were starting to take advantage of Linus, believing he was acting of his own accord. They felt this Roman soldier had no authority over their vineyards as long as they paid the taxes. I had to remind them it was my vineyard, that Linus leads on my behalf. They were disgruntled, but they agreed to comply. I let Linus know in front of them that if he had any trouble, I could begin to hire other workers.

Times are not good for the governed of Rome. We all need work, if for nothing more than to pay their exorbitant taxes. I think our laborers have a hard time separating Linus from the oppressive soldiers with whom he works. I can relate. People had a hard time differentiating Poppa and me from the run-of-the-mill tax collectors who burdened them excessively.

With that said, the businesses are doing well. Linus counted out the proceeds to me. He is honest. That is rare among the Roman soldiers. Roman centurions are generally the only officers of their army who have any trustworthiness at all.

Even then, they will buckle for Caesar and do anything. I am so thankful for Poppa's influence on Linus. I am also glad I grew up around Linus. Time has afforded us a trust. Poppa has successfully passed that relationship on to his next generation. I miss him so!

On the first month, the twenty-fifth day — Tonight, Atticus appeared at my door with a gift. I gave him a brotherly hug. I am infatuated. I had forgotten how handsome he has become. At our first encounters, he was a young man being led by the godless beasts called fishermen on the shore. He was different from them, though, even at our first introduction. He is more different today. He is upstanding. He is caring.

Tonight, I guess he feared I may have found someone else. He pledged his love to me. He even proposed. I was overwhelmed. He held me in his arms. I returned his embrace. He has honored me ever since I have changed. He has not been presumptuous. He has not shaded a line. He has treated me each moment as if Poppa is in our midst.

I want to be a disciple of Jesus. I want that privilege to go where He goes, to hear what He says, to see what He does. I also want a husband of my own. Peter has a wife. Philip does, too. A few of the other disciples are married as well. Now I have that opportunity. I pray I can have both. I wonder where Jesus is this week. He may be taking time to visit with His Father. He may be resting away from the crowds, or He may be knee-deep in them. Even at this moment, they may be pushing Him into the water, crowding for His attention. I hope to return to Him soon.

I am going to gather up our money to deliver to Judas. I have no idea where Judas stays. I may give it to Matthew to give to him. I thought of the widow giving her money at the Temple. She gave despite the corruption of the priests. She gave to God. She trusted God to take care of the abusers. I am going to do the same with our offerings for Jesus' care. I am giving to Him through Judas. What he does with it is between he and Jesus, between he and God.

On the first month, the twenty-seventh day — I have missed being with Jesus. I feel as though I am vulnerable when He is not near. Poppa is not here to help keep me grounded. Momma is not here to share my fears. I have Linus. He is a great help. I have Atticus. He and I are closer than ever before. Our moments alone are growing more heated. I feel the draw of my old habits. For some reason, I feel this sinful draw is controlled. Atticus and I are serious. He is the only man for which I long. He has shown love in the more respectful way. He is patient. He does not push. His love is measured not by emotions or by physical impulse. He has shown his love through commitment. I give him only kindness, nothing more. He is a complete gentleman around me. He does nothing more with me in private than what he does with me in public.

Nothing is hidden.

What I love about Atticus, too, is that he knows my past. I know I may have written this before. I have thought it more often. He was present on the shore when I was with many men on many different occasions. At our first meeting, he was the one I wanted. I had him. Then many men followed him. He knows that to marry me is to marry a woman who many men can snicker about when we walk the shoreline or enter a shop. I cannot imagine what it would be like to be married to a woman who has been had by so many friends. I grieve that I gave into sexual desires. The Roman world sees nothing wrong in these. My Poppa disagreed fully. Our God disagrees even more. I am a hand-me-down to Atticus. He could do much better, but at least I am now following the Lord. Most female choices on the Galilee do not follow the Rabbi. I honestly think I love Atticus. I believe he loves me, too.

On the first month, the twenty-ninth day — I have not been saying my prayers. I feel so distant. I have thought more of Atticus than God. Last night, we took it too far. I wanted him. He wanted me. It seemed so right. After all, we agreed to set a date to get married.

This morning, I realized it was all wrong. I have wanted to be a disciple of Jesus. I have never been happier than when I am walking with Him. Now, He is not here in Magdala. The disciples are probably with Him somewhere. I have failed Him. I have disqualified myself. I am so grieved.

Atticus knocked on my door this morning. I did not let him in. He tried to reason with me through the door. He called me "my love". I simply said I needed some time to think. He left my door, saddened. He calls me his love. That is the problem. I want God to be my love. I want God to be his love, too. I want to follow Jesus.

Now, I cannot even bear to face Jesus again. I believe firmly I may have lost my soul. I tremble to write this. I want eternal life. I want to go to Heaven. Jesus says He can give that. He can raise the dead. I have seen Him do it with my own eyes. I believe he forgave my sins of the past when He cast out the demons. He accepted me to travel with Him and His disciples. He let us care for them. He let me see so many things. I enjoyed the sweet fellowship with His inner circle. I had the privilege to be taught by Him. I want that. Nothing of the flesh can ever match what He can give me. Why would I settle for less? I feel so terrible.

On the first month, the thirtieth day — Today is the Sabbath. I could not go to synagogue. I wanted to go, but how can I go in my sin? I did not leave my house today. I am praying God will forgive me. I do not know how He can.

On the second month, the sixth day — Atticus came by again today. He has come every evening after his work. I have been occupying myself with our businesses. Linus has everything in order. I simply go to see what he is doing. Very few decisions need to be made. Everything runs so well without me. I receive the money each week. I have more money than most in this village. I have a nice home. I have fine clothes. The community does not hate me anymore. I have a handsome young man who loves me. So why am I not happy?

I feel lost. It was just one time since Jesus came into my life. Just one time. Many would say, "Let it go! Don't worry about it. Everyone does it. This is a new day. The old ways of morality were archaic." They say times have changed. Some believe society determines what is right and wrong. As a culture embraces something, the right-and-wrong label changes with it. The real determination of morality is whatever a society is willing to accept.

That all sounds good. Sadly, that did not work for Sodom and Gomorrah. That did not work for Korah in his rebellion against Moses. That did not work for the tribe of Benjamin. The history of the Judges in our nation proved to be a horrific thing. Then, everyone did what was right in their own eyes. It did not work during the Hasmonean period of our nation, either. Aaron's sons found out the hard way that doing what the rest of the world does can be deadly. And in Jerusalem, our religious leaders have sold us out to Rome. They lay hard rules on us. They then exempt themselves from those rules as a point of privilege. Lamech, in our first book, married two women. That was an affront to God. Then he killed a man who injured him accidentally. One violation of God's rules leads to others. Before long, we are building a tower near Babel and defying God by making our own morality.

All this is true. But how does any of this help me? I fell. I had intercourse with Atticus, a man who is not my husband. I gave in. I want to give in again. This is why I cannot let him in. I would be safer in the cistern, or would I? In the cistern, the guards took advantage of me. Where can I go where sin is not calling for me? And, if I have tasted of Jesus' righteousness and fell, how can I ever be a part of that holy life again?

I will pray what David prayed in Psalms: "Have mercy on me, O God, according to Your unfailing love; according to Your great compassion, blot out my transgressions. Wash away all my iniquity and cleanse me from my sin. For I know my transgressions, and my sin is always before me. Against You, You only, have I sinned and done what is evil in Your sight. Cleanse me with hyssop, and I will be clean; wash me, and I will be whiter than snow. Let me hear joy and gladness; let the bones You have crushed rejoice. Hide Your face from my sins and blot out all my iniquity. Create in me a pure heart, O God, and renew a steadfast spirit within me. Do not cast me from Your presence or take Your Holy Spirit from me. Restore to me the joy of Your salvation and grant me a willing spirit, to sustain me."

How did I remember that? God, are You still my Father? Will you truly wash these sins away? Are You willing to blot them out, to cleanse me? My greatest fear is that You will cast me from Your presence. O God, please do not cast me away. Please send me some comfort, some assurance, that I am forgiven. Please have mercy on me, a sinner.

On the second month, the ninth day — I let Atticus meet me in the courtyard of my house this evening. We had a good visit. He was very apologetic for our sin. I was, too. I talked to him for hours about Jesus. I shared with him my heart for him to know Jesus, too. He assures me that is his desire as well. The next time I have courage to go see Jesus, I will try to take Atticus with me. Maybe the second time I see Him. The first time, I will need to be without Atticus. I do not want Jesus to think I am flaunting my sin. I know He knows.

How can He not know? He knows everything. This is why I did not respond this morning to Matthew's message through a young messenger of his. Matthew said Jesus was back in Capernaum. He would be teaching where He fed the thousands. I cannot bring myself to see Him. But when will I be able to again?

On the second month, the eleventh day — Joanna came to my house today. She had been with the other ladies in Capernaum. They heard I had been invited, but did not attend. She was worried about me.

I have never opened up to another woman before. Momma was the first and last. I am so guilt-ridden, I could not suppress my failure any longer. I told her what I had done with Atticus. I also shared with her my past. I gave her details into what I could remember of the demonic possession. Joanna looked at me in silence. Tears rolled down her face. Without saying a word, she took me into her embrace. I laid my head on her shoulder. I soaked her expensive robe with my tears.

After a long time of silence, Joanna said she had something to tell me that she felt would radically change my perspective. She reminded me of our meeting Nicodemus in Jerusalem a while back. She said that she first met Jesus in the Temple courts not long after His encounter with the religious leader Nicodemus. When Jesus was in the Temple courts teaching, Joanna was present in the crowd. They were enthralled by His teaching.

They hardly noticed when some of Nicodemus's peers broke through the crowd, dragging a woman wrapped only in bed covers.

The Pharisees yelled out to Jesus, "Teacher, this woman was caught in the act of adultery. The Law of Moses commands us to stone such women. Now what do you say?" Joanna said she was horrified for the woman.

She knew her. She was married. Her husband was a business partner of Joanna's husband Chuza. She had always thought this woman had flirtatious ways, but never thought it was more than a game with her. At that moment, her sin was apparent to everyone. She lay before them in the covers of her lover who was also married.

The fear Joanna had was this: are we all going to stone my friend? The Law of Moses does say that. Joanna was greatly upset. She also knew the religious leaders were not to be playing favorites. They were not to take money from the Roman authorities. They were not to defile the Sabbath. These religious leaders had done all these forbidden things. She also had heard a few of them had women on the side. That was a rumor that she had not been able to verify. This woman before them was a confirmed adulteress. What would Jesus say? I was hanging on every word. For one reason, that woman could easily have been me.

Joanna said that, at that moment, Jesus bent down and started to write on the ground with His finger. She tried to read what He was writing, but the religious leaders were blocking her view. She heard the Pharisees continuing to agitate, to even goad Him to stone her. Jesus would not. He straightened up and said to them, "If any one of you is without sin, let him be the first to throw a stone at her." Again, He stooped down and wrote on the ground.

Joanna just knew one of them, perhaps many of them, would gladly throw the first one. They could easily defend themselves by saying the Rabbi told them to do so. It would be His word against theirs, after all. They had the high priest's favor. Jesus did not. My friend told me what happened next was shocking. Those religious leaders who heard Him began to walk away one at a time, the older ones first, until only Jesus was left with the woman still standing there.

She said that she and the crowd who were sitting on the Temple steps felt as though they were at some arena. The den of lions had been let onto the floor of the amphitheater with Jesus and Joanna's friend. The lions then left with no food for them to devour. Joanna said, "We all stared in silence. Jesus looked at the woman. He never looked at us, the crowd. It was as if we were no longer present. Jesus was still kneeling down, writing. He straightened up and asked her, Woman, where are they? Has no one condemned you?"

I pictured myself there. Does anyone condemn me? The Law of Moses condemns me. My spirit within condemns me. The teaching of my parents condemns me. The disappointed eyes of Jesus would condemn me. God's Word condemns me. Has no one condemned me? Yes, Lord. Mary from Magdala says, "Yes, Lord."

But this woman wrapped in a bed cover said, "No one, sir." Joanna told me the greatest thing I have heard to this point. She said Jesus looked her right in the eye and declared, "Then neither do I condemn you. Go now and leave your life of sin." Jesus did not condemn her, though He did admit what she did was sin. Jesus told her to leave her life of sin. I almost wish Jesus would have walked into my house two weeks ago. I would have hated Him catching me, but I would accept His words if He would say that He does not condemn me.

I told that to Joanna. She comforted me. She said, "Mary, I firmly believe Jesus does not condemn you. I believe He forgives. Remember the prayer He taught us on the road to Jerusalem? 'Our Father, forgive us of our sins as we forgive those who sin against us.' Mary, He will forgive." Jairus even told me months ago that the wonderful thing about Jesus is He even forgives those who say defaming things to Him.

Joanna then said, "I am staying with you tonight. Tomorrow, we will go together to Capernaum. We will find Jesus. Perhaps we can get a moment with Him. We both need assurance that He will forgive you — and me. I have made many mistakes myself, Mary. I have committed many sins. Yours is recent. Mine are not distant. Let us both go."

I agreed. I must get this load off of me. I need to know either way. My life's direction will hinge on His answer. I thank the Father He sent Joanna to me today. She slept in Poppa's room. I cannot sleep. I am nervous. I am filled with dread. Expectation also fills me. Could I find relief tomorrow? Is forgiveness waiting for me? Or is condemnation? The woman caught in adultery had not prepared a meal for Jesus. She had not stayed at Lazarus' home as His guest with the disciples. She had not heard Him teaching an intimate group of friends. I have had all those privileges. Sadly, my failure seems greater.

On the second month, the twelfth day — I made a nice breakfast for Joanna. We then headed off to Capernaum. We walked side by side until we saw a crowd at the shore of the Galilee. I knew who was there. I began to walk a few paces behind Joanna. She gleefully pushed forward toward Him, not realizing I had stopped at the back of the crowd. At that moment, there was no way she could find me. I wanted to run. I at least considered sliding back to Matthew's home. But I heard Him speak.

The crowd was pressed in. Jesus paused. The disciples had them all sit. I sat immediately. I did not want Him to spot me. He then began to tell a parable. "In a certain town there was a judge who neither feared God nor cared about men. And there was a widow in that town who kept coming to him with the plea, 'Grant me justice against my adversary.' For some time, he refused. But finally he said to himself, 'Even though I do not fear God or care about men, yet because this widow keeps bothering me, I will see that she gets justice, so that she will not eventually wear me out with her coming!'" And the Lord said, "Listen to what the unjust judge says. And will not God bring about justice for His chosen ones, who cry out to Him day and night? Will He keep putting them off? I tell you, He will see they get justice, and quickly. However, when the Son of Man comes, will He find faith on the earth?"

People began to ask questions. I was deep in thought. I am a woman who has been crying out day and night for God to forgive me. I have not let it go. I wake up with the words, "Forgive me, Father, please." I walk amongst our vineyards. I pause. I pray, "Forgive me, please." I kneel when no one is looking. I beg God to please, please, please forgive me. I admit I do not deserve it. I confess I have done wrong, that God would be right to cast me away. But, as David prayed after his adultery and the murder of his consort's husband, I plead for His forgiveness. It is the first thing on my breath in the morning. It is the last thing I pray at night. If a godless judge would hear the cries of a woman just to shut her up, will God not hear my cry and forgive me?

Jesus related another parable that really brought me hope. Many pious religious leaders were present to judge Jesus. They were there to catch Him in false teachings. They wore their flowing robes. They had the chief place on that shore. They were smug. Jesus looked right at them. I could see Him look them each in the eye as they sat beneath Him and to His right. He said, "Two men went up to the Temple to pray, one a Pharisee and the other a tax collector. The Pharisee stood up and prayed about himself: 'God, I thank you that I am not like other men — robbers, evildoers, adulterers — or even like this tax collector. I fast twice a week and give a tenth of all I receive.' But the tax collector stood at a distance. He would not even look up to Heaven, but beat his breast and said, 'God, have mercy on me, a sinner.' I tell you that this man, rather than the other, went home justified before God. For everyone who exalts himself will be humbled, and he who humbles himself will be exalted."

I am that tax collector! I am the tax collector's daughter. Why would He choose this of all vocations, on this particular day? He could have used a Roman soldier as an example. He could have used a zealot from Tiberias. He could have spoken of the woman caught in adultery. That would be fitting. But He said a tax collector. The Pharisee said he was not like other men — robbers (people said tax collectors were robbers; many were), evildoers (they said that was what our tax collector feasts were filled with), and adulterers (that was me — a tax collector and an adulterer). Jesus said that tax collector beat his breast, pleading with God for forgiveness, crying out, "Have mercy on me, a sinner." That has been my literal prayer ever since Atticus and I sinned. I am a sinner. I need God's mercy. I could write, how did He know? But does He not know? I knew He would know my sin. How did He know my prayer?

I am so relieved to write what happened next. It capped off everything for which I was searching. No sooner had Jesus commenced speaking, some men brought to him a paralytic lying on a mat. This was not odd. We have seen many interrupt Jesus' teachings to find healing. It is only when He is speaking, when He has a crowd, that people can have guaranteed access to Him. I have not yet seen Him turn one away. I believe everyone knows this. He does not send anyone away who desires healing.

Jesus looked down at the paralytic man. He said, "Take heart, son; your sins are forgiven." I heard the religious leaders gasp out loud! I was a little shocked myself. The man came for healing. Jesus says, "Your sins are forgiven"? I know this sounds bad, but I do not think those friends brought him for forgiveness. Laying on that mat, I do not think that man's first request was for forgiveness. He wanted healing. What he wanted and what he needed, though, may have been two separate things.

I know He told the guy at the Pool of Bethesda to sin no more. Clearly, Jesus knew he was in his frail condition because of sin. But, even with him, Jesus healed him. Now this man comes paralyzed. Jesus says, "Your sins are forgiven." I think we all wondered, "Would they then carry him out, still paralyzed?" I think the Pharisees would have preferred that.

That was the issue. The gasp on the shore was what captured our attention. The teachers of the law cried out for all of us to hear, "This fellow is blaspheming!" I know why they said that. Only God can forgive sins. I can forgive the fishermen on the shore who raped me. That is a human expectation from God. That does not remit their sins, though. They still have to come before God for what they have done. It is why we sacrifice sheep in Jerusalem, and lambs, goats, bulls, and doves. We have this yearning to placate God. We hope to avoid judgment after we die. God gives us assurance that with the shedding of blood, He forgives. Moses sprinkled the children of Israel with blood for forgiveness. God forgives. How can Jesus?

What I have learned of Jesus: He heals the sick. He gives sight to the blind. He feeds thousands with just a little boy's lunch. He calms the storm. He raises the dead. He knows our sins. He knows our names. He knows where we sit, even when He is nowhere near. I wrote a while back that I love Jesus as I love God. I love God as I love Jesus. I have felt that through Jesus, in obedience to Him, I can love God more. He says He comes down from Heaven. He is of the line of David. Many believe He is the Messiah. The belief exists that He was born of a virgin in fulfillment of an obscure text of the prophet Isaiah. So then, does He have the power of God to forgive sins? Can I know God has forgiven my sins by Jesus saying so?

I remember distinctly how Jesus looked at those gasping religious leaders. He said, "Why do you entertain evil thoughts in your hearts? Which is easier: To say, 'Your sins are forgiven,' or to say, 'Get up and walk'? But so that you may know the Son of Man has authority on earth to forgive sins." Then He said to the paralytic, "Get up, take your mat and go home." And the man got up and walked home. When the crowd and I saw this, we were filled with awe. The people around me began praising God. He had given this authority to this man, Jesus.

Which is easier to say: Your sins are forgiven, or get up and walk? I would say it is really easy to say, "Your sins are forgiven", though few would dare do that. Why is that easier? Who can know this side of Heaven if they really are? Who wants to wait to see if the sins are forgiven? I do not want to wait before I stand before God to see if I have been forgiven or not. I want to know now. I must know now. It is much harder in the fleshly realm to say, "Paralyzed man, get up and walk." That would be verified easily in a matter of seconds. If the man gets up and walks, he has received healing. If he stays on his bed, the man who acted as though he could heal would be viewed as a fake.

Jesus magnificently used His healing to vouch for His power to forgive! He said before God, "So that you can know I can forgive sins on earth, paralyzed man, get up and be healed." The man got up. He walked. He walked with new legs. He walked with his sins forgiven.

Am I forgiven? Joanna found me after Jesus dismissed us. She had a smile as broad as the Sea of Galilee. She asked me, "Do you feel better now?" I do! "Do you feel forgiven now?" I am. I began to reason with her regarding what we had heard as we walked back to Magdala. A woman begging for something night and day can be given that for which she pleads. A tax collector in sin can beg for mercy before God. He walks away forgiven. Can Jesus forgive? He tells the man before our eyes, for the scribes and Pharisees to hear, that He can forgive sins. He does forgive sins. I have done all of that. I have pleaded. I have asked for mercy. God is the God who is willing to forgive. David wrote that God does not punish us as our sins deserve.

Jesus said God has given Him the authority to forgive sins. I just want to hear Him say it to me directly. I suppose everyone in that crowd would like to hear it personally. Perhaps He did tell each of us personally at the same time. His use of the tax collector could not have been a mistake. On my very first visit since my sin, He spoke on forgiveness. I believe He has forgiven me. I told that to Joanna. She reminded me, "Don't forget my friend caught in adultery. Jesus told her that He didn't condemn her. He did say she needed to leave her life of sin." That is what I am trying to do. That is really what I have done. I have left the life of sin, but some sin is still in my life. His daily prayer that He taught us included "forgive us our trespasses" right after "give us our daily bread." We have a daily need for forgiveness.

I have to admit, sex with Atticus was not the first sin I have committed since I started to follow Jesus. It was the first of breaking my purity vow. Every day, I struggle with sin. Sometimes I do not think the best thoughts. Sometimes I still carry a bad attitude about those who were cruel to Poppa. I even bear a little grudge from the past against Simon the Zealot. Jesus knew all these sins, even when I was walking with Him. All this to say, I have left the life of sin. It is no longer my lifestyle. It is no longer what I desire.

I asked Joanna to pray with me. Together, I prayed, "Father, please forgive me of my sins today. Forgive me of my sin with Atticus. Forgive me for my grudge against Simon. Forgive me for my bad thoughts. Please, as David prayed, keep me from the sins I do on purpose. Do not let them rule over me." Joanna prayed something similar for herself. Together we said, "Amen." Now I can sleep. I am clean. Not because of anything I have done, but because of what God has done for me.

In the nineteenth year of the reign of Tiberius Caesar, on the second month, the twentieth day — I attended synagogue today. If ever anyone needed evidence of God's reality, they should go to synagogue or go to hear Jesus speak from God's scriptures. Every time I go, it seems the message is exactly what I need to hear. I would swear the synagogue ruler has Roman spies listening to my conversations. I know he does not. It is God.

Here is the text the synagogue ruler Simeon read today: "Blessed is he whose transgressions are forgiven, whose sins are covered. Blessed is the man whose sin the Lord does not count against him and in whose spirit is no deceit. When I kept silent, my bones wasted away through my groaning all day long. For day and night your hand was heavy upon me; my strength was sapped as in the heat of summer. Selah. Then I acknowledged my sin to you and did not cover up my iniquity. I said, 'I will confess my transgressions to the Lord,' and you forgave the guilt of my sin."

I left synagogue today with the assurance that I am forgiven! I have been washed with hyssop. I am clean. Two lambs were being offered in the Temple this Sabbath morning. Two more in the evening. These are to honor God and to atone for our people's sins. Mine is included. What a relief. I can pray again without any separation from my Father.

On the second month, the twenty-first day — I shared with Atticus what happened yesterday and the day before. He wanted to know if we were alright. I assured him we were. I want him to meet Jesus. I let him know that I want to see Him first. I hope to tell Him about Atticus. I want Jesus to know my intentions. He probably already does.

On the second month, the twenty-fourth day — Salome came to see me midday. She says her sons James and John tell her that Jesus is going toward Judea along the Jordan River to teach. Jesus would like for us to go. I had to clarify. "Us?" She replied, "Absolutely." She said He called our ladies by name. I confirmed, "And my name was included?" Salome chuckled, "Well, yes, Mary. What's wrong with you? You do not think He has forgotten you, do you?" Obviously, Joanna knows how to keep my confidence. I let her know that I would be ready.

I gave our money to Judas soon after we returned from Jerusalem. I asked her if they needed more. Salome did not think they did. I am taking some to be sure. I encouraged her to do the same. She said Zebedee's business has been great. She will have extra to bring also.

Jesus has invited me. He has forgiven me. He is not ashamed to be seen with Mary Magdalene. Father God, I thank you so, so much.

On the second month, the twenty-seventh day — Jesus came to Magdala! He spoke in our neighborhood synagogue! It has never been so packed. Thankfully, I was able to get in along with the disciples and my lady friends. The synagogue had never seen me in this light before. They knew my past. They knew of my ghastly behavior even in this synagogue, on that very bimah that bears the image of the Temple. They have seen the change in me over this year.

But never had they ever considered me a follower, a disciple of some sort to Jesus. I guess at some point, Jairus may have told our synagogue ruler he had seen me with the disciples of Jesus in Capernaum. That was all hearsay until today. Jesus was so gracious. He greeted me like He would His older sister. He was welcoming. He was loving. As I looked in His eyes, I could almost tell that He knew my sin and had forgiven me. It was not a twinkle in His eye. It was just this strong sense that He knew. I had an assurance deep down that He heard my prayers. He has forgiven me. Why else would He let me accompany Him in the synagogue where I am known best? If anything, this would be the place to keep me at a distance. He could, justifiably, have brought me closer to His followers when no one knew my past. But He did not do that. He brought me in with Him in front of the people who would have the most to protest. I could sully His name. Someone said Jesus is a friend of sinners. The Pharisees accost this. Jesus welcomes it. He is not a friend of sin. I think He came to take that away from us.

Jesus spoke. I honestly was unable to focus. All I have written above was what I was thinking. It was almost a private sermon to me, the very act of allowing me to enter with His disciples, to sit on the floor as a group near Him. There was James, John, Salome, Nathanael, Peter, Andrew, James the Less, Mary, his mother, Philip, Susanna, Simon the Zealot, Mary of Magdala, and the rest. I was hearing forgiveness the whole service. I am forgiven. I have been cleansed. I am washed.

When Sabbath was over, Jesus came to my house! He entered my family room. He saw where Poppa died. I showed Jesus and the others the rest of the house. They saw Poppa and Momma's room. They saw my room. Jesus saw the window of my bedroom. His back was to us, but I think He was rubbing His hands along the windowpane that I once crawled out of at night. He turned back. He comforted me with one look.

The ladies from the synagogue had delivered a portion of their Sabbath meal to my house so Jesus could eat. We sat in my family room — Jesus, the disciples, and the ladies. I felt like I was in Lazarus' home. We laughed. We shared. We asked Him questions. He let us know that we were heading to Judea, then to Jerusalem for the Feast of Weeks. He told us that we were all welcome to accompany Him.

This invitation could not have been more personal. I was told by Matthew that at His birth, the angels appeared to nasty old shepherds to let them know a Savior had been born to them. I see Jesus as my Savior. I am not sure how that all fits into God's plan, but I have been saved from my life, my intentions, my sins. He did that. Or God did that through Him.

Shepherds. Matthew said they were not just told of Jesus' birth, they were invited to go see for themselves. Nasty old shepherds from the Bethlehem area remind me of immoral young women from the Magdala area. I was invited to go. I would not hesitate.

One last great note for the day. Atticus dropped by as Jesus was leaving. He met Jesus. Our Rabbi welcomed him with great joy. He was thrilled to meet my friend, Atticus. Jesus did not act uncomfortable around him at all. He asked questions about Atticus. He worked to put him at ease. After He left, Atticus could not get the glow off his face. He said he felt like he had just met the kindest Caesar ever. He spoke of this royal feeling he had in His presence. I had not thought that way before. Atticus said he will be happy to go hear Him the next time He is near, if I am comfortable with that. I assured him I am. Atticus kissed me on the forehead. He left me to be with my friends in the family room.

On the second month, the twenty-eighth day — We are a day into our journey. The ladies and I made a fine meal this evening. I say "and I", but it was really Salome's recipe. We just helped. We sat around a common fire just up the hill from where the Jordan River runs out from the Sea of Galilee. It was wonderful. In the silent moments when conversations paused, I could hear the water rolling over the pebbles. It has some areas of depth. In those areas, no sound can be heard. It moves silently. Then when one walks a bit farther, the water shallows, the stones appear, and the sound returns. With my eyes closed, I can imagine the waters applauding that Jesus is near. The sound of the water rolling over the rocks has the distinct sound of hands clapping in adoration. The trees blew. The leaves rustled. It was as if the leaves were joining in His praise. The smell of the river was a delight — sharp, fresh, cool to my nose. What a peaceful day.

Nathanael walked us to the camp for the ladies. He made sure all were safe. He then made his way back to the Rabbi. I could hear them continuing to talk as they lay down on their mats. Once in a while, I would hear one speak a little louder, enthused, followed by men's laughter. It reminded me a little of my nights in Magdala. After Poppa and Momma would put me to bed, I could hear them visit into the night. They would sometimes laugh and joke. That was home to me. This riverbank is home to me, too. All because Jesus is near. He makes me lie down in green pastures. He leads me beside the still waters. He restores my soul. I am restored tonight.

On the third month, the first day — We were making our way down the Jordan River. At first, we saw a couple of young boys fishing. Jesus walked up to them. He greeted them. You would think they had found their long-lost uncle. It was not an hour later that they returned with crowds from the area villages in tow.

Jesus smiled. He welcomed them as always. We moved back so the people could draw near. He spoke for a few hours. They sat mesmerized on the bank of the river. Jesus had such a compassion on them. They invited Him to stay in the area for a while. They had heard so much about Him. They wanted their friends and family to have the same experience they had along the Galilee. Jesus agreed. He sent James and John to find a place to stay in that village not two miles from where we were. The people left, excited.

Jesus rested. We all milled around the river, waiting on James and John to lead us to the village. An hour or so later, James and John came back down to the riverbank to where Jesus was. I saw their look. I had not seen this look since the tax booth days. They had that uncontrollable angry look in their eyes. They said that when the people in that Samaritan village heard we were on our way to Jerusalem for the Feast of Weeks, they refused on no uncertain terms. They said Jesus was not welcome, nor were any of His disciples. Further, they demanded James and John leave immediately. They threatened their lives if they ever set foot in their city limits again.

I had heard the Samaritans hate the Jews. I know the Jews hate the Samaritans. Because I am half-Jewish, I never had any animosity toward them. They both hate tax collectors. When you are the most hated of sorts, you must do what you can to get along with everyone as best you can. John and James hated Poppa and me once upon a time. I guess they have never felt the hatred thrown back at them. I could tell that by how these two responded.

They rolled up their fists. John threw the excess of his robe over his shoulder, as if ready to fight. They asked Jesus, "Lord, do you want us to call fire down from Heaven to destroy them?"

James and John call fire down from Heaven? I knew Jesus had sent them out to work miracles, to preach the Good News, to cast out demons. Their words made me wonder, had they ever called fire down from Heaven, or was this a belief they could do such a thing if Jesus approved?

When Elijah prayed, fire fell down from Heaven, consuming His enemies. God does not change. I was frightened. I had never seen Jesus act in anger. I know He would be justified, but He had been rejected before. He never called fire down on those in Nazareth. He did not call fire down on the Pharisees. Was this the moment that we would see His wrath?

No, not at all! Jesus responded in a rebuke to both James and John. He said, "No servant is greater than his master. If they persecuted Me, they will persecute you also. If they obeyed My teaching, they will obey yours also. They will treat you this way because of My name, for they do not know the One who sent Me. If I had not come and spoken to them, they would not be guilty of sin. Now, however, they have no excuse for their sin. He who hates Me hates my Father as well. If I had not done among them what no one else did, they would not be guilty of sin. But now they have seen these miracles, and yet they have hated both Me and My Father. But this is to fulfill what is written in their Law: 'They hated Me without reason.'"

Jesus then led us to another village. There we found welcome for the night.

On the third month, the second day — Jesus found this entire village waiting at His door this morning. We were scattered throughout their community. When we awoke, the ladies and I headed to the house where Jesus was staying. We could not get to Him for the crowd. Jesus slid through the crowd to the town gate. There, He began to teach. The crowd sat in front of Him, behind Him, up on the town wall above. Some stood up on their mules. Wives sat on the shoulders of their standing husbands. He taught them about the Kingdom of Heaven. He told them the Father had sent Him to draw them to the Father. He shared all the things He had done. Many came with their sick. He healed them. Some had arguments. They brought them before Him. He was like Solomon in all His wisdom. He put everything in perspective. In the grand scheme of Heaven, nearly every argument was petty.

As He finished, the crowds began to head back to their daily lives. A few stayed around with us. It seemed they had the same desire I had. A man walked up to the Rabbi. He said, "I will follow You wherever You go." Jesus let him know the cost. "Foxes have holes and birds of the air have nests, but the Son of Man has no place to lay His head." With that, the man went away. We had not minded sleeping on the ground. Jesus had little or no money. All He had, God had given others to share with Him.

Another man walked up. This time, he did not ask Jesus to come after Him. Jesus invited him, just like He had invited Matthew. Jesus said to him, a Samaritan, "Follow me." I was thrilled. James and John did not seem as enthused. The man said to Jesus, "Lord, first let me go and bury my father." My first thought was, are we going to have to wait until this man buries his dad? Before that question was answered, Jesus said to him, "Let the dead bury their own dead, but you go and proclaim the Kingdom of God." The man walked away sad, James and John relieved.

Another came in his place. He said, "I will follow you, Lord, but first let me go back and say goodbye to my family." Jesus replied, "No one who puts his hand to the plow and looks back is fit for service in the Kingdom of God." Many say they want to follow Jesus, but the cares of this world snuff them out. It was like what Jesus shared at the Galilee about the farmer planting seed. I cannot boast in me, but I will admit, I want to follow Jesus so badly, I left everything in Linus's care. I feel I would have gone with Jesus at His word. I have waited so long for His word. Poppa said he would have followed if Jesus would have asked him.

Then again, when Poppa was sick, lying on the floor, dying, I do not think I would have followed Jesus then, either. I pray I would have. I think Poppa would have encouraged me to. I am convicted. I cannot judge these who walked away. I am elated that I did go with Him when the time came. Looking back, if I knew what I know now, I would have left Poppa's side. May I always keep Jesus first in all my decisions.

On the third month, the fourth day — The Rabbi is taking His time as we travel. He seems pensive on this journey. He left us last night to go and pray. We have kept camp south of Scythopolis, which was once called Beth-Shean. We wait for Jesus to return to us. Today is the Sabbath. I know He cannot be far from us.

While He was up in the hills praying, we had a good time of sharing. The ladies and I made a scarce meal for the disciples. We set back a plate for Jesus. We are running low on supplies. After we ate, Thomas began to talk about all we had seen. He said that never in his life had he dreamt of seeing masses follow, people healed, or the dead raised. Peter spoke about how he had never grasped the prevalence of evil until he heard the demons speaking. He related back to an event on the other side of the Decapolis where they met a man who was out of his mind, possessed by a legion of demons. Having seen the Roman army many times in Magdala, I knew a legion was somewhere between two thousand and six thousand men. I had seven demons in me.

They wrecked my life. How a man could house two thousand to six thousand, I will never understand.

Peter said Jesus demanded the demons leave. What made the hair stand on the back of his neck was to hear the demons begging Jesus all at once not to throw them into the abyss. Silence ensued. This oldest of the disciples, the one who seemed to have no fear in his body, said it was the most scared he had ever been in his life. He said Jesus allowed the demons to enter some pigs on that hillside. They immediately ran off the cliff and drowned in the Sea of Galilee. Andrew said he will never forget looking down at all those pigs floating in the water — probably two thousand or more, the whole herd of pigs.

Andrew said he looked back at the man from whom the demons came. His once distorted face was fair and pleasant. Peter said, "He could have easily been one of us. All he lacked were clothes. We quickly took our extras and clothed him." He sat there with us and Jesus. He posed questions to Jesus, which He answered. We asked him questions about his life. He answered them. Here was an ordinary man from a local village who had been possessed through his play with the false gods of this world. Thaddeus chimed in, "He asked to join us as a disciple. He even tried to get in the boat with us to head back to Capernaum. With all the men who said they wanted to follow Jesus, then gave excuses as to why they could not, this man was ready in a split second to go."

Peter jumped back in, "Yes, but Jesus showed us what a real disciple is to be in that man. He told him, 'Return home and tell how much God has done for you.'" I was so convicted at Peter's words. I am to do the same. I am to tell people in Magdala how much God has done for me. Peter was right. Nathanael closed that chapter by reminding them how many showed up at that shore the next time they made the trip. He said people from all over Decapolis came out to meet Jesus when they anchored. In the middle of them all was this man the Lord had healed, smiling ear to ear. He had done his job as a follower of Jesus.

The men and women of our group all shared what Jesus had done for each of us. I told of the cistern and my self-harming acts. Matthew told of his emptiness in his tax booth. John spoke of how he had tried to get into rabbinic school, but was not accepted. James shared how he had felt life was passing him by out on the sea, day after day, trying to catch fish. Philip shared about how his family, his wife and his daughters, were in such disarray. Arguing was always present. There was always this selfish bent. He did not think they would make it as a family. He wondered how long his wife would stay with him. He would be ugly to her and say sharp words to his daughters. He would then storm out of his house. He was just filled with anger. No sooner would he get away from the house, he would chastise himself for what he had done. He wanted to stop, but somehow he just could not. I knew that feeling.

Nathanael talked about his love for God. He had wanted to be a priest, but was born to the wrong family. He would hear rabbis speak about God's Word. So many of them seemed insincere. It seemed they preached sermons that glorified themselves, not God. He would look at the lives of the people of his synagogue. They were faithful, but they were living just like everyone else. He felt such an emptiness. He longed for Messiah to come to set everything right. Then Philip came for him.

Andrew shared about his personal hunger. He was one of the first to leave the fishing business to join up with John the Baptizer. He could not leave his side. He hung on every word John spoke. John's words were full of substance. He was not profiting from his ministry. John did nothing for himself. He wore the most rag-tag clothes, Andrew said. He ate a sparse diet. He had no close friends, but he had many disciples. He seldom opened up about his own feelings. He spoke God's Word without wavering. He dealt with what was to come. Truly, he wore the prophet's mantel. The religious leaders hated him. Andrew said he believed it was those leaders who told John the Baptizer of Herod Agrippa's affair, coaxing him to speak out against it. He felt they then instigated Herod's reprisal, whispering in the king's ear.

What Andrew shared next was something I had never heard. What am I writing? So much of what I record I had never heard before. It is all too wonderful not to note. Andrew said he was at the River Jordan about five miles north of the Dead Sea. John had been preaching repentance of sins, which was the focal point of all his messages. Jesus says the same. We cannot be right with God while holding on to sin.

Anyway, Andrew said John changed his message that day. He began to downplay his own ministry. After speaking a while, he said John stepped into the river. He waded out to a depth waist high. He then proclaimed he baptized with water, but that One would come after him who would baptize with the Holy Spirit and fire. The Baptizer said this One would be more powerful than he. He said he was not even worthy to carry this One's sandals. The crowd all questioned how there could be anyone greater than this prophet, John.

No sooner did John the Baptizer say that then Andrew saw Jesus for the first time. Jesus walked into the water. He waited in line behind many others to be baptized. Andrew was the second to be baptized. Afterward, he moved out of the way to watch others give their lives to God in repentance. He said as this Galilean walked up, John said to Him, "I need to be baptized by You, and You come to me?" Andrew was taken aback. Here was the man speaking of how all need to repent and be baptized. Then, all of a sudden, John was confessing that he needed to be baptized. Everyone who had been baptized and those waiting to be were confused.

The Galilean man said to John, "Let it be so now. It is proper for us to do this to fulfill all righteousness." Then John consented. It was not long after that, Andrew said that he went from John to meet this Galilean. His name was Jesus. Andrew stated he has been following Jesus ever since.

I did not realize Andrew was the one who told Peter. I believe Andrew was also the one who told John, James, and Philip. Andrew had done exactly what the demon-freed man had done in the Decapolis. Again, I am convicted. I need to tell the people of Magdala. They have seen me with Jesus. They have heard Him for themselves along the Galilee, and personally in the neighborhood synagogue. How many can I bring to Jesus?

Andrew interrupted my thoughts. He said what made him seek out Jesus was not John's words. It was God's words. That had my attention. He said the moment John brought Jesus out of the water, Heaven opened up, and he saw the Spirit of God descending like a dove and lighting on Him. He heard God's voice from Heaven say, "This is My Son, whom I love; with Him I am well-pleased." It was the first supernatural event Andrew had ever experienced. It was God's voice that prompted him to leave John the Baptizer and go to Jesus. It turned out to be the message of John all along.

Andrew's account made our visit divine. The rest shared their lives' encounters with Jesus. Joanna shared of hearing Him for the first time in Jerusalem. James the Less spoke of how he had always needed someone to follow. He had tried many, but each failed. He then met Jesus. He testified he watched constantly for Jesus to fail him, too. Now, he no longer looks for that. He is convinced Jesus will never fail. Salome spoke about how it was the change in her sons that caused her to follow Jesus. Now she follows Him for herself. Mary, the mother of James the Less, voiced the same. The two who were strangely quiet this day were Susanna and Judas. I expect Susanna to be quiet. That is her nature. But Judas? What is his story? Surely, he has one. I cannot judge him, though. He seldom ever speaks. That may be his nature.

On the third month, the fifth day — Jesus returned sometime last night. We went to bed in our respective camps. Jesus was not present when Nathanael and Simon the Zealot got us settled for the night. This morning, He was at the fire with the men. He was cooking fresh trout from the river for all of us. He is everything we spoke of yesterday, and more.

He then led us outside the village of Sychar to the actual well our forefather Jacob had dug. The water was pure and cold. I had not thought of being in touch with our Jewish history much until today. Since meeting Jesus, I have been focused on the now and the yet-to-come. Jesus does not forget the past. So much of what He teaches ties the present with the past. After we drank, He sent us into the village of Sychar to purchase food for the days ahead. He said He would stay by the well until we returned. We gladly went together.

Yesterday's testimonies brought the seventeen of us closer together.

The town of Sychar is a thriving, well-populated place. The people are open and honest. The market was well-stocked with meat, vegetables, fruit, and olive oil, along with spices and utensils. It was more of a farmers' market as opposed to the fishers' market in Magdala. The one difference is that we have access to more of the world because of the trade that goes on in my home village. We especially were pleased with the dates, olives, fresh bread, and quail. The men left us to ourselves. They milled around the market, observing the people more than anything. We had lunch together there. After a few hours, we headed back to the Rabbi with some food for Him.

We were glad to see Him still at the well. What surprised us was that He was there speaking with a woman. We seldom ever see Jesus alone with a woman. If He is, it is always in open places. The minute we walked up, she said to us, "This man told me everything I ever did!" She left her water jar with us and ran back toward Sychar.

Peter urged Him to eat, but He said He was not hungry. The other disciples urged Him to eat something. He said, "I have food to eat that you know nothing about. My food is to do the will of Him who sent Me and to finish His work. Do you not say, 'Four months more and then the harvest'? I tell you, open your eyes and look at the fields! They are ripe for harvest. Even now the reaper draws his wages, even now he harvests the crop for eternal life, so that the sower and the reaper may be glad together. Thus the saying 'one sows and another reaps' is true. I sent you to reap that for which you have not worked. Others have done the hard work, and you have reaped the benefits of their labor."

I could not help but think of the man in the Decapolis who stayed behind to tell his friends about Jesus. He was harvesting for God. We are being trained (at least, the twelve disciples are) to lead people to eternal life. Jesus says He gives eternal life. We have seen Him give life. Why can He not also make it last forever? The disciples were able to visit with Him, asking questions to understand better. At first, we thought the woman had given Him food. Then we understood we should be content — that serving God, leading people to Him, is the greatest nourishment of all.

That was surely displayed about an hour later. The woman we saw at the well returned with her whole village. We recognized many of them from the market. The very lady we purchased the bread from came and stood by me. The woman who brought all these people walked up to Jesus. She said, "This man, a Jew, asked me, a Samaritan, to give Him something to drink. He is the first Jewish man to ever speak to me. I wanted to know what He believed. Obviously, He is not a typical Jewish man. He looked at the well of Jacob. He said if we drink from this, we will be thirsty again later, but He said He can give me something to drink, and I will never thirst again. That sounded so good. I get tired of coming out here every day. I asked Him to give me some of that water. He asked me to bring my husband out here and He would. I told Him that I had no husband. All of you know I am not married to the man in whose house I stay. Here is a man I have never met before. Yet, He knew I had no husband. He knew I was living with a man who is not my husband. He also knew I had been married five times before. I was extremely uncomfortable that He knew that. It was as if He was judging me, but He was right. Guilt overwhelmed me. I needed to know what He believed. I began to speak of the difference between what we believe as Samaritans and what He believes as a Jew. He was not arrogant, nor was He condescending. He gently told me we worship with a lack of knowledge. He said that He and the Jews worship with knowledge of the truth. But He said that those who truly seek God will be brought together — Jew, Samaritan, and Gentile — to worship in spirit and in truth. He stated God wants those kinds of worshipers. I wondered how He knows what God wants? So, I asked Him about the Messiah. We look for the Messiah. The Jews look for the Messiah. I believe the Messiah would make it all clear. That is when this man — His name is Jesus — said to me, 'I who speak to you am He.' He says He is the Messiah, the One for whom we have been waiting. I believe He is exactly who He says He is, but I want you to ask Him questions. Please make sure I am not wrong."

I was overwhelmed. Here was a woman like me in so many ways. She has had five husbands and a live-in. I have been with many men myself. The question that came to my mind was, do I believe Jesus is truly the Messiah? I truly do, now more than ever.

The people of that village invited us back to Sychar to stay. Jesus led us back with them. Many of their leaders, civic and religious, grilled Him with questions, asking things we had asked. They also asked questions we had never thought of asking. All this time, the Jewish people had looked down on the Samaritans. For the first time for many of us, we actually got to know them without bias. Judas especially seemed surprised. I think he had the greatest prejudice toward these Samaritans. I was a little bothered that Peter shared that sentiment.

The townspeople opened their homes to us. Susanna and I are staying at the home of the bread-maker. The other ladies are staying at the city clerk's house at the request of his wife. Jesus is staying with a kind man. I think he is the father of the woman He met at the well. The disciples are dispersed amongst five homes. What a day we have had!

On the third month, the seventh day — We left Sychar this morning. We were blessed to leave with even more supplies than we had purchased with money. We had offered to use our supplies to make them food, but they refused. Jesus made a huge impact on this village. Many of them became believers. Their words caused all of our party truly to see Jesus for who He is. We heard them say to the woman from the well, "We no longer believe just because of what you said. Now we have heard for ourselves, and we know that this man really is the Savior of the world."

The Savior of the world? What does that mean? He forgives sins. He raises the dead. He has eternal life. For all these centuries, our forefathers thought the Messiah would throw off the yoke of the Romans, or whatever oppressing nation preceded them. We looked for a king like David or like Solomon who would bring us independence, who would set us up as a nation under our own rule. Now, we are seeing that Jesus is the Messiah, but His task goes far beyond the Jewish people's national sovereignty. He has come to cover our sins. He has come to fulfill all righteousness, which is what He displayed with John the Baptizer. He has come to undo what sin has brought. That includes giving eternal life. Jesus is the Savior of the world. He is my Lord. He is my Savior. I want to kneel before Him and tell Him that. I am just not sure if that is something I should do outwardly, though I will do so inwardly right now.

I pray to the Father in Heaven. I call Him "Father" because Jesus taught us we could do that. If Jesus is the Savior of the world, the Son of God, does that mean I can pray to Him, too? I am not comfortable asking that of anyone. I pray the Father shows me what I should do, or that Jesus Himself tells us. Either way, I am seeing God's eternal plan being played out before my eyes, before Mary, the once immoral woman from Magdala. Who would ever have thought I would have a seat on the front row to see what our prophets foretold?

On the third month, the eighth day — We are continuing our journey following the Jordan River. None of us had much to say. We have seen great miracles. We grappled with those. Now the truth of Jesus has come face to face with us. I am not sure any of us have words to describe what we feel.

Jesus circled back this evening about Samaritans when an expert in the law caught up with us as we were making camp. He asked Jesus what he needed to do to inherit eternal life. Jesus asked him, "What is written in the Law? How do you read it?" The man answered, "You should love the Lord your God with all your heart, with all your soul, with all your strength, and with all your mind. And that you should love your neighbor as yourself." Jesus told him he had answered correctly. He then told this expert of the law that if he does this, he will live.

This expert then asked Jesus the question, "And who is my neighbor?" I felt he was trying to qualify who he had to love. It is like so many of us — we can love others as long as we can put limits on who the others are.

Jesus told him (and us), "A man was going down from Jerusalem to Jericho when he fell into the hands of robbers. They stripped him of his clothes, beat him, and went away, leaving him half dead. A priest happened to be going down the same road, and when he saw the man, he passed by on the other side. So, too, a Levite, when he came to the place and saw him, passed by on the other side. But a Samaritan, as he traveled, came where the man was, and when he saw him, he took pity on him. He went to him and bandaged his wounds, pouring on oil and wine. Then he put the man on his own donkey, took him to an inn, and took care of him. The next day he took out two silver coins and gave them to the innkeeper. 'Look after him,' he said, 'and when I return, I will reimburse you for any extra expense you may have.' Which of these three do you think was a neighbor to the man who fell into the hands of robbers?"

The expert in the law replied, "The one who had mercy on him." Jesus told him, "Go and do likewise." I wonder how hard it was for that scribe to answer in that way. He is the kind of man who hates Samaritans. Jesus probably knew this was his problem. We have been with the Samaritans. We have seen they hurt like we do. They thirst as we do. They were looking for the answer to life just like we were. They can love as we can love. We saw them feed us, house us, and give us oil and wine. They even sent us with supplies for our journey. God made us all. Jesus makes no delineation between Jew, Samaritan, Gentile, heathen, or possessed person. He loves. He is calling us all to God.

On the third month, the tenth day — The news has spread. We are just east of Ephraim (according to Matthew), still following the Jordan River. The crowds are overwhelming. It reminds me of our days in Capernaum. Jesus has been speaking. He has been healing all kinds of diseases. So many we have never seen before. I saw a man who had a huge bulge coming from his left hip and his left knee. He could barely walk. Some friend was helping him reach Jesus. In just an instant after the Lord (my Lord now) prayed, the man was jumping, running — no bulges anywhere. All the people celebrated, emboldening even more to come forward.

I have to say, these are real diseases being healed. Yes, Jesus heals the mind. Yes, He mends broken relationships. Yes, He can take care of headaches, but these are harder to see in the moment. Jesus is taking those and the ones more observable. The healing is clear to anyone with vision, and He is giving vision to those who are blind.

The people come to Jesus by this river. They are dressed in an assortment of ways. As a woman, I will admit many women are coming very scantily dressed. They may be prostitutes, or they may be loose women trying to lure a man with money. They come very inappropriately, but they come. They hear. They cover their bodies as soon as they are moved by the words of Jesus. I have seen many women come barely clad who quickly cover themselves with the modesty of a matriarch. What our Savior (my Savior, too) is doing is awesome.

The disciples are entering the river just like John the Baptizer did. Jesus is openly declaring He is the Messiah, the Savior of the world. He is offering eternal life. He is offering bread from Heaven. He is the Bread. He is asking them to receive, to follow Him as He follows the Father. Those who accept Jesus as their Savior are being baptized in the River Jordan. All twelve disciples are baptizing. I know John baptized alone, from what I hear. He had masses. The masses Jesus is drawing requires twelve Johns to baptize. One would never get it done. People are repenting. They are wanting to be made clean. In the flurry of the moment, Jesus has touched me right to the heart. I feel the need to openly receive Him, too. I am laying down my parchments.

I rose from where the ladies and I were sitting. I walked right into the water at Jesus' bidding. I waited in line for the first available disciple. It was Thaddeus. He looked at me, a little surprised. He then saw my tears. He did not question me. He did not hesitate. He raised his hand toward Heaven. He looked toward Jesus who looked back at me and Thaddeus with the most approving expression. Thaddeus baptized me. I was elated. This was no mikvah baptism in Jerusalem. This was no ritual. It was real. I was letting the crowd, the disciples, the ladies, and Jesus especially, know that I have made my decision about Him.

No sooner did I get baptized, I saw Susanna run into the water. Salome grabbed Mary, the mother of James the Less, and entered. Finally, I saw Joanna. Her head was bowed on the bank. She was sobbing profusely. She then laid aside her expensive stola. She entered the water in her beautiful flowing dress. She reached her hand out to Philip, who raised his hand toward Heaven and baptized her, too. It was the most amazing movement of God's Spirit in our midst. Before long, I saw the disciples taking turns baptizing each other. They had made their decisions, too, or maybe it was a rededication. We were one.

Afterward, we all sat on the shore together. We were gleaming. We were excited. We saw a man walk up to Jesus. He had the clothing and the fanfare of a ruler with great authority. That surprised us when we saw his face. He was a young man. I am not sure how a man of his age had accumulated such prestige. He looked confident as he approached Jesus. But, if he really were so confident, why is he approaching Jesus? He was the kind of man who exudes weight. Everyone listened intently. Was this man there to accost Jesus? Was he there to reprimand Him? Was he there to pass on some commendation? Or was he just like us — a man with a void that needed to be filled?

It turned out, he was a man with a deep-seeded question. He fell to his knees before Jesus. Finally, someone fell before Him the way I want to. He asked Jesus, "Good Teacher, what must I do to inherit eternal life?" Jesus responded, "Why do you call Me good? No one is good — except God alone. You know the commandments: 'Do not murder, do not commit adultery, do not steal, do not give false testimony, do not defraud, and honor your father and mother.'"

Still on his knees, the man said to the Lord, "Teacher, all these I have kept since I was a boy." I wish I could have said, "Teacher, all these things I have kept since I was a girl." That was not true for me. No wonder this young man has reached such high position. Jesus looked at him with love. I was moved by that look of Jesus upon a man He just met. Jesus kindly said, "One thing you lack. Go, sell everything you have and give to the poor, and you will have treasure in heaven. Then come, follow Me." Jesus was asking this young man to join us. In the split second before his answer, I thought how wonderful to have a young man like that with us. I have many questions I want to ask him. What an invitation Jesus just gave him! Just leave it all. We have done that in a sense. I left my businesses. I left my home. I left Atticus, whom I pray I will soon marry.

The man's response was not what I expected. Then again, many had been invited. Most gave excuses as to why they could not at the moment. This young man dropped his head. He broke eye contact with Jesus. He said not another word. He gave no excuses. He just walked away. Why? He had all the answers. He had been obedient since his youth. He had achieved great accomplishments. He had wealth and power that surpassed that of Matthew. He walked away, sad. Jesus did not say, "You can't follow Me." He did not say to this man what He said to the demon-freed man at Decapolis: "Go tell your friends what God has done for you." Yet, this man walked away. The man gave no excuse about burying a father or saying goodbye to his family. He just left.

We all looked back at Jesus, who looked equally saddened. He said, "Children, how hard it is for the rich to enter the Kingdom of God! It is easier for a camel to go through the eye of a needle than for a rich man to enter the Kingdom of God." Then it was clear. This man would not sell all he had. Jesus said if he did, he would have treasure in Heaven. What if Jesus told me to sell all I have, give to the poor, and follow Him? I have already been following Him. I have used my money to give to the poor and to His ministry. I can gladly look the Lord in the eye and respond, "Lord, say the word, I will do what You told that young man. I will sell all I have. I will give it to the poor. I want to be with You. You are all I want. I will leave Magdala behind, my vineyards, our buildings, even Atticus. Jesus, say the word, and I will."

I thought that. Peter admitted he and the disciples had done just that. "We have left everything to follow You!" In my mind, the ladies and myself were included in his statement. We had been journeying together for a good while now. What Jesus said next filled me with joy.

As He looked around at our seventeen, Jesus said to Peter, "I tell you the truth, no one who has left home or brothers or sisters or mother or father or children or fields for Me and the Gospel will fail to receive a hundred times as much in this present age (homes, brothers, sisters, mothers, children, fields, and with them, persecutions) and, in the age to come, eternal life. But many who are first will be last, and the last, first."

What a blessing! The Lord told us that whatever we have lost for Him and the Father will be repaid a hundred times over in this life and in the one to come — Heaven. Heaven is where I want to be. I had never thought of building our wealth in Heaven before. Jesus continued in this thought. "Do not be afraid, little flock, for your Father has been pleased to give you the Kingdom. Sell your possessions and give to the poor. Provide purses for yourselves that will not wear out, a treasure in Heaven that will not be exhausted, where no thief comes near and no moth destroys. For where your treasure is, there your heart will be also."

How could anyone walk away from what the Rabbi is offering? Every moment we spend with Jesus, we are laying up treasures in Heaven. Every sinful inclination we reject, we are laying up riches for ourselves that will last forever. Every person we tell about Him is filling purses for ourselves to use in the Father's presence. Jesus has come from the Father. He is telling us what things are like in the land from which He comes. It is the land to which He is returning. He says He will take us there with Him. Not just us, though; all who come to God through Him.

On the third month, the fourteenth day — The crowds have overwhelmed us. We entered Jerusalem today. We got to the crest of the Mount of Olives. Jesus paused, as was His custom. We all saw Jerusalem spread out before us. This is a beautiful time of year. People come from all around to thank God for this year's harvest. It is a time of thanksgiving.

This pilgrimage feast is called the Feast of Harvest. I believe those who have followed us are part of the harvest. Jesus had called upon us to open our eyes to see the fields are ripe unto harvest. He is harvesting people for eternal life. We have seen people repent. We have seen people baptized. We have seen people accept that He is the Savior of the world. I wonder how many who have followed us into Jerusalem today had no inclination to worship God just a few weeks ago? But after meeting Jesus, after hearing Him, after seeing His miracles, now they are wanting to worship God. Now, God has consumed their thoughts. Jesus is bringing to God masses of people today. All of these are part of the harvest. How appropriate that at the Feast of Harvest, I can grasp this. Most of whom we have seen reaped have been in the last few days. It truly is a time to give God thanks. It is amazing what God can do with His Son. God is in Heaven. Jesus is on earth.

Together, they are working in perfect harmony.

Down below, I am sure we will see more come to Him. Below this mount, we will also meet the jealous, religious elite. I am confident He can handle whatever comes. Jesus entered the Temple. He was exceedingly upset to see the irreverence given to this holy place. At some point in the past, Joanna told me He had driven out all the buyers and sellers. She said not nearly as many were here today as the day Jesus drove them out.

I thought of that. How is Jesus able to decide who can be in the Temple of God over the priests? Joanna expressed the same question. She said Jesus invokes a fear in the high priest that Pilate cannot match. The majority hate Him because of the way they seem forced to comply to His wishes in their area of supervision. I saw a few moneychangers quickly close up shop when they saw us enter. The merchants of the doves silently moved their cages outside the Gentile courts without another glance in our direction.

Jesus called us to pray in the Temple. He reminded us of what Solomon prayed at the dedication of the first Temple. Solomon said, in part, "May Your eyes be open toward this Temple night and day, this place of which You said, 'My Name shall be there,' so that You will hear the prayer Your servant prays toward this place. Hear the supplication of Your servant and of Your people Israel when they pray toward this place. Hear from Heaven, Your dwelling place, and when You hear, forgive."

Suddenly, I saw a connection between God and this Temple. I had never thought as much of praying to God here. I thought of making our payments for sins here. I thought of showing our religiosity here. I thought of ritualistic gathering here. But it never occurred to me to make this a place to actually pray to God, realizing He is near, sitting within the Holy of Holies in person. Here was Jesus, God's Son, kneeling outside with us, ushering us before the Father inside. I cannot help but think, in our flesh, this was as close as we could ever get to God this side of Heaven. I felt if I could live through the experience, I could walk through the women's court, past the Jewish men's court, walk up the steps to the Holy Place, past the Veil of the Holy of Holies, and I could see God's brilliance in glory before me. His brightness would blind me. I would be no more able to see His face as I can make out the shape of the sun for its blinding brightness. Brighter still would be the Father.

He is there right now, even as I write this from Joanna's home. I am blocks away from where God dwells. I have sat at the campsite within feet of His Son. Jesus alone can see Him with the naked eye. Jesus has seen Him from the beginning. Jesus saw Him as He left Heaven's throne. Jesus talks to Him wherever we are. God spoke in an audible voice for all to hear Him acknowledge His Son when

Jesus was baptized. Andrew heard Him with his own ears. Heaven has come down to earth.

On the third month, the sixteenth day — Joanna brought a special guest to meet with us today. Sitting in her grand home was Susanna, Mary, the mother of James the Less, Salome, and myself. Who walked in but Jesus' mother, Mary. She was guarded as she entered. She walked with a cautious defense.

I cannot imagine how many attacks she has faced because of Jesus. If the crowds come from everywhere to where He is, or where they think He is going, how many crowds have waited outside her home in Nazareth? I wonder how many people have sought her prayers for healing, assuming that if she is the mother of One of such power, she must contain some herself. People may believe that if she could give birth to One such as Jesus, then she must be worthy of attribution. I do not doubt people even bow before her, pray to her.

Do they not see? Mary is not comfortable with Jesus. It was not too long ago that she and her sons tried to accost Jesus as one out of his mind. I wonder how much trouble she faced when her hometown tried to throw Jesus from the cliff of their town. I would assume some praise her, while others curse her. I am curious how often the religious leaders have shown up at her synagogue to confront her, to demand she get control of her son before something bad happens to Him.

I could understand her shyness. She easily could have assumed Joanna was setting her up. But for some reason, she came anyway. We chose to put her at ease. I knew it would be hard for her to believe us, but if we each shared what her son has meant to us, maybe she would understand that we mean her no harm.

Joanna opened our conversation to let Mary, the mother of Jesus, know we are here to be a support for her. Joanna has the political clout to give some protection. The guards posted outside should give credibility to that. One by one, we shared what Jesus had done for us. We shared how we had been with Him for many days and nights. We talked about the miracles we had seen. We gave Him praise for the changed lives. We shared about how we had all been baptized. I am sure she had heard these things before. Surely, by now, she must have some change in her attitude toward her son.

Giving her the option not to answer, I asked her, "Was He anything like this when He was growing up under your roof?" Mary hesitated. She then spoke about how He was like any normal boy. He needed chores. He went to synagogue. He learned with the other boys. He helped his father in the carpentry shop. He was loving to his four brothers and two sisters when they were born. As the oldest, He was great help.

Mary said His goodness was most evident when her husband Joseph passed. According to Jewish custom, the responsibility of the oldest son is to provide for the family if a father passed prematurely. She said Jesus did that. He worked the carpentry shop. He provided for His mom and siblings. He stayed in Nazareth the whole time until His brothers and sisters married. He helped raise His little brothers. He taught them the trade. He loved on them. He nurtured them. He corrected them. He was their role model for what God had instructed the children of Israel. He rousted them out of bed every Sabbath. He made sure they accompanied the family to synagogue. He set the example. He never ever missed one day at synagogue. He made sure they did not, either. What a testimony. He has not changed.

Susanna spoke up, which is rare for her. She asked Mary if Jesus had ever worked any miracles as a boy. Mary did not answer immediately. Susanna clarified. "Was there ever any evidence that He was capable of doing things other men were unable to do?" Mary told of a few instances when He provided something out of almost nothing. She always thought He was simply more resourceful than others.

Salome, with insight from her sons, asked Mary, "Can you tell us about the wedding in Cana? It is my understanding from James and John, my sons, that you had your son do something to help out at a wedding." Mary lit up, but still cautious. She said she had been invited to a wedding of a family friend. Jesus was invited, as were a few of His earliest disciples. She said she thought James and John were two who were there. She said it was embarrassing — this young couple had run out of wine for the wedding. They did not have much money, yet more showed up than they had expected. Mary said she knew Jesus was resourceful, so she asked Him to do something. She said He voiced a reluctance, but at her word, He ordered that the six stone jars of water being used for ceremonial washing be filled with water. Obviously, they had been emptied from all who came to the event. Jesus then told the attendants to draw some out and give to the master of the banquet for his approval. When they took it to the master of the banquet, he called the bridegroom to himself. Mary said she heard what he said. He complimented the groom, saying, "Everyone brings out the choice wine first and then the cheaper wine after the guests have had too much to drink, but you have saved the best till now."

She said, "My son, Jesus, did what I asked. He did more than I asked. He did not rely on connections. He did not call up old favors. He miraculously turned water into the finest aged wine they and I had ever tasted. I looked at Him with great surprise."

I asked her to tell us about when He was twelve, when He was separated from them in Jerusalem. Mary again smiled. "My son told you about that? That is interesting. His father and I went back for Him. We were worried sick. We looked everywhere. When we entered the Temple, there He was in the Temple courts surrounded by our teachers of the Law. He was asking them questions. They were answering. That was not a shock. What amazed us was that they asked Him questions about God, and He answered them. They were in awe. We were, too. They complimented us for what we had taught our son. We did not take credit. Jesus' insights and understanding did not come from us."

Finally, the big question. Mary, the mother of James the Less, asked her to tell them about His birth. Mary got quiet. She was not sure our group of women would believe something the public had never seen. Mary, the mother of James, asked her straight out, "Ma'am, Scripture told us that a virgin would give birth to a child, that He would be called 'Immanuel', God with us. Was that how Jesus was born? I ask this, because over the last few weeks we have come to believe God is with us every time Jesus is with us. From all He says to all He does, we have no other explanation."

Mary simply answered, "I have kept all of these things that you ask hidden in my heart. I have pondered them night and day. I can only answer that you are correct in how He was conceived. To this day, I do not understand how. I was treated as if I had been a loose woman. People thought Joseph and I had intercourse before marriage. That was not true. I know how Jesus was conceived. My struggle is why is it so hard for me to grasp who He is." She began to weep.

We comforted her. We asked no more questions. We simply let her know that we love her son. We love her. I let her know that I am still trying to wrap my head around all that Jesus is. I told her, "Please know we wish to be your help. We will never harm you if we can prevent it. Wherever this road leads, we will be here for you. I promise." Mary wiped the tears from her eyes. I think she believed she had found some friends who understood a little. With that, we walked her back to where she was staying with her younger son, Jude.

I have much to consider. What I feel is that the mystery is being revealed to us little by little. I cannot wait to see it fully displayed. I fear that as well.

On the third month, the seventeenth day — We arrived at the Temple courts. The people were all waiting for Jesus. I heard one of them cry out, "There He is." A few rushed toward us. Another yelled out to the crowd from the west of the Temple, "Hurry, He is over here!" More people rushed to us. The crowd was larger than ever. I saw priests and Levites walk past us to their stations. They showed a mixture of disgust and envy. Jesus began to speak within their hearing. They paused to listen. The Rabbi's message had a dual application, from what I gathered.

I am glad I brought my parchments with me. I was able to take copious notes while the Rabbi spoke. I truly am becoming a disciple, a student of His teaching. After visiting with John, I recorded what we recalled the Rabbi said. Jesus said, "The man who enters by the gate is the shepherd of his sheep. The watchman opens the gate for him, and the sheep listen to his voice. He calls his own sheep by name and leads them out. When he has brought out all his own, he goes on ahead of them, and his sheep follow him because they know his voice. But they will never follow a stranger; in fact, they will run away from him because they do not recognize a stranger's voice. I am the Good Shepherd. The Good Shepherd lays down His life for the sheep. The hired hand is not the shepherd who owns the sheep. So when he sees the wolf coming, he abandons the sheep and runs away. Then the wolf attacks the flock and scatters it. The man runs away, because he is a hired hand and cares nothing for the sheep. I am the Good Shepherd; I know My sheep and My sheep know Me — just as the Father knows Me and I know the Father — and I lay down My life for the sheep. The reason My Father loves me is that I lay down My life, only to take it up again. No one takes it from Me, but I lay it down of My own accord. I have authority to lay it down and authority to take it up again. This command I received from My Father."

I have reflected on these words all day. It dawned on me that Jesus opened with this teaching because the experts in the law were passing by us in that instant. Every eye turned toward them for fear they would break up our gathering. I, too, fixed my eyes on them. I expected them to interrupt as they have at times at the Galilee. Looking at them, Jesus seemed to call them the wolves or the hired hands who care nothing for the sheep. If we are sheep, none of us are following these religious leaders. We all flock to Jesus. People run to Him wherever He is. I do know His voice. When He calls, I do follow Him. I have tried strangers before Jesus. They all failed me. Now that I have met Jesus, I would dare not follow any other rabbi. We all were sitting on the steps of the Temple courts. We all were listening only to one voice — His.

What alarmed me was when Jesus said He would lay down His life for the sheep. He even said the Father loves Him because He lays down His life for His sheep. What can He mean? Does He mean He has put His life on hold for us, that He will break from living a normal life to teach us, then pick it up again when His appointed time to lead us has ended? I pray the time of His teaching will never end. But what if laying down His life means He will die for us? I am convinced He would die for us. I know He loves us that much. I have seen Him threatened. I have even seen His own people attempt to kill Him. A chill runs through my bones. What is He telling us? Is He saying they have not been successful yet, but a day will come when they will kill Him?

Then the question is, how is that for us? We follow Jesus. No one threatens to kill us. He has not stood between us and murderers or robbers. He is standing between us and false teachers. As far as laying down His life, it is only Jesus' life that we have seen threatened. So, how could He die for us? After seeing Him raise the dead, after seeing Him walk through those who wanted to kill Him, I believe the only thing that could kill Him is age. He is aging before us. He does get tired. And, if He dies, I have seen Him raise the dead. Is it possible He could raise Himself? I cannot see that. He stands outside of death. He speaks to those who are dead. If He dies, who can stand outside of death to call Him back to life? Is this what He is training the twelve to do? So many questions plague me. I pray someone will get Him to clarify some things.

I am content with one part of the lesson. He is our shepherd. The priests and religious leaders are definitely hired hands. They do what they do for money, for prestige, for accolades. Jesus said they do not even care for their parents. They hoard all they get for themselves. They show no love for us at all. I have never seen one with compassion. Nicodemus shows potential, but even he did not give me a warm feeling. When Jesus is around, all I feel is love.

On the third month, the eighteenth day — The ladies and I feasted for breakfast. Joanna prepared it all day yesterday. She presented it to us this morning as our Sabbath meal. I am surprised how slim she is with all of this at her disposal. I imagine the disciples did not get anything like this at the home of Lazarus where they stayed. This meal was fit for Jesus more than us.

We met Jesus and the disciples at the Sheep's Gate at the third hour. On our way to the Temple courts, we came upon a man begging for money. He was blind. Peter and the disciples were visiting among themselves. Then Peter pushed forward and asked the Rabbi, "Rabbi, who sinned, this man or his parents, that he was born blind?" That was a great question. People's infirmities always make me wonder if they had done something wrong. I had heard Jesus tell the man at the Pool of Bethesda to leave his sin or something worse would happen to him.

Jesus answered, "Neither this man nor his parents sinned, but this happened so that the work of God might be displayed in his life. As long as it is day, we must do the work of Him who sent Me. Night is coming, when no one can work. While I am in the world, I am the light of the world." He then spat on the ground and made some mud with His saliva. I had never seen Him do anything like this before. I expected Him just to touch him, or to say the words. But He made a mudpack and put it on the man's eyes. He then told the man to go and wash at the Pool of Siloam. That brought another surprise. The Pool of Bethesda was nearby. Why would Jesus send him to the Pool of Siloam, which is on the other side of the city? I will have to think about that. Regardless, the man left us. He was still blind, but he walked with his eyes covered in mud from the Rabbi's spit. I wanted to follow him, but I could not risk leaving Jesus.

Jesus continued His teaching about sheep. Yesterday, He spoke of Himself being the Good Shepherd. Today, He referenced Himself as the gate. As He spoke, He said, "I tell you the truth, I am the gate for the sheep. All who ever came before Me were thieves and robbers, but the sheep did not listen to them. I am the gate; whoever enters through Me will be saved. He will come in and go out, and find pasture. The thief comes only to steal and kill and destroy; I have come that they may have life, and have it to the full."

He surely has brought life. I have seen what the thief can do within my own life. The thief came to steal from me what God had planned. He came to kill me through fishhooks and knives. He came to destroy me with demons. Then Poppa took me to Jesus. He cast out the demons. He bound the thief. He gave me life, a life that is full. I never imagined I could have such a life. Before I thought I was living; instead, I was dying rapidly. Everything I reached for expedited my fall. Then I went to Jesus. He was my gateway to a joy unspeakable.

As I was reflecting on this, a commotion coming from the Court where the men pray interrupted my thoughts. We saw a man thrown out. Jesus turned to look. We did too. There were those priests, the hired hands, throwing out a man. It was the man who had been blind. His face was washed. His eyes were open. He could see! Jesus told him to go to the Pool of Siloam, not the Pool of Bethesda, which was closer to the Sheep's Gate when we first encountered him. I wondered why Jesus did not send him there, but now I get it. The Pool of Bethesda was attributed to having mythical properties of healing. If he had gone there, all would say it was the stirring of the waters that healed this man. Jesus sent him instead to the Pool of Siloam from which no one has ever claimed healing. Clearly, Jesus healed him, not some magical pool.

Anyway, the man walked up to Jesus. The disciples, the ladies, and I listened. Another man we did not know asked the one thrown out what had happened. The man said he had gone to wash in the Pool of Siloam as the Rabbi had instructed. He immediately received his sight. He then went into the Temple courts to praise God. Some of his neighbors began to argue in front of him whether he was the man healed from blindness or some other man. The man related how he told them he was Gaius, their neighbor. Instead of being happy for him, they demanded he tell them who opened his eyes. Gaius told them the man they called Jesus made some mud, put it on his eyes, told him to wash in Siloam, and he would see. He said, "I did just what He said.

Now I can see."

Gaius said they then brought Pharisees to him. They asked him the same question, "How did you receive your sight?" He told them the same. He then looked at Jesus and said, "They say You are not from God for You do not keep the Sabbath. Others defended You, saying a sinner cannot do such miracles. They asked me what did I have to say about You? I told them You are a prophet. They began to say I was never blind at all. They called me a liar. They then summoned my parents while they held me in custody in the Temple. I never saw God's house as a prison, but that is where they held me. None of them were happy, I could see. None of them celebrated what God had done through You. I was sick to my stomach."

We all listened with rapt attention. How could these religious leaders of ours not see what Jesus had done? How could they not celebrate someone made well? I cannot understand how they can equate healing with some violation of the Sabbath. Gaius said they brought his parents in as if for a trial. They asked them if he was their son. They grilled them to see if he was born blind or if they just said he was born blind. They told the Pharisees he was indeed their son, that this was no money-making scheme. He was born blind, to their great sadness.

The Pharisees drilled down, asking, "If he was blind, how is it that he can all of a sudden see?" The parents were hesitant to answer. They knew the Pharisees could have them banned from the synagogue and the Temple.

They directed the question to their son. Gaius said the religious hierarchy gave an order before the Feast of Weeks began. They made it clear that if anyone acknowledged Jesus was the Christ, they would banish them without exception. The Law of Moses gives stipulations for a person to be cut off from our people.

Going through my head, I thought of some of those reasons we were to ban people from our gatherings: if someone offers an unclean sacrifice, if someone dishonors the Sabbath, if someone is involved in sexual perversion, if someone spills innocent blood, if someone is unclean when they partake of the fellowship offering, if someone mimics the fragrance offering for their own pleasure, if someone eats anything with yeast during the Passover, if someone eats anything with blood in it; and there are many others. There was no stipulation to cut off a person from the Temple or the synagogue for acknowledging the Messiah. I thought our people were looking for the Messiah. I thought we pray for the Messiah. I thought at Passover, we all pray for Him to come. Now, one is here who meets every prophecy, who has power we never imagined, and yet one can be cut off for acknowledging what we so clearly see?

Gaius said they demanded he give glory to God, not to Jesus. They said Jesus is a sinner. This is when Gaius shared with them the most amazing statement I have ever heard. He replied to their inquest, "Whether He is a sinner or not, I don't know. One thing I do know: I was blind but now I see!" Hallelujah! What an answer! I looked directly at Jesus. He is the Messiah. He stands in the chaos of this hallowed place. He reigns supremely over it. It is as if there is a wall between Him and those who seek Him harm. Religious leaders threaten, then flee to their posh surroundings protected by the Temple guards. If they are really living for God, why do they need guards? Is God not enough guard for anyone? Look at Jesus — not one guard around Him. He does not need any. God protects Him. He protects us as our Good Shepherd.

Gaius said he tried to reason with them as they were hauling him out. They hurled insults at him, saying he was a disciple of Jesus. They insinuated they had no idea from what place He came. The last cut Gaius got out before he was rolled down the Temple steps was, "Now, that is remarkable! You do not know where He comes from, yet He opened my eyes. We know that God does not listen to sinners. He listens to the godly man who does His will. Nobody has ever heard of opening the eyes of a man born blind. If this man were not from God, He could do nothing."

They called him a sinner with their last shove. Here he was dusting himself off. He favored his right leg. His elbow was bleeding. His head was cut. He felt the blood dripping down the right side of his cheek. He grabbed a piece of his own sleeve, wiping it off. Jesus walked up to him and asked, "Do you believe in the Son of Man?" Gaius answered, "Who is He, sir? Tell me so that I may believe in Him." Jesus said, "You have now seen Him; in fact, He is the one speaking with you."

Gaius then fell to his knees again. He said to Jesus, "Lord, I believe", and he worshiped Him. I dropped to my knees, too. I have waited so long to do that. I saw the young, rich ruler fall before Him, but then he left Jesus, refusing to do what Jesus asked. I wanted to kneel then. It was not the right time. I did not get right beside Gaius. I fell to my knees a few feet away. Susanna reached down to help me up, thinking I had fainted. I patted her hand on my shoulder. I remained on my knees. With my eyes looking straight at Him, I whispered, too, "Lord, I believe."

The Pharisees approached at that moment. Jesus said to them, "For judgment I have come into this world, so that the blind will see and those who see will become blind." Those Pharisees would not let those words pass. They confronted Jesus. They accused, "What? Are we blind too?" They are blind. They do not see the Messiah standing right in front of them. He is the Messiah. It is not just what He claims. It is what He does. It is what the facts declare. He is what the scriptures foretold. They are blind. Jesus said to them, "If you were blind, you would not be guilty of sin; but now that you claim you can see, your guilt remains." With that, Jesus motioned, and the twelve disciples and the five of us women followed. He is our Shepherd. He is good.

I could write much more this evening, but I must get my rest. Every day is packed with the unbelievable, yet seen. I do not want to miss a thing.

On the third month, the nineteenth day — All made their offerings. We have been blessed with a harvest in Magdala. We have given our gifts at the Temple. Jesus took the disciples to Gethsemane for time away. I did some shopping with Joanna. The ladies and I tried to recount all the miracles we have seen.

Joanna had a few more, as she was near Him every time He came to Jerusalem. I write that, but Salome may have seen even more. Her two sons had been with Jesus throughout most of His ministry. We had a time of prayer, just the five of us. We thanked God for all He has shown us through His Son, our Messiah, my Savior — Jesus.

They all have turned in for the night. None have the night duty of wrapping up the notes from the day. I do not understand how they cannot take notes. It helps me reason through all I have seen, and I have seen a lot. The thought has come to me: There is one miracle I have not seen Jesus perform. He has healed the sick of every disease that we can fathom. He has given sight to the blind. He has given hearing to the deaf. He has given voice to the dumb. He has healed the deranged. He has given legs to the paralyzed. He has cleansed the leper. He fed thousands from a boy's lunch basket, like manna from Heaven. He has cast the demons. He has calmed the storm in the presence of the twelve. He has redirected lives. He has raised the dead. He has turned water into wine, as His mother Mary shared. He has done things that, at first glance, were considered resourceful, only to find they were miraculous. Jesus has walked through would-be killers. He has stymied the Pharisees. He has kept them at a distance. God's voice was heard at His baptism. He was born to a virgin, a miraculous birth.

What is the miracle He has not yet performed? There is one. It is a miracle we have seen in our history. It is a miracle God has performed. It is one an old priest prayed for, to see it fulfilled in the one for whom he prayed. What is that miracle Jesus has not performed? It is beyond my understanding that no one has yet noted this one missing act of God. Will He perform this one miracle? Or will it forever be absent from His divine acts?

We have many in this town who pray for this. I am sure many have come to Jesus as they came to Eli many centuries before. Husbands and wives pray this in their bedrooms. Wives pray in the Court of the Women for this one thing. They pray for God to end their barrenness. They want a child. Hannah wanted a child. Eli prayed, and God blessed. Sarah wanted a child. God gave her one. I understand John the Baptizer's mom, Elizabeth, and his father, Zechariah, wanted a child. It was too late for all of them. Yet, at the answer to prayer, these barren women became pregnant.

Not one time have I heard of Jesus touching a barren woman and she came back pregnant, nine months later, to present a baby to Him in thanksgiving. The question is why? Why of all the miracles, of all the longings couples and women have, why have we not seen one barren woman made pregnant? No sooner do I write that, the answer as to why strikes me.

The Pharisees have called Him a drunkard. They have called Him a partier. Others have called Him a man who sings the dirge, stating he is a stoic. How quickly would they call Him a womanizer or an adulterer? I do not doubt they search for such an opportunity. Then, if they look at the five women who follow Him — three are married, one is widowed, and then there is the woman from Magdala. Many could say He is an adulterer. Yet they watch our camps. They see we sleep a good distance away from each other. I am sure many have even watched us late at night to see if any of the men and women slip off together. They have never seen that. Even when Jesus was alone with the woman at the well, that was the most public place for a man to be seen with a woman this side of the town square. I am called Mary Magdalene. I believe part is to try to raise an awareness to all. There is a woman of immoral descent in His party. Yet, He lets me come. He bids me follow.

Back to my question of why Jesus has not worked this one miracle. Even if one had received this from the Lord, they would surely attest to it in the Temple courts. Their families and friends would be amazed, as they were with Zechariah and Elizabeth. God worked a miracle with Mary, from all I understand. She was a virgin and was given a child in her womb. All in Nazareth gave that claim no credibility. Some have even insinuated Jesus was illegitimately born. The miracle of Mary is considered a sordid affair, not an act of God. So, why has Jesus not worked this miracle? I believe because all would disclaim the miracle and accuse the sordid affair. They might even say Jesus has the power in His body to make a woman pregnant. Then they would say by natural means.

This is not far-fetched. I remember Judas the Galilean, who many thought was the Messiah. He claimed to be the Messiah. He used that adoration to seduce many women. If they would not be seduced, he raped them within his quarters. I know. He did it to me. He claimed I had received a gift of God when he forced sex upon me. He claimed he favored me in his sexual deviance. I do not doubt, years from now, many will still claim Jesus was an adulterer, that he had sex with multiple partners, or that He seduced his female followers, even fathering children. I would not doubt people would accuse Him with me above all other women. I have that reputation. I have slept with many men — if you can call that 'sleeping'. If only people could see His purity. If only they could see how guarded He is with women. I realize the one miracle He has withheld — opening a womb for children — is because He seeks to block the blasphemies that would certainly follow. I praise God for what He is doing through His Son. I praise the Father that He has given insight to His Son to prevent any falsehoods to have support.

On the third month, the twentieth day — We left Jerusalem. Joanna walked with us as far as Lazarus house. It was good to see Mary and Martha again. We did not get the time with them this trip, but that is okay. They are a blessing to all of us. The crowds are following us. I am sure they will be with us a few days until they start to peel off to go back to their homes. It has been a festive atmosphere. Each time we come to Jerusalem, it seems like we enter the arena for a competition of warriors. We left this time as we did the last, following our victorious warrior, Jesus. He does not lose in the arena of religion, in the arena of ideas, or in the arena of scholars. He reigns supreme. As the Good Shepherd, He leads us into Jerusalem. He protects us there. He then leads us out.

This evening, we camped near the Jordan River. As we listened, a mother and father brought their son to Jesus. They asked Him to lay His Hands on him and pray for him. Jesus obliged. Many more parents saw this. They began to bring their children to Jesus, too. The disciples were a little put out over it. I was, too. Jesus was speaking, but every time He got going, some parent would bring their child in front of Him, waiting for Him to bless the child. It was as if He could not get two sentences in without someone interrupting Him repeatedly. Though it did not seem to bother Him, it surely bothered us. We were accustomed to hearing Him speak without distraction. It did not seem respectful for the parents to continue this. The disciples took charge.

About ten sets of parents had lined up beside the bank where Jesus was speaking. Peter and John walked up to the front of their line. I saw them say something quietly. The parents would not budge. Then I saw Peter extend his arm, pointing harshly for them to sit back down on the hill where we were. It was then Jesus stopped what He was teaching. He looked at Peter and John. He spoke strongly: "Let the little children come to Me, and do not hinder them, for the Kingdom of Heaven belongs to such as these."

He then placed His hands on them. He blessed them with the widest smile. The kids went to play with their friends. Jesus stopped His teaching. He watched them with great joy. I watched the children for a minute. I was tickled by how they play. When their parents called them, they ran to their side. I watched how one mother took her child to Jesus. Then the little girl began to play with her little friends. When she saw her father approach, she lit out after him. She jumped up in his arms. She gave him a big kiss on his cheek, pressing her little face to his. I looked back at Jesus. That show of affection also touched Him.

Our Rabbi then turned back to the crowd, and to me. He called a little child back to Him. He had him stand among them. The Rabbi said, "I tell you the truth, unless you change and become like little children, you will never enter the Kingdom of Heaven. Therefore, whoever humbles himself like this child is the greatest in the Kingdom of Heaven. And whoever welcomes a little child like this in My name welcomes Me. But if anyone causes one of these little ones who believe in

Me to sin, it would be better for him to have a large millstone hung around his neck and to be drowned in the depths of the sea."

I thought about what He said. A young child seldom challenges his or her parent. There is a trust. There is also a respect. There is a fear of consequences. Mostly, there is just love. Even when chastised, the child will hug the parent. There is no separation, even with discipline. The child believes what the parent says. The child does what the parent orders. The child is afraid. The child trusts the parent to protect. In a crowd, the child can spot his or her parent. The child is not deceived, does not go after a different adult mistakenly. Jesus says we must be like that with our Heavenly Father. He loves us. We fear Him. We trust Him. We respect Him. But mostly, there is love. Even when He chastises us, we hold on to Him. As Job said, even if He slay me, I will serve Him. We are to do what our Father says. We are to accept His direction. He is our provider. We are to look to Him for our needs, as a child looks to the parent. How I yearn for that.

The warning Jesus gave was stark. If we cause a little child to stumble, to sin, it is better a large millstone be hung around our necks to drag us to the bottom of the sea. I will not keep a child from Jesus. I pray I will not do anything to cause any to turn from God. I pray I do not do anything to cause Atticus to turn from God, either. He is like a child in faith. He does not know much about God, or Jesus, for that matter. My actions with him must be such that he is drawn to the Father. I do not dare risk otherwise.

Jesus also gave us a warning. "Woe to the world because of the things that cause people to sin! Such things must come, but woe to the man through whom they come! If your hand or your foot causes you to sin, cut it off and throw it away. It is better for you to enter life maimed or crippled than to have two hands or two feet and be thrown into eternal fire. And if your eye causes you to sin, gouge it out and throw it away. It is better for you to enter life with one eye than to have two eyes and be thrown into the fire of Hell. See that you do not look down on one of these little ones. For I tell you that their angels in Heaven always see the face of My Father in Heaven."

We do not hear as much about sin from some rabbis. They want us to be secure in who we are. They want us to believe if we want something, then God wants it for us. Others give us God-like qualities. They act as if we can speak, things will fall in line according to our power. I have no power. I found that out quickly while chained in the cistern. The Pharisees only talk of sin. They define sin as anything that is against what they say, not against what God says. They believe if they order it, God has ordered it. We know better. They spend their time with us trying to convince us of their authority.

Yet, here is Jesus, One who speaks with an unprecedented authority never previously heard. When He says 'woe to the people who cause others to sin', there is great judgment for that. I had never heard such serious steps that we are to take not to sin. Jesus said cut off our hand, chop off a leg, or pluck out an eye if it causes us to sin. This is radical. I must deal radically with my sins. I must do whatever it takes not to sin against God. Otherwise, Hell is our destination. This scares me greatly. I still sin. What is radical enough to not sin, to quit sin, to be saved from the consequences of sin?

Back at the Temple, Jesus said He is the gate, that whoever enters through Him will be saved. I want to go to Heaven, not to Hell. Jesus says He gives eternal life. I believe He is saying He is the gate by which we can be saved from Hell and allowed to go to Heaven. The Samaritans declared He is the Savior of the world, the One who saves. I suppose the radical move for me would be to put off my attempts to save myself and, instead, to accept Him to save me. I can do that. I have done that. I hope I have done that.

On the third month, the twenty-fourth day — I have not written much the last few days. All Jesus has taught us since we left for the Feast of Weeks has overwhelmed me. I feel as though I have lowered my face into the River Jordan at flood stage, trying to drink everything that flows into my mouth. It is too much for me to grasp. There comes a time when I must take time to think. This may be the benefit that the other ladies have in not writing. They can dwell on each word of Jesus rather than try to record them in their entirety.

The disciples have continued on toward Capernaum. I bid them goodbye. I had the privilege, in their presence of course, to thank Jesus. I bowed before Him. I told Him, "Lord, I see You in a way I never realized. I cannot thank You enough that You would let me be with You and the disciples. I accept You are my gate to Heaven. I receive You as my Good Shepherd. I believe You are the Messiah. I have accepted You as my Savior. Wherever You lead me, I will go. Whenever You call or send for me, I will respond in an instant." I then said something with every ounce of my being. I have said the words before, but never to this depth, never to the fullness of who I am. I told Him, "I love You more than anyone or anything. I love You with my whole heart, just as God commanded us to do." He gave me the most accomplished expression. He had done what He set out to do. He saved me. I do not know what all that means. I have no idea how that will play out. I am content that He is the Savior of the world, and the Savior of me.

I have found myself singing all evening since I arrived home. Atticus dropped by. I welcomed him, but told him that I had things to do. If he would not mind, I asked him to let me get back to him in a few days. I have so much to think through. He was so kind. He agreed. He told me he loved me. I told him the same. It is just a different love for him than the one I have for God, or the love I have for Jesus.

On the third month, the twenty-fifth day — I was glad to be in the neighborhood synagogue today. Everyone welcomed me. Since they had seen me with Jesus, they all wanted to ask me questions after the service. I feel privileged to have this opportunity. As Jesus told the man in Decapolis to tell all his family and friends about Him, I am now getting that opportunity. I do not think they would have listened to me had they not known I had been with Jesus. Some saw me and the ladies with Him in Jerusalem. They saw us walk in together. They saw us walk out together. They see how I now dress. They see how I now speak. I am totally different, which gives them some confidence that Jesus is unique among the other rabbis to whom they have been exposed. I am also thankful they all had the privilege to hear Him speak from behind our very own bimah.

Afterward, I had the privilege to answer all sorts of questions. I first wanted them to realize He is not just a rabbi, nor is He just a uniquely gifted speaker. I shared with them the miracles I have seen. They did not have to take my word for it. Jesus has directly blessed many of the families of Magdala. He has healed their sick. He has ministered to their families through His Words. He has impacted how people see God. Even our worship in this synagogue has changed. I do not know if we will ever be able to measure the lives Jesus has already dramatically affected.

I shared with them the things we know about the Messiah. I felt as though I was a rabbi, a female one, anyway. I had them share with me what they expected from the One to come. I then began to lay Jesus' life before them in comparison to what they expected and what the Scriptures teach us. They were as in awe as I was. To think that in our day, in the nineteenth year of Tiberius, on the third month, we would see scripture come true. The prophets truly longed to see this day. Now we see it, or should I say, we see Him.

When they heard what I told them about the funeral procession coming out of Nain, they questioned if the boy was truly dead. They had all kinds of explanations. I simply told them they could travel to Nain themselves. It is a short trip. The widow still lives there, as does her son. The townspeople know all about it. That is the beauty of sharing about Jesus. Plenty of eyewitnesses are available to attest to what I say (or to what the disciples say, all the more).

I was sharing when Julia, a respected lady from our synagogue, shut me down. She told the others not to listen to me. She reminded them I am nothing more than a tax collector's daughter. I am the one, she said, who fleeced their village, who built my wealth off of their labor. She accused me of trying to do the same again as a collector of disciples. She told them I had been gathering money. She saw it herself. She was right. I had gathered money for Jesus, but never from anyone in our synagogue. The only one I think she was aware of was when she saw Salome and me in the market. It was then that I first asked Salome to help support the Rabbi.

I could sense the tension. People wanted to stay and ask me more questions. Even so, they did not want to draw her ire. Just as the parents of the blindman, Gaius, feared being thrown out of the synagogue, I believe these feared they would face the same here in Magdala. The last question asked before Julia came was, "Was He born to a virgin or was He born illegitimately?" I never got the chance to answer. I pray the issue comes up again.

On the third month, the twenty-sixth day — I found bad news today. Linus has been gone for over two weeks. His centurion sent him to Rome. Our businesses have suffered since. I have no one to oversee the work, no one to gather, much less account, for the money. It is a fearful thing to realize I can go from wealth to poverty in a matter of weeks. The timing of my return could not have been more fortunate. I am going to have to spend the next two weeks working to get things back in order. My finances are in jeopardy, even more my support of Jesus.

This brings the question of that young, rich ruler. Why do I not sell everything, give to the poor, and follow Jesus? Then I would have nothing to have to manage. I could be undivided in my attention to Him. If the Rabbi asked me to do it, I would immediately. The reality is, He has not asked me. I fear if I did it without His request, I might be making a mistake against His will. I do not want to presume anything. How can I know if He will ever call me to go with Him again? I remember Poppa saying, "If He wants us to follow Him, we will. If He does not call, we will follow Him here in Magdala." I would prefer to be with Him. However, He may have a purpose for me here. I had a little taste after synagogue.

On the fourth month, the twentieth day — I have been faithful to memorize God's Word. I am in synagogue every Sabbath, though I believe Julia is working to have me removed. I think of going to the synagogue by the shore. I believe I would be accepted there. The people there seem willing to listen to different points of view. With that said, how can I let someone run me off? I stand on the truth. Julia may not want to hear it. She may hate my presence, for it reminds her of Jesus. Our whole lives, it would have been easy to disengage from society. Poppa never would let us, even as hated tax collectors. He taught me to love, to show the people they were wrong by how we lived among them. I must do the same here. Besides, if Jesus is the Messiah, if He is the way to eternal life, and if I really care for others, I must be willing to share this Good News, debate, persuade, and convince. Whatever it takes, people need to live beyond their daily existence to consider what lies at the end of this life. I am already getting that opportunity. I have had the privilege of several women visiting me, wanting to know more about Jesus. I believe He is the One at the end of life who can carry us to Heaven.

He has not been around this side of Galilee for a while, nor has His twelve disciples. I miss Jesus, but His impact on my life has stayed. I am living for God. I am emboldened to share. I have a peace, regardless of pushback. I am finding strength over my temptations. Atticus comes to mind. He has been attending synagogue with me. We are talking marriage a lot. I have agreed to be his wife. To use the formal word, we are "betrothed". I am not sure when. That is the problem. He is ready at this moment to wed. My only concern is, I do not want to be restrained by a husband should Jesus ask me and the ladies to accompany Him again. I know Atticus would understand. He might even go with me if he could get off work. If we were husband and wife, he could even run our businesses for me at some point. I am not sure how equipped he is businesswise. The best scenario would be for Linus to return. Until then, I will continue to run the businesses. If we were married, I could train Atticus. I would then have the freedom to go with Jesus as Salome and Joanna do.

Again, the dilemma I feel is that I do not want family to interfere with my time with Jesus. I do not believe I can have a child with my age and all that I have done to my body. God is able, but I do not even have the desire for a baby, nor do I foresee that changing. Atticus and I have visited about that. All he wants is to have me for his wife. Even so, as near as the Lord is with God, I could see Him ride off in a chariot like Elijah. As close as He walks with God, I could see Him be like Enoch, walking with the Lord and then being no more, for God might carry Him to Heaven. Enoch pleased God. How much more does Jesus please God? If God brings Jesus straight to Him, I want to be like Elisha. I want to be present when it occurs.

I do not believe this is far-fetched. Jesus said Himself that He has come from Heaven. He has been called Immanuel, meaning 'God with us'. We know our history. The Angel of the Lord would come and go at will amongst our forefathers. Jesus may, again, be just like that. He is with us now, and then He is gone. For all I know, He has already gone to be with His Father. That could be the reason I have not heard from Him. At this very moment, the disciples could be spreading the news of His being taken up. I would be crushed if I have missed that. What an event I could tell the people about in this neighborhood and in our synagogue!

On the fifth month, the second day — The businesses are getting back in shape. I have learned to be strong when dealing with the men who work our vineyards, our properties and the like. People often ask me if I regret having been a tax collector, working for my father. In view of the hatred, it would be easy to say I wish we would have never been in that field. It is easy to wish something had never happened.

Then I realize I have learned from every situation where God has placed me. Even in the harmful positions I put myself in, God brought good from them. I can relate to people who are hated. I know what it is to be left out. I can reason with someone who is sexually promiscuous. I have the ability to communicate with people who are destroying their lives. I have been there. I also have skills of record-taking because of my tax booth experience. I have gained the added attribute of operating in the face of animosity. I can make demands on our workers when I am in line with God's Word and the law. All these things have equipped me. God used Poppa and Momma to equip me to live life after their deaths. For these things, I am grateful. The one thing I keep in mind is that I never want to make the same mistakes again. It is fine to learn from them.

There is wisdom in experience. However, I would rather have the wisdom of obedience. God told Adam and Eve not to eat from the forbidden fruit, or they would surely die. The wisdom of obedience is to not eat the fruit, then you will not die. Instead, they chose the wisdom of experience. They ate the fruit, only to find that death and destruction came, as God said. When I was a child, Momma told me not to touch her pot sitting on the fire because it would burn me. I did not listen. I touched it. Guess what happened? I got burned. The scar is still on my left hand today, almost thirty years later. What did I learn? The wisdom of obedience is better than the wisdom of experience. It is one thing to know I will get burned and to avoid it in obedience. It is another thing to have the painful burn from experience. I want to choose the wisdom of obedience every time.

On the sixth month, the twenty-second day — Today was a fulfilling Sabbath. I had the privilege to visit with the ladies again in my home after synagogue. Increasing numbers of women are coming each week. I take time to tell them about Jesus. I then go over different lessons I have learned since being with Him.

One Sabbath, I told them about Jesus feeding the thousands. I shared with them how the Psalms came alive for me. "The Lord is my shepherd. He makes me lie down in green pastures. He leads me beside the still waters. He restores my soul." I have learned another part of that scripture. "He prepares a table for me in the presence of my enemies." Even as I write in my parchments today, Julia is having a meeting with the elders to have me removed from the synagogue. The ladies tell me that she is pushing this every week. They do not believe she will be successful. I have the favor of the synagogue ruler Jairus from Capernaum's synagogue. He supports my claims about Jesus. He opens his synagogue to Jesus every time He is there. The ladies meeting in my home are also standing with me against her. I rejoice in the table He has prepared for me.

A few weeks ago, I told our women friends about how Jesus taught us to pray. I shared a week before how Jesus described the Pharisees. He has opened our eyes to their false pretenses. A week prior to that, I shared what Jesus revealed to us in the widow bringing her offerings in the Temple. I told them about the blind man He healed and how people in the Temple hassled Gaius. I gave them my firsthand account of Jesus' hometown of Nazareth turning against Him. It has been a blessed experience. I prayed to be a disciple. I am now having the opportunity to be that in my own hometown. I have never found such satisfaction this side of being with Jesus. I would rather learn from Him than teach others. That may be why He has been gone so long from me. I believe He has a purpose for my life. He is not physically at all places at once. I can serve His purpose here.

On the sixth month, the twenty-fourth day — Matthew is back! He and the disciples just returned from a wonderful time with Jesus. He said he has so much to tell me, but that would have to wait. He let me know Jesus would be meeting the disciples north of Capernaum. He said we were welcome. Matthew did not want me to miss being there. I am going to be there for certain. I am hopeful Atticus can accompany me.

On the sixth month, the twenty-fifth day — It was an amazing day. Jesus welcomed me personally. His warmth and love overflows toward all who come to Him. I introduced Him again to Atticus. Atticus was nervous. He could not speak. At first, I thought he was upset about something. As we took our place in the meadow, I asked him if he was okay. He gave me a nervous grin. He said that it was as if Jesus had known him his whole life. He had this notion he was being totally exposed. Every sin he had ever committed came rolling into his mind. When Jesus shook his hand, he said it was as though Jesus was aware of each one. Conviction poured over him. He noted the presence of a sense of grace too.

The more we talked, Atticus related it to being with a childhood friend. The beauty of friendships that are longstanding is that the friend knows where you come from, who your parents are, the mistakes you have made, the struggles you have faced, the efforts you have extended to do right, and the fears you still harbor. Friends from our youth know the questions you have. Nothing is hidden. Atticus said that is exactly what he felt the moment he saw Jesus. His eyes were familiar. There was a feeling of home in His presence.

I had never thought of that description before. My betrothed could not be more accurate. The best part is that Atticus said he knew Jesus loved him. Atticus said he understood fully how I could love Jesus in a way that is not a romantic love, but a godly love. He said he felt the same draw. With that, Atticus tenderly said, "Thank you for letting me come with you, Mary. I do not think I will ever be the same." Oh, if my husband can love Jesus like I love Jesus, what a marriage we are going to have!

We sat next to Susanna. Salome was present with her sons. Mary, the mother of James the Less, was beside her. I had the pleasure of introducing Atticus to my lady friends again. I had told him all about them. They all welcomed him. I was proud to be sitting by his side.

Back to Jesus speaking. His message was different from any I have ever heard Him share. He had warnings to those who refuse to believe after seeing all His miracles, hearing all of His Words. I thought of Bethsaida. I thought of Capernaum. No city of people has ever seen or heard what Capernaum's residents have. No sooner did I have that thought than Jesus said, "Woe to you, Korazin! Woe to you, Bethsaida! If the miracles performed in you had been performed in Tyre and Sidon, they would have repented long ago in sackcloth and ashes. But I tell you, it will be more bearable for Tyre and Sidon on the day of judgment than for you.

And you, Capernaum, will you be lifted up to the skies? No, you will go down to the depths. If the miracles performed in you had been performed in Sodom, it would have remained to this day. But I tell you that it will be more bearable for Sodom on the day of judgment than for you."

I wondered what Jesus had been seeing in those towns? It sounded as if they had turned on Him like Nazareth had. Bethsaida, the hometown of James, John, Peter, Andrew, and Philip, had witnessed many miracles, as Jesus visited there often. Did their synagogue have a Julia in their midst? Korazin? Jesus spoke at synagogues all around the Galilee. Gamla was one that I have never had the privilege to visit. I have been to Korazin, but never their synagogue. What had been their response? Jesus said they had seen His miracles. They did not believe? Tyre and Sidon were guilty of idolatry. They rejoiced in the persecution of the Jewish people. God destroyed them for a time by the hand of Alexander the Great. Is Jesus saying God will do the same for Bethsaida and Korazin? It would make sense. Jesus is drawing people to God. He is working miracles. He is calling people to repent, just as John the Baptizer did before Him. What a harsh pronouncement of villages in our midst.

That could not compare to the judgment Jesus foretold for Capernaum. I was shocked by His words. I have been to Capernaum many times to see Jesus. I have seen the crowds. The city, the visitors to the city, and I have seen His miracles. We have heard His Words. Jesus says they have not repented. I began to search through my mind: When did the people of Capernaum reject Jesus? I had thought the crowds to hear Jesus in Capernaum were the residents of Capernaum. The more I thought about it, the more I realized that the crowds that came to see Jesus in Capernaum were mostly nonresidents. I came to hear Him in Capernaum. I am from Magdala. Joanna came to hear Him. She is from Jerusalem. Salome came to hear Him. She is from Bethsaida. Jairus was the synagogue ruler. He followed Jesus. I wonder, would he have, had Jesus not healed his daughter? Peter followed Jesus. He lives in Capernaum. Then again, he lives in Capernaum after a move from Bethsaida to reduce his taxes.

Miracles were being performed all over Capernaum. People were carried in and left walking. People guided to the town were now seeing. Lepers who had shouted from a distance were cleansed. Demon-possessed people were set free — those who, just hours before, had been so destructive to the city. I then thought of the demon-possessed man healed in the synagogue of Capernaum. Why were they not convinced? Or did they prefer he be possessed in their midst? My mind was racing. I wonder if the people at that synagogue were so far from God they never realized a demon-possessed man was one of their leaders?

I thought of what Matthew told me about the demon-possessed man from Gadara. He haunted the people in their village. He lived among their graves. He ran naked around their villages. He had the strength to break any chain that had been placed upon him. Then, Jesus healed him. He sat in their midst in his right mind. The people of Decapolis were not elated. They demanded Jesus leave their shores at once. Is this what Capernaum has become?

Jesus stated Capernaum will be brought down. He said if He had performed the miracles He performed there in wicked Sodom, Sodom would have repented and remained to this day. Sodom. In my mind, there is no more wicked city than

Sodom. God judged them because their men had sex with men. Their men sought to have sex with any male visitor who entered their boundaries. God destroyed them with fire. To this day, the name for such a sexual perversion is still called "sodomy". I will never understand a civilization accepting such a distortion of how God created us. Then again, many things about my past I cannot understand either. Once we accept one sin, it becomes easier to go a little farther into other sins. Before long, we find ourselves doing things we never imagined. I remember the men I entertained on the shore before I met Jesus.

Capernaum does not believe in Jesus as the Messiah. They will not break from making money and making merry. How much more is that the case for Magdala? Our reputation is not nearly as respectful as Capernaum. Abraham pleaded with God for Sodom. I will plead for Magdala. I will also plead for Capernaum. I am confident Matthew is doing the same.

Of all the lessons to which I could expose Atticus, I was uncomfortable having his first exposure to Jesus be His condemnation. I looked over at Atticus. His eyes were wide open. I leaned toward him. "Are you okay?" He whispered back, "I would not have missed this for the world. He brings judgment. Yet, He does so in love. He speaks of punishment. Yet, I believe He is pleading for the cities He just named. He does not want them to face that. Can you not see the hurt in His eyes, Mary?" I looked back at Jesus. I did see His hurt. I thank the Father in Heaven that He has revealed this to Atticus.

No sooner had I prayed that then Jesus prayed, "I praise you, Father, Lord of Heaven and earth, because you have hidden these things from the wise and learned and revealed them to little children. Yes, Father, for this was your good pleasure. All things have been committed to Me by my Father. No one knows the Son except the Father, and no one knows the Father except the Son and those to whom the Son chooses to reveal Him.

Come to Me, all you who are weary and burdened, and I will give you rest. Take My yoke upon you and learn from Me, for I am gentle and humble in heart, and you will find rest for your souls. For My yoke is easy and My burden is light."

Jesus practically heard my prayer. Perhaps He heard it exactly. Here was Atticus. I know he is wise in many ways, but in the things of God he is a little child. Jesus prayed in the instant I prayed, thanking the Father for revealing His truths to little children. It is not the wise or the learned. It is Atticus. It is me. Jesus admitted in His prayer that He knows the Father. The Father knows Him. I prayed to the Father. I believe Jesus heard my prayer. He prayed the "Amen" to it.

The sweetest words followed. He has called me, Atticus, these disciples, and these ladies to come to Him. We are heavy-laden. We are weary. We are burdened. He is offering us rest. I felt a rest sitting in that meadow. I was overwhelmed with peace. I was refreshed. After so many days of not seeing Him, in His presence again, I received rest. I was having a Sabbath without it being the Sabbath. He is the Sabbath for me. I was drawn to God. Atticus was, too. I glanced at him. He has been calling me his "love." In that meadow, it was as if I was not there with him at all. He was oblivious to my presence. He locked his eyes on Jesus. He hung on every word. I thanked the Father again. This is what I wanted for my husband-to-be.

Jesus dismissed us. He and His disciples left. The last I saw of them, they were walking through the grainfields up from the meadow. Atticus and I watched. Atticus smiled. He told me this was one of the most amazing days he has ever lived. As we walked back to Magdala, he could not quit talking about Jesus. He thanked me over and over for bringing him. He then asked questions about what I had seen on other occasions. I shared with him what I have been sharing with the ladies from the Magdala synagogue. His mind has never been so open to the things of Jesus than they are right now. He bid me goodbye at my door. I asked if he was going to his home. He said he could not sleep. He was going to walk up to the synagogue to think. I close this entry with a praise to Heaven! How good is Jesus! He may have harvested another soul in the man I love.

On the seventh month, the tenth day — Today I have fasted. Atticus did too. We gathered for a sacred assembly in our synagogue as our Father prescribed. I noticed most of the people in the synagogue this morning were taking this time very seriously. I found one exception — Julia. She is filled with hatred toward me. If she knew what this day is about, she would confess that. She would reach out to me. I would love her. I would forgive her. She is unwilling.

I am. I have gone over the sins I have committed. My past haunts me. I will never be able to undo these. I trust them to God to forgive me of all my sins. I rejoice that in Jerusalem, at the Temple, the high priest washed himself this morning. He put on white robes. He trusts he is offering a bullock for his and the priests' sins. I pray they are truly repentant. After what I have learned of their hypocrisies, I place little comfort in them mediating for me. He is to sacrifice a goat for our sins. He is to sprinkle the blood on God's Mercy Seat. He is then to lay his hands on another goat, we call him the scapegoat. He leads that goat out into the wilderness. The goat is separated from our people so far that he will never return again. That is the forgiveness God offers. He will cover our sins and then carry them far away from us. It is as if we had never sinned. I want that for me.

Atticus wants that, too. He had no idea what went on at the Temple on this day. He was amazed at the beauty. He was also comforted at how readily God is to forgive us. I shared with him a remarkably interesting thing Jesus showed us. Jesus forgives sins. Atticus objected with a limited understanding. "I thought only God could forgive sins?" I told him that is correct. He then finished my words with a question. "Then Jesus is equal to God?" I told him this is the thing with which I am struggling. Jesus says He is from God. He says He can forgive. He says He can give eternal life. I have seen Him raise the dead. I have also seen Him back His power to forgive by raising the paralytic. Atticus felt an affirmation. "This would explain how He is able to do what only God can do, Mary!" I told him that is my belief as well.

The grief of today, other than my sins, is the fact that while this is a solemn day in which God said all are to engage in fasting and none are to work, we walked down to the shore. Business was going on as usual. God commanded us to do no work at all on this day. Yet, in this town in Magdala, at the fish factory, in the shops, and practically everywhere else, people were doing business as if this day did not exist. I mentioned that to one of the ladies from the synagogue. She said, "So what, Mary? People have to make money. I do not think that command applies to us in our day."

She does not think this applies to us in our day? God's Word we hear read in synagogue and the commands we hear rabbis explain do not apply anymore? If one can discard that part, then how can we know we are forgiven? If we pick and choose, can God not do the same? How can we have confidence that He hears us in this day? Until Jesus came, most did not believe miracles were part of God's activities anymore. For me, the world stops until I can know my sins are forgiven. If my sins are not forgiven, death holds a special terror for me. Job said, "In my flesh I will see God". In my flesh, I am a sinner. I need those sins cleansed. I cannot see how mortal man can blot out one part of God's Word and choose to keep another. Have we made ourselves God's peers?

I wonder if anyone who was at synagogue remembers the message from one of our speakers. The synagogue ruler Simeon quoted Malachi: "I, the Lord, do not change. So you, O descendants of Jacob, are not destroyed. Ever since the time of your forefathers you have turned away from My decrees and have not kept them. Return to Me, and I will return to you, says the Lord Almighty." God does not change. His commands are the same. His call to repentance is the same. He still longs to save.

Some believe Jesus, or the Messiah, will undo the commands of God. Matthew sent me a letter recently. I found it a few minutes ago. I am so thankful I remembered it as I reason through this generation's laxity toward the things of God. Matthew wrote that Jesus was on a mountainside, teaching. He was asked about what changes He was going to make to God's Word. Jesus told them (Matthew wrote it for me), "Do not think that I have come to abolish the Law or the Prophets. I have not come to abolish them, but to fulfill them. I tell you the truth, until heaven and earth disappear, not the smallest letter, not the least stroke of a pen, will by any means disappear from the Law until everything is accomplished. Anyone who breaks one of the least of these commandments and teaches others to do the same will be called least in the Kingdom of Heaven, but whoever practices and teaches these commands will be called great in the Kingdom of Heaven. For I tell you that unless your righteousness surpasses that of the Pharisees and the teachers of the law, you will certainly not enter the Kingdom of Heaven."

I wish Jesus would have been here to speak this in all our hearing. Jesus said not one command of God's, not even a stroke of Moses' pen recording God's words, would be changed. We have people amongst our religious leaders adding to God's Word. We have others taking from what He has said. He said we cannot enter the Kingdom of Heaven if we are guilty of such. God said it. Jesus reinforced it. He always does. He never contradicts God's Word. He never brings some far-out philosophy to benefit Himself or to endear Himself to His listeners. He speaks. His words can be sourced right back to our holy scriptures. There is no wavering with Him.

I would love for Atticus and me to go see Jesus today. I am sure He is on His way to Jerusalem for the Feast of Tabernacles. I cannot make the trip this year, but

I will be living in a booth to remember what God has brought us through. Atticus is going to be making a booth for himself. He is getting profoundly serious about the things of God. We are going to do exactly what God commands. Right now, I am the lead in the things of God. I pray Atticus will one day be that for me.

On the seventh month, the twenty-second day — Atticus gained insight this week while living in a booth. He had never studied what the Jewish people went through in the wilderness. He had never considered the miracles God provided for His people. He visited with me tonight about the similarity between Moses then and Jesus now. We had a great time fleshing out all the ways Jesus is shepherding us through this wilderness of Rome's government rule and our religious leaders' hypocrisy. Both are harming our nation.

We decided we would not go through the motions with God. Without exception, we want to live entirely by God's Word. We believe we will be blessed in doing so. Joshua wrote that God spoke, "Do not let this Book of the Law depart from your mouth; meditate on it day and night, so that you may be careful to do everything written in it. Then you will be prosperous and successful. Have I not commanded you? Be strong and courageous. Do not be terrified; do not be discouraged, for the Lord your God will be with you wherever you go."

If I were reading this as a stranger who just happened to pick up some discovered parchments, I would assume the woman who wrote this was very righteous. I would read how she once lived, but then I would read her hunger for God. My conclusion would be that this woman, Mary, and her fiancé, Atticus, are now upright in all their ways. In case some stranger ever does read what I have written, I want to make clear that I am messing up every day. Atticus is, too. We still cross the line in our physical relationship, but less and less. We both grieve when we fall. We take measures not to fall again. Every time sin raises its head, we do what we can to avoid that happening again.

No sooner did I honor the Day of Atonement, I said ugly things about Julia to the women who meet with me. I have caused them to falter by my vitriol. I have given a new believer, Atticus, an idea that some sin is acceptable. I find myself excusing some of my sins as being natural or normal. Jesus did not come to change one part of God's Law. God does not change. The things He has called sin are an abomination to Him. They are also of great harm to us. He never calls something sin unless it brings hurt. He does not speak to hear Himself speak. He does not command for the mere purpose of exercising His authority, but I find a battle within me. I want to live for God. I also want to live for me. I want Him to win. I want me to lose. Oh God, please have the victory in me. I cannot win on my own. I am trusting You to step in. I need You to fight my battles all the way to victory.

This is most true when Jesus is not around. I must confess also to any stranger who may read this: I sin when He is around, too. I carry great skepticism toward Judas. It may be warranted. I do not know. Because I do not know, I am judging him rather than praying for him. I carry a grudge at times against Simon the Zealot. I have not forgiven Peter completely for how he acted at the tax booth. I see people coming to Jesus. Some turn me off. Some I would not help if I were Him. Daily, I am asking God to forgive me. I plead with Him to change me. I believe He is. I want it to be faster. I write that, realizing I am the hold-up, not Him.

On the eighth month, the fifth day — Jesus has been in Capernaum all week. I have had the privilege to go with Atticus to hear Him teach in their synagogue. Rolling around in my mind are His words concerning that city's unbelief. Until He said it, I never noticed it. Today, I saw how cold the townspeople are to Jesus. Some regulars at the synagogue choose not to attend when He is speaking. Others walk out when He gets up to speak. Jairus has tried to stop the flow, but has been unsuccessful. My understanding is that talk ensues of replacing Jairus. The rumors are that he has become enamored with Jesus. They say he has ceased to be a synagogue ruler who stands on our religious traditions.

This has grieved Peter. He said he has seen Pharisees coming in and out of the synagogue of late. Peter's home is near the synagogue. He and his wife have a better feel for what goes on there than most. Some are withholding their offerings as well. I do not know how long Jairus will be here. I hate his young daughter is enduring this. The man her father brought healed her. I have seen her in the synagogue when Jesus speaks. Of all the local youth, she seems to have the sincerest heart for God. Most synagogue rulers' kids are spoiled. They tend to rebel against all the teachings of God. It is almost as if they do not believe them, because they have heard them from birth. They are not moved. They are not convicted. They may see their parents living differently than what they teach. I do not believe this is the case with Jairus.

Andrew took Atticus and me aside near the millstone factory. We were walking behind Jesus. When we got near the portico of the main building, he motioned for us to stop. I did not want to, but I figured he had something to share. He did. He said, "Watch the townspeople when they approach Jesus from the opposite direction He is heading." We did. Every one of them walked to the other side of the road. They each looked away from Him. Some even turned down a side road. Seeing it once or twice could be a coincidence.

However, it happened time and time again. Almost unanimously, they turned away.

Had they not seen His miracles? I know Jesus blessed them, or they knew someone else He had blessed. How can they be touched, healed, and taught, and then reject Him? It makes no sense. From a woman who was possessed, I could never understand turning from the One who rescued me. But these are. Jesus' words north of Capernaum made sense. He is experiencing things we had never imagined. Why? Why send Jesus out of Decapolis when He had tamed their greatest fear? Why? Why reject Jesus when He had made family members whole?

Andrew commented. His grief over this was more than he could express. He then motioned for us to join back up with the disciples. We caught up relatively quickly. A Roman centurion had stopped Jesus. I expected trouble. Had the townspeople of Capernaum appealed to Rome to have Jesus removed? I expected as much.

That was not the case after all. Andrew ushered us close enough to hear the centurion's conversation. He was asking Jesus for help. He said, "Lord, my servant lies at home paralyzed and in terrible suffering." Jesus told him He would go immediately to heal his servant. Again, I was reminded that so many who come to Jesus in Capernaum are not from Capernaum. This Roman officer was a perfect example.

The centurion replied, "Lord, I do not deserve to have You come under my roof. But just say the word, and my servant will be healed. For I myself am a man under authority, with soldiers under me. I tell this one, 'Go,' and he goes; and that one, 'Come,' and he comes. I say to my servant, 'Do this,' and he does it." I could not believe my ears. If one of my vineyard workers were sick, or if Linus himself were sick, I would ask Jesus to go and heal him. I would never think to say, "Don't come. Simply say the word." This man was a Roman centurion. He had the might of Rome to command Jesus to follow. They never hesitate to tell us what to do. They expect us to do it. We always do, for fear of reprisal.

Jesus was as astonished as we were. He turned to the twelve, me and Atticus. He said, "I tell you the truth, I have not found anyone in Israel with such great faith. I say to you that many will come from the east and the west and will take their places at the feast with Abraham, Isaac, and Jacob in the Kingdom of Heaven. But the subjects of the kingdom will be thrown outside, into the darkness, where there will be weeping and gnashing of teeth."

Unbelievable! Here we were in Capernaum amongst many children of Abraham. I have been with Him in Jerusalem where the vast majority were of the children of Abraham. Jesus said there will be people in the Kingdom of Heaven who are not of the children of Abraham. That is a surprise. We at least thought we would have some advantage. Even a person who is half of Abraham, like me, feels a preference. I was thankful for Atticus' sake. When Jesus said He gives eternal life, I have trusted that He would get Atticus into Heaven, and my mother.

The alarming part was Jesus saying some children of Abraham will be cast into Hell, where there is weeping and gnashing of teeth. That would include people of Bethsaida, Korazin, and Capernaum. We heard Jesus say it about Capernaum. At that moment, we were hearing Him say it in Capernaum within their hearing. I wonder how many who had not taken a side street in time heard this judgment. I am grieved that some sons and daughters of Abraham will not be in Heaven. I am heartbroken. These are my relatives. These are my people. Nothing else matters in life other than what happens after this life. How I wish all would turn to God so that they can enjoy all God has made for us together in His Kingdom.

Jesus then said to the centurion, "Go! It will be done just as you believed it would." With that, the centurion rushed off to his home, praising God, expecting to welcome his servant back to health. That was the confidence he had when he left.

When Poppa was dying, if I could have left his side to find Jesus, I would ask Him to come. If Jesus had said, "Go, your father is well," I would probably not have left Him until He returned with me. If I had to leave Jesus to go on His Word alone, I would have rushed back praying, hoping, but unsure. This Roman centurion left with a confidence his servant was already healed. He left joyfully, not sadly. He left certain, not pessimistic.

On the eighth month, the sixth day — We stayed the night at Matthew's. I slept in my room. Atticus stayed where Poppa usually slept. We had a nice breakfast.

As we were about to leave, someone pounded on Matthew's door. He rushed, fearing some bad news. He found it was Jairus. He said the Roman centurion sent a soldier looking for Jesus. When he could not find Him at Peter's home, he came to Jairus.

What he told us was amazing, miraculous news. The soldier said the centurion was sending his gratitude to the Rabbi. He returned to his quarters to find his servant fully well. When he inquired what time the servant was healed, his soldiers told him. It was the exact time Jesus told the centurion, while in Capernaum, that his request was granted.

Above all of us, Atticus was amazed. He had heard of Jesus' miracles. Now he has seen one for himself. Little does he realize he is betrothed to one of Jesus' miracles. He has stayed at the home of one of Jesus' miracles in Matthew. He was led to the side by another one of Jesus' miracles — Andrew. Atticus saw a father, Jairus, of one of his miracles in his little girl. I have not seen Atticus more excited. I believe his excitement today surpasses the day I told him that I would marry him!

On the eighth month, the eighth day — Matthew came by the house this afternoon. He had told me when they returned with Jesus, he had a lot of things to share with me. He said today that chief among them was what Jesus had told them at Caesarea Philippi. Matthew was saddened. He said, "Mary, the Lord says that He must suffer many things and be rejected by the elders, chief priests, and teachers of the law, and that he must be killed and after three days rise again."

I clasped both my hands in a cup over my mouth. I sat down in silence. Tears began to roll down my eyes. Matthew's tears matched mine. He could not speak beyond that tragic news. It all made sense. The religious leaders have been contesting Him every step of the way. His own hometown tried to kill Him. Reports have circulated that the Pharisees have been meeting to find a way to take Him out, and murder was an option. The people in Capernaum are rejecting Him; the people in Korazin and in Bethsaida, too. Yet, I see the crowds who love Him, who follow Him. Surely they would not let this happen? But then again, Jesus has never lied to us. He has never misled us. He told the twelve He would be killed.

I have believed Jesus would ride a chariot out of this earth, or that He would walk right out of here with God as Enoch did. I envisioned a glorious effect. Jesus says He will be killed. Enoch walked with God after he had his son whom he named Methuselah. God then took Enoch to be with Him after three hundred years of walking hand in hand. I remembered again Enoch's son, Methuselah. Methuselah's name means, "It will be sent when he is dead". In the year Methuselah died, some say on the day he died, God sent the flood to destroy all living things on the earth. If Jesus is killed, can we expect anything less on this earth?

I broke the silence to discuss these things with Matthew. All we could focus on was His death. I then asked Matthew about the last part. "What did you say He said would happen in three days afterward?" Matthew reported Jesus said He would rise from the dead three days later. If anyone else were to say this, I would say they were out of their mind. I could digest a modified statement if someone said they would die and Jesus would raise them up in three days. I could see Him do what He did for the Nain widow's son. I would think that one has to be living to have the ability to raise the dead. How does a dead man raise himself? How does an ox pull himself out of a well into which he has fallen? He cannot. Someone has to do it for him. Jesus says that He will rise in three days. If anyone can, He can. I could also see God doing that for Him. God is continually active in Jesus' life. They walk hand in hand. If Jesus is God's Son, and Jesus is killed, it would be very easy for me to see God raising the One He loves from the dead. This would show all mankind that man does not have the final say. God does.

Matthew left my house with two hopes. One, we pray it does not happen. Two, if it does, we pray He will rise from the dead. No greater miracle than that one could occur.

On the ninth month, the first day — Tomorrow is the Sabbath. Matthew informed us Jesus was back in town with the disciples. Jairus has dared to announce that Jesus will be speaking in the synagogue. The religious leaders are deciding Jairus' fate at the present in Jerusalem. Jairus seems undeterred.

Atticus made the journey with me back to Capernaum today. I was sorrowful. I shared with Atticus what Matthew had told me a few weeks back. I wanted to see Jesus' face. I had to see Him.

On the ninth month, the second day — Jesus was wonderful this morning. He was handed the scroll of Jonah. He shared about Jonah's rebellion. He then spoke of the gigantic fish that swallowed him. For three days, Jonah languished there. He had time to consider his actions. He vowed to serve God if only God would deliver him. It is amazing to me the impact God made on the city of Nineveh through Jonah. Even their animals were made to fast. The people cried out to God for mercy. They repented. God spared them. I looked around the synagogue as the people listened. Jesus was speaking to them. For them to avoid the judgment of God, for me to avoid His judgment, too, we must repent.

His final words before He sat were the most riveting. Jesus said, "When evening comes, you say, 'It will be fair weather, for the sky is red,' and in the morning, 'Today it will be stormy, for the sky is red and overcast.' You know how to interpret the appearance of the sky, but you cannot interpret the signs of the times. A wicked and adulterous generation looks for a miraculous sign, but none will be given it except the sign of Jonah."

What did Jesus mean — the sign of Jonah will be the only sign given? Will we be swallowed up by the Romans, languish under their iron fist, then come out repentant? That makes the most sense to me. Jonah was in the belly of the great fish for three days. I believe for our nation to repent, it will probably take more than three days. It could be three hundred days or three thousand days. Jonah was in the belly of the fish for three days.

Tomorrow, Jesus is leading the disciples to Mount Tabor. It is about a nine-hour walk. Atticus asked Andrew if we, too, could go along. He has found a sort of kinsmanship with Andrew. Andrew reported back that we were welcome to follow. I did not want to travel alone with Atticus for that distance. Not just because we might be tempted, but because I did not want to give anyone any cause to gossip. I know people like Julia will be looking for a reason to disparage my walk with God. We are engaged, not married. I asked Susanna to go with us. She was excited to go along.

We are staying at Matthew's home. Atticus is staying in the room Poppa used. I am in my usual place. I will trust my laborers and foremen to tend to our businesses without me. I feel we have things back in working order. Magnus, a peer of Linus, is stepping into the role of overseer for me. He came to me with a letter of recommendation from Linus. I was glad to get the help. I was even more glad to know Linus was thinking of me. He sounds as if he is doing well in Rome. He is up for a promotion. I rejoice in God's blessings. It is good to know there is a man in Rome who admires Jesus.

On the ninth month, the third day — Jesus had already gone ahead of us. He took Peter, James, and John. The rest of the disciples are leading Atticus, Susanna, and me. We are probably a few hours behind them. I was surprised to see so many people join us at different intersections of our journey. Jesus is not with our party, but the people in this community now recognize the disciples. They know that where the disciples are heading, Jesus may be at the destination. They have also heard that the Lord has empowered the disciples with miracle-working abilities. They have the same hope my father once had. They will do anything, see anyone, if only they can find healing or help.

We arrived at Tabor this evening. A huge crowd was waiting on us. Another crowd was following us. Nathanael asked one of the men where Jesus had gone. He replied that Jesus was up on the mountain with three of His disciples. We knew that was Peter, James, and John. There was nothing to do but wait.

Simon the Zealot made the fire for us. The masses around us built theirs. People flocked the nine disciples with us asking for prayer, for healing, for help, for casting out demons, even to travel with them to pray over a dead relative in the hope they would be revived. I have never seen these disciples more overwhelmed. It was almost more than they could handle. There is just one Jesus. He could handle this massive gathering on His own. These nine disciples could not even divide the crowd into nine groups and manage the push.

The disciples did what they could. God did work miracles through them. I saw Matthew, my friend, pray over a man who was blind. He asked God in Jesus' name to give this man back his sight. In an instant, the man could see. Matthew's face showed no surprise, nor an ounce of pride. We all knew it was Jesus doing it through them. I cannot explain that. Atticus was in awe the entire time. He never blinked. He never spoke. I do not think he even closed his mouth. He was seeing Jesus and His power that we had become remotely expectant of, but to which we were never accustomed.

I looked all around. Simon the Zealot was seeing miracles through his hand. Strong Nathanael was filled with compassion, praying in Jesus' name, and witnessing the occurrence of miracles. James the Less, the meekest of them all, had the biggest line of people. His face welcomes all. As humble as he is, the miracles performed by this man were heaven-sent. Power emanated from him, power I have never seen in any of the disciples.

Again, not an ounce of pride. None of the disciples were taking credit. All of them were in full awareness that Jesus, up on that mountain, was working through them. It is like borrowing a fine boat, riding it out onto the Galilee. A storm hits. While other boats are sinking, that one hardy vessel weathers every wave. When the storm is over, the man who borrowed the boat takes no credit in surviving the squall. He returns the boat, thanking the owner who let him use it. Jesus lent these disciples the power. They were using that power to overcome every storm that walked up to them. At some point, when Jesus does come down, all they can do is thank Him. That is all I can do, too, as one whom He has rescued.

On the ninth month, the fourth day — It has been a long night. I was able to slip in a few little naps, probably a total of thirty minutes of sleep. I am exhausted. Susanna was active throughout the night, bringing people to different disciples. She was helping keep order. I tried to help. I would get water for the nine. I would bring them bread while they worked. Atticus was a soldier all night. He helped carry people to disciples. He broke up fights when someone cut in line. Before long, many had mistaken Atticus for a disciple. He caught me as he passed by. He said, "They think I am a disciple of Jesus. It is a lot of work. I think it would be an honor to be one!" As he was moving past me, I hurriedly told him, "We will serve Him here as disciples or at home as witnesses." He looked back at me, smiling as he raced to the next problem. That was the last I saw of him for hours.

Jesus still has not come down. I pray He does soon. An argument has broken out. Most of the crowd have had their prayers answered. But one man has not. He brought his demon-possessed son to the disciples for healing. The man told the disciples this boy is always trying to kill himself. He speaks in voices. He is calm one minute, uncontrollable the next. The disciples did all they could. Matthew prayed over him. He just went into convulsions. Philip prayed over him. He spat at Philip. They called James the Less. Everyone had been seeing the mighty effect he had been experiencing. The boy swung at him. The nine grouped together as the father held his son down with the help of other men. Again, no deliverance. The boy threw off the men, running toward the fire. They were able to knock him away from it.

I thought of where I was not too long ago. I had demons in me. They spoke through me. They tried to kill me. They tried to use my body to kill me. They struck at my family. They led me to do despicable things. I say 'they', I was a willing party until it was too late. Then I met Jesus. He cast them out. They have never returned. I do not believe they will ever be allowed to return, thanks to His mighty Name. I could not help but weep as I watched that boy. Is that what I looked like? Is that how I acted? Is that the demonic power that once flowed through me? I know it is. I see the face of Poppa in the expressions of that helpless father.

The teachers of the law wandered up. I had not seen them all night. I am not sure if they recently arrived, or if they had been standing in the shadows watching the miracles in Jesus' Name. Then, when a boy could not be healed, they joined the father to criticize the disciples and the Lord. Nathanael took exception. He flexed his muscles, bowed up to them as if ready to fight. After all the disciples had done that night, the crowd seemed ready to stone them for not being able to work one last miracle in Jesus' Name. Of all the miracles Jesus performed, they want to discount Him as a phony for the one His disciples cannot perform. I was flabbergasted.

As I watched, the faces of the crowd all fixed upon the mountain Tabor. Silence filled the crowd. I turned to look, too. Jesus was coming down. His face shone, almost glowed, like the moon on a winter's night. I envisioned what Moses had to have looked like when He came down with the Commandments of God. I am not sure if the glow was from Jesus or the rising sun lighting upon Him as He walked down. He looked troubled by the crowd.

The crowd rushed toward Him. Jesus continued His steady walk in their direction. He did not flinch. He did not stop in His tracks. Jesus called out as He walked toward us, "What are you arguing with them about?" The father of the boy knelt before Him. "Lord, have mercy on my son. He has seizures and is suffering greatly. He often falls into the fire or into the water. I brought him to your disciples, but they could not heal him."

Jesus looked at the disciples first. He then looked at the religious leaders. Finally, He looked at the crowd. He said, "O unbelieving and perverse generation, how long shall I stay with you? How long shall I put up with you? Bring the boy here to Me." Jesus rebuked the demon in our hearing with His echoing voice that reverberated off Tabor.

The spirit shrieked, convulsed him violently, and came out. The boy looked so much like a corpse that many said, "He is dead." But Jesus took him by the hand and lifted him to his feet, and he stood up. He was healed at that moment. All was calm. Jesus.

The religious leaders were the first to scamper out of the camp. Their efforts to discredit Jesus had failed again. You would think they would give up. If they truly sought God, they would follow Him with us. But they are not really seeking God. The crowd, satisfied, left for their homes. No one stayed to hear Him teach. No one asked if He needed anything. They got what they wanted. They saw a show. They left. It was as if they had attended a Roman theater. They saw the play. They left to live the way they lived before they came.

The quickness with which the crowd disappeared was strange. It was just me, Atticus, Susanna, the twelve, and Jesus. Even the crowd following us disbanded. I cannot explain it. Another thing I have a hard time explaining is Peter, James, and John were eerily quiet. Peter has always been the boisterous one. I heard Philip address them. They were sheepish. Andrew asked Peter what they had been doing up on the mountain. He simply said, "Worshiping." Andrew pressed. "Anything else?" Peter said, "That is all I can say. It was wonderful." I guess, as brothers, they can read each other. Andrew seemed to know there was more. He also read the facial cues. Peter was going to say nothing else.

We sat down, exhausted, at the foot of the mountain. Jesus seemed energized, but His face looked tired. Peter, James, and John laid down to nap. The other disciples could not rest until they got one question answered.

They asked Jesus, "Why couldn't we drive it out?" I wondered the same. They had tried everything. Jesus replied, "Because you have so little faith. This kind can come out only by prayer. I tell you the truth, if you have faith as small as a mustard seed, you can say to this mountain, 'Move from here to there' and it will move. Nothing will be impossible for you."

I pondered the lesson with Susanna and Atticus. Jesus had never empowered us to do any of this. The disciples had been. Evidently, they had become too nonchalant in their prayers for healing and in using Jesus' Name. They had forgotten to truly pray first. They had forgotten that when the totality of evil is in their midst, it is overpowering. They must pray and know Jesus can cast out one demon or two thousand. He is able. That is where their faith must be. This is where our faith must be, too. He is able. I am not.

We all were able to rest. Jesus even laid down for a while. Susanna and I had our own area. Atticus laid down on the ground near Andrew's mat. As always, we did everything that was right, even for the sake of appearance. We are to have no hint of compromise.

When we awoke, Jesus distributed some food to us. He told us we were headed back to the Galilee. He said, in our hearing this time, there was more disturbing news. "Listen carefully to what I am about to tell you: The Son of Man is going to be betrayed into the hands of men." Jesus has been referring to Himself as the "Son of Man." This has not been a surprise to us. That is the term used for the Messiah. We are convinced Jesus is the Messiah. He has laid out the case without coming right out and telling the masses. I am not sure why He does not. If He were to announce He is the Christ, would He not get a second look from His accusers? People long for the Messiah. We need Rome's yoke thrown off. We need corruption removed from our faith. We want God's Kingdom to come, and His Will be done on earth as it is in Heaven. But who am I to question Jesus?

Back to betrayal. Matthew said Jesus was going to be killed. It would stand to reason that for Him to be killed, someone must carry it out, but betrayal means someone who is a friend will turn a loved one over to an enemy. I looked around our group. Who would betray Jesus? We have a saying that comes down from one of our prophets (I assume), "The treacherous betray." I cannot help but think it is no one here. I could see Jesus' hometown betraying Him, even one of His brothers, from what I am told. I do not think Mary, Martha, or Lazarus could. I thought of

Joanna. I feel bad that I thought of her. She is one connected to Rome. She is respected among the religious elite because of her husband's power. If everything were on the line for her, would her husband not force such an act?

Jesus told the twelve He would be killed and rise from the dead. He tells us that He will be betrayed into the hands of men. What lies ahead? I feel the walls are closing in on us. It is the same feeling I had in the cistern when I was imprisoned there. I pray that nothing like what I fear will happen.

On the ninth month, the sixth day — We have returned to Magdala. Susanna walked with us until we reached Capernaum. We did not stop talking the whole walk. Jesus had gone with the disciples, leaving her, Atticus, and myself to walk most of the trip back. Our conversation was filled with wild ideas on how to tie together all Jesus had taught us, shown us, and what little the disciples had divulged with us. It is funny. Nothing makes sense before an event. It is only afterward that all the signs tie together. I am hoping we can tie it all together beforehand.

Once Susanna left us, Atticus asked many of his questions. He wanted to understand more about what the prophets said about Messiah. He wanted to know how sin first began its hold on humanity. He sought to grasp the necessity of animal sacrifices. I could only tell him that without the shedding of blood, there can be no forgiveness. He has a simple logic that is hard to explain away. In fact, his questions raise up questions of my own. The things I have accepted as fact, or tradition, or something we do fell into the category of why?

He reasoned that if we sin, how can an animal's death make us right with God? So, we steal a neighbor's purse. God will forgive if we go out and kill a lamb on a hillside? It was not the lamb who took the purse, we did. Why does the lamb get killed when we did the crime? He had a great question. My only answer was, "God said to." That really is the acceptable answer, but God does not do anything simply to do it. Everything He does is well thought out. Jesus taught us that. If God commands it, there is a reason, a good reason, other than, "I said so." So why do we kill a lamb or a goat or a bullock or a dove for our transgressions? I could not answer that. I cannot answer that. I pray Jesus can answer this among other questions the next time I am with Him. I seldom ask Him questions. The disciples usually beat me to the punch. That works great for me. God always seems to know what my question is. He answers it before I have the chance to ask. But not always.

Atticus walked me to my door. He went through my house quickly to make sure no one had broken into it. He then went back outside the door. He kissed me on the cheek. He thanked me for bringing him with me. He says he wants to follow Jesus with his life, too. I am thrilled. This is the man I want to marry. His name is Atticus.

On the tenth month, the ninth day — Jesus is back in Capernaum. He spoke at the synagogue. Jairus was not there. No one answered where he went. Even in his absence, Jesus spoke. Another man stood in Jairus' place. I suppose he is temporary. The people seemed less attentive to Jesus. I fear they are taking Him for granted. The crowds in the city also have declined.

I asked Matthew about this. He told me Jesus has been speaking about sacrifices a lot lately. He intimates that He is our bread that we must eat. Many are unclear on this. Sure enough, at the synagogue Jesus preached, following a reading from Moses' writing about sacrifices. He said, "I am the bread of life. Your forefathers ate the manna in the desert, yet they died. But here is the bread that comes down from Heaven, which a man may eat and not die. I am the living bread that came down from Heaven. If anyone eats of this bread, he will live forever. This bread is My flesh, which I will give for the life of the world."

He did not get far into His message before a Jewish leader interrupted Him. The leader stood near the bimah. He turned his back on Jesus. He faced the crowd and exclaimed, "How can this man give us his flesh to eat?" I had not even considered that. We are not to eat the blood of any animal, certainly not another human being.

Jesus took back over. He said to us, "I tell you the truth, unless you eat the flesh of the Son of Man and drink His blood, you have no life in you. Whoever eats My flesh and drinks My blood has eternal life, and I will raise him up at the last day. For My flesh is real food and My blood is real drink. Whoever eats My flesh and drinks My blood remains in me, and I in him. Just as the living Father sent Me and I live because of the Father, so the one who feeds on Me will live because of Me. This is the bread that came down from heaven. Your forefathers ate manna and died, but he who feeds on this bread will live forever."

A huge commotion occurred. The religious leaders said they were not going to stick around and listen to this heresy any longer. They called for those who are on the side of God to come with them. Practically, the whole synagogue emptied. Even those who had been as faithful to follow Him as I have, left. One lady looked at me. She said, "No more! I have had it with this teacher!" The walls are closing in.

We walked out of the synagogue alone. Just the twelve, me, Salome, Susanna, Mary, the mother of James the Less, and Atticus. None of us knew what to say. We returned to Peter's home to eat. Jesus was as quiet as we were. We ate. The food had no taste. The conversations were superficial.

After our meal, Jesus spoke about what He had said in the synagogue. "Does this offend you? What if you see the Son of Man ascend to where He was before? The Spirit gives life; the flesh counts for nothing. The words I have spoken to you are spirit and they are life. Yet there are some of you who do not believe. This is why I told you that no one can come to Me unless the Father has enabled him."

He did not offend me. I did not quit believing. I looked at those in this family room of Peter. I could not tell if any did not believe Him still. Yet, Jesus said some of us do not believe. He also said He would be betrayed. It makes sense that the one who does not believe Him would be the one who would betray Him. In this little room of disciples, I have no doubts of any of our sincerity. Perhaps Jesus was being more universal when He said "some of you." We were in the unbelieving Capernaum after all.

His words snapped us all back to attention. We were going to be with Him, no matter what. Peter reiterated what Matthew stated he had said before. "Lord, to whom shall we go? You have the words of eternal life." Peter is right.

On the eleventh month, the second day — I do not know where the time goes. When I am with Jesus, I cannot help but write of every second. When I am in Magdala, I am consumed with business. Courtship also distracts me. Atticus and I had our first adult friction a few days ago. He asked me to put up security for a loan he was seeking so he could buy his own fishing boat. I understand him not wanting to be around the men on the shore any longer. His coworkers are evil men. Also, when they break for lunch, they say vile things about me. They talk about how good I was for sex. They ask him if he is keeping that all to himself or if he would not mind sharing with them, as they did for him once upon a time. He is sickened. He has had many fights over such vile talks. He wants to get away from them as I want him to.

This is why he was hurt when I told him I would not pledge security for him. The Scriptures tell us we should never do that. I offered to buy a boat. He could then begin a fishing business for me. He refused. He does not want to work for his future wife. I understand that as well.

He stormed away from my courtyard when I declined. Thankfully, he just left the house this evening. He apologized. He reassured me he loves me. He would never want to hurt me. I know that. It was a little awkward tonight. I can see, though, that we have made it through this disagreement. This is what couples in love face in marriage. It is better we have gone through this now, rather than later. I would not have had confidence we could survive such things if we would have faced this only after we were a married couple.

I remember many times Poppa and Momma argued. They especially struggled when Poppa was traveling for the fish factory. It is the reason he took the job at the tax booth. He wanted to be home for Momma and me.

At times, their conversations were terse, but they always made up. They tried their best not to let the sun go down on their wrath. I explained to Atticus that this must be our next step. He is not to go away for a few days, then return to patch things up. We must deal with the issue, even if it takes an all-night conversation in my courtyard. I assured him that once we are married, what I have is his. What he has is mine. I will gladly submit to his leadership with his acknowledgement that there be no lording over each other. We are a partnership, much like what James and John had with Zebedee. He could relate to that analogy. Zebedee had the final say, but they seemed to always come to an agreement that suited all three of them.

On the eleventh month, the seventh day — Matthew showed up at my house this evening with friends. Peter and John were with him. They were talking over each other. I could not make out what they were saying. Peter then took control. He said, "Mary, we were on our way back from Judea. The Jewish leaders tried to stone Jesus. We thought He was going to be killed as He forewarned us, but they were unable to get Him for some reason. God's Hand is upon Him." This is the reason why I cannot see Him being killed. God's Hand is upon Him.

Peter continued. "We made it to Samaria, on our way to the Galilee. A runner caught up with us. The messenger handed a note to the Rabbi that said, 'Lord, the one you love is sick.' Jesus looked at us and said, 'This sickness will not end in death. No, it is for God's glory so that God's Son may be glorified through it.'" John said they assumed all would be fine, because they stayed where they were for two days. They assumed it was to keep apprised of any updates. Then Jesus told them that they should go back to Judea.

I wanted to know if Lazarus was okay. I tried to interrupt, but they would not let me. It was as if they did not want to spoil the surprise. I soon found out why they stopped me.

Matthew said they were worried about returning when the Jewish leaders had attempted to stone the Rabbi. Jesus was unconcerned. Jesus said He needed to go wake Lazarus up, for he was asleep. Peter said he protested, "Lord, if he sleeps, he will get better." Peter said Jesus answered bluntly. "Lazarus is dead, and for your sake I am glad I was not there, so that you may believe. But let us go to him."

That answered my question. Lazarus was dead. The man who had opened his home to us. The sisters who had loved on him, on Jesus, and cared for us. Lazarus. I cannot help but think this is Jesus' best friend — next to God, of course. I gather no other person puts Jesus more at ease than Lazarus. I could not wait to hear the result.

Matthew said Thomas was resolved. He challenged the rest of the disciples, saying, "Let us also go, that we may die with Him." I looked at Matthew, at Peter, at John. They were going to put their own lives in jeopardy? Matthew said, "So we went." When they were near Bethany, Martha ran out to meet them. She seldom speaks. She always serves. But it was Martha who went out to meet them. They said it seemed she was agitated toward Jesus. She said to the Rabbi, "Lord, if You had been here, my brother would not have died. But I know that even now, God will give You whatever You ask." John said she was clearly upset that the runner she sent returned without Jesus. Peter added, "Give her credit. She believed God would do for Jesus whatever He asked. That is more than I could say."

Peter said Jesus told her that her brother would rise again. That is the hope for all of us who lose loved ones. He said Martha said the same. But Jesus then made a statement that all three of my disciple friends repeated at the same time. "Jesus said to her, 'I am the resurrection and the life. He who believes in me will live, even though he dies; and whoever lives and believes in me will never die.'" It was as if they were singing in the synagogue to a familiar song, but one they had only sung this one time.

I stopped them. I asked them, "Jesus told Martha that He is the resurrection and the life, that whoever believes in Him will live though he dies, that those who believe in Him will never die?" All of a sudden, Jesus' teaching became Jesus-focused. He was telling her in the disciples' hearing that eternal life with God comes through Him, through Jesus. The Son of God. The Messiah. The holder of eternal life. The forgiver of sins. The healer of the sick. The caster of demons. The calmer of storms. The one who raised the widow's son to life, and, I believe, Jairus' daughter. These thoughts were rolling through my mind. The three friends paused, almost as if they knew I needed to process their words.

They told me Martha had said something unexpected. It was a statement Jesus had shared privately with the disciples but told them not to repeat. Now that Martha said it aloud, they wanted to repeat it to me. Matthew, the one I trust the most, said, "Martha, she said, 'I believe that you are the Christ, the Son of God, who was to come into the world.'" The Christ. Jesus told them He was the Christ? They had held that to themselves all this time. It has been my belief, too. He had never stated it before in my hearing. The Samaritans said He is the Savior of the world. Jesus is clearly supporting our beliefs by the demonstrations of His Power.

"Then what?" I asked. I just knew where this was going. With a sparkle in his eye, John said, "He had been dead four days. Unlike the boy from Nain who had just died a few hours earlier, Lazarus had died four days before. He had been in his tomb that long. He probably died before the runner even reached us. Jesus asked them to take Him to the tomb. We went. Jesus began to weep in a way we have never seen before. Yes, we have seen tears well up in His eyes. We saw His sadness at the funeral of that boy. But He wept profusely, almost uncontrollably. Everything stopped."

John continued. "Jesus commanded, 'Take away the stone,' Martha protested he would smell. The Lord told her, 'Did I not tell you that if you believed, you would see the glory of God?' So they took away the stone. Jesus looked up and prayed, 'Father, I thank You that You have heard Me. I know that You always hear Me, but I said this for the benefit of the people standing here, that they may believe You sent Me.' When He said this, Jesus called in a loud voice, 'Lazarus, come out!'"

I was on the edge of my chair. All three had sat with me in the courtyard. Each would jump up to speak, then sit back down when another spoke. They got so excited in telling me this. Again, they began to speak over each other. I had to stop them. I wanted to know what happened next.

Matthew said, "The dead man came out, his hands and feet wrapped with strips of linen, and a cloth around his face. Jesus said to them, 'Take off the grave clothes and let him go.' Mary, we had supper with Lazarus, Martha, Mary, and a lot of their friends and family that night. It was exquisite!"

They were speechless from that moment. All they could do was laugh in wonder with their eyes lifted to Heaven when not looking directly at me. I was speechless, too. We saw Jairus' daughter raised when I am sure she had just died. We had seen the boy from Nain healed many hours after he had died. But to hear of Lazarus healed after four days in the tomb, body decomposing, eyes dried out of the sockets perhaps, his organs collapsing inside his body. This was no rumor. These three men came to my house. They were not sharing second-hand information. They witnessed it all. They ate with Jesus and Lazarus afterward.

I could almost see them at the table in the house with which I am so familiar. I imagine Jesus had to wipe the tears from His own eyes throughout the night. That is how He loves. He does not want to be separated from the people He loves. Death is not acceptable to Him. He seems determined to not allow it to separate Him from those who belong to His circle. Would He do the same for me? I pray so, but I am not as close to Him as Lazarus is. Would He have done that for Martha? I think so. Would He have done it for Matthew? I believe so. And what about Atticus? I think He would for him and for me. For whom would He raise me up? In thinking about that, I believe He would for Himself, because of His love.

The three disciples ate with me. I sent word for Atticus to join us, along with Magnus. We had a great fellowship. Before they left, they told me Passover was near. Jesus is going. He gives them insight that this may be a monumental visit. He would love for me and the ladies to come too. I looked at Atticus. He gave me his blessing. He was unable to go himself. He found a man willing to sell him his fishing boat provided Atticus works for him for a year. The man is near retirement. Atticus wants this for us. I want this for him. Magnus assures me he can manage our businesses for the period of time I will be gone. He has been doing a good job. He may even be more conscientious than Linus. It may be because he is still in his trial period. Regardless, I am going to Jerusalem with Jesus. We will be leaving in a few weeks. I will make sure all is in order before I go. I also need to make sure I settle any big decisions beforehand.

In the nineteenth year of Tiberius, on the twelfth month, the twenty-third day — Jesus and the disciples came through Magdala for me. Salome, Mary, the mother of James the Less (I want to write Mary the less to save writing, but then that could make people think I am Mary the greater. I will stick with the full term), and Susanna. Joanna is going to meet us near Jericho.

We are camping for the night. This first day has been uneventful. As is the case when we first leave for Jerusalem, not a lot of people are journeying with us. The crowds grow as we make our way.

Nathanael got our campsite set up. Simon set our fire. We ate together. Not a lot of talk tonight. A sense of danger fills the air around us. I am not sure why; maybe because Jesus had said He would be betrayed and killed. He did not say when. As a result, the disciples are more watchful. Nathanael follows behind us all. Peter walks on one side of Jesus, John on the other. We all prayed together. We then retired to our respective camps for the night.

In the nineteenth year of Tiberius, on the twelfth month, the twenty-fourth day — We got to the edge of Samaria today. I expected a lot of people to run out to see us. Some did come out, but when ten lepers approached us from a village nearby, the small group of greeters disbanded.

The lepers posed no threat to anyone. They kept their distance from the group and from us. They called in a loud voice from where they were, "Jesus, Master, have pity on us!" No disease deserves as much pity as leprosy. Their faces rot, their ears, their limbs, their fingers. The sores are nauseating. One day a person is fine. He or she may be married with children, a home, a job, and a future. Then a sore appears. They are quarantined. They pray it is not the worst thing they can imagine. The sores spread. They are examined with caution. Then the diagnosis is given. They have leprosy. In that instant, they are separated from everyone dear. No goodbyes. No gathering of their clothes. No collection of money. They are sent away by sword to live with other lepers. They die alone. Only the lepers bury lepers. Most of the time, they drag them out of the camp. Few have strength in their limbs to do the digging. Leprosy is highly contagious. It spreads rapidly.

I saw them at a distance. I was sick at my stomach. I looked at Jesus. He has encountered individuals before with this. At the sight of Him, most run to Him without regard for anyone else. They yearn to be healed. They do not care who they expose to get healed. From what I have seen, Jesus has never turned one away. He has healed every one of them.

But these ten lepers, they were more respectful than any I have seen. They cried out from afar, respectfully, not demanding healing, but asking for mercy. I looked at Jesus. He looked at them. He did not say what I expected. He told them, "Go, show yourselves to the priests." That was it? It was probably the priests they had seen at the first. It was probably a priest who sentenced them to the leper colony. Go see the priest? If I were them, I would have said, "But Lord we have. We need You to heal us. Heal us, please!"

They did not do that. They heard Him. They left. I watched them go. When they had gotten about two hundred yards away, I saw them stop. They were looking at each other. They then looked at their own hands and feet. I heard a yell, like of celebration. The next thing I know, they are running toward Jerusalem. Were they healed? I know Jesus heals. This is only the second time where I have not seen the results. The first was when Jesus told the centurion his servant was healed. The servant was healed at that very moment. I did not see the healing. The centurion sent word back that it was so. But these lepers?

On the twelfth month, the twenty-eighth day — We had a quiet day of walking. We walked in pairs or threes, each having our own conversations about different things. Even so, John and Peter walked beside Jesus. Nathanael followed behind. James moved to our westward side.

Before separating for the night, Jesus called us together. He said, "I have come to bring fire on the earth, and how I wish it were already kindled! But I have a baptism to undergo, and how distressed I am until it is completed. Do you think I came to bring peace on earth? No, I tell you, but division. From now on there will be five in one family divided against each other, three against two and two against three. They will be divided, father against son and son against father, mother against daughter and daughter against mother, mother-in- law against daughter-in-law and daughter-in-law against mother-in-law." He then prayed for us. In the silence, I could sense He was also praying for His own strength. I know I was.

I do not understand all of this mystery. I made my way to a tree between our two camps. I saw Nathanael standing guard. I could see Jesus on His mat, a small distance away from the others. He usually sleeps right in the middle of them all. If Jesus is in danger, why would He allow us to come along? When He has been in danger, the enemies have not been able to harm Him. He has the capacity to keep danger away. He did that in the boat during the storm with the disciples. He was as much at risk as they. I am at the extent of my reasoning. I am trying to bring to mind scriptures of the Messiah to help me make sense of this. The verses are not coming. He is to be the Prince of Peace? But Jesus said He has come to light a fire. He is to be our Wonderful Counselor. Jesus says families will be divided because of Him. His Kingdom is to have no end. Jesus says He is going to be killed. It does not make sense. I write this. I pray Father God, please help me understand. Please protect Jesus. I believe He is Your Son. I love Him. You must love Him far beyond my ability. Help us Father, please.

The Twentieth Year of Tiberius Caesar

In the twentieth year of Tiberius, on the first month, the first day — We are nearing Jericho. Before we set out this morning after a restless night's sleep (at least for me), Jesus called us together. I prayed for some understanding. My hope was this was the answer to my prayer.

Jesus said, "If anyone would come after Me, he must deny himself and take up his cross and follow Me. For whoever wants to save his life will lose it, but whoever loses his life for Me and for the gospel will save it.

What good is it for a man to gain the whole world, yet forfeit his soul? Or what can a man give in exchange for his soul? If anyone is ashamed of Me and My words in this adulterous and sinful generation, the Son of Man will be ashamed of him when He comes in His Father's glory with the holy angels."

I wrote exactly what He said. He does not seem to mind that I keep such copious records. I do not want to forget a word. We walked all day. Now, we are encamped just on the outskirts of Jericho. We ate in silence. We retired to our respective camps. Andrew now keeps watch. Simon left us just now. Susanna, Salome, and Mary, the mother of James the Less, retired to their mats. I have tried to question them — especially Salome. They have no idea. Susanna has the only unflinching confidence in our group. She says, "It will be okay.

Trust Jesus. I do, even when I do not understand."

But is no one concerned about His statement concerning the cross? He said He would be betrayed. Anyone who sides with the Romans is called a traitor. I know firsthand. As tax collectors, Poppa and I have been called that. We were traitors. We were said to have betrayed our people. The Romans crucify. Jesus said He would be killed. The Romans kill using crosses when they want to make a public display of someone. Is that what Jesus is in for?

He asked us to take up our crosses and follow. Is that it? We are all going to be crucified on crosses? It makes sense. He said if we try to save our lives, we will lose them. But, if we are willing to lose our lives for Him, we will save them. If we back down, will Jesus be ashamed of us in His Father's Glory? I am afraid now. I am fearful mostly for Him. His warnings have been about Himself. Now, His warnings seem to include us. Am I willing to die for Him? I believe so firmly. I do not love my life. I did not have a life until I met Him. My whole life has been Him. If He is not in this life, I do not want to be either. So, yes, I will die for Him.

Thomas was willing when they headed back for Lazarus. But crosses? Crucifixion is the worst way to die. It is for animals. It was used for rats long ago, if my history is right. It is for the worst criminals. It is to make a public spectacle of them so no one else will follow in their steps.

If Jesus is crucified, that would mean the Romans want all to know this is what happens to those who follow in Jesus' steps. I follow in His steps. The disciples follow in His steps. I wanted to be a disciple. Now I get to follow Him. It makes sense that those who follow Him will get crucified so that anyone else who considers doing so will think twice.

But what has He done to warrant this? He has healed our sick. He has raised our dead. He has cast out our demons. He has explained God in a way never before conceived, and all in perfect alignment with the scriptures. He has not threatened Rome. He has not tried to become the next high priest. He is from the line of David, but I have never heard Him speak of a kingdom here. He constantly speaks of the Kingdom of Heaven. It would be a reach for Herod or Caesar to take that wrong. He has said those who want to go to Heaven must go through Him. That narrows the pathway. Most want their own pathway. This is the only reason I could see anyone taking offense.

Oh, and He corrects our religious leaders. Why is that offensive? God corrected Aaron. God corrected Miriam. God even corrected Moses. Priests often offer sacrifices for their sins. This is an admission they sin, that they get it wrong. The Scriptures say if we love someone, we will correct them. So, why are His corrections so untenable? Unless the ones He corrects feel they are beyond question. That is true for these leaders of ours.

I see the disciples on their mats. They, too, are restless. I can tell by their movements. They are trying to sleep. They cannot. They have a lot on their minds. I do, too. I look back at the ladies. Other than Susanna, Mary and Salome seem to be struggling, too. It is a hot night. We could excuse it with that, though I do not think that is the reason.

On the first month, the second day — Today was more joyful. Joanna joined us before we broke camp. We had another visitor, too, before we left for the city of Jericho. One of the lepers returned. He was shouting at the top of his lungs, "Jesus! I found You! Jesus! I found You!" He threw himself at Jesus' feet and thanked Him over and over. I could tell from his dialect, and in keeping with when we first saw him, he was a Samaritan. Jesus gladly received him.

Then the Lord asked him a convicting question, but not for him, "Were not all ten cleansed? Where are the other nine? Was no one found to return and give praise to God except this foreigner?" I had not thought of their nationalities. I suppose the other nine were not Samaritans. The man just shook his head. "I have no idea, Jesus. But I am here. I thank You so, so much." He then fell at Jesus' feet again. Jesus said to him, "Rise and go; your faith has made you well." He left with great joy.

We joined in his elation. I felt gratified. I saw the ten lepers leave Jesus. I saw them look at each other about two hundred yards away. I saw them look at their own limbs. I heard some sort of excitement. I saw them run toward Jerusalem. Jesus must have healed them just then. That is why He sent them to the priest. The priest, by law, must declare them cleansed so they can move back in with their wives, children, families, villages, and homes. Those men got to bid farewell to the leper colony. I can understand them wanting to return home after being away. What I am so impressed with is that before this man even went to share the good news with his family, he wanted to thank Jesus first. What a lesson for me! I cannot wait to tell Atticus about this.

My concern in our world is how often do we ask God to do something for us? We need a miracle. We pray for divine intervention. We ask God to do what only He can do. Sometimes, it is a whole community praying for someone tragically hurt in their midst. Oftentimes, we see the person die or continue in their affliction. But sometimes we see them made well. I am grieved that when God does give us the supernatural, we quickly give thanks to the doctors, or the diet, or the medicine, or the love of the family, or the will of the person. We tend to sweep it under the rug as if the miracle came through some natural means. We ask God or Jesus to do something. He acts. We then act as if He did nothing. We do not return to Him, and Him alone, to give thanks. I rejoice in the one. I am regretful in the nine. I pray I will be in the category of the one.

Not long afterward, I saw a great crowd coming toward Jesus from all directions. This leper must have been spreading the word everywhere he went as he looked for Jesus. We entered Jericho with masses. People were running toward us. Many pushed past us to get near Jesus. He welcomed each and every one. He spoke to the different people who came up. Many wanted just a word with Him. Some wanted merely to touch His garment or shake His hand. I felt as though this was how Jericho would welcome the prophet Isaiah, or the king David, or the priest Mattathias to their town. He was One they had heard about. His fame had spread throughout the entire region. Jesus had come to their town.

Jesus walked along, taking His time. He would stop often to visit with this lady or that elderly gentleman. He came under a sycamore tree. Under the shade, He visited with many. He sat on a rock wall there. One by one, they came before Him as if He were Solomon readily giving wisdom. I watched. After a few hours, Jesus looked up. I looked up, too. There above His head, high up, were legs dangling. The leaves covered his face. Jesus raised His voice just a little to be heard above the crowd. He said, "Zacchaeus, come down immediately. I must stay at your house today."

Zacchaeus! I knew a Zacchaeus from Jericho. I met him at one of Matthew's tax collector gatherings with Poppa. He was the chief collector for the region around Jericho. He was a short, feisty man. Sure enough, he made his way down the tree, going from one lower limb to the next lower limb. He hung by his arms on the lowest limb and dropped to the ground. It was our Zacchaeus! He welcomed Jesus gladly. The people did not have the same response when they saw him dismount from his ledge.

Jesus told my father's tax collector friend, in their hearing, that He was going to stay at his house today. The people from Jericho were vocal in their displeasure. One distinct voice yelled out in anger, "He is going to be the guest of a 'sinner.'" Zacchaeus heard the man. He responded back, looking at Jesus, but speaking so all could hear: "Look, Lord! Here and now I give half of my possessions to the poor, and if I have cheated anybody out of anything, I will pay back four times the amount." The crowd began to cheer. That meant they were going to get back money he had taken from them unfairly. I am thankful Poppa never did business like that. The poor in the crowd also cheered. This wealthy man was going to give half of his vast wealth to them. They assumed, as did I, that they were the poor who would be direct beneficiaries of his largesse.

Jesus smiled broadly. He said, "Today salvation has come to this house, because this man, too, is a son of Abraham. For the Son of Man came to seek and to save what was lost." I thought of that young ruler who had all his wealth. He had kept all the commandments to the best of his ability, but was unwilling to give away all he had and follow Jesus. On the other hand, Zacchaeus volunteered to give half of his wealth, and then more, to settle with those he had cheated. He wanted to see Jesus. He wanted to follow Jesus. I do not know his heart, but the Lord does. Zacchaeus accepted Jesus as his Lord. I did the same months ago.

Later, I had the privilege to reacquaint myself with Zacchaeus. He knew my father, Jared. He talked about all the things they had been through. They were both Jewish. They both had faced the criticism and hatred of our people. They had both made money. The people of Israel had called each of them traitors. I let Zacchaeus know that Poppa gave his heart to Jesus, too. He did not have near the insight that I have now, but with all Poppa grasped, he accepted Jesus for himself.

The more we visited, the more Zacchaeus was comfortable to ask me about myself. He had heard of my meltdowns. Poppa shared concerns at their last meeting together about my erratic behavior. He asked me what changed. I shared with him how Poppa took me to see Jesus in Capernaum, and how He cast seven demons out of me at the front door of Peter's house. We both celebrated together. I told him about Matthew. Zacchaeus knew Matthew. He had heard Matthew had quit the tax booth, but had no idea he was now following Jesus, that he had become one of His twelve disciples. I could tell Zacchaeus was thinking. He got quiet. He then asked me, "Was Matthew in my house earlier?" I said, "Yes." He said he knew one of the disciples looked strangely familiar. Matthew heard his name and walked up. He and Zacchaeus had a grand reunion. Here we were, three tax collectors, each of us following Jesus, each of us having been given a new life. That is what Jesus does!

We are staying in Zacchaeus's fabulous house this evening. He and Jesus are visiting. The other disciples are sitting around them, marveling. I bet Simon the Zealot is feeling awfully odd. He once protested tax collectors. He hated us. Now, he is a disciple with one. He is staying in the home of another; even while yet another tax collector prepares his evening supper. Talk about the walls closing in. Simon is changing. That's what Jesus does.

On the first month, the third day — We left Zacchaeus's house this morning. He had a nice breakfast prepared for all of us. As we were making our way out of town, we heard someone up ahead shouting Jesus' name. He yelled other things, but I could not make out what he was saying. The crowd was following Jesus. They had decided to join us on our trip to Jerusalem for Passover. I had felt everyone was turning against Jesus in Capernaum. Since we left there, our crowds have grown larger by the day. It seems the whole world is not turning on Him but turning to Him. Perhaps all the talk of betrayal and death were spoken in hyperbole to cause us to be alert to the ebb and flow of public sentiment.

Anyway, the man was yelling. Trying to hear Jesus as He spoke, the crowd began to yell back for him to be quiet even as we approached him. The closer we got to him, I could tell he was blind. He had a cup out. He was begging for money. Obviously, some family member set him up there every morning on that main thoroughfare to help him raise money for his basic needs. He could hear us drawing near. His cries were heard clearly over and over again: "Jesus, Son of David, have mercy on me! Son of David, have mercy on me! Jesus, Son of David, have mercy on me!" Many rebuked him and told him to be quiet, but he shouted all the more. "Son of David, have mercy on me!"

Jesus stopped and said, "Call him." The irritated crowd's attitude changed immediately. The ebb and flow of public sentiment was on display. They called to the blind man, "Cheer up! On your feet! He's calling you." Throwing his cloak aside, he jumped to his feet and came to the sound of Jesus' voice.

Jesus asked him, "What do you want Me to do for you?" The blind man said, "Rabbi, I want to see." "Go," said Jesus, "your faith has healed you." Immediately he received his sight. I watched. His eyes were clouded over. His pupils were barely detectable. When the Rabbi informed him his faith had healed him, he blinked several times. On about the third blink, his eyes became as clear as anyone's there. He had the darkest brown pupils. The clearest white of his eyes surrounded them. No blood veins showing. He focused on Jesus. His eyes actually opened wide in excitement. He saw for the first time, a human being. I never want to be blind. I would rather lose any sense than my eyesight. But, if I were born blind, Jesus would be the first human being I would want to see. Spiritually, I had the same experience. Spiritually, when my eyes were opened, Jesus was the first person I saw. I fell in love with Him that moment — the Son of God.

I can still hear him now. He said to Jesus, "My name is Bartimaeus." Jesus nodded as if He already knew that. There was no need to tell Him anyone's name. Jesus told him to go. He received his sight. He could go — no more begging, no more being led to a main road, no more being dependent. He could go and live a normal life. What thrills me as I write this evening is Bartimaeus did not go. He is camping with us now. He did not go. He followed Jesus. He is going to Jerusalem with us for Passover. Who knows? He may follow Jesus back to Capernaum.

On the first month, the fifth day — Our progress has been terribly slow. The crowds are overflowing around us. I think of the crowds around the Temple to worship God, to pray to God, and to wait for God to do something extraordinary. The crowds following Jesus are coming to Him after waiting to see God do something extraordinary. They come with their requests, their prayers for Jesus to do that needful thing.

When He does, they worship God, as well as Jesus.

Salome has been especially engaged. She has been walking with her two sons. Her eyes grow bigger by the day. She visited with us last night, talking about how she truly believes what we are experiencing are the precursors for the coronation of Jesus as the king of Israel. In a way, it makes sense. Joanna has her hand on the pulse of such things. She said last night that Israel is in turmoil. There is disgust with the Roman rule, with the puppet Herod Agrippa's rule, and with the Caiaphas-led religious rule. The people are looking for someone who is good, who is holy, who is pure in all motives. They want someone, too, who has power to bring about change to this nation. They realize it will require someone almost miraculous to hold all enemies at bay. Jesus has that ability. Salome was in full agreement.

Even with last night's conversation, great disgust arose among ten of the disciples when Salome made her move toward Jesus. She led her sons James and John in front of Jesus. The whole crowd stopped. Jesus stopped. There was no way to continue unless He chose to walk around them. He has never done such a thing. Salome knelt before Jesus, pulling her two sons down with her.

Salome said that she had a favor to ask of Jesus. The Lord asked her to tell Him what it is. She made her request. "Grant that one of these two sons of mine may sit at Your right and the other at Your left in Your Kingdom." Judas grumbled, as did the others. Jesus had told us that God desires humility, that our only desire should be to please God. That is contrary to our culture.

What we heard from Salome was a vein of ambition all have fought to keep concealed. I suppose everyone has some vision of grandeur. This is especially true when we see crowds clamoring for Jesus. It was true when we saw all the people running after the disciples at Tabor. At this time, when we are hearing of coronations, it makes sense small men of Galilee could conceive an opportunity for them in the capital of our nation and her people.

Jesus paused. I wondered, is He going to grant this request? If He does, how many of the men will wish they would have asked first, if it was that easy to gain position? There was no doubt who would be on the throne. That certainly would be Jesus. But to be on one side of Him or the other would be the loftiest position one could desire.

Jesus then answered, "You don't know what you are asking." He looked at James and John. He asked them, "Can you drink the cup I am going to drink?" Both answered simultaneously, "We can." Jesus then said to them, "You will indeed drink from My cup, but to sit at My right or left is not for Me to grant. These places belong to those for whom they have been prepared by My Father."

James and John stood. Salome fell back into the crowd. I think she was embarrassed, but more disappointed. She wondered how we would act, especially Mary, the mother of James the Less. Mary would have never asked such a thing. James the Less would have silenced his mom at the very mention of trying something as brash as that. The other ten disciples began to chastise James and John. Peter was not exempted. He is the oldest of the disciples. One would think he possessed the seniority for such a position.

A mother's zeal was trying to upend that. Arguing occurred. I could see the sons of thunder, James and John, were ready to fight. The ten's rebuke offended them, but the comments about their mother made them really angry. There we were, so close to our entrance into Jerusalem, perhaps to see Jesus enthroned, and His twelve are at each other's throats. Is this what power does? They had no power. The mere scent of it was dividing these once humble men.

Jesus called them together and said, “You know that the rulers of the Gentiles lord it over them, and their high officials exercise authority over them. Not so with you. Instead, whoever wants to become great among you must be your servant, and whoever wants to be first must be your slave — just as the Son of Man did not come to be served, but to serve, and to give His life as a ransom for many.” With that, the arguing ceased. All were disciplined with loving words.

How I love Jesus. Look at how He is with people. He treats everyone the same. He gives no preferences. He also gives no one special privileges to sin. He strictly follows God’s commands. He calls for all who follow Him to do the same. We are seeing, in His presence, the Kingdom of Heaven. I believe that how He lives, how He calls us to live, is the ethic of all who are in Heaven today. Abraham had faults on earth. None in Heaven. Moses had weaknesses on earth, but not in Heaven’s city limits. If we could all live like Jesus, no bickering would occur. There would be no one-upmanship. He listens. He sees. He backs the crowd down for the pleading blind man. He weeps when someone dies. He calls His friend back from the dead. He rebukes the storm from scaring those He loves. He eats with a tax collector when the world says no. He stands in between the adulteress and the men with stones. He walks through the crowd of haters. He forgives sins. He gives entrance to Heaven. He changes lives in between.

I do not know if anyone else caught it. I write in my parchments to record, but also to reason out what I have seen or heard. Jesus said, “The Son of Man did not come to be served, but to serve, and to give his life as a ransom for many.” Jesus came to give His life as a ransom for many. There is that hint of what lies down the road. He said He would be betrayed. He said He would be killed. Now He qualifies it: He will give His life. That makes sense. I have seen some attempt to kill Him, but they could not. The disciples recently witnessed another attempt. He walked right out of it. I do not believe anyone can kill Him. But I suppose if He wanted, He could voluntarily give up His life. Is that what He is doing? Or is that another statement of hyperbole?

Truly, in all the time I have known Him, nothing has been about Him. Everything He does, He is doing for others. It is as if His only purpose in life is to help, bless, deliver, and heal others. I see this as Him giving up His life.

On the first month, the sixth day — We stayed in camp for the Sabbath. Jesus taught us this morning with great clarity that He is the Son of Man, the Christ, the Messiah. He also made it clear He will assume the Throne beside His Father, God. Such things I have never heard uttered from His lips before. I look and I see a man with flesh and bones. I see His feet are dirty. I have seen Him tired. I have seen Him prepare a meal. I have seen Him sleep as I gazed from the women's camp. He loves on people. He puts His arm around this disciple or that as He walks. He smiles. He weeps. His stomach growls when He is hungry. We all laugh. That one element shows He is fully man, a neighbor from Galilee.

The next thing we know, He gives this hard-to-imagine discourse. I took down nearly everything He said. I am still thankful for the record-keeping training I learned in the tax booth. He said, "When the Son of Man comes in His glory, and all the angels with Him, He will sit on His throne in heavenly glory. All the nations will be gathered before Him, and He will separate the people one from another as a shepherd separates the sheep from the goats. He will put the sheep on His right and the goats on His left. Then the King will say to those on His right, 'Come, you who are blessed by My Father; take your inheritance, the Kingdom prepared for you since the creation of the world. For I was hungry and you gave Me something to eat, I was thirsty and you gave Me something to drink, I was a stranger and you invited Me in, I needed clothes and you clothed Me, I was sick and you looked after Me, I was in prison and you came to visit Me.' Then the righteous will answer Him, 'Lord, when did we see You hungry and feed You, or thirsty and give You something to drink? When did we see You a stranger and invite You in, or needing clothes and clothe You? When did we see You sick or in prison and go to visit You? The King will reply, 'I tell You the truth, whatever You did for one of the least of these brothers of Mine, you did for Me.' Then He will say to those on His left, 'Depart from Me, you who are cursed, into the eternal fire prepared for the devil and his angels. For I was hungry and you gave Me nothing to eat, I was thirsty and you gave Me nothing to drink, I was a stranger and you did not invite Me in, I needed clothes and you did not clothe Me, I was sick and in prison and you did not look after Me.' They also will answer, 'Lord, when did we see You hungry or thirsty or a stranger or needing clothes or sick or in prison, and did not help You?' He will reply, 'I tell you the truth, whatever you did not do for one of the least of these, you did not do for Me.' Then they will go away to eternal punishment, but the righteous to eternal life."

So much of this discourse to understand. My immediate take-away is that Jesus will sit on His throne judging all nations, every group of people, every person individually. That means I will stand before Him, too, on that day. He will not simply have the power to judge, but He will separate in judgment. Those who followed Him, who served Him through others, will enter Heaven. Then, this Jesus who loves, who is merciful, who is willing to forgive, will cast those who did not follow Him, who did not show their love for Him by serving others, into Hell. I tremble at the thought. He did not take pleasure in sharing that last part. It was with grief and hesitation that He shared that.

I thought I had heard the full of the teaching when He dropped in one last statement that made all the rest of His lesson fall by the wayside. He said, "As you know, the Passover is days away— and the Son of Man will be handed over to be crucified." There it is. Jesus was not talking in hyperbole. He actually believes He is about to be crucified. He reiterated it again. I suppose it is to prepare us in some way. If it does happen, none of us can say, "He didn't tell us." I cannot think of Him on a Roman cross. I refuse to. The twelve do not even seem to want to speak of it. They act as if He never said such a thing. Is this what Salome wants for her sons? A cross? Jesus said they would drink from the same cup. I will go as far to say, if this were to happen to my Lord, He has told us ahead of time. I would hope we would not jump to the conclusion that Jesus did not foresee this. Or, that we followed Jesus in vain, that somehow we misread who He was. That is all I will write on the subject.

We are leaving in a few hours for Bethany. I will make ready.

We arrived in Bethany this evening. Who was at the end of the road but Lazarus! He ran to hug Jesus. Jesus hugged him back, lifting him from the ground in delight. They laughed. They would share. They would embrace again. Smiles were everywhere. To think this man was dead. Jesus did not want him to be, so Jesus fixed the problem. He brought him back to life.

Lazarus said the village of Bethany has prepared a banquet in His honor to thank Him. No greater evidence testifies to what Jesus has done. This was not some rumor resurrection. The entire village knew their neighbor was dead. They all attended his funeral. They oversaw his burial. They were present when Jesus arrived. They saw the stone rolled away. They heard Jesus call him out. They saw their friend Lazarus, a man of the village, walk out in dead-stinking burial clothes. They unwrapped him themselves, to see their friend alive again. This was no secret. All of Jerusalem knows, too. They say the priestly sort are fit to be tied. Bethany did hold a banquet in Jesus' honor. I was invited. There was another surprise. It was not held at Lazarus' home, but at the home of a man named Simon. Oh, by the way, he is called Simon the Leper. So, we ate at a leper's colony? No. We ate at a man's home, a man named Simon who was once a leper. Jesus healed him on one of His trips to Jerusalem. Simon was restored to his family. I looked at him closely. He was not one of the ten Jesus had healed on our way in this time. Imagine, we are eating in the former leper's home with a former dead man, along with many from Bethany who owe Jesus so much. They are not ashamed to show it.

The food was delightful. They treated the disciples with great respect. There was no question, though, that Jesus was the center of attention. He was the man, or the Son of Man, they all sought to honor. Martha joined the ladies of Simon's household preparing the meal. Salome, Mary the mother of James the Less, Susanna, Joanna, and myself did all we could to help. We would go into the kitchen, then be run out as they declared we were guests. Ultimately, we surrendered to sit around the huge tables. Ours was one away from Jesus' table, Lazarus to His right, Simon to His left. James and John were at my table, not theirs. They very humbly sat with Salome.

When the meal was finished, I began to smell a strong scent of perfume. I thought perhaps one of the children had broken one in their play. I saw Jesus push away from the table. There on the ground before Him was a woman. I sat up. From my place, I could see it was Mary, Martha's sister — Mary of Bethany. She took about a pint of pure nard. This was no cheap perfume. This was an exceedingly expensive perfume.

Poppa had bought Momma a jar when he got his first proceeds from the tax booth. This was a once-in-a- lifetime purchase. One uses it rarely, only for special occasions. It is taken just in little increments to make it last. Yet, Mary poured a large portion onto Jesus' feet. She began to wipe His feet with her hair. Mary then poured the remainder upon His head. It was her way literally of pouring out her love on Jesus. I watched, almost jealous. I wish I would have thought of that! I still have Momma's pint of pure nard in Magdala. The idea never crossed my mind to do something so extravagant.

In that beautiful moment, I was offended to hear Judas say, "Why this waste? This perfume could have been sold at a high price and the money given to the poor." How dare he interrupt! That was not his money. That was not his place to judge another. Everything we have learned from Jesus, has Judas heard anything? I was gladdened when Jesus confronted him. Jesus defended her by saying, "Why are you bothering this woman? She has done a beautiful thing to Me. The poor you will always have with you, but you will not always have Me. When she poured this perfume on My body, she did it to prepare Me for burial. I tell you the truth, wherever this Gospel is preached throughout the world, what she has done will also be told, in memory of her."

With that, Judas left, humiliated. He should have felt that. I hear Jesus has corrected other disciples publicly. He has corrected Peter. He has called out James and John. They all have learned from it. I pray Judas does, too. Again, what I heard is a continuation of what Jesus has told us. He would be betrayed. He would be killed. He would be killed through crucifixion. He would carry a cross. He said tonight that she has prepared Him for His burial. I want all of this to be hyperbole. How can it be? Jesus is being very specific. My prayer tonight is, "Please Father, do not let Your Son be killed. Please protect Him, even above us."

On the first month, the seventh day — We had a great time of honoring Jesus at Simon's last night. Many stood and shared with the dinner guests what Jesus had done for them. It was the most amazing time of praise. People teared up as others shared how Jesus had changed their lives. The scent of Mary's perfume spread throughout the room, as did the words of gratitude. Jesus listened intently to each. He smiled.

Sometimes, He got up, walked over to the one who shared, and gave them a warm embrace.

I shared about Poppa and Momma's struggle with me. I told of the demons. I told of the attempted suicides. I shared with them how I almost killed a man. I was sharing this with strangers. I was the only one not of Bethany or Bethpage who shared. I may have overstepped my bounds. I could not stay silent. I wanted to get in on the praise. When I told how He healed me, how He allowed me to go with Him, to learn from Him, He looked at me. He smiled with joy. I walked over to where He was seated. I gave Him a hug. He returned it. There was love for all. I walked away from Him with that smell of Bethany Mary's perfume. By the end of the evening, we all carried that aroma of love. It was sweeter than any man can mix.

We returned last night from Bethpage. We stayed in Bethany, in the home of Lazarus. This morning, we are setting out for Jerusalem. Much of the crowd left us when we broke for Bethany yesterday evening.

This morning, Martha prepared breakfast. We did not eat much as we were still satisfied from the night before. Jesus then led us to Jerusalem. The twelve followed Him. Nathanael walked behind. He is still leery of trouble. James and John returned to walk beside Him. Andrew walked to the right of our party, Simon the Zealot to our left. Peter followed behind Jesus. The rest of the disciples followed, as did Lazarus, Mary of Bethany, Martha, Mary, the mother of James the Less, Salome, Susanna, and myself. Salome has been very quiet since our walk out of Jericho. I decided to walk a while with her so she would know she is loved even when she falls. I have fallen many times.

We reached the top of the Mount of Olives. As I expected, Jesus stopped. He gazed upon the city of Jerusalem. He called two of the disciples to Him and said, "Go to the village ahead of you, and just as you enter it, you will find a donkey tied there with her colt. No one has ever ridden on the colt. Untie the colt and bring it here. If anyone asks you, 'Why are you doing this?' tell him, 'The Lord needs it and will send it back here shortly.'"

We waited. Joanna met us at the crest of the Mount of Olives. As she greeted everyone, I thought about the colt no one has ever ridden on before. What will Jesus do with a donkey's colt that is not broken? I had no idea. Obviously, the men had no trouble procuring the donkey's colt. They were back in a short amount of time. They brought it to Jesus. They threw their cloaks on the colt. I cannot help but think Jesus motioned for them to do that. I do not know a lot about donkeys or their colts. I am not sure the disciples know much more. But, at Jesus' beckoning, they got an unbroken colt and threw their garments on him. Jesus had them help Him get on its back. The colt did not buck. He did not resist. Under the Lord, he complied like the tamest of all animals. I write yet another thing Jesus has done that defies logic.

As we made our way down the Mount of Olives, the unexpected occurred. Crowds began to rush toward Jesus. They laid down their cloaks on the path in front of Him. Others cut palm branches with their knives, rushing to lay them ahead of Him on the pathway toward the Temple. I stepped back to where Joanna was. I asked her, "Is this what you expected here?" She was overjoyed. She said, "The time has come for a coronation!"

No sooner did she say that, I heard the crowds cheering, shouting from the front of us, "Hosanna to the Son of David! Blessed is He who comes in the name of the Lord! Hosanna in the highest!" From the sides, they shouted, "Blessed is the King who comes in the name of the Lord! Peace in Heaven and glory in the highest!" From behind I could hear them, "Hosanna! Blessed is He who comes in the name of the Lord! Blessed is the King of Israel!" It truly was a coronation. Jesus is loved. The people do not even seem to be here for Passover, but for Him. Or maybe He is the event we have waited for since Moses proclaimed the first Passover. I was overwhelmed. I was overjoyed! I joined in the shouting, "Blessed is the King who comes in the name of the Lord! Peace in Heaven and glory in the highest!"

Thousands upon thousands of people filled the streets. They formed a moving wall in front of us. With each step toward them, they separated at just the right time to make way for our King. I have never felt so much optimism in my life. If Jesus takes the throne, Rome may lose to our own people, or the Romans may withdraw in fear. Agrippa will run to one of his palaces a long way away. Pilate will have no reason to stay. I can imagine if Jesus is made king today, or this week, there will be no more sickness, or blindness, or paralysis, or deafness, or leprosy. He may even put an end to death. God the Father's kingdom may come this week. God's Will may be done. Before long, all nations will meet us here in Jerusalem to worship the Living God. Has this not always been our hope? I wish Poppa and Momma were here now. If I understand Jesus' teachings, they may come down to join us here. I am weeping with joy and excitement, fearful to write more on this subject, too. I do not want to get my hopes up too much.

We did see some resistance today to sober our joy by a mustard seed's size. Some of the Pharisees in the crowd fought their way to Jesus. They shoved to the ground many who were gathered around Him. No love for the people exists in these "leaders." They are just as Jesus had said. They made it to Jesus. They grabbed the reins of the colt to stop Jesus. They said to Him, "Teacher, rebuke your disciples!" How dare they! I half-expected them to try to knock Him off the colt and mount it themselves. I wish they would have tried. They would see how a colt that has never been ridden responds to the hands of a stranger. Before they could do more, Jesus corrected them, "I tell you, if they keep quiet, the stones will cry out." With that, the crowd cheered all the more. It was deafening. I looked to the right where, behind the colt, Bartimaeus was leading the cheers. The Pharisees slithered away. My ears are still ringing.

Our procession lasted hours. We went down the Mount of Olives slower than a crawl. We entered the Sheep's Gate but were stopped as so many were gathering. They would separate with each step of the donkey's colt. In normal circumstances, no donkey could have stayed to the path with so many people yelling, reaching, throwing down coats, casting palm branches in front, but this little colt was under the Master's hand — his Master. He calms the storm. He guides the unbroken donkey's colt.

We reached the Temple courtyards. The crowd was in a frenzy. Every one of us was yelling at the person next to us just to be heard. I saw some men with Andrew and Philip at the Gentile court. They appeared to be Greeks by their attire. I moved near them. I heard them yell to be heard above the cheering. They shouted to the two disciples who were no more than a foot away from them that they wanted to see Jesus. Andrew and Philip walked up to tell Jesus. I followed in their wake. Jesus said to them, having to shout, too, to be heard, "The hour has come for the Son of Man to be glorified. I tell you the truth, unless a kernel of wheat falls to the ground and dies, it remains only a single seed. But if it dies, it produces many seeds. The man who loves his life will lose it, while the man who hates his life in this world will keep it for eternal life. Whoever serves Me must follow Me; and where I am, My servant also will be. My Father will honor the one who serves Me. Now My heart is troubled, and what shall I say? 'Father, save Me from this hour'? No, it was for this very reason I came to this hour. Father, glorify Your name!"

I wish Jesus would take time to explain what He says. Then again, who would be able to hear over this bedlam? I gathered Jesus was conveying to His disciples that if someone wishes an audience with Him, they must follow first. The two Greeks looked like men of wealth or power. Perhaps they figured their status would delight Jesus. He was not moved. I also think this is not the time for consultations. Jesus stated this is the hour the Son of Man is to be glorified. He surely is being glorified. It started at Simon the Leper's house (Simon once-the-leper's house). It has exploded today over all Jerusalem.

Again, in all this glory, Jesus spoke of a kernel of wheat being buried; that if we love our lives, we will lose them, and if we hate this life in this world, we will gain a superior, eternal one. Jesus said He was troubled. I do not know if He is troubled because He fears the position of king, or He fears the attempts on His life as king. The Romans are good at killing their rivals. The Herods are even worse.

I will not be dismayed. In the twentieth year of Tiberius, I believe Israel has ushered in her king. I bet even the people from Capernaum have joined in this mass of humanity. They were shouting His name with the people of Korazin and Bethsaida. Everyone is turning to Him now! Just then, a loud thunder blast struck our ears, rumbling for perhaps four or five seconds. It was the only thing that overpowered the crowds' shouts. It hit with a volcanic explosion and rumbled like thunder following a long string of lightning. The thunderbolt served as a crescendo to today's event. A buzz is arising all over the city. This Passover is different from any other.

Each step took what seemed like hours. By the time Jesus dismounted at the Temple, darkness was falling. He had the two disciples return the donkey. They made their way through the crowd. He talked with all who were around Him. I lost sight of Him. I knelt and prayed in the women's court. I could not thank God enough for this day. He brought me to His Son. He brought me to the highest point in my life. I traveled with His Son and His disciples. I have made them meals. I have sat at His feet. I have been changed. I am being changed. God is in His holy Temple. His Son is ministering in His stead outside it. We had always wanted God to rend the heavens and come down. It appears He has.

When we returned to Bethany this evening, we were exhausted. Joanna asked us to stay with her. We could not. How can we leave Jesus at this moment? What would we miss? We won the discussion, so much so that Joanna stayed with us at Lazarus's home. Mary and Martha shared their room with us.

I heard Andrew talking in the other room about the sound of that thunderclap. I went in to hear what he had to say. He believed he heard God speak like He spoke at Jesus' baptism. He said that Jesus had prayed at the top of His lungs above the noise of the crowd, "Father, Glorify Your Name." Andrew believed he heard God answer, "I have glorified it, and will glorify it again." The Greek men thought it was the voice of an angel.

Andrew, who saw Jesus baptized, said he recognized that voice. He said it was God's voice. With that, I returned to my room. All I could do was pray and rejoice.

On the first month, the eighth day — I had a difficult time sleeping last night. I was so excited by the crowds. I had no idea what this day would bring. I could see the crowds drive out Herod and Pilate. Both are here in Jerusalem for the Passover. I could see Caiaphas and Annas slipping out with the escort of the Pharisees, of all groups. If the Lord was escorted in yesterday, surely plans are being made to seize this opportunity to make true the prophecies of the Messiah. I miss Atticus. He has no idea what a joyous time these days are.

I got up early this morning. Martha had made some breakfast for us. I enjoyed visiting with her while the others were getting ready. The Lord had gone out early this morning, I suppose to pray. Everyone had eaten by the time He walked back into the house. Martha offered Jesus some food. He graciously declined. He then headed out the door with the disciples, the ladies, and me following.

I had gathered my money along with that from the ladies. I gave the money to Judas as we were heading out the door for whatever needs the Lord might have today with His disciples. We easily could have paid for the things as they came. We planned to be with them, but we felt it would be better for the Rabbi's own men to be seen paying for what they needed. This would prevent any slanderous accusations.

I need to write of an odd occurrence. As I wrote, Jesus left without eating. We noticed the smells of the food coming from the different houses we passed. He seemed to be hungry. Seeing in the distance a fig tree in leaf, Jesus walked up to its trunk. He looked up, seemingly to grab a fig from it. He reached up, pulled on some limbs, and opened up a few clusters of leaves. He found nothing. My understanding is that fig trees do not bear fruit this time of year, but Jesus was looking for some. Perhaps this is a kind that bears in this season. I am a tax collector, not an orchard expert. Jesus then said to the tree in our hearing, "May no one ever eat fruit from you again." I heard Him. The disciples did too. James looked as dumbfounded as I felt.

As we topped the Mount of Olives, the Lord paused. There was a simple, silent prayer. No call for a donkey was made. No crowds lined up with palm branches. I found that odd. As I looked toward the Temple, I did see the crowds. I assumed they were waiting on us there.

When we approached the Sheep Gate, people began to follow us. Many resumed the cheers from yesterday. As we neared the Temple courts, the odor shocked me. Beneath our feet was excrement from oxen, bulls, sheep, goats, and doves. The atmosphere was carnival-like. Booth after booth was set up in the Gentile courts.

One gruff-looking man called us over to his table. He showed us his lambs. He boasted of how he alone had the blessing of the high priest for his stock. He had a ribbon on every lamb to indicate each was priest- approved.

I was curious. I recognized him from our tax booth days. Many things were shipped in and out of our port. He knew my face. He struggled to remember my name, but he kept saying, "Jared's daughter." I told him he was correct. I told him my name. He reminded me his name was Rufus. I think Rufus thought I was still working the tax booth in Magdala. He gave me special courtesy. He even offered me a lamb for free. It was his way of trying to gain favor for some perceived violation he had committed. He spoke to me as if we were of the same ilk. I felt comfortable to ask him how he had gotten so close to the high priest here in Jerusalem.

He winked. He said he does not know the high priest personally, but they allow such claims as long as the vendors give money to the priest's official who comes through the courtyard each day. I was upset that such graft was going on here in the house of God. I looked up to see the Lord looking right at me. I felt He knew everything this dealer was doing.

The disciples were called to one table after another. Some had scantily clad women calling men to their male-friends' booths. This was not appropriate in all of Israel, yet there they were in the Temple courts — granted, the Gentile portion. Each operating booth was attempting to cut a better deal than the one before. Each claimed to have priestly approval for their livestock. How could anyone believe any of these had such endorsements? Then again, each animal purchased was receiving approval at the altar inside the Temple. The same went on for the sellers of doves and the merchants of cattle.

A man with a patch on his eye called out to Salome. She went over. He was a money-changer. They were charging an exorbitant amount for worshippers to obtain the only coins the Temple priests would accept. What was sickening about that coin or shekel was that it had the head of a Greek god on one side and the graven image of an eagle on the back. I believe the priests desired this coin regardless of its image, because its silver content is known to be greater than that of the Roman coins. They forbid the Roman coins with the excuse that these held the graven image of the emperor. They declared the accepted money with the graven image of a Greek god as clean, provided it be used for the Temple. The coin was only deemed unclean if it was used for immoral purposes. What greedy hypocrisy! Does no one see that?

To me, the more fitting coin is the lepton, which Jesus pointed out as the gift the widow gave. It appropriately has a star on it signifying our coming Messiah as God foretold through Balaam: "I see Him, but not now; I behold Him, but not near. A star will come out of Jacob; a scepter will rise out of Israel." The other side has an anchor with the inscription, "Gift of Jehovah." If the priests really wanted to honor God, why not mint this one in silver? I know why. Herod would hate it, for he is no Messiah and has no plans to be replaced by one.

The clamoring for our attention was annoying. The begging for our money was even worse. Who can worship God in the Temple with all of this corruption going on before our eyes? I was nauseated by it all. I silently prayed God would stop all of this, that He would turn us back to Him. I prayed for His spirit to sweep over our nation. Then again, is this not what Jesus has been doing? He has been turning hearts toward God. He has been doing what Andrew said John the Baptizer said He would do.

No sooner did I have this thought, I heard a loud noise. Tables were crashing. People were running out of the courtyard. Doves were flying everywhere. Sheep and goats were running by me with their keepers following after. Several cattle ran, knocking over people and more tables. I heard the sound of money bouncing on the limestone pavement. Down on the ground, many were scurrying to pick up what they could. The money-changers were cursing them: "Give me back that money! That is mine! Stop! Thief!"

I looked to see Jesus' reaction, just to find He was the instigator of the action. He was overturning the tables and benches of the sellers. Even as people were gathering their animals back, trying to upright their tables, Jesus flipped them back. He would not let anyone carry merchandise through the Temple courts. He ran out every one of the buyers and sellers. The priests and their guards tried to put down the uprising. They were unable to. Someone screamed a warning, "Governor Pilate's guards are on their way, run!" Jesus yelled over them, "Is it not written: 'My house will be called a house of prayer for all nations'? But you have made it 'a den of robbers.'" He was looking eye to eye with several of the priests. What did they care about God? They did not even believe in life after death. Hence, they feared no judgment beyond this life. No wonder they were so brazen as to make this little Temple fiefdom their personal kingdom.

The guards came toward Him, but when they heard Jesus, they ran. I suppose they never had heard anyone speak with the authority of Jesus. I have never heard anyone speak like this, either. I have only heard Jesus speak this way when He was casting demons out of people. Is this what He is doing? Are there demons here for Him to cast?

I am having a hard time writing what happened next. I can only describe it as a pristine calm sweeping over the Temple. I imagined it being like the Galilee after Jesus calmed the storm. A peace ensued, as if a burden was lifted. From every corner, the blind and the lame came to Jesus. This One who scared the guards, the merchants, and the priests, posed no threat to the true worshippers. Many had come with a prayer to be healed. There Jesus was. He heals. Naturally, they went to Him.

It was not only the sick. Children from all around were coming to Him. They began to shout, "Hosanna to the Son of David." I envisioned them hiding during the chaos of Jesus throwing out the crooks. But I think they were hiding before Jesus came. God has given these little ones an innate sense of people. I believe they felt endangered by these merchants. I think they sensed darkness in the Temple. After the vendors were gone, they felt the weight lifted, too. They began to sing songs about Jesus. He would hold their hands. He would kiss their heads. He would join in a circle with them, enjoying Himself. This One, who moments ago had the power to throw people out, suddenly had the compassion to draw in children. Parents were unafraid of Him. It was surreal.

When they sensed it was safe, the cowardly priests reared their ugly heads. They tentatively walked up to Jesus. They waited for Him to acknowledge them. Giving them permission to speak, they asked the Lord, "Do you hear what these children are saying? They are calling You the Son of David. They are singing Hosanna about You?" That was true. These kids were crying "Hosanna to the Son of David", and "Save us, Son of David!" Save us. That is what we want. That was what their silent cry was in the Temple, while the traders of evil were holding court. Jesus, save us. Jesus, save me. That was my thought.

Jesus answered them, "Yes, I hear what they are saying. Have you never read, 'From the lips of children and infants You have ordained praise?'" The religious leaders left. One lifted his fist with an angry gesture. He whispered some threat to Jesus, but I could not hear it. Later, Matthew said the man told Jesus He was as good as dead. What kind of crime family is running this Temple?

Jesus continued to heal in the Temple courts. He would share different things with different people. I think He gazed back several times toward the Temple itself. The front of the Temple was in view. It was like He could see through those front doors, through the Holy Place, into the Holy of Holies. I imagined Jesus was hearing God, His Father, speak. He would then obey and do what He was told from inside the Temple. He received an overwhelming air of approval from on High. We did not hear thunder or a voice, but we knew our Father was approving.

We arrived back to Lazarus's home tonight. Jesus and Lazarus had a great time of fellowship after our meal. We ladies helped Mary and Martha clean up. We then joined the men to listen to the stories. They spoke of old times together. Mary and Martha added a few things here and there. The disciples and I were noticeably quiet after what we had seen today — the anger of the Lord followed by His gentleness. Jesus showed a mastery over the Temple and its inhabitants. It was as if it was His house. It made me wonder if this was why Jesus never had a home of His own as an adult?. Could it be the Father's house is His house, too? I did not have the opportunity to visit about this with the ladies or the disciples. Everyone was tired.

Every day, there is so much to internalize. The one other surprise of this day was that no one tried to make Him king except for the children in the Temple.

What will tomorrow hold? I admit in writing, I love Jesus more today than ever before, and I believe more than ever He is divinely sent.

On the first month, the ninth day — This morning, we began our habit. The one exception was that Salome got up earlier than the rest of us. She took some of the food we had been carrying and made a delicious Galilean morning meal for us all. The Lord joined us at the table. He blessed the food. We talked around the table about what the day might hold. The Rabbi listened without giving us anything specific. As we pray for the Father to give us each day our daily bread, I believe He is leading us each day to meet the events as they come in faith.

After we finished our meal, the Lord led us out again. We came upon the fig tree Jesus had cursed yesterday morning. It was withered from the roots. Peter brought it to the Lord's attention. "Rabbi, look! The fig tree You cursed has withered!" Jesus responded, "Have faith in God. I tell you the truth, if anyone says to this mountain, 'Go, throw yourself into the sea,' and does not doubt in his heart but believes that what he says will happen, it will be done for him. Therefore I tell you, whatever you ask for in prayer, believe that you have received it, and it will be yours. And when you stand praying, if you hold anything against anyone, forgive him, so that your Father in Heaven may forgive you your sins."

The Rabbi was true to His title. He was teaching us with every step. We had no idea what lay ahead as we walked out of Bethany. We were to walk by faith, pray in faith, and believe God will take care of us. More than anything, I never imagined we could pray for a mountain to be moved and it would be done as we prayed, if only we believed. I think that also depends on if what we ask is according to God's Will.

We paused at the top of the Mount of Olives. Jesus bowed His head and prayed. We then continued down into the Kidron Valley, back up toward the Sheep Gate. We saw masses of booths outside the Sheep Gate. There were moneychangers, sellers of bulls, goats, sheep, and doves. All of them were outside the city gate. It looks like they took seriously Jesus' demands. As we passed by them, they were silent. The buyers also were silent. They obviously were trying to avoid another display of Jesus' power. The Lord greeted them each as He passed like nothing had happened the day before. He was so kind to them. Why? Because they were doing what He had requested on the Father's behalf.

We walked through the Sheep Gate, toward the Temple courts. As we walked, the crowds were waiting for us again. They let us pass. They followed close behind. No merchants were anywhere in the Gentile courtyard. Jesus took His place to speak. The crowd gathered around. The twelve disciples stood behind them. They were courteous to these. We have had the privilege to walk with Jesus, to camp where He camped. We lived where He spent most of His time. These did not have that luxury.

Jesus began speaking on a passage from Isaiah. "Here is My servant, whom I uphold, My chosen One in whom I delight; I will put My Spirit on Him and He will bring justice to the nations. He will not shout or cry out or raise His voice in the streets. A bruised reed He will not break, and a smoldering wick He will not snuff out. In faithfulness He will bring forth justice; He will not falter or be discouraged till He establishes justice on earth. In His law, the islands will put their hope." I am blessed to be able to write on my parchments as He teaches. I do not want to forget a thing. The way the Rabbi quotes the scriptures is impressive.

As He broke down this Scripture, I could see the crowd hear His words. Their eyes, and ours, were wide open. Everything He quoted, written thousands of years before, described Him to the letter. I had seen Him firsthand. He never raised His voice except during His entry when the crowd was so loud. All had to yell to be heard then. He also raised His voice when He was driving out the merchants from the Temple. He came to the bruised reed and the smoldering wick of lives. He did not break them or snuff them out. He tenderly cared for them. He did not rule out a life of one who had squandered their years in licentious living. Rather, He offered forgiveness. He gave the promise of hope with repentance.

Jesus is tender. He is kind. He is patient. His face shows a willingness to receive any who come. He has expressed that welcoming face toward religious leaders, Pharisees, prostitutes, tax collectors (thankfully), fishermen, rich men, immoral women, successful scholars, and failed businessmen. His love is on display. The whole crowd felt it. I think I can speak for them. Jesus has a practice of making eye contact with every listener when He speaks. His eyes often meet mine. When He speaks, I experience a conviction that He is speaking directly to me. I have heard others say they felt He was talking directly to them and their individual situations. Beyond that, a certainty exists that He knows every intricate detail of each life that is listening. It is remarkable.

Just as He spoke of the Messiah not being discouraged, up walked our religious leaders. The reigning chief priest and his predecessor made a rare appearance together in the Gentile courts. They confronted Jesus publicly in all their regalia. "By what authority are you doing these things? Who gave you this authority?" I wondered to what were they referring. Jesus' authority to heal? Jesus' authority to speak publicly each day on the most holy of occasions? Jesus' authority to drive out greedy merchants? Jesus' authority to correct the religious leaders? Or Jesus' authority to take over the Temple every time He came to town? I think they were referring to all the above.

Jesus replied, "I will also ask you one question. If you answer Me, I will tell you by what authority I am doing these things. John's baptism — from where did it come? Was it from Heaven, or from men?" Andrew and Philip had told me about how the religious leaders had tried to thwart the popularity of John the Baptizer.

They set traps for him. Ultimately, the belief is they whispered in Herod Antipas's ear to have him arrested, and finally killed.

The chief priest, Caiaphas, visited with Annas, his father-in-law. They were in a heated discussion. Jesus began to answer questions from the crowd while they debated among themselves. I was able to move closer to them. I heard them reasoning, "If we say, 'From Heaven,' he will ask, 'Then why didn't you believe him?' But if we say, 'From men,' we are afraid of the people, for they all hold that John was a prophet." They broke their discussion, walking back toward Jesus, interrupting His answer to one of the questions from the crowd. Caiphas said, "We do not know." They do not know! I thought these men knew everything! They are the ruling religious elite. They project they have the answer to every question. They do not know? They do not want to say. I heard their reasoning. Jesus was not nearby to hear them, but they sure thought He had.

Jesus said to them, "Neither will I tell you by what authority I am doing these things." It was not that they did not know; it was that they would not tell. Jesus continued with a shocking assessment of their lives. "I tell you the truth, the tax collectors and the prostitutes are entering the Kingdom of God ahead of you. For John came to you to show you the way of righteousness, and you did not believe him, but the tax collectors and the prostitutes did. And even after you saw this, you did not repent and believe him."

Jesus' words elicited cheers from the crowd. Others jeered the religious leaders. I joined in the cheers and the jeers. Here is the Rabbi in the Temple courts calling out the reigning leaders of Israel. Yes, we have Herod, but all bend to these two men. I say all — all but Jesus.

The Lord would not let them go. He kept them fixed in their place. He never broke eye contact. He held such a command over them. It was as if He could speak to them, and say, "You will leave when I say you can leave." Those are my words, not the Lord's.

Jesus said to them, "Listen to another parable: There was a landowner who planted a vineyard. He put a wall around it, dug a winepress in it and built a watchtower. Then he rented the vineyard to some farmers and went away on a journey. When the harvest time approached, he sent his servants to the tenants to collect his fruit. The tenants seized his servants; they beat one, killed another, and stoned a third. Then he sent other servants to them, more than the first time, and the tenants treated them the same way. Last of all, he sent his son to them. 'They will respect my son,' he said. But when the tenants saw the son, they said to each other, 'This is the heir. Come, let us kill him and take his inheritance.' So, they took him and threw him out of the vineyard and killed him. Therefore, when the owner of the vineyard comes, what will he do to those tenants?" Jesus looked at Caiaphas. He waited on their answer. He did not say another word. The silence was as deafening as the cheers two days before.

Finally, they answered Jesus, "He will bring those wretches to a wretched end, and he will rent the vineyard to other tenants, who will give him his share of the crop at harvest time." Jesus said to them, "Have you never read in the scriptures: 'The stone the builders rejected has become the capstone; the Lord has done this, and it is marvelous in our eyes'? Therefore, I tell you that the Kingdom of God will be taken away from you and given to a people who will produce its fruit. He who falls on this stone will be broken to pieces, but he on whom it falls will be crushed."

The Rabbi spoke directly at the chief priests and their Pharisee counterparts. I can still hear Him saying, "I tell you that the Kingdom of God will be taken away from you and given to a people who will produce its fruit." These men felt they had the monopoly on the Kingdom. Jesus let the crowd know they should not follow these religious leaders. They are not leading anyone to the Kingdom of God or to Heaven. I knew He was speaking to them. They knew it, too. They left in a huff. The crowd was closing in on them. I truly believe if Jesus would have said the word, the crowd would have stoned them in their tracks. Fear was the only emotion I could read in our chief priests' faces as they moved quickly back to their luxurious quarters to regroup. The Pharisees that were with them stayed. They had the respect of the people more than the priests. One of their members came to Jesus with a known Herodian who loved Rome's rule. They asked Jesus, "Teacher, we know you are a man of integrity and that you teach the way of God in accordance with the truth. You aren't swayed by men, because you pay no attention to who they are. Tell us then, what is your opinion? Is it right to pay taxes to Caesar or not?"

That was a good question. They could honestly acknowledge Jesus is no respecter of persons. He just undressed the high priests to display their hypocrisy. I thought these men were warming up to Jesus. The Lord clearly did not think so. He said, "You hypocrites, why are you trying to trap Me? Bring Me a denarius and let Me look at it." They brought one to Jesus. He asked them, "Whose portrait is this? And whose inscription?"

I reached into my purse. I had several. I handed one for Joanna to look at, another for Salome. We shared them with Mary, the mother of James the Less, and with Susanna. I had never paid much attention. The Pharisees replied it was Caesar's portrait on the coin. Oh, I love what Jesus said next: "Give to Caesar what is Caesar's, and to God what is God's."

They tried to trap our Lord. If Jesus would have said not to pay taxes to Caesar, the Roman authorities would have arrested Him immediately under the Herodian's report. If Jesus would have said pay taxes to Rome, the Pharisees would have riled the crowd against Him. How marvelous is our Savior! I was exultant to see them leave, whipped just like the chief priests.

Before Jesus could start to speak to the crowd, the Sadducees came in their royal robes. They were not as ornate as the chief priests, but they were not far behind. They asked Jesus a question. "Teacher, Moses told us if a man dies without having children, his brother must marry the widow and have children for him. Now, there were seven brothers among us. The first one married and died, and since he had no children, he left his wife to his brother. The same thing happened to the second and third brother, right on down to the seventh. Finally, the woman died. Now then, at the resurrection, whose wife will she be of the seven, since all of them were married to her?"

It was a riddle. I had never dreamed of such a twisted question, but it was a legitimate one. I had a feeling we were in a Greek gymnasium pursuing the highest form of education with Jesus as our instructor. What He says is right. Everything He says is worth taking note. So, the question, whose wife will she be? I do know this, though: the Sadducees do not believe in life after death. As a result, I was confused by their question. This seemed more fitting for the Pharisees to ask, as they believe in eternal life.

Jesus was not near as terse with them, but He did let them know they were wrong. He said to them, "You are in error because you do not know the scriptures or the power of God. At the resurrection, people will neither marry nor be given in marriage; they will be like the angels in Heaven. But about the resurrection of the dead — have you not read what God said to you: 'I am the God of Abraham, the God of Isaac, and the God of Jacob'? He is not the God of the dead but of the living."

How I love Jesus. I was falling more and more in love with who He is. He let these men know they did not know the power of God! They worship God yet believe He has no power to raise the dead. What good is life if it ends in a grave? What good is religion if there is no judgment at the end of this life? If there is no life after death, we should live like the Sadducees — get all you can, do all you want, let everyone else suffer. I could tell the crowd was as in awe of Jesus' answer as I was.

What thrilled me more was the statement the Rabbi made about Abraham, Isaac, and Jacob. They are alive today. They are in Heaven with the Father at this very moment. God creates each of us with an eternal life. The question is not if we live beyond the grave, but where we will live beyond the grave. This is why I rest in Jesus as Savior. I cannot save myself. I proved that in Magdala. Jesus saved me in this life. I believe He will save me in the next. I am trying to understand more of how.

One after another, the questions kept coming from one group of our leaders to the next. The Pharisees walked up to join the Sadducees before Jesus. These two rival groups joined together. I saw them visit together. I then saw them nudge one of their members forward. He was dressed in the scholarly robes of a scribe. Speaking of a Greek gymnasium, here was one who most likely had such training. He posed the question: "Teacher, which is the greatest commandment in the law?" This was another great question. The crowd and I were learning much today. Which is the greatest commandment? There are ten main ones, but others given in the Law of Moses. Which is most important to follow, I wonder? I was glad they were asking these questions — not for the entrapment of Jesus, but for our knowledge.

Jesus replied: "'Love the Lord your God with all your heart and with all your soul and with all your mind.' This is the first and greatest commandment. And the second is like it: 'Love your neighbor as yourself.' All the Law and the Prophets hang on these two commandments." Jesus summed them all up for us to understand. I looked over at Matthew. He looked at me. We both smiled broadly. I could tell, he was like me — so glad to be out of that tax booth. We would be dealing with counting money, investigating records, and facing insults. Instead, we are walking with the Son of God!

Jesus had them (and us) captivated. He posed His own question to these elitists, "What do you think about the Christ? Whose Son is He?" The religious leaders answered, "The son of David." I knew that was the correct answer from Scriptures. The Christ would be of the line of David. Jesus then posed a confusing question to them, "How is it then that David, speaking by the Spirit, calls Him 'Lord?' For he says, 'The Lord said to my Lord: Sit at My right hand until I put Your enemies under Your feet.' If then David calls Him 'Lord,' how can He be his son?"

What an amazing twist was in the Lord's question. He had posed what is written in our scripture as questions for these experts in the law. I could not answer the Rabbi's questions. No one would expect me to — a woman from Magdala. But these experts could not answer either. Without a reply, they walked away humiliated.

Jesus looked around at every man, woman, boy, and girl sitting before Him on those Temple steps. He paused for a minute to make sure every eye was upon Him, every ear open to Him. He said for all to hear, "Beware of the teachers of the law. They like to walk around in flowing robes and love to be greeted in the marketplaces and have the most important seats in the Synagogues and the places of honor at banquets. They devour widows' houses and for a show make lengthy prayers. Such men will be punished most severely."

No one asked any more questions. Jesus dismissed the crowds. He then led us outside the city, going toward the Mount of Olives. I followed toward the back of our group with Salome. As we walked outside the courtyard of the Temple, Jesus stopped. I could not make out who it was, but one of the disciples pointed out to Jesus the size of the stones that make up the Temple walls. They are remarkable. I am told they weigh around two to three tons each. Some of the stones are fifty feet in length, twenty-four feet in height, and sixteen feet in depth. This edifice has a sense of great permanence. We looked at it with pride.

Then the Lord said, "Do you see all these things? I tell you the truth, not one stone here will be left on another; every one will be thrown down." Every one of them will be thrown down? Not one left on top of another? I thought in my mind, that would be complete destruction. How could this ever happen? Who would ever be able to carry off such a feat? Jesus said it would happen. I let myself drift for a moment to what Jerusalem would look like in complete ruin. At this moment, it seems our Jewish leadership is in harmony with the Roman leadership. At times, friction is present. Rome's governor kills our people for some manufactured reason. Our people reach an uproar. It subsides with cheap acts of appeasement. We continue on.

Jesus rode into this city with great triumph. People were calling to make Him our king. Those cries are not heard anymore. I felt He would be made king, that He would save our nation. Now, He tells us this city will be destroyed. The only way that can happen is if this nation is defeated by an invader on the way in. I see inner corruption, but the evil inside our leadership would never take the ghastly step to destroy the Temple of God. I could see them using it for themselves, which they do, but destroy it? No. That is our identity as a nation.

We walked up the Mount of Olives. He sat us down on the Jerusalem side. The Rabbi stood between us and the city. He faced us, His back to the city. We faced Him. The beautiful city was spread out before us. Peter, James, John, and Andrew were visiting. Jesus looked at them. Peter voiced the question for the group. "Tell us, when will these things happen? And what will be the sign they are all about to be fulfilled?" Obviously, these four had the same question I had. How could this Temple be destroyed? When? By whom?

We awaited Jesus' answer with fearful anticipation. The Rabbi answered, "Watch out that no one deceives you. Many will come in My name, claiming, 'I am he,' and will deceive many. When you hear of wars and rumors of wars, do not be alarmed. Such things must happen, but the end is still to come. Nation will rise against nation, and kingdom against kingdom. There will be earthquakes in various places, and famines. These are the beginning of birth pains. You must be on your guard. You will be handed over to the local councils and flogged in the synagogues. On account of Me, you will stand before governors and kings as witnesses to them. And the gospel must first be preached to all nations. Whenever you are arrested and brought to trial, do not worry beforehand about what to say. Just say whatever is given you at the time, for it is not you speaking, but the Holy Spirit. Brother will betray brother to death, and a father his child. Children will rebel against their parents and have them put to death. All men will hate you because of Me, but he who stands firm to the end will be saved. When you see 'the abomination that causes desolation' standing where it does not belong, then let those who are in Judea flee to the mountains. Let no one on the roof of his house go down or enter the house to take anything out. Let no one in the field go back to get his cloak. How dreadful it will be in those days for pregnant women and nursing mothers! Pray this will not take place in winter, because those will be days of distress unequaled from the beginning, when God created the world, until now — and never to be equaled again. If the Lord had not cut short those days, no one would survive. But for the sake of the elect, whom He has chosen, He has shortened them. At that time, if anyone says to you, 'Look, here is the Christ!' or, 'Look, there he is!' do not believe it. For false Christs and false prophets will appear and perform signs and miracles to deceive the elect — if that were possible. So be on your guard; I have told you everything ahead of time. But in those days, following that distress, the sun will be darkened, and the moon will not give its light; the stars will fall from the sky, and the heavenly bodies will be shaken. At that time, men will see the Son of Man coming in clouds with great power and glory. And He will send His angels and gather His elect from the four winds, from the ends of the earth to the ends of the heavens. Now learn this lesson from the fig tree: As soon as its twigs get tender and its leaves come out, you know summer is near. Even so, when you see these things happening, you know that it is near, right at the door. I tell you the truth, this generation will certainly not pass away until all these things have happened. Heaven and earth will pass away, but My words will never pass away. No one knows about that day or hour, not even the angels in Heaven, nor the Son, but only the Father. As it was in the days of Noah, so it will be at the coming of the Son of Man. For in the days before the flood, people were eating and drinking, marrying and giving in marriage, up to the day Noah entered the ark; and they knew nothing about what would happen until the flood came and took them all away. That is how it will be at the coming of the Son of Man. Two men will be in the field; one will be taken and the other left. Two women will be grinding with a handmill; one will be taken and the other left. Be on guard! Be alert! You do not know when that time will come. It is like a man going away: He leaves his house and puts his servants in charge, each with his assigned task, and tells the one at the door to keep watch. Therefore, keep watch because you do not know when the owner of the house will return — whether in the evening, or at midnight, or when the rooster crows, or at dawn. If he comes suddenly, do not let him find you sleeping. What I say to you, I say to everyone: 'Watch!'"

I wrote down everything the Rabbi said. I was horrified as I wrote. Not one disciple interrupted. When He concluded, not one person said a thing. The vast majority of us were overwhelmed. My hand trembled about halfway through my record. I could not stop the shiver. I am still shaking this night as I finish my writing for the day.

I cannot make sense of any of the things I wrote. All I know, they are all horrible. Is this what is to come to this world? Is this what is to come to this city, to our people? I must write that it is what we deserve for leaving God, for trying to create our own heaven without Him. It is like being in the city of Babel. We have built a tower to our own credit, for our own edification and pleasure. We boast in this Temple. We believe that as long as we have it, we are safe. Yet, the Ark of the Covenant is no longer inside those curtains per my understanding. The last time we rebelled against God, it was taken away. If God allowed that to be taken, will He not allow the Temple to be next? He has allowed the Temple to be destroyed before. Are we to go into exile again?

I have a hope that Jesus can save us. That was my thought as I wrote His words. But can the Lord save us after what He closed with this evening? Jesus dismissed the ladies and me with one final statement. "As you know, the Passover is two days away — and the Son of Man will be handed over to be crucified." Jesus moved toward an olive grove. He called the twelve to Him.

They left us there on the Mount facing the city. I could see the rooftop of Pilate's praetorium. Before that place is Gabbatha, where the governor frequently passes his sentences of death. Rome crucifies. The Jews do not. Jesus had told us He would be betrayed, that He would be killed, that He would be crucified. He has stated that several times in my hearing. Even more times in the disciples' hearing. Based on Jesus' words, will His crucifixion come after He is crowned king? I cannot see all this evil if He is king. I can see people trying to kill Him after He becomes king. That seems to be a human response when someone rules, and another wants to take his place. Does Jesus mean He will be crucified soon or later? Or will another who follows in His place be crucified?

All I can write are questions. I am putting my pen down. I have nothing left in me. I am drained emotionally. I am in Joanna's house. We left the Mount of Olives and came here when Joanna asked the ladies and me to stay with her to give Mary and Martha a break. We are each in our own comfortable quarters inside the city. I am going to pray.

On the first month, the tenth day — We woke up this morning to a grand feast, but it was not for us, but rather for the royal friends of Chuza and Herod Antipas. Off to a side room, Joanna hosted the ladies and me. She had their servants bring us a portion of all they were having in the grand ballroom. The food was plentiful, some of it we loved. Other portions were of a strange delicacy that did not suit those of us from the Galilee. Joanna laughed at our responses. She was not at all offended that we were not fond of some of the peculiar dishes.

About halfway through the meal, a servant came to Joanna and whispered in her ear. She quickly excused herself. About twenty minutes later, she brought in a familiar face. It was Mary, the mother of Jesus. Again, she was quiet when she entered. You could see a sense of relief when she realized it was just the five of us who had followed her son again to Jerusalem.

One could never tell by Joanna's humble ways that she is a woman of wealth and power. When she is with us, she is just one of the women following Jesus. She sits and listens to Him like we do. She cleans a dish as quickly as any of us. She is not slow to sweep the floor or do laundry. She gladly sits anywhere there is room when He speaks. She even gives up her chair for others who seem more needful. I believe this is why Jesus' mother is comfortable around her.

We all let Mary know what has been happening. She was especially amazed to hear of how the crowds welcomed Jesus on the first day of the week. She could not believe the outpouring of love for her firstborn. We told her of the Pharisees, Sadducees, Herodians, and scribes. We shared with her the questions they asked. We told her how her son never flinched. He answered every question with authority. Jesus truly was comprehensive in His understanding of people.

I am sad to say, I did most of the talking. About an hour into our visit, I realized I had taken over the floor. I quickly sat back in my place. I asked Mary, the mother of Jesus, how she and her family had been doing.

She let us know she had received a message from her son, Jesus. He was staying in Bethany today. He wanted to take time to pray. He also wanted to give some personal guidance to the disciples. She thanked me specifically for the love and care I had shown her son. She was grateful to know about Sunday's entrance into Jerusalem. She said that explained what she had been facing this week.

Very timidly, Mary opened up. She said people had buffeted her with requests for miracles. She has been plagued by people flocking to her in hopes of getting to Jesus. Mary said the most disturbing thing was that people were starting to bow to her, to pray to her, to ask her to lay her hand on them. She said people would bring their children to her to bless. She was horrified. Mary said, "No one really knows who I am. They know who Jesus is, but they have no idea what a sinner they bow before. I have not always followed God. I have made mistakes with Jesus. I still sin against God. I need a Savior myself. Yet, I have doubts as to the claims my son makes."

Mary stopped herself. She apologized to us in our little circle. She said, "I know you all believe that Jesus, my son, is the Christ, the Savior. I know you call Him 'Lord.' I know how He was born. I know what the angels said. I was a virgin at His birth. I have seen Him do unexplainable things." Mary then looked around the room. We could catch just a slight resemblance between her eyes and those of Jesus.

She said, "I just am not sure what has happened to Him. One minute, He is my son. The next minute, He is the talk of the nation. One minute, He attends a wedding with me. The next day, He supposedly is healing people. He was a carpenter in my husband's shop. As the oldest child, He helped raise my kids after Joseph's death. Then, I am told He is raising the dead, healing lepers, giving the blind their sight. These things do not make sense to me. I pray He is who you say. My fear is that He is not right in His mind, but is so influential that you all are under His spell."

She began to cry. We tried to comfort her. It is hard to embrace a woman like Mary. She is distant. She does not seem to appreciate the invasion of her space. Joanna told her, "Mary, you do not offend any of us. I am hearing the same doubts you express. But Mary, I truly believe if you had seen the things He has done with your own eyes, your doubts would disappear. I am a woman of position. I have seen fakes come and go in this city of Jerusalem. Many of them are eating with my husband Chuza in the other room. I have developed an eye for the counterfeit. Your son is not one of them."

Joanna took a breath, as I stepped back into the conversation. I told Jesus' mother, "Ma'am, I was there at Nain. I saw a boy being carried out. He was stiff. He was in a coffin. The whole city mourned. Jesus then touched the coffin. He spoke, 'Young man, I say to you, get up!' In an instant, the boy sat up. I have heard Samaritans call Him their Savior. I have seen Him cast the demons. As I told you before, He cast them out of me."

Mary listened intently. She sobbed for a while. Wiping her eyes, she said, "That is just half of my struggle. The high priest called me to their quarters the other day. They questioned me about my son. They had heard from some in Nazareth that Jesus was illegitimate. They pressured me. They demanded I tell them who His father was — Joseph or some other man. I would not back down. I told them plainly, 'Joseph raised Jesus. I was a virgin when He was born. God placed Him in my womb'. They threatened to stone me. I saw a few pick rocks up to do so. One tore his robes, but then a Sadducee stopped them. He said if they stoned me, then all would want to know my offense. It would undoubtedly anger the crowd against them even more. They would say, 'You cannot get Jesus, so you attack His widowed mother!'"

Mary continued, "I have come to Joanna's today for shelter. I need a place to hide. I do not mean you any harm. I do not want you to think that I do not believe you with regard to my son. At this moment, you five are the only people with whom I feel safe. My greatest distress is that people would worship me of all people!"

Mary reminded us of a passage from our prophet Jeremiah where the nation was enamored to worship some female goddess called the Queen of Heaven. She quoted the scripture, "We will not listen to the message you have spoken to us in the name of the Lord! We will certainly do everything we said we would: We will burn incense to the Queen of Heaven and will pour out drink offerings to her just as we and our fathers, our kings and our officials did in the towns of Judah and in the streets of Jerusalem. At that time, we had plenty of food and were well off and suffered no harm."

She shook in fear. "God says there are no other gods beside Him. Yet, these people want to worship me? I can somewhat understand the worship of my son. If He is who He says He is, if He is who the angels declared, He should be worshiped — Immanuel. I know His actions back that up. His words say the same. I am His mother. Why can I not believe?"

Mary stopped for a moment. She composed herself. She continued in the line of her being a goddess to whom to be prayed. She said that she sins every day. Sometimes in thoughts. Other times in words. Even sometimes in deeds. She doubts God. She said that she had the most amazing revelation given to her over thirty years ago. She still cannot grasp it. Oftentimes, she refuses to believe it. Mary said, "I am not sure of much. I am sure of one thing. Anyone who worships me brings a curse upon themselves. God has been very clear. He leaves room for worshiping a Son. God said through the Psalmist, 'Kiss the Son, lest He be angry and you be destroyed in your way, for His wrath can flare up in a moment. Blessed are all who take refuge in Him.' God spoke of a king to come from the line of David, just as the angel told me, 'For to us a child is born, to us a son is given, and the government will be on His shoulders. And He will be called Wonderful Counselor, Mighty God, Everlasting Father, Prince of Peace. Of the increase of His government and peace there will be no end. He will reign on David's throne and over His Kingdom, establishing and upholding it with justice and righteousness from that time on and forever. The zeal of the Lord Almighty will accomplish this.'"

Mary then pulled out her own parchments. They were much like mine. While she looked through them for something, I showed her my own. I informed her I had been keeping copious notes about her son and His teaching. She told me she had been treasuring everything that was told her. She had kept her own diary of events. She told us what her cousin Zechariah had said of her baby boy: "Praise be to the Lord, the God of Israel, because He has come and has redeemed His people. He has raised up a horn of salvation for us in the house of His servant David (as He said through His holy prophets of long ago), salvation from our enemies and from the hand of all who hate us — to show mercy to our fathers and to remember His holy covenant, the oath He swore to our father Abraham: To rescue us from the hand of our enemies, and to enable us to serve Him without fear in holiness and righteousness before Him all our days."

The mother of Jesus then stood in our midst and said, "I have not shared this with anyone but my husband. He is gone now. I try to talk to my other four sons. They will have none of it. They are harder than I am toward Jesus. My daughters are the same. Their husbands will not even let them come near me. They are skeptical of Jesus. They are angry that I have not publicly denounced Him. With you ladies, I feel free to say I am working through all these things. I believe I am seeing played out before me that which was told to me. It breaks my heart. It also encourages me. God was with me in my pregnancy when no one would speak with me. When Joseph and I had to travel to Bethlehem alone for the census because no one wanted to be near an immoral woman, God was there. I knew we had not had sex. Joseph knew he had not had sex with me. He thought I had cheated on him, but God sent an angel to tell him the truth. God was there with me."

The last thing Mary said before she resumed her quiet pose was, "Joseph and I took Jesus to the Temple when my time of purification was over to offer our sacrifice. The Temple that is just a few blocks from here. I remember it like it was yesterday. An old man walked up to us. He took our baby, Jesus, into his arms. He said these haunting words that I wrote down. He said, 'This child is destined to cause the falling and rising of many in Israel, and to be a sign that will be spoken against, so that the thoughts of many hearts will be revealed. And a sword will pierce your own soul too.' He looked right at me. Is this what is being played out this week? I do know my heart is broken for many reasons."

With that, Mary put her head in her hands. She began to weep silently, withdrawn, as if alone in this world. Joanna called for some water for Mary to drink. Susanna spoke up, saying, "Let us pray." We sat in a circle around Mary. We began to pray to God for her. We prayed for Jesus. We prayed that God would show

Mary who her son really is, that God would confirm the truth to us all. A tenderness permeated the air. After about an hour, Mary, the mother of James the Less, closed our prayer in the humble way she always does.

Mary said she felt better. We stayed around Joanna's house most of the day. We would gather to visit, then separate to different areas of her home to rest. We ate together again this evening. When it was dark, Joanna said, "We need to get out of the house. Come, my chariots and guards will lead us out. The people are used to us. They will pay us no mind. They will assume it is just more of Herod's officials going out. Sure enough, for an evening, we were royalty. Jesus' mother was one of us. We were no longer the five. We were pleased to be the six.

I cannot wait to share this with Jesus. Then again, if I share we were able to comfort Jesus' mother, would I not be clanging a cymbal for my own good deeds? I decided He knows so much about me without it ever being spoken. I do not think I can spend time with His mother without Him knowing.

Joanna decided we all should stay with her for the remainder of the feast. We agreed. My only reservation is that I want to make sure we know where Jesus is, so we can be with Him throughout the day. Joanna assured us that would not be a problem. Herod's men were watching Jesus around the clock. Even now, they know where He is. Joanna uses their spying to assist her in caring for Jesus. She gave us one ominous bit of intelligence. She said that the priests are talking to a particular disciple. She said, "Jesus was not wrong. There are men planning to kill Him. One of His own disciples, I am told, is working on a plan to betray Him." Joanna said if she knew more, she would act through Chuza, if possible. Regrettably, she knows nothing more than that.

Why is it that every time I am near sleep, someone brings me frightful news? Last night, Jesus said He was going to be crucified. I had trouble sleeping last night. Tonight, Joanna informs us people are plotting Jesus' murder, and one of His disciples is working to betray Him. My mind raced. Which disciple is seeking to betray Jesus?

I first thought of the twelve, naturally. I worked through them in my mind. The quietest one comes to mind. That would probably be Thaddeus. I cannot imagine him betraying Jesus. He is always tender toward Jesus. He hangs on every word. He never leaves Jesus' sight. I thought of Simon the Zealot. He may be angry Jesus is not speaking more against Rome. It seems, from my perspective,

Jesus speaks more of our own religious leadership than the Romans. But, then again, Simon was present when Jesus was ushered into Jerusalem a few days ago. I do not believe any were more elated than Simon the Zealot.

My personal suspicion is Judas. But how can it be Judas? Of all the disciples, Jesus trusts him with the money. He is the one who comes and goes, freely conducting business for the Lord. He never singles Judas out. I then began to think of others who joined us with Jesus. He has many disciples, more than twelve. I thought of Matthias. I thought of Justus. I thought of Nicodemus. I thought of Mark. I do not think any of these have the capacity. Besides, they are not always with us to know where Jesus is, or where He is going. Then again, they could have enough insight to help the haters of the Rabbi.

I know it is not me. I know it is not Matthew. Or could it be Matthew? No. He loves the Lord like I do. He informs me where the Lord is going. Would it not be just as easy for him to do the same for the religious leaders? Could Matthew be regretting the loss of his wealth? No. Could it be Salome is angry that her sons were not designated immediately to rule on His right and on His left? Could Salome be ambitious enough to want her sons to take the place of Jesus? They have the impatience for such a traitorous act. They also can lose their temper easily. Yet, I have never seen them do anything but submit willingly to Jesus.

Could it be Joanna? She could be throwing shade over the others for her husband Chuza's sake. Jesus called Herod Antipas "that fox." Could Herod be pressuring Chuza who, in turn, is pressuring Joanna? Here in her palace is Jesus' mother. Could they not use her as a hostage to bring Jesus in? My mind is out of control. How dare I question these! They could easily do the same concerning me. I will not dwell on this any longer.

On the first month, the eleventh day — Philip came by Joanna's mansion to let us know we would be eating the Passover together this evening. He said he would come back when he knew where the room is. We spent the day with Mary. Joanna took us around and showed us things about the city of Jerusalem that most do not see. She took us to Hezekiah's tunnel. She showed us the site of David's ancient palace. She guided us to a close-up view of David's tomb. Joanna is quite a historian. She unrolled for us the history of our nation. I was so gratified Poppa gave me this ancestry. Mary, the mother of Jesus, was intrigued. She even had moments of being just one of the ladies. Her burden would lift, then it would fall. She would speak as if she were just a pilgrim coming to worship God. She would then revert to being the mournful mother of a son she could not figure out. Joanna let Mary wear some of her clothing so she would not be the sought-after figure of Nazareth.

We had a delightful private lunch together. Mary, Jesus' mother, sat between me and Joanna constantly. She never wanted to leave our side. I was thankful that, though I could not get this close to Jesus because of what people would say, I had the freedom to befriend His mother. Everything with Jesus is morally proper in what is seen and unseen.

Philip came for us this evening. He led us to a room not far from David's tomb. It was a large, spacious, open room. The twelve sat around a long table, washed and ready. I found it odd that as Philip entered, the Lord had a towel over His shoulder. Without saying a word, Philip sat down. Jesus washed his feet. Let me write that again: Jesus washed Philip's feet. We had seen Mary of Bethany wash Jesus' feet. Now Jesus washed Philip's? I looked around; all of the disciples' feet had been washed. I wonder if Jesus did the same for them? I do not know.

Placing this question in the back of my mind, the ladies and I took over the service of the courses. Jesus led our Passover remembrance. John and Peter had prepared the meal. They did a good job. All of this time, the ladies and I had prepared their food on our trips. I felt they needed us. After eating this meal, I realize they were more than capable of fending for themselves. It was their way of letting us take part. We were grateful. Jesus had been sharing in many conversations around the table while we were eating our last portions of bread and drinking our last cups of wine of the Passover. He then reclined with the twelve. We sat on the outer circle around the table. Jesus said, "I tell you the truth, one of you will betray Me."

It was exactly what Jesus had stated before. It confirmed what Joanna had heard. Each disciple questioned the Lord about themselves. Jesus said, "The Son of Man will go, just as it is written about Him. But woe to that man who betrays the Son of Man! It would be better for him if he had not been born." No more was said in our hearing.

After a while, Jesus told Judas to go do what he needed to do. I suppose he had to pay for the room where we were having Passover. After Judas left, the Rabbi continued His teaching. He passed the bread around. He gave thanks for it. He broke it. He then said the oddest of things: "Take and eat; this is My body."

He then took the cup of wine. He raised the cup. We raised ours. He said, "Drink from it, all of you. This is My blood of the covenant, which is poured out for many for the forgiveness of sins. I tell you, I will not drink of this fruit of the vine from now on until that day when I drink it anew with you in My Father's Kingdom."

We sang a hymn. Jesus and the disciples headed up to the Mount of Olives to pray. They have been doing that a lot lately. The ladies and I cleaned up. We waited for Judas to tell him where they had gone. He did not return. We decided not to wait any longer. He probably knew to go to the Mount of Olives as well.

I am back in Joanna's place. Each of us ladies are blessed with our own room. Mary, Jesus' mother, sleeps in the room beside mine. I am thinking about what Jesus said. We were told to eat the bread for it was His body. I am not sure what that means. He then passed the wine. He told us to drink the cup, for it was His blood poured out for the forgiveness of sins. I remember Atticus' question a while back. How can the blood of an animal cover our sins? Jesus said it is His blood that is poured out for the forgiveness of sins. Now, I know that wine did not taste like blood. It tasted like the wine we drank before, and the wine we drank afterward. Jesus said that was His blood poured out for forgiveness of sins. I do not understand. I pray He will explain more the next time we are with Him.

I wish I were with Him and the disciples at this moment. I have no doubt the disciples have already asked this question. He will certainly have answered them. Perhaps I can get Matthew to share with me what this different sort of Passover was all about.

Break in the Diary

Giuseppe Campise gently turned the page, finding the next several pages matted together. He put down the fragile bound book. It had taken weeks for him to work through the faint print, taxing his brain to recall the Koine Greek words while trying to fit them into a meaningful sentence. His heart pounded again, as it had the many days before. If he was not mistaken, these truly are the words of Mary Magdalene. But how could he be sure? To his mind, this had followed the Gospels' account to the letter. There were no gnostic heresies. There were no apocryphal references. The author had not varied from the historical record. She had even stayed true to the Old Testament scriptures. It was as if Mary Magdalene herself had actually taken time to record humbly all that she had seen and heard from this historical figure, Jesus of Galilee. It all fit into place. It all made sense.

What did not make sense was why these next few pages were all stuck together? More importantly, he felt he was at the climax of Jesus' life in Jerusalem. If the next pages recounted Mary Magdalene's experience at the Cross, he wanted to know it. He wanted to know what Mary saw, heard, and felt. How could he unravel the mystery without separating these pages? He tried gently to pull them apart at the bottom corner. The parchment broke off. Thankfully, no ink appeared there. He would not try that again. This was beyond his expertise. He was the one who cordoned off areas, built matrixes, and oversaw the digging. He was not the one who analyzed artifacts, much less old parchments.

He reached out to Father Corbo after the next day's dig. He shared with him all that he had found. He was grateful the friar did not demand to see the parchments, or force himself into taking over Guiseppe's project. Father Corbo said he remembered some papyrus scrolls found in Pompeii had been carbonized by the intense heat and buried by the eruption of Mount Vesuvius. These scrolls, which in the past were nicely rolled pages of papyrus, had become nothing more than long thick chunks of coal. All the pages were practically melded together. They could not be read. He told Guiseppe that these were taken to an Italian research group that developed a way to read ancient documents without using mechanical or chemical techniques to separate them. Such approaches had brought irreversible damage to many before. This research group was having success using a technique called x-ray phrase-contrast tomography, or XPCT, to read the individual pages. They did so with a particle accelerator.

Guiseppe asked if the friar would make the contact for him. Father Corbo had better news. This group was currently in Jerusalem working in conjunction with the Hebrew University's Institute of Archaeology. They had lent their newly developed mobile particle accelerator to the University from their main headquarters in Grenoble, France. Father Corbo was glad to accompany Guiseppe with his sacred treasure and make all necessary introductions.

On the short two-hour drive to Jerusalem, Guiseppe shared great details with Father Corbo about his find. The priest/archaeologist was thrilled. Guiseppe shared the background of Mary Magdalene and gave her demon-possession account. He also told of the things Mary saw with Jesus. Father Corbo was beside himself. As much as he wanted to delve into this more, he respected Guiseppe as a peer, not a hired hand.

The Italian research group welcomed Father Corbo, giving him passage through all the security requirements. Because Guiseppe was with the friar, he received the same courtesies. Finally, they met the chief scientist, a Dr. Robinet. He was impressed with Guiseppe's discovery. He was also relieved the pages were held together, not by some carbonized heating event, but by another substance.

They ran some tests. A few hours later, Guiseppe was told the substance that stuck the pages together was composed of water, electrolytes, proteins, lipids, and mucins. They were more clearly defined as having prolactin, potassium, and manganese. Guiseppe had no idea what this meant. He asked Dr. Robinet. The scientist smiled. "Mr. Campise, what has held these pages together is nothing more than emotional tears."

It all made sense! Here was Mary Magdalene writing about what seemed to be the last days of Jesus' life on earth. Naturally, she would be weeping while she wrote. It was the most emotional time of her life, the most important moment of our world.

Guiseppe asked the scientist how the pages could be separated. Dr. Robinet said, "Because this is parchment, I would suggest using a gentle humidification technique." Guiseppe looked perplexed. Dr. Robinet winked at Father Corbo. He asked, "Would you like our people to do it? We will not charge you. I am sure our scientists here will be delighted to help. It may be for the greater good of all mankind. This is why we do what we do." Guiseppe was thrilled. He did ask one question, though. "Will you let me continue the translation once you have finished?" Dr. Robinet agreed. He even told Guiseppe he could be present for the entire process.

After a day of watching, the parchment pages broke away, forming individual pages again. Guiseppe could continue with this journey he assumed was with Mary Magdalene and Jesus. He took precautions by staying in the Hebrew University facility as he read the remainder of this precious book.

Turning to the next page, he read:

Diary Resumes
The Twentieth Year of Tiberius Caesar

On the first month, the twelfth day — I have just awoken to Joanna banging on our doors. She is yelling with alarm, over and over, "Jesus has been arrested! Hurry. He has just left Herod Antipas's palace. He is on His way back to Governor Pilate's judgment seat." I rushed out in my gown. Joanna told me, "Go back inside. Put on your clothes. I will explain while we rush to be by Jesus' side." I hurriedly closed my door. I threw on my clothes and was out in no more than five minutes.

All the other ladies soon appeared out of their rooms. Mary, Jesus' mother, looked the most frantic. I rushed to her side. I hugged her. She was lifeless. She did not return my embrace. She said nothing. Susanna asked me if I knew what was occurring. I had no answer. Joanna had left the mansion. She told a servant to tell us to hold back until she returns. I have gone back into my room to get my parchments. I do not dare take them with me. I do not see time to write. I am just making a note before she comes.

I am glad I have had time to change, but I am not concerned about my appearance. I must stand by Jesus. While we wait for Joanna, Salome is with Mary. Jesus' mother keeps repeating over and over, "I knew this was going to happen. I knew this was going to happen. I knew this was going to happen." Salome asked Mary what she was saying. She repeated it again, "I knew this was going to happen." Susanna came to her side. She said nothing to Mary. She just held on. Mary then lamented, "He said a sword will pierce my own soul, too.

My own soul, too."

Joanna is calling, "Let's go. Hurry!"

I cannot write for weeping. All I can do is cry. The world must be ending. Methuselah's name keeps ringing in my ear. "It will be sent when he is dead." Jesus has been sentenced to death.

(tears stain page)

Up and down these halls, there is nothing but crying. Chuza gave the order for me and the ladies to be returned to his palace. We did not want to leave Jesus. He ordered that we do. I cannot stop weeping. Mary, Jesus' mother, demanded to be left alone. I hear her next door crying out to God. I am praying too, O God! Why is this happening? I know Jesus said He would be crucified. He has been saying that for a while. But what happened to the first day of the week? What happened to that triumphant entry? Where are the crowds calling Him their king? I do not understand. I cannot understand. I will never understand!

Chuza called us together just a few minutes ago. He let us know what has happened. The chief priests arrested Jesus while he was in the garden on the Mount of Olives. That place is called Gethsemane. I asked about the disciples. Chuza said, "They were not arrested. There has been no sight of them since Jesus' arrest." We could not contain our bitter sadness. Chuza was patient. He wrapped his arms around his wife Joanna. She was beside herself in grief. He kept saying to her, "Shhhh! Shhhh! Joanna, we cannot do anything. It is out of my hands."

He continued. "Pilate interrogated him with the religious leaders present. Jesus was silent. Pilate took him inside his quarters. I have no idea what was said. The one thing is certain, Pilate was nervous. You would think Caesar had called for his own life. The tension was unbearable. He then sent Jesus to our king. Herod found no fault. He returned Jesus to the governor. The governor had remembered a choice that is made each Passover of letting a Jewish prisoner go free. I believe he had hoped it would get Jesus off this path. The people demanded that one of their most notorious criminals be released instead of Jesus. The soldiers then led Jesus away. That is about all I know."

Salome challenged Chuza, despite his graciousness toward us. I understand her pressing the subject fully. She asked him, "What about King Herod Antipas? Do you not have any influence over him to stop this? He is the king of Israel after all!" Chuza responded, "The king found no fault in Jesus. He has always been afraid of him, thinking he is John the Baptizer returned from the dead to haunt him from the grave. Such nonsense, but he believes what he believes."

Joanna was able to find her voice, "Chuza, Herod has influence! He can pardon! Pilate knows his security rests on the silence of the king." Chuza told her, "Yes, but we are still at Rome's mercy. Pilate has been looking for a reason to depose the whole Herod family for quite a while now."

Joanna snapped, "You act as if Antipas is innocent in all this! You told me the king mocked Jesus, put a scarlet robe on Him, laughed at Him, and made sport of Him! I think he is behind this, too. Stand up to him! I am willing to lose everything to save Jesus! You know He is innocent. You would not let me follow Him if you had found fault in Him. I have told you all the good He has done. I have shared with you how He only thinks of others. You relished the fact that He calls the religious leaders out for their hypocrisy. Where are you in all of this? Come on, Chuza!"

Chuza was quiet. He simply said, "Joanna, I cannot do a thing. Even if I put my life on the line, it would do no good. The decision has been made. One of his own disciples has come forward to fuel the complaints against him. None of his other disciples have stood up to defend him. It must all be true. And where are the people to stand in his defense? If he truly worked the miracles you say, where are the beneficiaries of his power? The will of the Jewish people could stop this. Other than you ladies, no one is willing to put their neck out for him. There must be something about him that you do not know."

I stood up. I put my right arm around Joanna. She lay her head on my shoulder. My robe was drenched in tears — Jesus' mother's tears, then Joanna's. I told Chuza, "I have been with Him as we traveled. He has done nothing wrong. He is the same in private as in public. He does not even come close to doing wrong. Nothing He does is questionable. He even pays His taxes down to the last cent. One of our former tax booth associates, Matthew, has been with Him every step of the way. We are trained to sniff out fakes. We have the innate sense to identify lies. There is none of that in Jesus. Matthew concurs." Chuza answered, "Then where is Matthew to present that to the Governor?" I had no answer.

(tears stain page)

Mary, the mother of James the Less, was kneeling in the corner of the hallway. She wept, but she made not one sound. Mary, Jesus' mother, spoke. "Sir, I want to be with Him. He is my son. Can you please get me an escort to His side? Every condemned criminal has that right." Chuza agreed. I asked Jesus' mother Mary, "Can I go with you?" All the other ladies asked the same. Chuza looked at the mother of Jesus. "Is that okay with you, Mary?" She nodded her head, trembling. "Yes."

(tears stain page)

We arrived at the place near the praetorium where they flog criminals. I had heard of this heinous act inflicted on whomever Rome willed. Most of the time, they were criminals we all agreed had earned the punishment. Except for the very worst, no one deserved what I saw.

There were metal hooks. Jesus was stripped of His clothing. He stood leaning over the whipping post to which He was chained. I saw the Roman soldiers laughing as they prepared to begin. They flinched Him a few times, swinging toward Him without making contact. They would swing the whips in the air over Jesus' head so He could feel the wind of them whisk by. I heard the sound. There was Jesus, my Lord, my Savior, my Rabbi, the Christ. He had always been clothed fully in our midst. I focused on His Face. He looked at His mother. I could tell He wished she had not been there. I wish none of us were there, foremost Jesus.

(tears stained page)

How could we not be there? He was there for me. I deserved what I was getting from those demons, from those fishermen at the shore, from the people in Magdala, from the soldiers. Jesus heals people. He raises the dead. He defends those persecuted. He throws leprosy off men. He casts demons out of people. He speaks in love. He feeds people. He calms storms. He helps the broken. Jesus loves God. He speaks for God. He draws all people to God, all who are willing. He should not have been there.

(tears stain page)

They began the whipping. Mary, the Lord's mother, screamed, "NO! Stop! Take me! Take me, please!" A guard yelled at me, "Shut her up or you will be escorted out! That is the rule." I grabbed Jesus' mother to me. I placed my hand gently over her mouth. I asked her, "Do you want to go? We can go. I will go with you." Mary said, "No, please. I will be quiet. I promise." I told her I did not mind her defense. I was on the verge myself. I felt we had to stay. We had to do whatever was necessary to stay. I was embarrassed for Jesus. I was hurting for Him.

(tears stain page)

Whip after whip. Roman soldiers would not do this to their enemy's dogs. We are called dogs. But if they would not do this to their enemy's dogs, why Jesus? He is not their enemy! He is not Linus's enemy. Oh, if Linus had been there. I would like to think he would have done something. I know he would have. He has no idea.

(tears stain page)

When it seemed He could take no more, He stood. Blood soaked the pavement. Blood splattered on me, on His mother. We stayed. People crowded in to see more. Others cried out, "Do it again!" They laughed. With fury, the Roman soldiers continued. Not one person on that pavement did not have blood stains — Jesus' blood.

(tears stain page)

Pilate ended the beating by word of a messenger. They threw the scarlet robe of Herod's back on Him. We were led back to Gabbatha, the judgment seat elevated above the crowd. Jesus' fate rested in what Pilate would decide. The only way the Lord could have lived through all of that is He willed Himself to live through it. He willed Himself to walk while every inch of His body was bleeding. He was striped up and down the back of His body, blood highlighting every stripe the whip left.

(tears stain page)

Pilate stepped out. Jesus was called from behind the pillar for the crowd to see. He did not look human. Somewhere on His way to Pilate, the soldiers crammed a circle of thorns upon His sweet head. I heard a soldier say, "Here is the King of the Jews, Governor." The soldier laughed. Another soldier patted him on the back. Jesus winced in pain. Another solider pretended to place a crown of thorns on his peer.

Pilate faced the religious leaders and said, "Look, I am bringing him out to you to let you know that I find no basis for a charge against him. Here is the man! What do you want me to do to him?" They began to rally the people to shout, "Crucify! Crucify!" The man behind us yelled it. The woman in front of us shouted it. The children to our right giggled, mimicking those around them, and shouted the same.

It was the first time I sensed any humanity in Governor Pilate. He asked, "Why? I find no charge against him. You crucify him." They said, "We have a law, and according to that law he must die, because he claimed to be the Son of God."

I could see Pilate look at Jesus. He was unable to hide his concern. He took Jesus back behind the pillar. I did not hear what he asked Jesus.

The religious leaders are demonic. They are worse than anything that ever embodied me! He does claim to be the Son of God. His words and miracles prove it. Even God affirms this with His own voice. If only they would realize the truth, that they are wanting to kill the Son of God. They do not care. They have no fear of God or of Hell.

(tears stain page)

I wanted to cry out, "Jesus walk through this. Walk out on them! You did it in Nazareth. You did it here a year before. You have mastery over them. You drove them out of Your Father's House. You can do this Lord." I turned to Mary, His mother. I could not say it to her. I turned to Susanna and said, "Why does He not do something? He has the power to walk out of this. He can freeze them in their tracks. He can raise the dead. I believe He can speak and cause these living enemies to die. Why does He not do something Susanna?" She simply answered, "I do not know. I do not understand."

(tears stain page)

Finally, Pilate handed Him over to them to be crucified. Jesus was too weak to carry His cross. We were helping carry His mother. Mary could hardly walk. She was inconsolable. I was in the same state, but how can I take this time to grieve for myself when His mother needs me? I held her on one side. Salome clung to the other side.

The Romans grabbed a man from the crowd. They forced him to carry Jesus' cross or to suffer on it. It was his choice. The man chose to carry it.

(tears stain page)

It was a long walk. Crowds shouted at Jesus. They called Him names. They spat at Him — the One who healed their sick, the One they rallied to hear each day in the Temple courts. We were allowed to follow Jesus. Two thieves led the way. I could not tell if they had been beaten at all. They had blood on them, but I saw no stripes. They had no mother nearby. They had no family. Jesus was the only one with any family member following, and it was His mother alone. No one else. Where were the disciples? I kept asking myself. Where is Matthew? Where is Peter? Where is John? Where is Andrew, the first to follow Him? Why is Andrew not following Him now? Thomas? Where is Thomas? It was said he volunteered to return to Jerusalem months before to die with Jesus. Were those just words? How sad! It was just the women from Galilee following Jesus. I no longer saw Joanna. Did Chuza make her go back to their safe, luxurious confines? I cannot say.

(tears stain page)

Some women stopped us. Jesus said something to them. The Roman whip was swung over their heads. They quickly stepped back. The man helped Jesus carry His cross. We followed. I always said I wanted to follow Him. My worst nightmare would not have had Him leading in this way. But I would follow. I had hoped He would turn around. I prayed He would drop the cross, that His voice would let out the command, that the soldiers would freeze as they did at the Temple, that He would walk between them, have me and the ladies follow Him back to Galilee, but no.

(tears stain page)

As we walked, it was a punch in the stomach to hear some cursing Mary, Jesus' mother. I do not think many knew who she was, but the ones who did lambasted her, cursing her for giving birth to Jesus. As I stared at one of the women flaunting her hatred, the multicolored silk coat of a man caught my eye. I had seen this man before. His face had a youthful look with wavy hair, but his face was filled with deep-seated wrinkles.

These were the wrinkles of an old man, but a young man carried them. I had seen him a few days before. This very man had taken off that silk coat as we came down from the Mount of Olives to enter Jerusalem. People were laying out palm branches in front of the donkey's colt, as well as their everyday coats and robes. But this multicolored silk coat was of great value. It stood out above all other garments. I saw the donkey's colt tread that coat under foot. The man with the wrinkled face was shouting with the rest, "Hosanna, Blessed is the king! Blessed is the One who comes in the name of the Lord!"

As we walked in this pre-funeral procession of Jesus who, if God did not intervene, would soon be dead, this same man was not laying down his silk multicolored coat. He was cursing Jesus. He was spitting at Jesus. He cursed Mary, Jesus' mother. He cursed me for weeping behind Him. What changed in this man? How could he go from sacrificial praise to overt hatred? I had been with Jesus. I never saw Him do a thing that would draw this ire other than from the religious leaders. This man was not a religious leader. They were cursing our Rabbi. They were calling for His crucifixion. They rejoiced in His stripes. They screamed, "More blood! We want more blood!"

(tears stain page)

Jesus collapsed at Golgotha. They dropped His cross beside Him. They rolled Him on top of it. Several soldiers shoved us out of the way. Groups were assigned to each execution. For Jesus, for my Lord, one held the hammer. Three carried the nails. Two more assisted holding Jesus down. Mary, Jesus' mother, covered her mouth. She collapsed behind the soldier who bent at the feet of Jesus. She was covered in His blood. I was, too.

As the soldier with the nail to His right reached for His right hand, Jesus stretched it out for him. The soldier looked surprised. The two men to assist were ready to force His hand out, but Jesus, my Savior, laid it out for him. He held it still. The soldier placed the nail below His hand, forcing the point of it into His wrist. Jesus winced. The two men moved over. One sat on His chest. The other on His legs. The man to the left with a nail stood on His left hand with both feet. The man with the hammer swung. I heard the clink of the hammer meeting the nail. I heard a gasp.

(tears stain page)

Why write this? Why am I doing this to myself? It is how I reason. It is how I cope. I cannot imagine ever reading it again.

(tears stain page)

The soldier hit the nail four more times, driving it into the wood of the cross. Satisfied, he looked over to the soldier with the nail to Jesus' left. Mary, Jesus mother, was on her knees, her body bent forward, her face buried in the dirt. She'd look up. Her face was covered with mud from the tears wetting the soil. Blood was mixed. She buried her face again, letting out the loudest scream yet.

(tears stain page)

The soldier to the left reached for Jesus' left hand. The two soldiers moved to that side to force Him. But again, He extended His hand with His teeth clinched.

He looked them right in the eye. It was as if the Rabbi was giving His tacit approval. I turned away for a moment. How can Jesus be working in concert with these murderers? I looked back. Where another might turn his head, Jesus watched the nail being forced into His wrist. Again, blood began to run down on both sides. One soldier sat on His chest. The other on His feet. The one from the right stood to watch. His smile had turned to almost a grimace of pain. The man with the hammer watched Jesus' eyes as he raised the hammer, then softly lowered it to tap the nail. He grinned. He raised it again. He acted as if he was coming down with all his might, but he pulled back to gently touch the nail again. He laughed. Jesus never made eye contact with him. He looked at the nail.

(tears stain page)

The soldier drew the hammer back, making full contact. The sound of metal on metal echoed off the walls of Jerusalem, outside the Damascus gate where the world fell headlong into evil. Five more strikes. A gasp each time. A cry.

(tears stain page)

The soldier with the nail at Jesus' feet then stood. The two soldiers came around. They forced one foot down. I say 'forced'. Jesus laid it on top of the wood, moved the other out of the way. The soldiers looked at each other. One said, "If I did not know better, I would think He is wanting this." No one laughed. He pushed the nail into Jesus' foot, pushing his whole body's weight upon it. It was in the Lord's foot. The man with the hammer then came. Jesus looked to Heaven from where He lay. Mary reached, but they shoved her away. I pulled her back. She threw herself face down in the dirt again. She began crying His name, "Jesus, Jesus, Jesus, my son, my dear boy."

The man raised his hammer and drove the nail through the wood. Then the most horrifying thing happened: They ripped the nail out. The loud gasp like when one's wind is knocked out was heard. They shoved that foot with the hole in it out of the way. They reached for the other, but the Rabbi moved it over the wood without looking down toward them. The soldiers shook their heads. One said, "This is one for the books." Just then the centurion approached,. "Get on with it. Quit playing. We have done enough damage to this one already."

(tears stain page)

The man with the bloodstained nail then pressed his body weight upon it again. The head of that nail was flat from the previous swings. I looked down at Mary. She was frozen. I looked back up. The man pulled off the nail. He had cut his hand on it. The soldiers began to laugh. He cursed them. He cursed Jesus. In that moment, Jesus looked down at him. He then looked beyond the soldier to His mother. He made one glance into my eyes. He then looked up to the sky again. Jesus closed His eyes. He moved His lips ever so slightly.

What is He thinking? Is He praying? I was. I was begging God to stop this. One minute, Jesus is the king coming to save us. Another, He is the One masses wait for in Capernaum. They pay for rooms. They wait without complaint. When He arrives, they run to Him. Here is the One they bring their children to for Him to touch, for Him to bless. Then, here He is at Calvary.

(tears stain page)

The man wrapped his bleeding finger. For all he knew, it was Jesus' blood on his finger. How could he tell if he was bleeding? He pressed back down on the nail. He moved it around to bore a bigger hole. The man with the hammer then came. He swung. He swung again. He swung a third time, a fourth time. He drove it into the wood.

In horror, he pulled it out of the wood of the cross. Jesus' foot was still attached to the nail. The solider with the hammer then slid the other foot under it. He drove the nail through the hole he had already made in that foot. Then he swung his hammer until the nail was pressed through the wood, pressing into the feet of Jesus. Had it not been for the jagged nail's head, it would have gone through.

(tears stain page)

The centurion ordered Jesus be lifted. They shoved me and Mary farther back, cursing us, demanding more room. Mary looked up. Her face was covered in tear-drenched dirt. I knelt beside her. I wrapped both arms around her shoulders. I pressed my head against hers. Only three times in my life have I ever seen her. Just two times have I ever been near enough to hear her speak. At the foot of Jesus' cross, we found ourselves inseparable. Some jeered curses at her and her daughter (meaning me). They had no idea. They cursed her son. They called Jesus my brother. They cursed my brother. They had no idea. Hatred.

They dropped the cross into the hole. It hit with a jerk. Jesus let out a nightmarish scream of agony. The soldiers laughed as His blood was blown onto them and us again. They placed stones in the hole to steady the cross. They then threw dirt into the hole. The depth of the hole made the cross lean forward with Jesus on it, but it was too deep for the cross to fall out. The rocks were used to straighten it. The dirt was shoveled into it to make it immovable in the wind. They took every earthly belonging of Jesus. They laughed, saying, "Now for the spoils, gentlemen."

(tears stain page)

Who cared about things? That was my Lord on that cross. That was Mary's son. We stood there for a moment. Mary grabbed hold of His feet. She pressed her face against them to assure Him she was there, that she loved Him. I placed my arm around Mary. We both looked up. I had never been this close to Him by myself, but even then, I was not alone. His mother was present. He had always kept a proper distance from women. I wanted to touch His feet, too, but I could not. How can I take a privilege that He always avoided? Even with Him on the cross, I would maintain all proper appearances. His sister. They think I am His sister. He has spoken to me and the women as sisters. That was not such a misclassification after all.

John walked up. I looked for the other disciples. They were nowhere to be found. I was angry at Matthew. He had stared at great opposition from that tax booth. Where was he? Where was Simon the Zealot? He hated the Romans. He hated the Herodians. Where was he? He had risked his life many times before Jesus to bring down their rule. Where was his courage when Jesus needed him? Peter? Andrew? Nathanael? He was Jesus' acting self-appointed guard. Where is Nathanael? James the Less? James, the brother of John? The sons of thunder? Only one comes. John came sheepishly, but at least he came. He stood on the other side of Mary. I was just glad he was there. We needed him. I needed him. I no longer had to be the strong one.

(tears stain page)

I collapsed at the foot of the cross. I threw myself facedown just like Mary. I wept. I threw dirt in the air. I moved closer to where the cross met the ground. I felt a drip. Then another drip. I thought it was going to rain. It was not rain. I looked at the drops on my hand. They were Jesus' blood. I wanted the blood off.

I felt if I could rub it off, this whole thing would merely be the worst dream ever, surpassing those I had in the Magdala cistern. I rubbed and I rubbed. The blood smeared. I did not wake. I was awake. This was real!

Priests had been taunting Him, saying, "You saved others. Save yourself!" They laughed. He had saved me. I was one. He had saved Himself in Nazareth. He had saved Himself a few months before here in Jerusalem. But why not at the crucifying moment?

The wrinkle-faced man with the silk multicolored coat yelled out, "Come down if you are the Christ. I will throw my coat before you again. I will get the donkey's colt myself!" How dare he! I heard His voice. He raised it over the clamor. It was loud. It was as strong as ever. He cried out, "Father, forgive them for they do not know what they are doing."

If I could speak then, I would have said, "Lord, they know what they are doing. They are killing You. Lord, forgive them? How can I? How can your mother? And Your Father? How can God forgive this? You are His Rabbi, His Son, His Christ. You are the most righteous, loving, kind man to have ever lived. They are hating You. They are killing You!"

(tears stain page)

The criminals, Barabbas's allies, had been cursing Jesus. With every exhale, they mocked Him. There they were dying, facing an eternity of torment, and they would rather use their last breaths to curse rather than survive? I could not understand. Before long, either they all quit cursing Him, or I ceased to listen. It was silent. I could hear my crying. I could hear Mary's. I could hear John trying to comfort Mary. I felt so sorry for her. She has four other sons. Where are they? She has daughters. Where are they? None were there. Two strangers were with Jesus' mother — me and John.

(tears stain page)

Salome came near. Mary, the mother of James the Less, came too. Joanna walked up a few minutes later with Susanna. They knelt beside me. They comforted me with their tears. I was not alone. I write that. It was not me who mattered. Jesus was not alone.

I could not get up. I would look up. I would try to get up, but grief pulled me back down. It was as if I was tied to the foot of that cross. The women tried to get me up, but they were all on their knees. They had no ability. At some point, we gave up trying to regain composure. We each wept individually together. Jesus had touched each of us. Each of us had chosen to follow, to help, to support Him. He had drawn us together. We did not have a relationship with each other before Him. Nor had we a relationship with Mary before now.

We all wept together. While I grieved and prayed silently, I heard the criminal to Jesus' left continue to berate Him, saying, "Aren't you the Christ? Save yourself and us!" I was too exhausted to give his hideous remarks another thought. But then I heard the thief to Jesus' right, saying, "Don't you fear God, since you are under the same sentence? We are punished justly, for we are getting what our deeds deserve. But this man has done nothing wrong. Jesus, remember me when You come into Your Kingdom."

I lifted my head. Jesus' Kingdom? "Your Kingdom come. Your Will be done on earth as it is in Heaven." I have followed Jesus for the way He loves. I have been attached to Him because I know, from all I have seen, that He wants to give us eternal life. He has promised He will give us entry into God's Kingdom. This thief repented? I could not believe it. It was the right response. It was more appropriate than what he had been doing. I then heard that sweet voice of love. I felt myself back on the shore of Galilee, hearing Jesus comfort, heal, restore. That voice — I heard Him speak to the coffin of a teen boy. "Young man, I say to you, get up!" It was Jesus' same voice. I had to look up at Him again. His voice was as serene as if He were not hanging like a murderer on a cross. He said gently, but clearly, "I tell you the truth, today you will be with Me in paradise."

Even on the cross, He can give eternal life to anyone He chooses? Oh Lord, give that to me, too! His blood dripped down on my forehead, rolled down the side of my cheek. I looked over at the thief. He rested for a moment. Then, he continued to push up and down on the nails to breathe. All three in unison were pushing up and down on the nails to breathe. One would stop, sometimes to talk, then begin back. Another would stop, almost to take a break, then begin the push again. I do not understand. I could only tell it was necessary to breathe.

(tears stain page)

I noticed a darkness settling on the horizon. Jesus, pushing up and down on the nail through His feet, looked down and made eye contact with Mary, His mother. Jesus said, "Dear woman, here is your son." To John, He said, "Here is your mother." I could sense Jesus saw what I had seen: No family member with His mother. She was bearing His torture without one family member, without one friend from Nazareth. Jesus loved John. John was always in the inner circle of three with James and Peter. They were at Jairus' house when Jesus raised his daughter. They were with Jesus on the top of Mount Tabor. John was the only disciple at the cross.

I saw Jesus taking care of the last remaining details before He died. He wanted someone to look after His mother. I would gladly have taken the responsibility. Perhaps Jesus knew I would. What Mary needed was the strength John was giving her at that cross.

Darkness swept over us. We went from mid-afternoon to total darkness. Torches were lit. Many left, fearing a storm. I cannot know for sure how long, but I think, for almost three hours, we sat in the dark below Jesus' cross. The guards kept their posts. The centurion watched over the whole crucifixion area. He gave breaks to the soldiers. He filled in for them. We did not move. Our energy was gone. I wanted to sleep. Grief has a way of making one feel that way. I could not leave Jesus. It appeared that I was there for Mary. I was really there for Jesus. I was there for me, too. For the full time of darkness, I relived all I had heard Jesus say, all I had seen Him do. What I focused on most was the reflection in my mind of His smile, of His laughter, of His banter with His twelve and Lazarus. I thought of watching Him from our ladies' camp, visiting with the disciples around the men's fire. I could not hear them. But I could watch. I remember seeing Him sleep by the fire. I could not take my eyes off Him. Ultimately, I would tire, return to my mat, and sleep.

Jesus was silent up on that cross. He continued pushing up on the nail to breathe. The rhythm like clothes blowing in the wind to dry, rising and dropping, rising and dropping. What was He thinking? How was He managing? I knew He hurt. I could hear His groans of agony. I felt this yearning to take His place. I cannot heal people. I cannot raise the dead. I cannot give life. I cannot return a leper to his family. I cannot speak and draw the masses to God. He can. But I can die. I can suffer if that means He does not have to.

I am designed for such an ending because of my sins. He is not. I thought of all my sins as He pushed up and dropped on that nail. I thought of all my sinful words, my sexual acts, my violent stabbing of that fisherman. I remembered the hurtful things I said to Poppa and Momma. I grimaced at the thought of what I did on the bimah in our Magdala neighborhood synagogue. I continually shook my head to chastise myself. "I should be up there, Jesus. You should be down here, or better yet, You should be back in Galilee helping people. Leave me here on the cross. I deserve it. I deserve to be alone. I deserve to be embarrassed. I deserve to be stripped naked. I have done that for myself many times. I deserve the curses. I am Mary Magdalene. I should be hated. I should have the nails."

My tears were overrun by my anger at myself. I hate my sin. I hate me myself for what I have done. Why would He let me be with Him? Why would He ask me to go with the disciples following in His footsteps? What have I ever done to have the privilege to sit at the same table with Him and His friends Lazarus, Mary, and Martha? Who am I, Jesus, that You would love me?

(tears stain page)

As the darkness lifted, I think it was around three o'clock per one of the soldier's statements, I heard Jesus cry out, "My God, my God, why have You forsaken Me?" I looked up at Jesus. I was dumbfounded. Why does He think God has left Him? I no sooner thought that, then it made sense. How could He be going through this if God had not forsaken Him? God had protected Him, empowered Him, blessed Him, spoken boldly for Him in public. Looking at the men on either side of Jesus, this is what someone goes through when God has left them. Or better stated, this is what someone goes through when they have left God. But the man on the middle cross; this is not what One whom God approves of should be going through. Was Jesus feeling abandoned by the Father, the One about whom He spoke so lovingly? I wanted to speak to Jesus. I wanted to reason with Him, "God is here Lord. He has not abandoned You. He has let man do what man does, kill the innocent. Jesus, this is not God's doing, it is our sins. It is my sins."

Jesus then looked down at one of the soldiers, the one nearest the bucket of some liquid that the other two had been given while they were suffering on their crosses. Jesus said, "I am thirsty." The soldier soaked a sponge in it, put the sponge on a stalk of hyssop plant, and lifted it to Jesus' lips. I could see Jesus' mouth clutch the sponge between His dried lips. He attempted to suck on it for a moment. He then turned His head from it. The soldier lowered the stalk. Jesus said in a hoarse voice, "It is finished." Yet, He continued to push upward and drop down. It dawned on me. He appears to be living for us. Why else is He pushing up repeatedly? He has lived for us all this time.

I waited. I watched Jesus. After all these months of clamoring to hear Him. I spent every waking moment willing to drop everything to be where He was, to hear what He had to say about God, to see what He would do with every malady presented to Him. I did not want that to end. I did not want Him to be finished. I prayed, "Please God, do not let this be the end."

(tears stain page)

I never saw this coming. In the back of my mind, Jesus said this would be His fate. I have heard people say often that our people persecute and kill any prophet God sends to us. Jesus has been no different. There He was on the cross. His ending was no different than the many who have come before. He said the owner of the vineyard sent his servant to collect the rent from the laborers. They killed the servant so they could have the vineyard for themselves. The owner sent his son. They killed him too, believing that finally the vineyard was theirs.

Jesus pressed upward one more time with an exhale. His voice rang loudly over all who were at Golgotha. All looked to the center cross. All heard Him say, "Father, into your hands I commit My Spirit." With that, His head dropped. No more pushing. No more dropping. The thieves on each side continued their labor. They pushed up. They dropped. Jesus hung still. The voice that set me free was silenced.

The ground began to shake beneath us. The few remaining near the crosses fled, including the religious leaders. The whole earth shook. The centurion fell against Jesus' cross. He looked up with fear in his eye, saying, "Surely, this was the Son of God." That is who Jesus said He was. I believed Him. Why did they not believe before it was too late?

(tears stain page)

I crawled over to Jesus' mother. Mary let out a haunting cry. She threw herself into the cross over and over. It seemed she wanted to feel the pain. John and I grabbed her. She pushed us away. She threw herself again into the cross. John grasped her tightly. When she tried to break free from his arms, they both fell to the ground. Joanna, Susanna, and Salome helped them up. Joanna told John, "Take her back to my home. I will lead you back there." Joanna looked at me and

Mary, the mother of James the Less. I told her I would stay. Mary, the mother of James the Less, said the same.

A few minutes later, the religious leaders came to the Roman guards. One of the guards had an edict from the governor. I could not read what it said, but they immediately did a ghastly thing. They broke the legs of the thief on Jesus' right. He gasped a few times, slumped, and died. They did the same to the one on the left. He screamed as they swung. He fought to push up, but the bones of his legs would not connect beneath. He died weeping as the air exited for the last time.

They came to Jesus. He was already still. No pushing. No movement. One of the soldiers drew back to break His legs, but the centurion stopped him. He handed the guard a spear. The guard approached the cross of Jesus, plunged the spear up into His chest. The centurion pronounced, "He is dead."

(tears stain page)

From the corner of my eye, I saw two more religious leaders arrive. I tried to ignore them. I expected some last insults. I closed my eyes, grabbing the bottom of the cross.

One of the two softly placed his hand on my shoulder. He could see me weeping. I was holding on to the cross in Mary's place. I looked to see what religious leader would offer solace to a friend of Jesus.

It was Nicodemus. He had tears flowing down his cheeks. He approached Jesus reverently. He softly said, "Rabbi" as he looked up at the Lord. He then spoke to the man next to him, saying, "Joseph, we must get Him down."

The man he called Joseph spoke to the centurion. The soldier who had charge of the hammer grabbed the two men who had responsibility for nailing His Hands. They leaned a rudimentary ladder against the Lord's cross. They were going to pry Jesus' hands and feet from the wood and let Him drop. Nicodemus caught on to what they were about to do. He extended a long linen cloth to them. He demanded they wrap it under His arms from the top of the cross. He ordered, "The Rabbi must be lowered down with respect. Do it that way!" The centurion nodded at the soldiers. Jesus was let down gently to the ground.

I stared for a moment at His precious face. It was marred beyond most people's recognition, but I could still see Him beyond the blood, bruising, and cuts. For a moment, I touched His head, then held His hand. I whispered in His ear, "Thank you Lord. I love You. You are my Savior." Mary, the mother of James the Less, took away the thorns from His head. The soldiers had labeled them His crown. I watched as she ran her hands through His hair. She thanked Him for loving her.

(tears stain page)

Nicodemus and the man he called Joseph wrapped the linen around Him. They rolled apart two poles to reveal a stretcher made of a hardy cloth. The two of them moved Jesus' body onto the stretcher with the help of the centurion. They were silent. We were, too. I wondered what they would do next, but with the care they were showing, I trusted them with the Rabbi's body. Salome returned. She said nothing about Mary, the Lord's mother.

Nicodemus laid a heavy bag at the end of the stretcher below Jesus' bruised, blood-stained feet, the gaping holes apparent, yet pooled with blood. His friend went to the other end near the Lord's head. Nicodemus knelt, grabbed hold of the poles on his end. He faced away from the stretcher. Joseph did the same at the Lord's head, facing toward the Lord. They lifted at the same time. They turned away from Skull Hill, moving slowly east. We followed behind. As they walked with only the sound of their sandals moving along the gravel, I looked ahead of them. I saw a garden. We were headed toward a garden.

We entered this beautiful place. We walked by a grape press made of stone. We followed a winding path deeper into the garden, going lower and lower. The garden was at the foot of the hill near where Jesus was crucified. I saw an opening in the side of the mountain. Nicodemus and his friend carried the Lord's body into that opening. It was a tomb much nicer than the one below Mount Arbel where Poppa and Momma were buried. Salome, Mary, the mother of James the Less, and I walked to the entrance of the tomb. Joseph looked up at us after they laid the stretcher down on an outcrop of limestone rock. While Nicodemus lit a lamp inside, Joseph said, "I had this dug for me and my family. I am giving it to Jesus. He deserves it more than I ever could." This was truly an expensive tomb.

With a mixture of myrrh and aloes, the two of them wrapped the Lord's body with the spices in strips of linen. They were following our Jewish burial custom. Why would they not? Nicodemus was a member of the Sanhedrin. The way Joseph was dressed, I assumed he was too. While they were wrapping Jesus' body, Salome said she would go and purchase additional spices before the Sabbath began. All shops would close within the hour.

Nicodemus and Joseph took their time, applying great care. Once they were finished, they walked toward us with the stretcher rolled back up. We moved back outside the tomb. A huge stone rested on an incline, sitting in a groove cut into the limestone base. It took both men to roll it downhill in front of the opening to the tomb. Once it began to budge, its weight carried it to the stop carved for it, positioning it completely over the entrance. The men looked at us. They shook their heads in grief. They walked away, leaving us alone. We stayed for a few moments, praying. I wept. Mary, the mother of James the Less, wept too. We then made our way back to Joanna's.

(tears stain page)

Joanna was waiting for us when we returned. Mary, Jesus' mother, had gone to her room. We could hear her cry out from time to time. Then we could faintly hear her sniffling. We let Joanna and Susanna know where Jesus was buried. We were thankful for Nicodemus and Joseph. I never considered what we would do with His body, nor had we the time to plan. Had these two men not taken Jesus' body, the Romans would have disposed of Him with the two criminals in the city dump, Gehenna. We thanked the Father for providing a place for His Son, His Prophet, His Christ to be buried.

We visited about the disciples, or should I say, about their absence. I never considered the possibility that they had been arrested and were being held in some Roman prison. Joanna told us that John said the disciples were fine. He had gone to let them know what was happening. They had been able to return to the room where we had observed the Passover the night before. The disciples were hiding for fear they would be next. With all that has gone on, that was not a far-fetched fear. I was still upset with them. Jesus had stood for them. They crouched in hiding when He needed them. These bold men were frightful little boys when it mattered most. Only women were with Him, and, thankfully, John later.

That Passover supper together seemed so long ago. Jesus was there alive. He was loving. He taught us as always. He laughed with us. He asked about things that concerned us. He gave us His undivided attention. He spoke of what lay ahead. We never saw its fulfillment coming any time soon. Now He is dead.

(tears stain page)

We talked a little longer, then each of us retired to our rooms. I have been writing ever since. As I go back over what I have written, I see tears. The ink is smeared. What shocks me most is that there are remnants of red on these pages. I never washed after being with Jesus. I looked at my reflection. His blood was not just on my fingers. Jesus' blood was on my face, my clothes, my feet. I cannot imagine ever reading this again. In the same way, I cannot keep myself from wanting to relive all I have written. I do not want to forget the depravity of man, the sinfulness of us all. He was spotless. He was perfect. He is gone. He did not have the honor to ride out on a chariot or to walk away with God into Heaven like I had hoped. He was tortured like a traitor to His nation. He was killed like a murderer.

(tears stain page)

In the twentieth year of Tiberius, on the first month, the thirteenth day — I could hear crying all night. It was not Jesus' mother alone. Weeping came from every room, including mine.

As I look out the window of my room. I smell food being cooked from other houses around ours. I see children playing. I see others joining their families. They are dressed nicely. They are walking toward the Temple to worship God. The streets are full of worshipers going to worship God, the Father. Jesus, His Son, was killed not hours before. They act as if nothing has happened. I hear the shofar from the Temple. At this moment, I feel as though they have swept Jesus under the rug. They all act as if He never existed. One minute here, the next minute gone. How can this be? I am numb.

We did not go to the Temple this morning. We stayed in our rooms for most of the morning, praying. Joanna coaxed us out for a bite to eat. All we could do was move our food around on the plate. We had traveled all the way from Galilee with the Master. What are we to do now — go back to Galilee, me go back to Magdala, without Jesus? The center of our lives is gone. We are to pick up where we left off? I cannot even think of Atticus. Then again, what will I say to him? How will I be able to tell him what has happened? Will what our religious leaders did make him turn away from God entirely? Will he think Jesus was a fraud? I hope not. I know He was not.

I find myself praying like I never have before. I am in the mindset of wanting to be alone. Sadly, being alone is torture. To have to talk to others right now would be even worse. I need this time with the Father. I need this time to think. I must try to sort out what has happened. I must write down all that I can, perhaps I can make sense of this. I doubt it.

Ringing in my ears are the Lord's words. He said He would be betrayed. I wonder who did it? Which of the disciples is absent in that room where they hide? Jesus said they would kill Him. He said He would die. He said He would be crucified. Everything He said has occurred as He said. I am clean now. I have put on fresh clothes. Still, the pages of my parchments are crumpled from the tears. There are still dark patches on the pages — Jesus' blood.

I thought of Atticus' question about an animal paying for our sins. We both realized it made no sense that an animal could take the punishment for our sins. But God said to do it. Would God say to sacrifice an animal so we could realize sin must be punished? Was God willing to take a small deposit on our sins rather than require the full measure be paid? He is merciful. He could do that for us. But God is also just. How is it just for an animal to shed its blood for my sins? That I would have a hand cut off for my sins, or a foot, or my tongue, would make better sense. That would be a fair deposit, though not full payment.

I remember Jesus saying at the Passover supper, "This is My body broken for you. This is My blood shed for you." I am also reminded of what Andrew said when we were around the fire near Samaria, when Jesus left us alone to pray. He said John had pointed to Jesus one day when He was walking by. John the Baptizer said, "Behold the Lamb of God who takes away the sins of the world." My mind is racing. Does this all make sense? God is just. He cannot let sin slide. The spilling of a sheep's blood is unfair. One day a lamb is grazing on a hill. The next day, it is taken from the flock by a rough fisherman who has raped, stolen, and pillaged.

The fisherman cuts the throat of the lamb, saying, "This is for my sins." He goes back living the way he has. That is not right. That is not fair. I cannot see any way God would equate that to atonement.

But Jesus. The Lamb of God. He said, "This is My body. This is My blood shed for you." He is the perfect human. He is also Divine. He is the Son of God. Abraham said God told him He would provide the lamb for the sacrifice. Jesus was born to a virgin. He is called the Son of God. He said He would die for our sins. He never sinned. I can almost see Jesus coming for the express purpose to pay for my sins. Because He is God's Son, because He is perfect, the sacrifice of Himself is sufficient, I would think, for the whole world of sinners if He chose to be.

I believe He has chosen to be. I recall the sweet time when He taught us about shepherds and sheep. Jesus said He was the Good Shepherd who lays down His life for His sheep. It all makes sense. I never thought I could love Jesus more, but I love Him more this very moment! I remember the passage of Isaiah: "He was despised and rejected by men, a man of sorrows, and familiar with suffering. Like one from whom men hide their faces, He was despised, and we esteemed Him not. Surely He took up our infirmities and carried our sorrows, yet we considered Him stricken by God, smitten by Him, and afflicted. But He was pierced for our transgressions, He was crushed for our iniquities; the punishment that brought us peace was upon Him, and by His wounds we are healed. We all, like sheep, have gone astray, each of us has turned to his own way; and the Lord has laid on Him the iniquity of us all. He was oppressed and afflicted, yet He did not open his mouth; He was led like a lamb to the slaughter, and as a sheep before her shearers is silent, so He did not open His mouth. By oppression and judgment, He was taken away. And who can speak of His descendants? For He was cut off from the land of the living; for the transgression of My people, He was stricken. He was assigned a grave with the wicked, and with the rich in His death, though He had done no violence, nor was any deceit in His mouth."

That is it! Jesus was despised and rejected a day ago, even longer when I think of how the religious leaders treated Him the whole time I was with Him. I also saw such hatred in the people of Capernaum. He said it was the same for the people of Bethsaida and Korazin. He was pierced for our transgressions. We strayed as sheep, but God laid on Him, the Good Shepherd, the sins of us all. He was led as a lamb to the slaughter — He, not some lamb from a hillside.

My mind is rushing. I cannot write fast enough. He was killed with wicked thieves, though one seemed changed while hanging on that cross. When it came time for His burial, what did I see but a rich, religious leader hand over his tomb to Jesus? Everything has been as God foretold. Everything was as Jesus told us while He walked with us! I must share this with the women. I pray they will listen. It all makes sense. We have been forgiven. I have been totally forgiven. No sheep can do this. God provided the Lamb.

The women were enamored by what I shared with them. They all added other things to what they remembered of scripture. We were elated at the plan God laid out in our day for our forgiveness. Even so, Jesus is not here for us to thank. I do not doubt for one minute that He is with His Father again in Heaven. All of this does not remove what we saw, what He faced. It does bring solace. It does make sense. Sometimes, I guess, we must go through pain to find joy. The pain is not forgotten. The joy makes it worth it. I hear that is what childbirth is like. I will probably never know that.

Sabbath is over. It is night now. We are going to set out for the disciples. Joanna cannot send any guards. They will draw attention. Besides, the disciples will probably not open a door if they see soldiers. We will have to go, and hope no one follows us. I am sure we will not be, since we are leaving Joanna's home, the wife of Chuza. Mary, Jesus' mother, has decided to stay in. I shared what I felt about how Jesus was the sacrifice for our sins from God, that her son even said so Himself. She was upset. She said that she was hurt that we could look at the death of her son as some far-fetched benefit for sinful men. I understood. When we began to share, I felt it sounded silly to a mother whose son was the sacrificial lamb. She ran back to her room, weeping. Joanna agreed to stay with her.

I had to get to Matthew. I wanted to hear from Peter. I longed to understand why they were not with Jesus. I also wanted to tell them what I believe was insight from the Father. They may have already come to the same conclusions.

We took the dark streets, the long way around, to get to the room where the disciples were supposedly staying. It was me, Susanna, Salome, and Mary, the mother of James the Less. We got to the door. Salome decided she would knock. Her sons would know her voice. She did. After a hesitation, they opened the old door. It squeaked as it opened. The sound was deafening. We had gone through it before, but the last time were not afraid, so the squeak had not drawn our attention.

We entered the room. It was as large as before, but it was dark except for one lantern sitting on the table where we once ate. The disciples would not speak at first. Salome asked questions. Her sons whispered back, cautioning us to do the same. They were trembling in fear. I found Matthew at the end of the table, next to Nathanael. I asked him where they had been. He said he did not want to talk about it. I said, "Matthew, I know you are afraid, but you all act as if Jesus never existed. You appear to be only concerned for survival for yourselves." I thought back to the Levi I knew at the tax booth. That was the Matthew of old I felt I was talking to, only concerned for himself. Is that it? Do we all revert back to the lives before Jesus?

Andrew, James, and John spoke of returning to their fishing. I could not believe my ears! I cannot go back to what I was. There is no way. I would be dead if I returned to what I was. I would be dishonoring Jesus. I told that to them. They listened without response. I looked around to see if all the disciples were present. It was then I remembered that one had betrayed. I did a count of the dark shadows of men. There were only eleven.

Who was missing? I walked up to each one as they sat, or cowered, or knelt. I saw John and James. I saw Peter alone. I saw Andrew. I saw Nathanael next to Matthew. I saw James the Less next to his mother. I saw Thomas. I found Thaddeus next to Philip. I was angered when I saw Simon the Zealot. All those threats toward me in front of Roman guards never deterred him. Jesus gets arrested, he slithers away in fear!

Judas? Where was Judas? I made my way to Peter. He is the oldest. He is the leader now. I asked Peter to tell me where Judas was. Peter was extremely pensive. He said in a somber tone, "Judas betrayed the Savior for thirty pieces of silver. He is gone. We received the news a few hours ago. He hung himself." How ghastly, I thought. I told Peter, "He deserves that and worse! How dare he betray the Rabbi. How dare he eat with Jesus, walk with Jesus, be blessed by Jesus, and then betray Him. It is as if he had denied ever being with Jesus."

Peter's response floored me. Peter began to weep. I looked at him. He fell to the floor. I looked at Matthew. Matthew whispered, "He's been this way ever since Jesus' arrest." I fell down beside him. I sat. I handed him a cloth. His chest just shook. His tears were uncontrollable. I have never seen such a man broken like this. I told Peter, "We all understand Peter. We are all saddened. We are all shocked. We are all confused. Please know we are here together just like the Rabbi would want." He said to me, "You do not understand. You do not know." I said, "What do I not know Peter? I was at the cross. I saw it all. I saw Him buried. I understand."

Peter wept even more. He asked, "You were at the cross?" I answered, "Yes Peter. I was there." He asked, "Were you not afraid?" I answered, "Yes, I was afraid, but I would gladly lose my life to be with Him." Peter wept even more. I sat beside him again in confused silence. He was inconsolable.

Peter broke the mystery. He confessed, "I told Him I would die for Him. I meant it. I really thought I could. I told him that at Caesarea Philippi. I told Him that at our Passover meal here. I told Him that again on the way to the Garden where we pray. I tried when the soldiers came for Him. I really did try. I drew my sword. I struck a guard. I was ready to die. Jesus stopped me. He told me to put it away, that this was the Father's plan. I was so confused. Jesus was dragged away. John grabbed me to follow. The High Priest knew John's father Zebedee and his whole family very well. He was able to get me into the courtyard. Mary, I was so afraid. I could see Jesus being tried. I felt we were next. Many asked me if I was with Jesus." Peter began to weep more.

I waited. Peter composed himself, "Mary, I told them I was not with Jesus. I lied and said I was not one of His disciples. I swore. I cursed. I said that I did not even know who this man Jesus was. On His worst day, Jesus, while being tried, looked out of the window to see me in the courtyard. He bowed His head in sadness. He was alone. I left Him alone. The rooster crowed. I remembered at that moment that Jesus had said I would deny Him three times. I said I would never. But I did, Mary. How can I be His? How can I enter Heaven?" Peter lowered his head to cry.

I had no answers. I never dreamed Peter would prove such a weak man. I looked around. All these men were no different. I could not feel any pride for myself. I did not speak up for Jesus, either. I did not try to take the hammer from the soldier. I had stabbed a fisherman, but I would not challenge the soldier with the nails. I was no better. I thought of Jesus being our sacrifice. I had intended to share my thoughts with these. At that moment, I felt incapable to speak at all. The ladies and I left that upstairs room. We let the men know we were going to the tomb at daybreak. We wanted to anoint Jesus' body. We invited them to come with us if they would like. None of them seemed willing. Just sweep Jesus under the rug, I suppose, as if He never existed.

In the twentieth year of Tiberius, on the first month, the fourteenth day — Early this morning, I awoke before sunrise. I want to get to the tomb of Jesus. My longing is to spend all day with Him. I know He is dead, but I want to have time with Him. I want to talk to Him. I went to Salome's room. She was awake and ready. She had the spices for us to use to anoint Jesus' body further. Mary, the mother of James the Less, and Susanna were also ready to go.

Joanna decided to stay back with Jesus' mother. Mary has not left her room. Joanna attempted to rouse her from the outside, but no response. She went in. A few minutes later, Joanna came back out. Jesus' mother was bed-ridden in grief. I was sorry we could bring her no comfort. I wish her sons or daughters were here. I have no idea where they could be. Do they even know their older brother was killed?

I have the most amazing thing to write. We just returned from the tomb. When the four of us approached the tomb, we had not thought to bring a few men with us. We had seen the difficulty Nicodemus and Joseph had in rolling the stone down the slope to close the tomb. Who would roll it back up the slope and put the stop to hold it back for us? We hoped a gardener would be nearby. The garden was a very luxurious, functional one after all.

As we neared, we saw the Roman soldiers sprawled out on the ground. They seemed to be unconscious, but their eyes were wide open. The tomb was even more so. At first, we were hesitant to walk inside. Something had gotten to these soldiers. Were we next? We stood still for a minute. My thoughts were, if Jesus' body is still in there, then we must do what we came to do.

We walked hand in hand, except for Salome, who carried the spices. She followed close behind. We stepped to the entrance. I looked in. Susanna walked in past me. We were broken. The body of our Lord was not there. We walked back toward the soldiers to ask. Their eyes were trained on something behind us, but they would not speak. Their mouths were wide open. They blinked. But they remained frozen. They watched to see what would happen to us, I assumed. I wanted to ask them what had happened.

At that moment, the soldiers began to run. I looked back toward the tomb. Two men in clothes that gleamed like lightning stood beside us. There were four women, but now there were six of us, including these two brilliant, blinding men. No wonder the soldiers ran. Mary, the mother of James the Less, began to step back. Salome dropped the spices, backing up with her eyes fixed on these two. If they were going to harm me, I could do nothing. They both were within an arm's length of me. One of the men cleared his throat. We all knelt, Susanna and I side by side. Mary, the mother of James the Less, knelt where she was. Salome bowed with one knee on her sack of spices, the other on the ground. She was lopsided as she knelt but did not adjust. Everything within me felt fear like those Roman soldiers. The men spoke, one after the other. One began a sentence, the other finished it. They said, "Why do you look for the living among the dead? He is not here; He has risen! Remember how He told you, while He was still with you in Galilee: 'The Son of Man must be delivered into the hands of sinful men, be crucified, and on the third day be raised again.' Come and see the place where He lay. Then go quickly and tell His disciples."

The women and I looked at each other. Susanna said, "Don't you remember? He did say He would die and rise." I had thought of that last night. I saw no way. Peter could not raise Him. He was not alive to raise Himself. Neither Elijah nor Elisha were anywhere around. I could not see this one promise He made being fulfilled. The angels said He has done it. The tomb was empty. If I was not mistaken, these were not two ordinary men in flashy attire. These were angels! The shepherds saw angels at His birth. We were seeing angels at His resurrection!

We ran to tell the disciples. We did not walk. We ran as fast as the Roman soldiers but with a different purpose. We did not hide where we were going. We had no concern for the safety of the disciples. We ran right up to that upstairs room of the Passover in broad daylight. I banged on the door, shouting, "Let us in now!" They swung the door open. The squeak could not be heard over my voice, "Jesus has risen! We just saw angels at His empty tomb!"

The disciples shook their heads. They acted as if we were out of our minds. I went to Matthew. He would not budge. I went to Peter. I reminded him of the conversation last night. I told him, "Peter if you are ever going to get past this, it is time for you to stand now. If you do not believe me, believe Him. Go see for yourself." John walked up to Peter and said, "The Lord said He would rise, Peter. Should we not go see?" Peter nodded. Off they went. I followed behind them.

Once they got outside their hiding place, they began to run. I did my best to keep up, but they were way too fast. When I finally caught up to them at the tomb, Peter was fully inside. John stepped through the entrance to join him. I walked in behind John. They kept looking at the linen lying by itself on the crypt. The head piece was lying by itself, holding its form as if Jesus' head was still in it. They both looked perplexed. They did not see Jesus. I did not see Him either. I could tell by their faces that their worst fears had been realized. Someone had stolen or moved Jesus' body so no one could gather to honor Him. Peter and John left the tomb. They left the garden. They left me.

I had the same empty feeling as them, but I had seen the two men in brilliant clothing. They said Jesus was risen. I do not know why, but I was doubting my own eyes and ears. I stood in the tomb for almost a half-hour. I walked out. I collapsed on the ground near the big stone, weeping. I heard some talking. I looked back into the tomb. The two men were present again. One was seated where Jesus' head had lain, the other where His feet had rested. They both looked at me, eye to eye. I stood up. They asked me, "Woman, why are you crying?" I told them, "They have taken my Lord away, and I do not know where they have put Him."

I heard someone walk up behind me. I turned to see another man. He asked me the same question. "Woman, why are you crying? For whom are you looking?" I assumed he was the gardener I was counting on to roll the stone away when we first arrived early this morning. I said to him, "Sir, if you have carried Him away, tell me where you have put Him, and I will get Him." I turned away from him, hopeless. I wanted to be alone. I had all these people asking questions, no one giving me answers. Just then, the man I thought was the gardener said, "Mary." I knew that voice! I turned. I stared at the man. He was not a stranger. He was not one to tell me where the body was, He was the body. He was the Lord! I fell to the ground again. I grabbed His feet. I could see the nail marks. I said, "Rabbi!"

Oh, what a glorious moment. Jesus said, "Do not hold on to Me, for I have not yet returned to the Father. Go instead to My brothers and tell them, 'I am returning to My Father and your Father, to My God and your God.'" Every ounce of grief was gone. Every memory of the cross was as good as erased. I was no longer tired. I felt this amazing vigor traveling from my eyes to my mind and to my legs. I looked back at Him. He smiled. I could sense His directing me., "Go."

I ran back to the city of Jerusalem. I rushed back to that upstairs room. The traffic in and out of that room made it clear it would not be a hiding place for long. I saw all the disciples gathered in that room. They were as sad as the moment I found them last night. I told them this time even more than before. Not only was I told He was risen, but I also announced, "I have seen the Lord!"

I related what happened after Peter and John left. I told them about seeing the two angels again. I told them of hearing a man behind me. I told them I bowed when He said my name. I told them Jesus sent me to tell them that Jesus is alive! Just like He said! Excitement overwhelmed me. Surely, I thought, they will believe me this time.

But they did not. They did not believe me. They thought I was out of my mind. They heard I saw angels. They saw no angels. They heard I saw the Lord. They did not see Him. I dare say they saw me as that struggling thing from Magdala. They probably would have had compassion on me if they had not had such contempt at that moment. They clearly were ready to move on. No more of this talk of Jesus or His resurrection. I was beside myself. He was alive. No one was able to believe.

I gave one last plea. "My friends, what did He say He would do after He died?" No one answered. I answered for them. "He said He would rise from the dead." I then asked them, "Do you remember when someone asked Jesus for a sign? He said no sign would be given but the sign of Jonah? Do you men remember how long Jonah was in the belly of that great fish? All thought he was dead and gone. Three days later, he was walking around in Nineveh. Brothers, this is the sign of Jonah! He has given us the sign of Jonah. He is the Christ!" Not one budged. It was useless. I looked around. Only nine of them were in the room. Peter was missing, as was Thomas.

I waited. I prayed Jesus would appear to them in some way. A few hours passed. I had nowhere to go. Salome soon came, as did Mary, the mother of James the Less, and Susanna. They tried to convince the disciples, too, but there was no moving these.

Peter returned. His countenance totally changed. He said, "My brothers I have seen the Lord Jesus! He met me as I was leaving Jerusalem. I had made my mind up to go to Galilee without you. I was so despondent over how I failed Him. He met me. He told me He forgave me! He told me to come tell you." I jumped with joy. I gave Peter a great big hug. I told the disciples, "Will you believe now? Two witnesses have come forward — me and Peter. That is enough for any court." They still would not believe. Two more men walked into the room. One named Cleopas. I did not recognize the other. I had seen Cleopas a few times when Jesus was in Jerusalem. I think he was a friend of Lazarus. They entered the room as excited as I was. They said, "It is true! The Lord has risen and has appeared to

Peter." I called out, "Brothers, that makes four of us!" I looked over at Matthew. He looked like he wanted to believe, but he just could not fathom it.

They quizzed Peter. They questioned Cleopas. They asked me not one thing. Not an hour later, I asked the disciples, "What are you going to do now? Are you giving up what the Rabbi has called you to do? He trained you. Now that you do not see Him physically, are you resolved to return to your old lives?" I could tell the men were tired of me. They seemed ready for me to go back to Joanna's.

As darkness came upon the city, Andrew lit the one lantern on the table. They began to make their plans to leave the city secretly by twos so no one would see them together. They made their plans. I was flabbergasted. At that very moment, while the doors were totally shut, no knocks on any doors, Jesus appeared at the head of the table where He had conducted our Passover. No one noticed until He said, "Peace be with you!" After He said this, He showed us His hands and side. The disciples were overjoyed when they saw the Lord. I wanted to say "I told you so", but I knew that had I not seen Him for myself, I probably would not have believed, either.

Jesus then said, "Why are you troubled, and why do doubts rise in your minds? Look at My hands and My feet. It is I Myself! Touch Me and see; a ghost does not have flesh and bones, as you see I have. This is what I told you while I was still with you: Everything must be fulfilled that is written about Me in the Law of Moses, the Prophets and the Psalms."

All embraced Him, but a holy fear arose as if being in the presence of a ghost. Jesus ate with us to prove otherwise. He visited with us. He took the bread and broke it just as He has done hundreds of times before. It was surreal. It was like He had never been gone. The last few days were like a nightmare. We felt as though we had awakened, but how could we all have the same nightmare over the same few days? He was killed on a cross. We were reminded of that as He handed out the bread. We could see His wrists as they extended beyond His sleeves. We saw the nail marks. As I looked closely at Him, I could still see the thorn pricks at the top of His head. This was Jesus. Everything He said had occurred.

Thomas was not present. Philip said, "I cannot wait to tell Thomas!" I felt the liberty to speak as Jesus looked right at me with another warm smile. I said, "Yes, and he will not believe you anymore than you all believed me." They all began to laugh. I looked back at Jesus. I said, "Rabbi, thank You for appearing to me. Thank

You for letting me see You at that tomb. Thank You for dying for my sins as the Lamb of God. Now that You have conquered death, I have no doubt You can take us to the Kingdom of God either now or when we die. I can close my eyes one day in death, if God chooses, I know You will be there to raise me back up again."

Jesus looked at me with approval. He then looked around the room at the ten disciples and the four of us ladies. Jesus said, "Because you have seen Me, you have believed; blessed are those who have not seen and yet have believed." I began to think while all of this was going on, I wish I could have believed without seeing. I know it is harder. I have no idea what Thomas will think. He was the one willing to go to Jerusalem and die with Him a few months back. He also is the one who ran and hid. He is not here now. I wonder if he is heading back to his hometown like Peter.

I am at Joanna's now. She and Jesus' mother have gone to see Jesus. I would love to be with them. I believe Mary, Jesus' mother, deserves time with her son alone. I also believe Joanna deserves time with them. She sacrificed much to always stay behind for Jesus' mother. I believe she felt that responsibility since she was Mary's first friend of our group. It was her home in which we were staying. Those were her guards who responded to her orders, not ours.

I cannot put into words what I am feeling right now. I did not want to go back to Galilee without Jesus. He told us to go without Him, but He assured us He will meet us there. Anyone who says they will rise from the dead, and does, we certainly can trust to meet us in Galilee. All I have is love in my heart. I am overflowing with joy. Life has meaning. We are eternal. We have our sins covered. We have the guarantee of eternal life sitting in the upstairs room of the Passover with His mother and disciples. Death no longer has any hold on any of us. I am assured to see Poppa and Momma again. There was hope before. Now there is unshakeable certainty.

In the twentieth year of Tiberius, on the first month, the twenty-second day — Thomas made it back to the disciples. He did not believe, as I feared. Matthew, who is now convinced of our Lord, met me at Joanna's. He let me know Jesus met them in the Passover room again, this time to challenge Thomas. He showed Thomas His hands and feet. He had Thomas reach into His side where the spear had gone. Matthew said Thomas's only response was, "My Lord and my God." What a blessing!

We are all headed back to Galilee today. The Lord said He would meet us there. Traveling with the eleven is me, Salome, Susanna, and Mary, the mother of James the Less. To travel as Jesus' disciples without Jesus is strange. I cannot imagine what the crowds will do when they see us. I am sure many have heard what happened in Jerusalem to our Rabbi. I am sure they will not believe He has risen, any more than did our group. Whether they believe or not, the truth is Jesus the Christ is risen from the dead. I cannot write or say that enough.

In the twentieth year of Tiberius, on the second month, the first day — We arrived in Magdala today. The disciples walked me to my home. They saw me in, then hurriedly continued to Capernaum. They could not wait to spread the news to their own towns and families. Granted, we have shared this amazing truth the entire journey.

Jesus did not give us a place to meet Him. I asked Matthew, John, and Peter to be sure to come get me when He appears. They promised they would. I cannot wait to be reunited with the Lord.

I was not home an hour, when there was a knock on my door. I had hoped it was Matthew. It was not. It was Atticus. I was not disappointed at all. I wrapped my arms around him. He looked at me. He asked me, "Mary, is it true? Jesus was crucified in Jerusalem?" He obviously had not heard the Good News. We sat outdoors in the courtyard. I pulled my chair next to his. I held his hand. I reminded him how much I loved him. I told him that I am ready to marry when he is. I then told him, "Before we do anything else, you need to know something, Atticus." He braced himself as if for bad news. I said, "Atticus, do not be afraid. What I want to tell you is what happened at the tomb where Jesus was buried." I told him all that occurred. I then reinforced the amazing truth. "Atticus, Jesus has risen from the dead! He is alive! I have seen Him. I have eaten with Him since. I have spoken with Him. He is going to be back here in Galilee any day."

Atticus had all kinds of questions. I knew he would. My greatest delight was sharing with him the conclusion of our discussion, that the blood of lambs cannot take away our sins. Jesus, the Lamb of God, did that for us. All the other lambs were pointing to the Lamb of God, Jesus. He was overjoyed. He kept saying, "I knew animals made no sense. I knew animals made no sense. It all fits together so divinely." I reiterated what he said. "It does indeed, my betrothed."

We had a sweet fellowship together. We prayed to end our visit. Atticus had been studying diligently in my absence. He shared with me the many things he had learned about God and His goodness. He asked me to promise him one thing. I asked him what it would be. He said, "When Matthew sends for you to go where Jesus is, will you take me with you?" I assured him with delight, saying, "Unless Jesus says otherwise, I will not leave here without you."

In the twentieth year of Tiberius, on the second month, the third day — Matthew sent a runner to let me know Jesus was meeting us near the place where He multiplied the fish and loaves of that little boy. I hurried to where Atticus was working. He received permission. We left with just the clothes on our backs. I had some money in my purse. But other than that, we rushed out of Magdala.

We arrived at the hillside facing the Galilee. The eleven disciples were present. Thomas was grinning ear to ear. I hugged them all. The ladies were there, Joanna included. Even Chuza was with her. He had never been with us to see Jesus. The news of what happened in Jerusalem captured his heart. While we waited on Jesus to walk up, Chuza said the Roman soldiers were paid off by the high priests to say Jesus' body was stolen. He said the vast majority did not believe that. He said the city is filled with fear. After their rejection of Jesus, they are certain of retribution in the order of Sodom and Gomorrah. I cannot see Jesus responding this way. At least not until it is His time to judge the world, if I understand what He taught as we sat on the Mount of Olives.

Jesus walked up just as Chuza finished talking. Jesus looked as serene as always. He had the mastery over everything. Crowds came out to hear Him. Many doubted He had died. Most believed it was a rumor, nothing more. Some skeptics said it was a hoax to try to cause a movement to make Him king of Israel. Jesus put all that speculation to rest.

He asked the crowd, "What were you discussing together as you walked along?" No one answered. Jesus reminded us how He had been a prophet, powerful in word and deed before God and all the people. He told us about how the chief priests and our rulers handed Him over to be sentenced to death, and consequently crucified Him. He talked of how everyone had welcomed Him and then rejected Him. He reminded us how, multiple times, He had said these things would occur. He softly rebuked us all, saying, "How foolish you are, and how slow of heart to believe all that the prophets have spoken! Did not the Christ have to suffer these things and then enter His glory?" Beginning with Moses and all the Prophets, He explained to us all that was said in all the scriptures concerning Himself. Cleopas was there. I heard him say with delight, "That is exactly what Jesus said to me at my house!" The Lord smiled at him.

Atticus was dumbfounded, as was the crowd. I was gratified to see how all of scripture came together at one intersection — Jesus. It was as if He had opened our minds to understand and believe the scriptures. He stood before us. He held out His Hands. He removed His sandals. He showed us the scars. He then said to us, "This is what was written: The Christ will suffer and rise from the dead on the third day, and repentance and forgiveness of sins will be preached in His name to all nations, beginning at Jerusalem. You are witnesses of these things." Amazing!

Every disciple had a new lease on life, on everlasting life. I count myself with them, though I am not one of the twelve. I am just like Poppa said, a person willing to serve when He calls, or serve Him in my hometown when He does not. We felt as if we had all been to the greatest rabbinic school in the world and now were graduating. I write that, but we know it will take eternity and even more to grasp a fragment of who our Lord Jesus and our Father God are.

Jesus gave us a command., "All authority in Heaven and on earth has been given to Me. Therefore, go and make disciples of all nations, baptizing them in the name of the Father and of the Son and of the Holy Spirit, and teaching them to obey everything I have commanded you. And surely I am with you always, to the very end of the age." I thought of what Jesus said would come the last days, as in the days of Noah. Clearly, dark days lay ahead. Jesus had said if they hate Him, they will hate us. He said if they persecute Him, they will persecute us. It is not a leap to imagine that since they crucified Him, they well may do the same to us.

I talked with Atticus after Jesus left us to pray. I told him of my disappointment in the disciples when they deserted the Lord. Atticus began to talk like he would not have left Jesus. He said he would have been there with me. I told him that this could be the case, but then again, we never know what we will do until the time comes. We should all pray for the Father to give us strength. The disciples are changed now. They realize death is not the end. I see it, too. Atticus has seen with his own eyes. We are going to live forever. He promised everlasting life. He has delivered.

In the twentieth year of Tiberius, on the second month, the seventh day — We met Jesus in Capernaum at Peter's home. He attended the synagogue. We were right there with Him. Whispers surrounded us. Some thought they had seen a spirit. Many of His greatest adversaries stayed away this Sabbath when they saw He was walking toward the synagogue. I could see people make an about face like they forgot something. They never returned. Jairus is no longer the synagogue ruler here. The new one did all the speaking. He did not acknowledge Jesus, nor ask Him to speak. Some wanted to touch Him. Some asked to see His wrists after worship. Jesus obliged. Many left with a joyful hesitancy.

In the twentieth year of Tiberius, on the second month, the eighth day — The crowds were at Peter's door again. Jesus was there! People came from everywhere to see Him. They brought their sick, their paralyzed, their deaf, their blind. It was like all was the same as before. But then again, He had returned with a convincing power that could make even the hardest of hearts melt.

The perfect example was when many of the priests and Pharisees from Jerusalem appeared on the shore of Capernaum. The crowds were large. These priests and Pharisees bowed before Jesus. They called Him "my Lord". They asked Him to forgive them. He did. They declared for all to hear, "Jesus is the Christ, the Son of the Living God, the Son of David. He is the Messiah we have been told about, prayed for, hoped for. He has died. He has risen!"

I saw another group come to Jesus at the shore. They were Roman soldiers. In their midst was the centurion I recognized from the cross. He came before Jesus with his contingent. I would have feared he was there to arrest Jesus, but I had felt a tenderness in this man as Nicodemus carried Him from the cross. Many of the people moved forward, ready to challenge the soldiers on Jesus' behalf. Peter was the first to come to His aid. Jesus raised His hand for Peter to stand down.

This centurion, with his soldiers, took their helmets off. They bowed before Jesus. I heard the centurion say, "Master, we have come to give our lives to You. We believe You are the Son of God. What will You have us do?" Jesus told them to go back to their homes, to their posts, and tell everyone that God has sent His Son to pay for the sins of the world, and that He is risen from the dead. He told them to spread the Good News that salvation, forgiveness of sins, and eternal life are given in His name to everyone who calls upon Him. The centurion and all his men gladly agreed. They rose from their stance. They faded back, but they would not leave until He had finished. They watched Jesus in awe. They were not alone. We all did.

In the twentieth year of Tiberius, on the second month, the tenth day — We had stayed at Matthew's home — Atticus in Poppa's room, me in my usual one.

We met once again with the Lord near Magdala this morning. He taught us about the Kingdom of Heaven. He challenged us with a message that He had shared before:

"Blessed are the poor in spirit, for theirs is the Kingdom of Heaven. Blessed are those who mourn, for they will be comforted. Blessed are the meek, for they will inherit the earth. Blessed are those who hunger and thirst for righteousness, for they will be filled. Blessed are the merciful, for they will be shown mercy. Blessed are the pure in heart, for they will see God. Blessed are the peacemakers, for they will be called sons of God. Blessed are those who are persecuted because of righteousness, for theirs is the Kingdom of Heaven. Blessed are you when people insult you, persecute you and falsely say all kinds of evil against you because of Me. Rejoice and be glad, because great is your reward in Heaven, for in the same way they persecuted the prophets who were before you."

The eleven, the ladies, Atticus, and I were blessed to have a private meal with the Lord down on the shore. Afterward, I had the impression Jesus wanted to spend the next few days with His disciples. We gladly excused ourselves early in the afternoon.

Atticus and I arrived back in Magdala. My betrothed let me know of something that happened at the shore when Jesus had finished speaking. I had gone to visit with Matthew for a moment. Atticus said he approached Jesus and personally asked Him to be his Savior. Jesus placed His hands on Atticus' shoulders. He looked him in the eye. He asked Atticus if he believed Jesus was the Son of God, that He died for his sins, and that He rose from the dead to give eternal life. Atticus said, without flinching, "I believe all of it, Rabbi. I believe in You with my whole heart. I have seen what You have done for my fiancé. I have seen what You have done for others. I know what You have done for me. I give You my life. Use me however You choose." Jesus welcomed him into the Father's family. He told him that this very day, he has been saved. Atticus did what everyone else seems to do. He wept tears of joy.

I took his hand. I kissed him on the forehead. I said, "We are now complete." After a long visit, we decided to get married on the twenty-eighth day of this month. I had no family to notify. Atticus only has a brother. It would be at the beginning of the Feast of Weeks. I cannot express how genuinely happy I am. The Lord has risen from the dead. He is alive! I have made Him my Savior. He has blessed me with forgiveness. He has given me experiences that will never be replicated. He has saved my Atticus. For what more could I ever pray?

In the twentieth year of Tiberius, on the second month, the thirteenth day — I traveled to Capernaum to see Jesus. He had a crowd around Him. He was as awesome as ever. His face glowed in glory. I do not know if that is what I saw in Him, or if that was what He displayed to all. More people lined up to see Him. I heard many giving their lives to Him.

I took Matthew aside. I let him know of Atticus and my decision to get married. I asked Matthew if he would stand in for Poppa. He was delighted. Matthew was practically giddy. He told me he could not get over the honor I had bestowed upon him. He then shared with me that he would not be able to be there. Jesus had asked the disciples to meet Him in Jerusalem for the Feast of Weeks. He said, "The Lord has asked us to stay in Jerusalem until we are clothed in power from on high." I did not know what that meant. Matthew did not either. I was not disappointed. If I were given the same choice, I would delay my wedding to be there. Matthew apologized. I let him know there was no reason to apologize and that we could have a celebration when he returns.

In the twentieth year of Tiberius, on the second month, the twenty-eighth day — Today, I gave my hand to Atticus in marriage. It was a small gathering, but it was one of the most joyous occasions of my life. I praise God that He would give me a man who would know my past and still love me. I thanked God that He had given Jesus to pay for the sins of my past, present, and future, and that He would give me a man who had given Him his life, too. I am now the wife of Atticus.

We paid off the fishing boat. He now has his own business, effective next week. I was pleased to let him know I had been with no other man. It was a joy to share that I had not been alone with a man for a long, long time. When with Jesus and the disciples, we always had a separate camp for the ladies. I had never even been alone with Jesus. Even at the tomb, we had two angels in our midst. Jesus called for holiness. He modeled it not only in action, but privately, just as in public. What a blessing to consummate my marriage with the man I desire to spend the rest of this life with, serving Jesus.

We made a commitment to be Jesus' witnesses in Magdala, in our synagogue, on the shore, in business, to our neighbors, and with everyone we meet from this day forward. We also pledged to honor the Jewish feasts each year, for that is what Jesus does. We decided he would move in with me in Poppa's and Momma's home, which is now my own.

In the twentieth year of Tiberius, on the third month, the eighteenth day — Matthew came by to see us. Atticus and I welcomed him into our home. He said if it was alright with us, he wanted to host a celebration for our marriage this evening. We agreed. He was glad because he had already ordered the food.

We laughed! I asked Matthew if Jesus was coming with them tonight. He said, "No, Mary. You missed the most amazing thing yet. Jesus led us out to the Mount of Olives. You know, the place He always stops to look and pray for the city?" I nodded yes. Matthew continued, "Jesus sat us down and began to teach like He always does.

"James asked Jesus a question, 'Lord, are you at this time going to restore the kingdom to Israel?'" We all were wanting to know. It seemed to be the next logical step for our Lord.

Matthew said, "Jesus answered, 'It is not for you to know the times or dates the Father has set by His own authority. But you will receive power when the Holy Spirit comes on you; and you will be My witnesses in Jerusalem, and in all Judea and Samaria, and to the ends of the earth.'"

There was a long pause. Matthew's eyes watered. As he spoke, his voice took a higher excited pitch. He said, "Mary, after He said this, He was taken up before our very eyes, and a cloud hid Him from our sight. Mary, Jesus literally lifted from the Mount of Olives. He looked at us as He ascended. He smiled. He spread His arms. He looked into Heaven. He became as bright as lightning." I started screaming to Matthew, grabbing Atticus, "I knew He would leave like Elijah or Enoch! I knew it! This is why I never wanted to miss being with Him! I did not want to miss out on His ascension. I am so thrilled. I am so angry. I wanted to be there."

I looked over at Atticus. I had not considered his feelings. I was getting married to Atticus, which was why I was not there. I quickly grabbed my husband's hand, saying, "I told you I was so thrilled. I am thrilled Jesus went up the way He did. I am angry in one way that I was not there, but know this, my husband, if Jesus had wanted me to be there, He would have had me there, us there. He shows us what He desires. I am fully content. I believe it was His will for us to be in Magdala getting married. I have no regrets." Atticus smiled. He was going to be fine.

Matthew said, "Mary, Atticus, while we were looking intently up into the sky as He was going, suddenly two men dressed in white stood beside us. They said, 'Men of Galilee, why do you stand here looking into the sky? This same Jesus, who has been taken from you into Heaven, will come back in the same way you have seen Him go into Heaven.' Mary, Atticus, Jesus is coming back!" I asked Matthew, "When?" He said he did not know.

What a wonderful surprise. I am in love with Jesus even more today. It is hard to believe my love can grow. His goodness exceeds all limits, drawing my love beyond its limits, too. Matthew said that all twelve disciples would be joining us this evening. I was taken aback, and said, "Twelve, Matthew?" Matthew said, "I knew you would catch that. While in Jerusalem, we prayed. With Peter's direction by the Holy Spirit, we chose Matthias to join us."

I knew Matthias somewhat. He seemed like the perfect choice. I asked Matthew if Matthias was the gift Jesus spoke of them receiving in Jerusalem. Matthew said, "Oh no, Mary. He gave us His Holy Spirit to live inside us." He said Jesus had given His Spirit to the disciples and all those who were following Jesus, including the priests, the Pharisees, and the soldiers who had converted. He said that Mary, the mother of James the Less was there. Salome was there. Susanna was there. Joanna and Chuza, too. Even Jesus' mother Mary was there. Matthew said, "You would not believe it, Mary! We all received the gift of the Holy Spirit. He was the most amazing gift. All of a sudden, we did not just believe we were saved. We had an affirmation inside of us." I leaned forward in my chair and asked, "How?". Matthew said, "When the day of Pentecost came, we were all together in one place. Suddenly, a sound like the blowing of a violent wind came from Heaven and filled the whole house where we were sitting. We saw what seemed to be tongues of fire that separated and came to rest on each of us. All of us were filled with the Holy Spirit and began to speak in other tongues as the Spirit enabled us. People from all over were in Jerusalem that day. You have seen them, Mary. They speak in many different languages. As the Holy Spirit moved, we were speaking in other languages that we had never spoken before. Someone would walk up who had that native language. We would converse with them. We were able to tell them about Jesus. It was amazing. Jesus told us to be witnesses throughout the world. Now we can, because He will enable us to speak the languages and understand them wherever we go, by His precious gift, the Holy Spirit."

"Mary and Atticus," he continued, "people began to gather where we were. Peter spoke to the crowds who gathered. Over three thousand gave their lives to Jesus at that moment. You have never seen such love. You have never seen such harmony. Jesus was taking over the city of Jerusalem. More priests, Pharisees, Sadducees, Herodians, scribes, soldiers, tax collectors, prostitutes, and people from every nation were receiving Jesus as their personal Savior. It was Heaven on earth. Every day, increasing numbers of people were being saved, Mary. Jesus, even in Heaven now, has us in awe. We feel His Presence stronger every day."

We asked all kinds of questions. Matthew was not even able to leave. Later this evening, the food arrived. Peter came with the most welcoming, loving, celebratory embrace. He was profoundly changed. He reminded me of our Rabbi. John came, smiling. James, too. Philip and Andrew joyfully entered our home. Nathanael came. He never said much. His face said everything. Simon the Zealot had never set foot in our home. He came in as if he had been a long-time friend of tax collector Poppa. Thomas congratulated Atticus. He was joined by Thaddeus. Before long, all the men were around my husband. They were cheerfully visiting, laughing, embracing. The ladies tended to my every need. Salome, Susanna, Joanna, and Mary, the mother of James the Less were all with me. We took time in the family room to talk about all we had seen and heard with Jesus.

Before long, Zacchaeus entered. I was shocked. What a change Jesus has made in him. Then the surprise of all surprises: Jesus' mother came with two of her sons, James and Jude. For a couple who had no family on my side, one brother on his, we suddenly had the largest party of guests. I say 'guests'. I sat back late this evening as they were all fellowshipping. I began to thank Jesus. He has given me a family like I have never known. I was an only child, a hated daughter of a tax collector. I had few friends. Now, I am loved. I am embraced. My life has meaning, all because of Jesus.

We are in our room now. All our guests have left. Atticus and I prayed together. He has given me time to write my final thoughts before we blow out the flame in our lamp. Joy is mine. Jesus said He came to give us life, and that life abundantly. He has given me that with a promise of eternity to be even better. I am blessed. I have only three pages left in my parchments. I will keep this in a sacred place in our home. I know I will refer to it repeatedly to remember, to rejoice, and to look forward to the promises. I thank You, Father. I thank You, Jesus. I thank You, Holy Spirit. By the way, as we prayed, the Holy Spirit came upon me and Atticus, too. Not in an overt way like they had in Jerusalem, but just as powerful. I feel His presence flowing through me.

Mary Magdalene's Death — In the Eleventh Year of Nero Caesar

In the eleventh year of Nero's reign, on the third month, the second day — The soldiers came into Magdala today. They targeted the followers of the Way, the followers of Jesus. We have seen persecution on the uptick since Caligula was killed. Emperor Claudias began it subtly. Now, Emperor Nero has come to Israel with a vengeance. He blames all his troubles on our "Christ-following sect" as he calls us. We have done nothing but love people and live at peace with everyone.

It is just as Jesus said: they persecuted Him, so they will persecute us, also. They came for me, saying I was the cause of this movement in our village. We have seen many turn to Christ over the last three decades.

Atticus met them at our door. They demanded he hand me over. He refused to let them take me. They killed my husband before my eyes with a sword. I fell to help him, but they snatched me up. All I could say was, "I love you, Atticus. I will see you soon." The soldiers looked at each other in confusion.

(tears stain page)

They ordered me to go. I asked to get my coat. They said I could only take one thing. I left my coat. I grabbed my parchments from our shelf. If ever I needed them, it is now.

They threw me into the deepest part of the cistern. I spent several nights here years ago. It has remained closed for almost thirty years. Over the last few weeks, the Romans dug out the majority of the dirt, replaced the roof, anchored stronger chains, and divided it into three small cells with bars. We knew arrests were to be made soon.

This cell is dank and dark. Only a gleam of light shines in from a crack in the roof. I have sat under this beam to write. I am surprised they let me have my bound parchments and a pen. I wonder if they are hoping for some confession, or maybe some suicide note. They will get a confession for sure. I do believe Jesus is the Christ, the Son of the Living God, that He was born to a virgin, lived a perfect life, worked miracles, was crucified, dead, buried, and He rose from the grave offering forgiveness of sins and eternal life. I believe that as many as receive Him, they will inherit eternal life in Heaven. I believe if Jesus is rejected, they will face the sad eternity of Hell. I believe only one God exists, God the Father, His Son Jesus Christ, and His Holy Spirit. That is the confession I will never recant.

Atticus and I had spoken of this eventuality. We weighed the options of moving. We decided the Lord had us here for a reason. We prayed together a few nights ago. We committed our lives to the Lord's hand. Our resolve expressed was, "If we die, we will die honoring Jesus. If we live, we will live bringing glory to His Name". My sweet husband of over thirty-seven years died honoring Jesus. I very well may follow. I am ready. After seeing Jesus risen from the dead, I have no fear of an end to life, just a graduation to the next.

We could never have children. I believe we were married too late for that. We have seen much fruit, as many have heard our testimony and received Jesus as their Lord. There are no better offspring than these.

So here I am. From what I know, the outcome of the Lord's twelve has been expected. Our dear James was the first to die. He was put to death by the sword at the hand of Herod Agrippa. To my knowledge, John is somewhere in prison after surviving being thrown into boiling oil. We pray for him. Peter was hung on a cross upside down in Rome. He had denied the Lord three times, but for the rest of his life, he stood for Christ, refusing to shrink from death.

Andrew was crucified in Achaia. Thomas was martyred in India by a spear. Philip was crucified in Hierapolis with his daughters, because they refused to worship the emperor along with God. Nathanael was flayed and then crucified in Armenia. Simon the Zealot was killed in Persia because he refused to give a sacrifice to the sun god. Thaddeus was beaten to near-death with a club and then crucified. James the Less was thrown from the pinnacle of the Temple in Jerusalem and then stoned to death. Matthias was stoned to death in Judea, then beheaded. Our dear friend Matthew was stabbed to death in Ethiopia for speaking against the immorality of their royal family.

My precious brothers have all suffered for Jesus. The world has not been worthy of them. I now await my verdict. If what they did to my precious husband is any indication, my death is imminent.

In the eleventh year of Nero's reign, on the third month, the third day — I have been returned to the cistern after my short trial. They asked me to recant and be silent, or be beheaded. I chose the latter. They have given me until the ninth hour to change my mind. I will not.

My concern? What do I do with my bound parchments? I know Matthew has written of his experiences with Jesus. I know Mark recorded all that Peter could recall. But what of mine? I want as many people as possible to read what Jesus did for me. The Rabbi called us to be His witnesses. If I am dead, I want my witness to live on. How can I save this for others? I am praying for an answer. I have five short hours left.

I have found in the corner of this cistern a thick layer of dirt. I have dug around it. An exceedingly small clay pot is covered over. It has a lid on top. I praise the Lord! The pot is empty. I am going to place my parchments there. I believe I can cover them over again. It is so dark, no one can see what is here.

Here is my last entry. Jesus is my Lord and my Savior. In the days that He walked these shores, I dropped everything to join the crowds to be with Him, to hear Him, to watch Him. I am about to drop everything again to join the crowds in Heaven to be with Him, to hear Him, to watch Him. I know the eleven are there as before. Atticus is there now, too. Poppa and Momma are with Jesus, I know, hanging on every Word. I am leaving to join the crowd.

The Conclusion

Guiseppe Campise pushed back from the ancient bound parchments. He was embarrassed as a few tears began to roll down his cheeks. He looked around. The students and professors had all gone home for the Sabbath. Guiseppe was alone.

The immediate question was, what should he do now? He has read the ancient documents that he found — his first real discovery. He was excited. He had been the foreman on many discoveries for the friars, but his work ended with the dig. The authentication process was never part of his responsibilities. If a find were authentic, access of the discovery would be made available to the academic community. Following that would be the money-making promotion to the museums and the public.

All of which was foreign to Guiseppe. He had no idea where to start as a novice. Thankfully, he had Father Corbo and Father Loffreda in which to confide. These were godly men, highly ethical, and kind. They cared more for the find than the credit. They had been involved in every aspect of new discoveries. He made the decision. In the morning, he would meet with the two to begin the process.

The bigger question with which to be dealt was what does he do with Jesus? Guiseppe had never thought of life and death issues. He dealt with the past. His present work was the past. His future vocation would continue to be the past. Guiseppe was aging. He was finding it harder to work the physical hours he once had. He noticed Father Corbo's health failing, too. How long until his own health deserts him?

Guiseppe's entire work has really been about the dead. He never quite thought of his own mortality. Now, he reads of Jesus. He had read of Jesus before, but purely as a historical reference point. He had never read the Bible for himself. Again, he had seen the Bible referenced over the shoulders of the two priests in discerning where to dig and what to look for, but never for himself.

The foreman began to think over his own life. He had committed many sins. He had never really seen any infraction as a sin, but rather a freedom. Now, he has come face to face with the reality of sin, the need for freedom from sin, not freedom to sin. He had tried to stop his excessive drinking on a few occasions. His love for it always won. He was not inexperienced at womanizing. Being out on digs for months at a time, he found recreation in whatever female companionship could be had or purchased. Granted, the friars had no idea, but all his men did. He lived for money. He lived for pleasure. He lived for himself. All his life had been on the horizontal plane.

Conviction swept over Guiseppe. If Mary Magdalene was truly the author of this find, she wrote that Jesus is the one who will judge. He will send some to Heaven and the rest to Hell. Jesus said He is the only way to forgiveness and eternal life. Guiseppe began to think over the facts. It was not just this writing that attested to Jesus' resurrection. There was evidence in the Bible, and in extrabiblical sources. Josephus had referenced it. Nero had feared it. Herod Agrippa was haunted by the thought. Could Guiseppe face death like Mary Magdalene did — ready and excited? Or would he face death like his own father — frantic, fearful, fighting for every breath, begging not to die? He did not want his father's death for himself.

He searched back through his own notes he had taken as he read these ancient bound parchments. Could it be as easy as it was for Atticus? Everything he had ever read said it was. Guiseppe could not leave that university without settling the issue. Often, missiles were flown into the areas where he was digging. Every time, relief occurred after the misses. Some had been close, but never a direct hit where he worked. How long will this luck continue?

Guiseppe found himself melting from his chair to his knees. He clutched the bound parchments in his hand. Perhaps the very ones Mary Magdalene clutched in that cistern on that last day. He bowed before Heaven. He prayed, "Oh God, I am afraid of You. I am afraid of death. I do not want to go to Hell. I do not want to dread my own death. I want to know that when I die, I will continue to live. I want that life to be in Heaven with Jesus. I do not know how to say this. I will try to follow what I have read. I believe, Jesus, that You walked this earth. The evidence is overwhelming. I believe You were born to a virgin. I believe You lived a perfect life. I believe You worked miracles. How else could Your fame extend beyond little Israel? I believe You were crucified, dead, and buried. There is no question to that. I believe You rose from the dead. How else could such acclaim be given to Your name? No one has ever discovered a grave for Your body. We have one for every other religious leader down through history. Only Your body is unaccounted for. I believe You are the judge of all mankind. I am not worthy to enter Heaven. I am not worthy to have eternal life. I am empty inside. I am selfish completely. Lord Jesus, I am asking You to come into my heart and save me. I give You my life. Please come into mine and save me. Like that thief on the cross, I come to You. Like Atticus, I come to You. Like that centurion, I come to You. Jesus, I am taking You at your word, that whoever calls upon Your name will be saved. Please fill me with Your Spirit. Please give me the assurance that I am saved."

All of a sudden, a peace swept over this foreman of Friars Corbo and Loffreda. He had just asked Jesus to come into his heart. He felt certain Jesus had. The fear left him. Old things were passed away. All things had become new. He felt he could leave the university knowing that if he were to be killed, he would be joining the crowd in Heaven with Mary Magdalene and the disciples.

His last conviction as he walked off the campus was, "I must get this story out to everyone. I have been saved because of it! Others need to read this. They must hear while there is still time. In Jesus' Name I pray. Amen."

Epilogue

This book, The Lost Diary of Mary Magdalene, was written with great caution. John, under the inspiration of the Holy Spirit, wrote in the last book of the Bible, "I warn everyone who hears the words of the prophecy of this book: If anyone adds anything to them, God will add to him the plagues described in this book. And if anyone takes words away from this book of prophecy, God will take away from him his share in the tree of life and in the holy city, which are described in this book." This book is not Scripture. It was not written by the hand of Mary Magdalene, but it is based solely on what we know of her, and the life of Jesus as told in God's Holy Word, the Bible. I have written this book following scripture and exercising artistic license. We know very little about Mary Magdalene, though many have written wild heresies about her with Jesus. Some say she was a prostitute. Scripture does not say that. Some say she had an affair with Jesus. That could not be true. Some say Jesus and Mary Magdalene had children. That is false. Others have written that Jesus said that in the end times, Mary Magdalene would be made a man to make her complete. That is farcical.

This book is about the life of Jesus. It imagines what it would be like to travel with Him, to listen to Him, to watch Him, and to observe the responses to His life. As preachers of God's Word, we often fill in historical gaps and give entries to help the congregation step into the history we share, so that they are not just hearing what is being said, but feeling it, relating to it. In that vein, to make the book more accessible to the readers, names were given to Mary Magdalene's family and friends. Details of the travel and meetings with Jesus were created to give a feel for the context we have read in scripture. To set the scenario for the book's discovery, real historical archaeologists were used, as well as noted scientists. Again, these men had no input into this book. What is written was not these men's historical experiences. They were used in a fictional way to lay the groundwork for the premise of the book's discovery and contents.

With all of this acknowledged, the biblical account of Jesus is true, one hundred percent accurate. This book was written to counter falsehoods about Mary Magdalene, but more, to help the reader step into the experiences she had with the historical and living Lord, Jesus Christ. I pray that as you read it, or have read it, you will come to the same conclusion that our fictional Guiseppe Campise reached. Heaven and Hell are real. Death is certain. Sin is inherently our nature. Jesus is the way to forgiveness and eternal life in Heaven. I have made Him my Lord. I pray you have, too. My whole eternity rests in who He is and in what He promised.

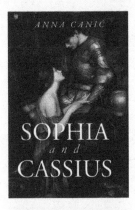

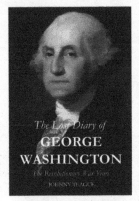